s Printing Office

A Witch's Printing Office

story
MOCHINCHI

art
YASUHIRO MIYAMA

3

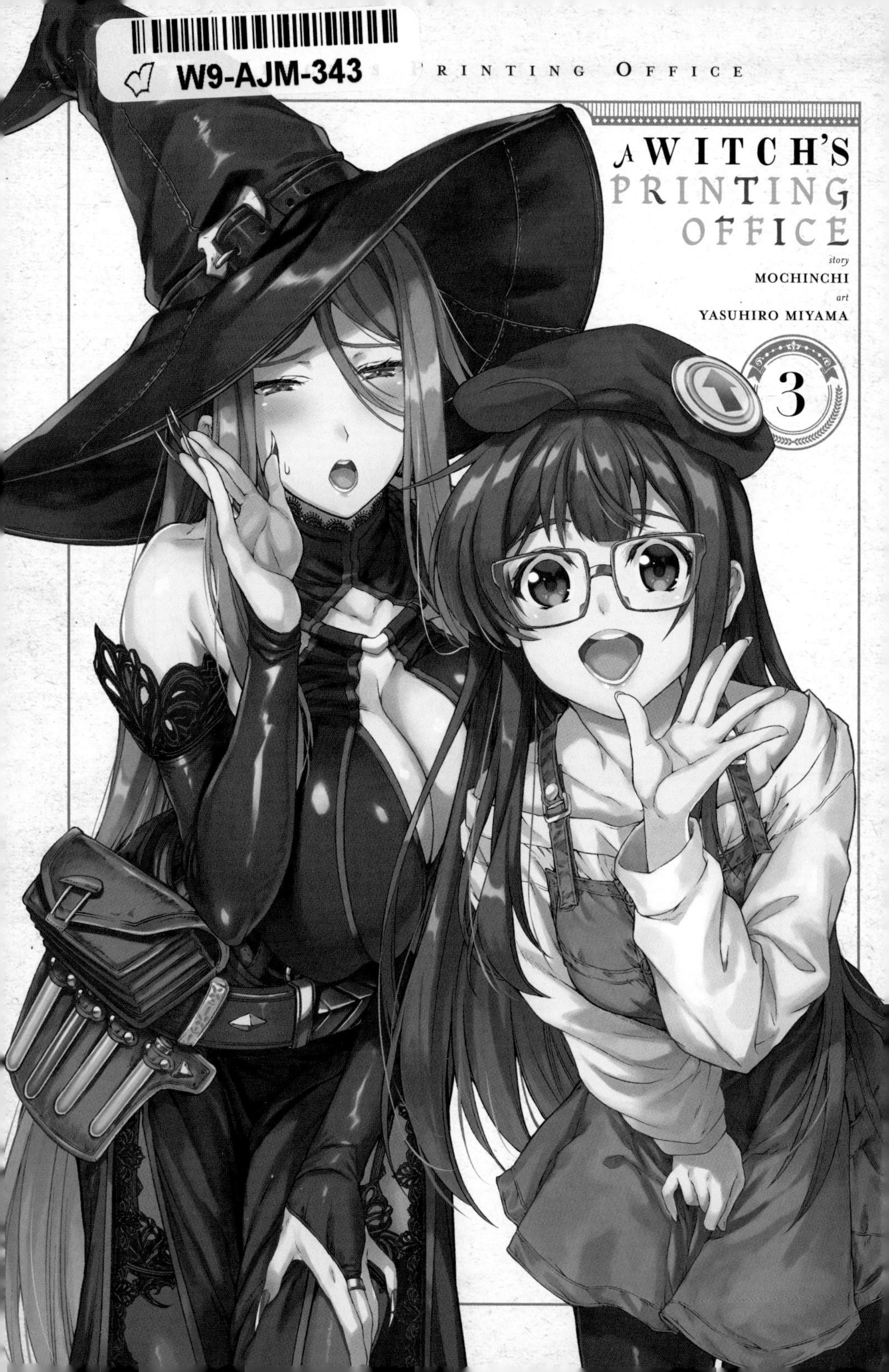

A WITCH'S PRINTING OFFICE

CONTENTS

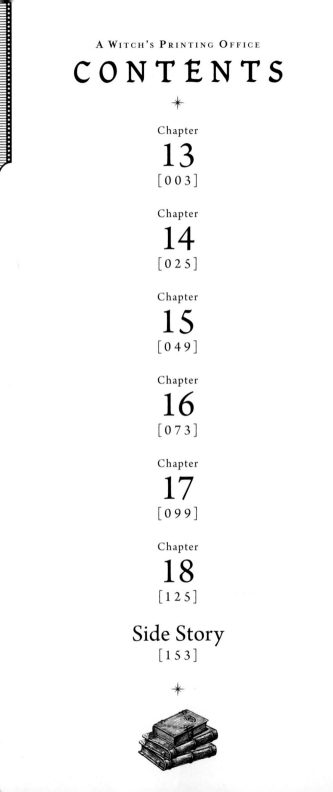

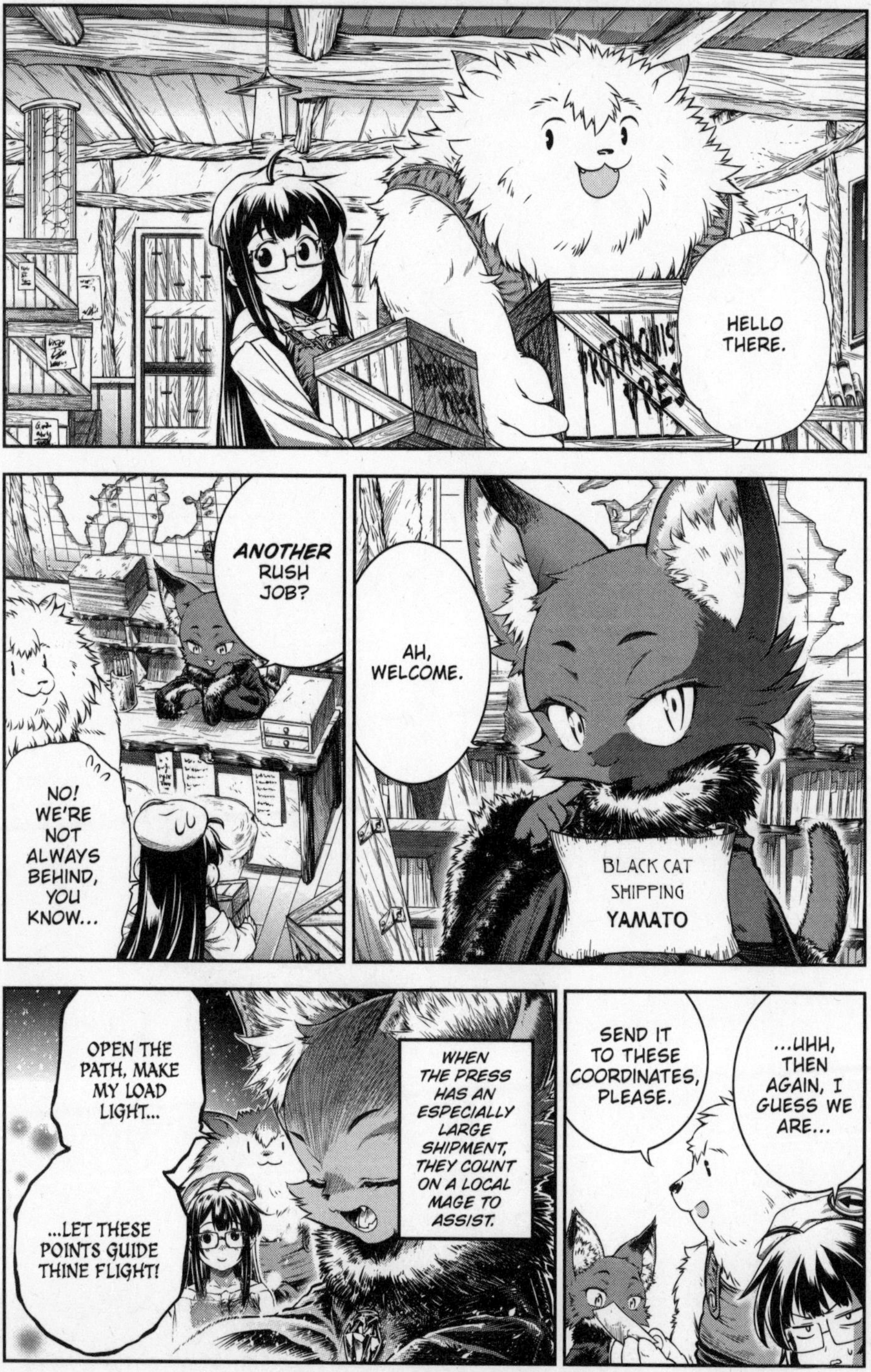
HELLO THERE.
PROTAGONIST PRESS
AH, WELCOME.
BLACK CAT SHIPPING YAMATO
ANOTHER RUSH JOB?
NO! WE'RE NOT ALWAYS BEHIND, YOU KNOW...
SEND IT TO THESE COORDINATES, PLEASE.
...UHH, THEN AGAIN, I GUESS WE ARE...
OPEN THE PATH, MAKE MY LOAD LIGHT...
WHEN THE PRESS HAS AN ESPECIALLY LARGE SHIPMENT, THEY COUNT ON A LOCAL MAGE TO ASSIST.
...LET THESE POINTS GUIDE THINE FLIGHT!

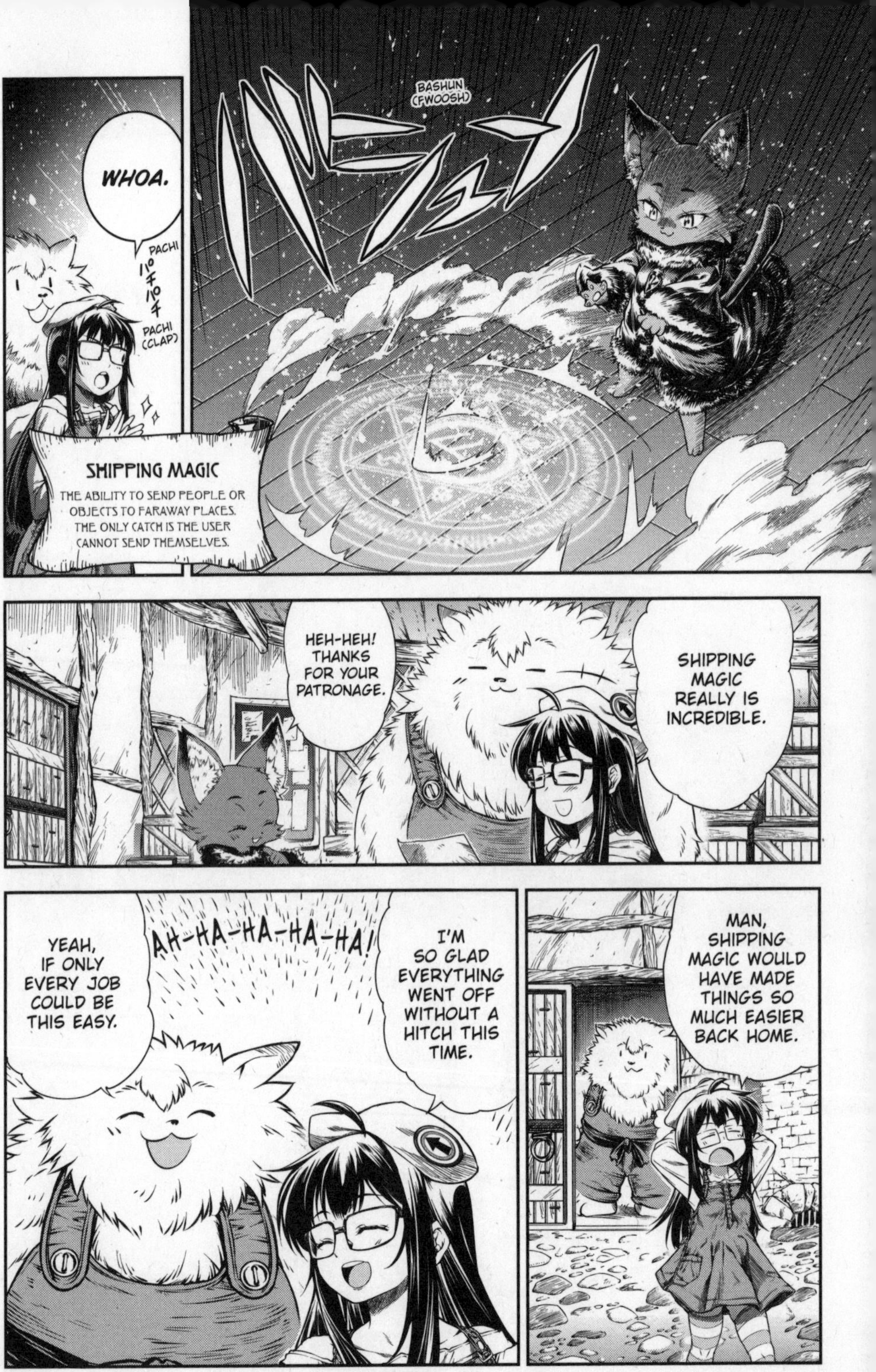

BASHUN (FWOOSH)
WHOA.
PACHI パチパチ PACHI (CLAP)
SHIPPING MAGIC
THE ABILITY TO SEND PEOPLE OR OBJECTS TO FARAWAY PLACES. THE ONLY CATCH IS THE USER CANNOT SEND THEMSELVES.
SHIPPING MAGIC REALLY IS INCREDIBLE.
HEH-HEH! THANKS FOR YOUR PATRONAGE.
MAN, SHIPPING MAGIC WOULD HAVE MADE THINGS SO MUCH EASIER BACK HOME.
I'M SO GLAD EVERYTHING WENT OFF WITHOUT A HITCH THIS TIME.
AH-HA-HA-HA-HA!
YEAH, IF ONLY EVERY JOB COULD BE THIS EASY.

Chapter 13

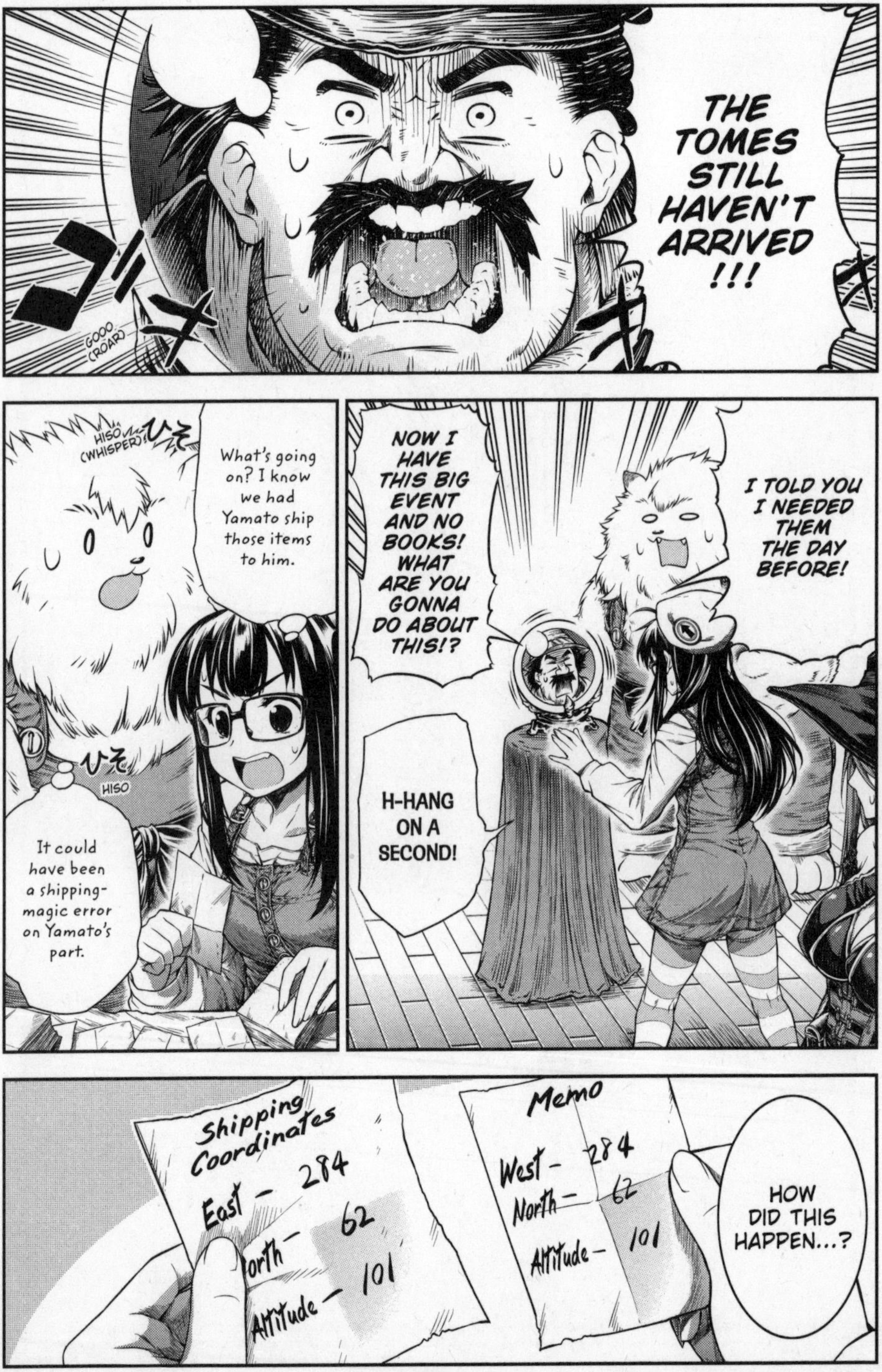
THE TOMES STILL HAVEN'T ARRIVED!!!
GOOO (ROAR)
I TOLD YOU I NEEDED THEM THE DAY BEFORE!
NOW I HAVE THIS BIG EVENT AND NO BOOKS! WHAT ARE YOU GONNA DO ABOUT THIS!?
H-HANG ON A SECOND!
What's going on? I know we had Yamato ship those items to him.
ひそ HISO (WHISPER)
ひそ HISO
It could have been a shipping-magic error on Yamato's part.
HOW DID THIS HAPPEN...?
Memo
West - 284
North - 62
Altitude - 101
Shipping Coordinates
East - 284
North - 62
Altitude - 101

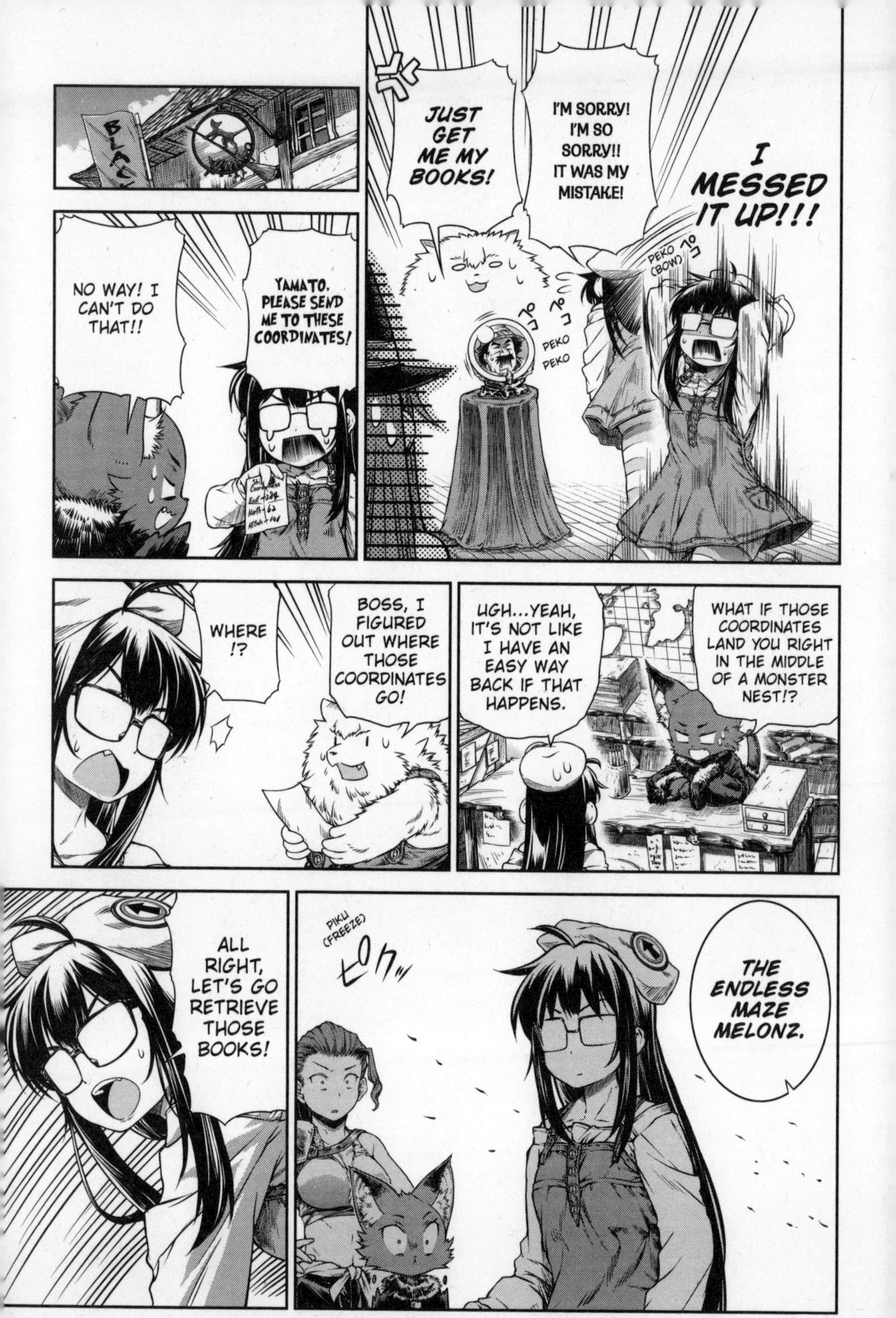
I MESSED IT UP!!!
PEKO (BOW)
I'M SORRY! I'M SO SORRY!! IT WAS MY MISTAKE!
JUST GET ME MY BOOKS!
PEKO PEKO
YAMATO. PLEASE SEND ME TO THESE COORDINATES!
NO WAY! I CAN'T DO THAT!!
WHAT IF THOSE COORDINATES LAND YOU RIGHT IN THE MIDDLE OF A MONSTER NEST!?
UGH...YEAH, IT'S NOT LIKE I HAVE AN EASY WAY BACK IF THAT HAPPENS.
BOSS, I FIGURED OUT WHERE THOSE COORDINATES GO!
WHERE !?
THE ENDLESS MAZE MELONZ.
PIKU (FREEZE)
ALL RIGHT, LET'S GO RETRIEVE THOSE BOOKS!

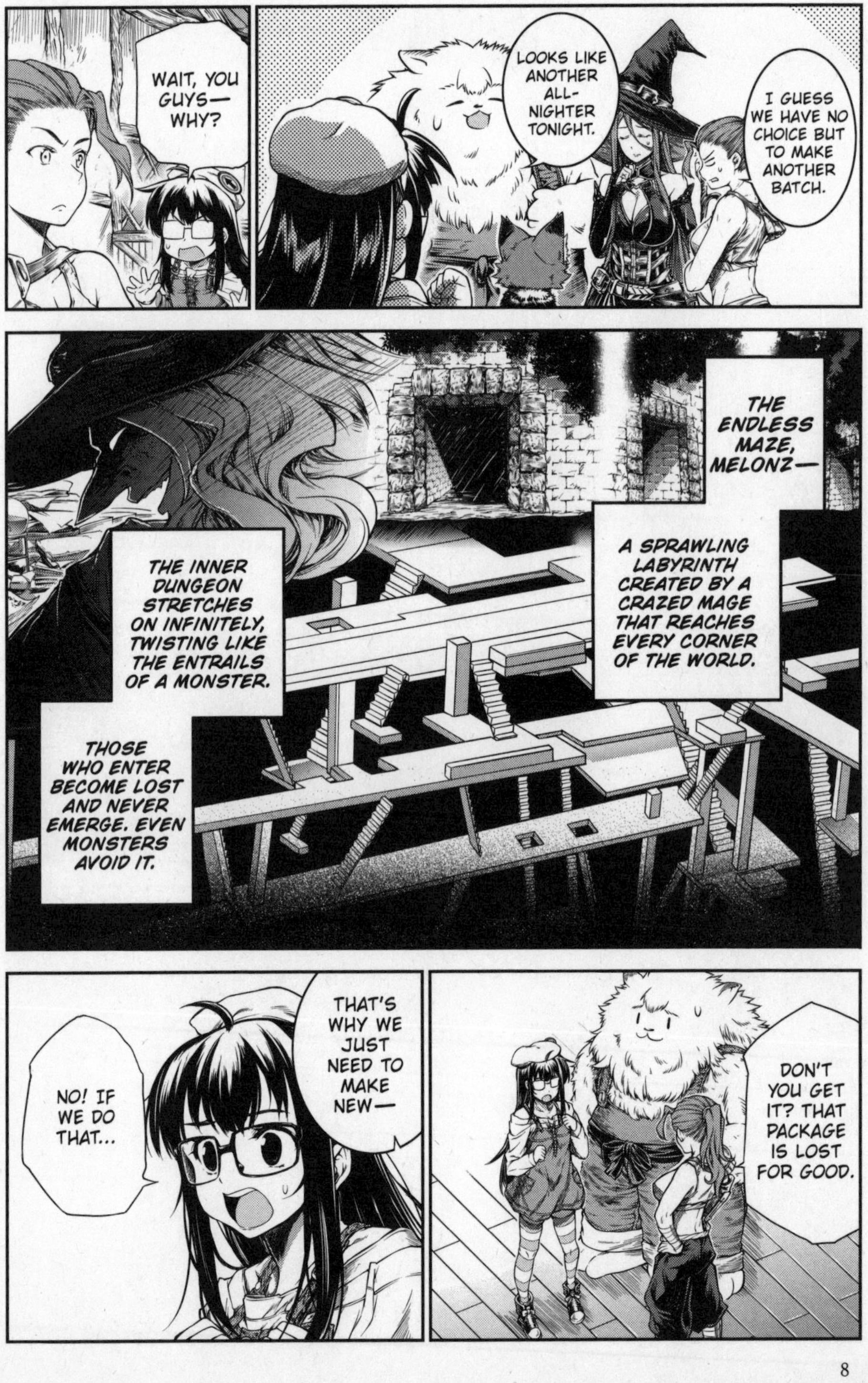
I GUESS WE HAVE NO CHOICE BUT TO MAKE ANOTHER BATCH.
LOOKS LIKE ANOTHER ALL-NIGHTER TONIGHT.
WAIT, YOU GUYS— WHY?
THE ENDLESS MAZE, MELONZ—
A SPRAWLING LABYRINTH CREATED BY A CRAZED MAGE THAT REACHES EVERY CORNER OF THE WORLD.
THE INNER DUNGEON STRETCHES ON INFINITELY, TWISTING LIKE THE ENTRAILS OF A MONSTER.
THOSE WHO ENTER BECOME LOST AND NEVER EMERGE. EVEN MONSTERS AVOID IT.
DON'T YOU GET IT? THAT PACKAGE IS LOST FOR GOOD.
THAT'S WHY WE JUST NEED TO MAKE NEW—
NO! IF WE DO THAT...

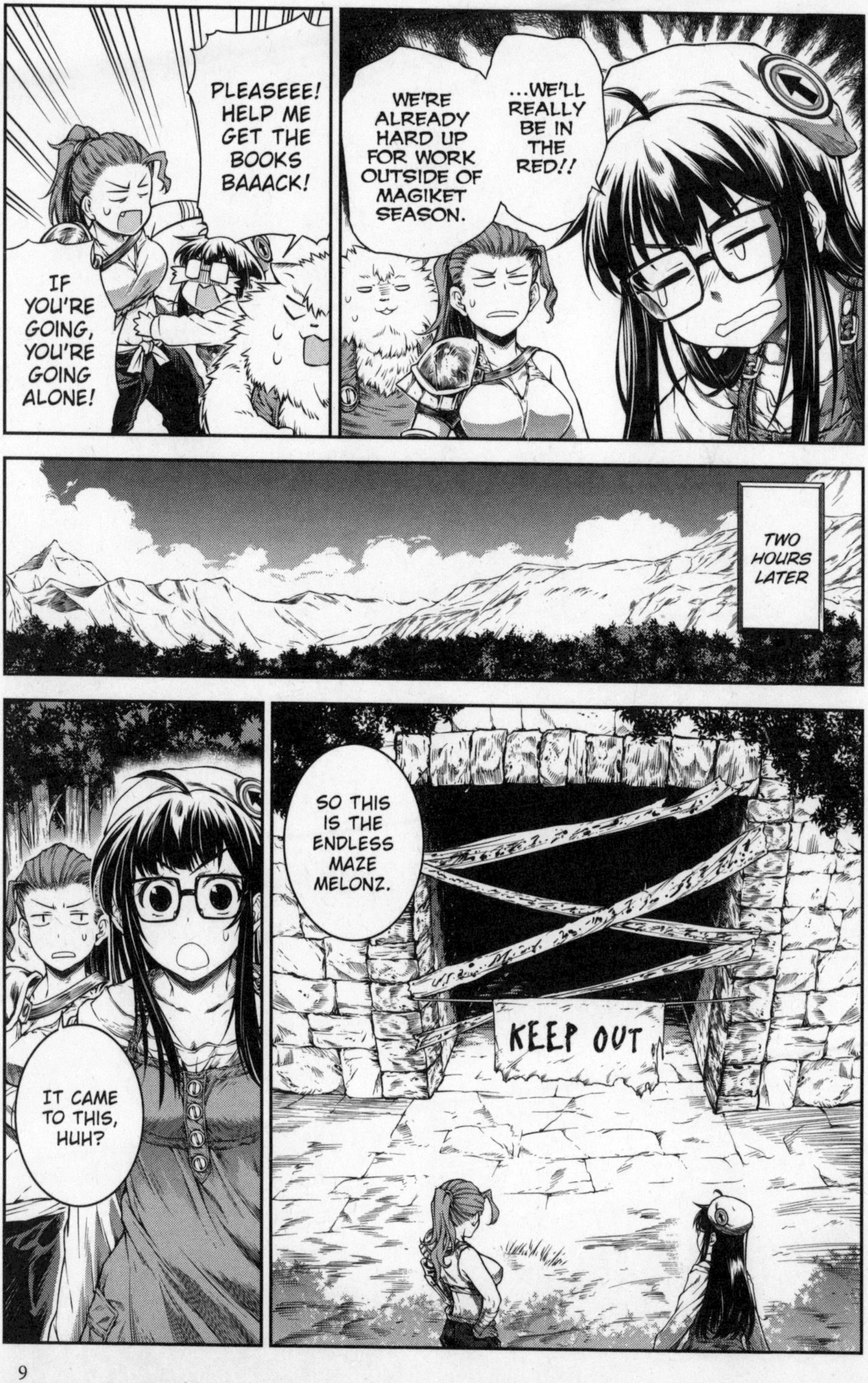
...WE'LL REALLY BE IN THE RED!!
WE'RE ALREADY HARD UP FOR WORK OUTSIDE OF MAGIKET SEASON.
PLEASEEE! HELP ME GET THE BOOKS BAAACK!
IF YOU'RE GOING, YOU'RE GOING ALONE!
TWO HOURS LATER
SO THIS IS THE ENDLESS MAZE MELONZ.
KEEP OUT
IT CAME TO THIS, HUH?

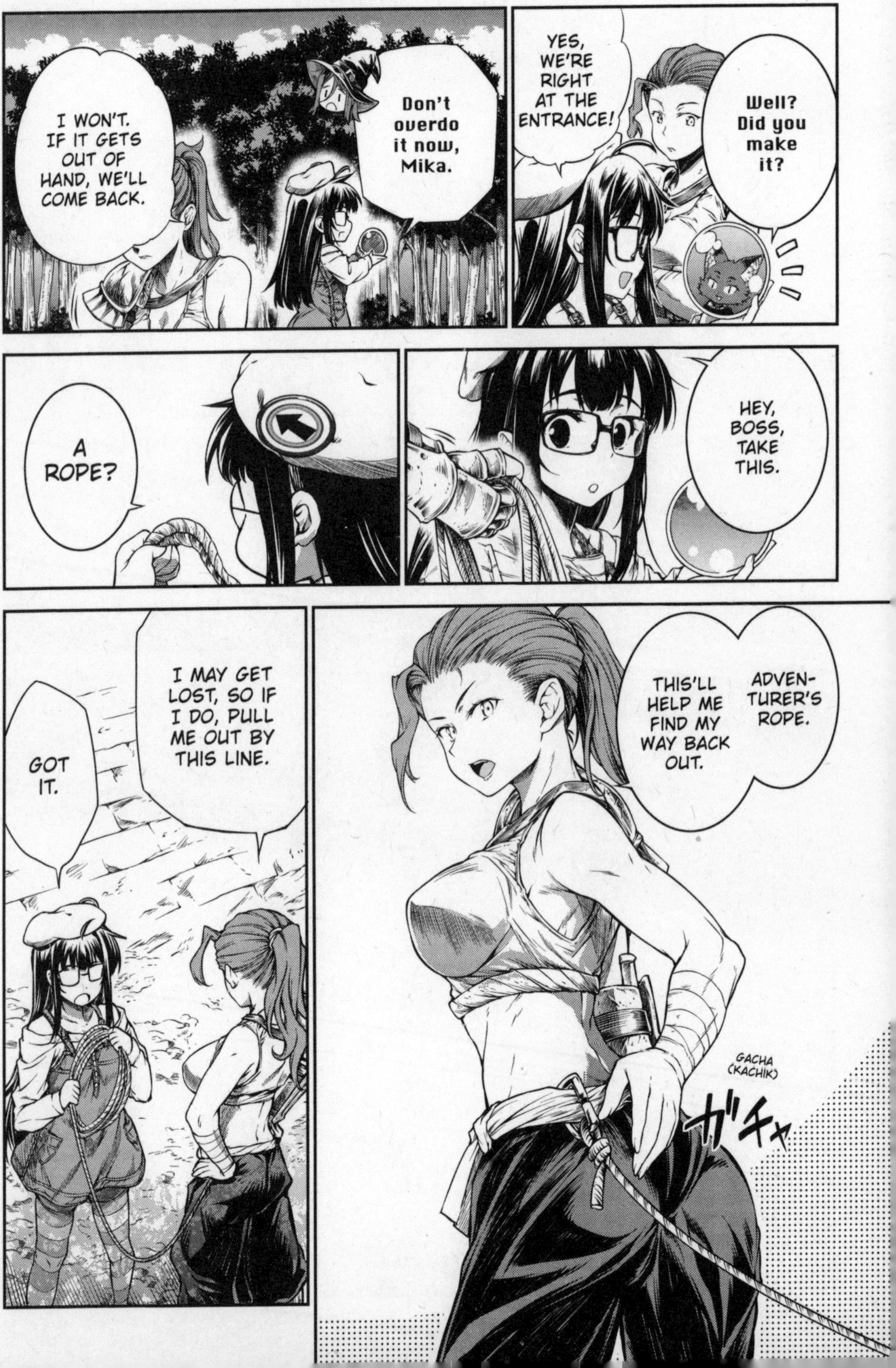
Well? Did you make it?
YES, WE'RE RIGHT AT THE ENTRANCE!
Don't overdo it now, Mika.
I WON'T. IF IT GETS OUT OF HAND, WE'LL COME BACK.
HEY, BOSS, TAKE THIS.
A ROPE?
ADVENTURER'S ROPE.
THIS'LL HELP ME FIND MY WAY BACK OUT.
ガチャ
GACHA (KACHIK)
I MAY GET LOST, SO IF I DO, PULL ME OUT BY THIS LINE.
GOT IT.

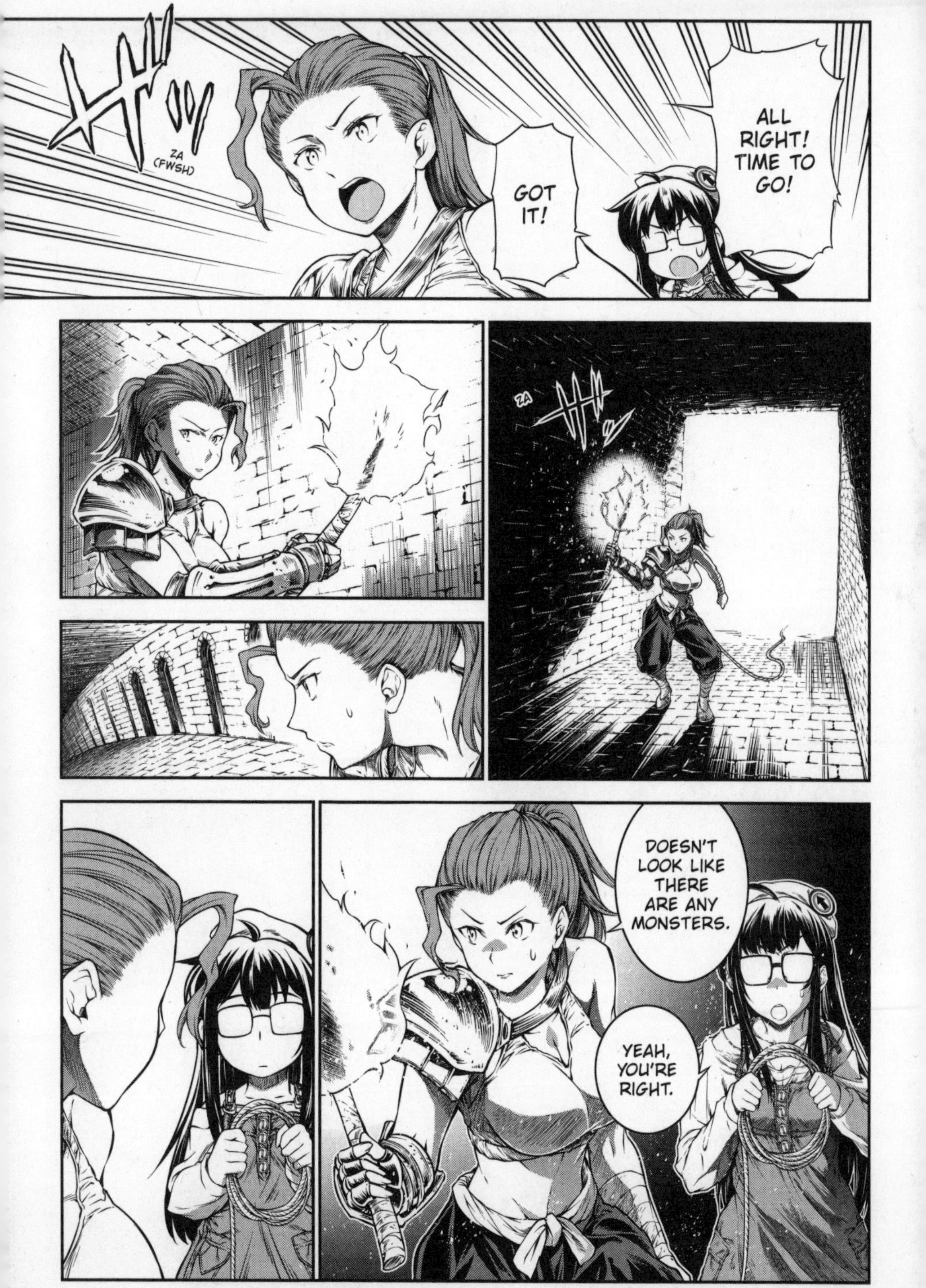
ALL RIGHT! TIME TO GO!
GOT IT!
ZA (FWSH)
ZA
DOESN'T LOOK LIKE THERE ARE ANY MONSTERS.
YEAH, YOU'RE RIGHT.

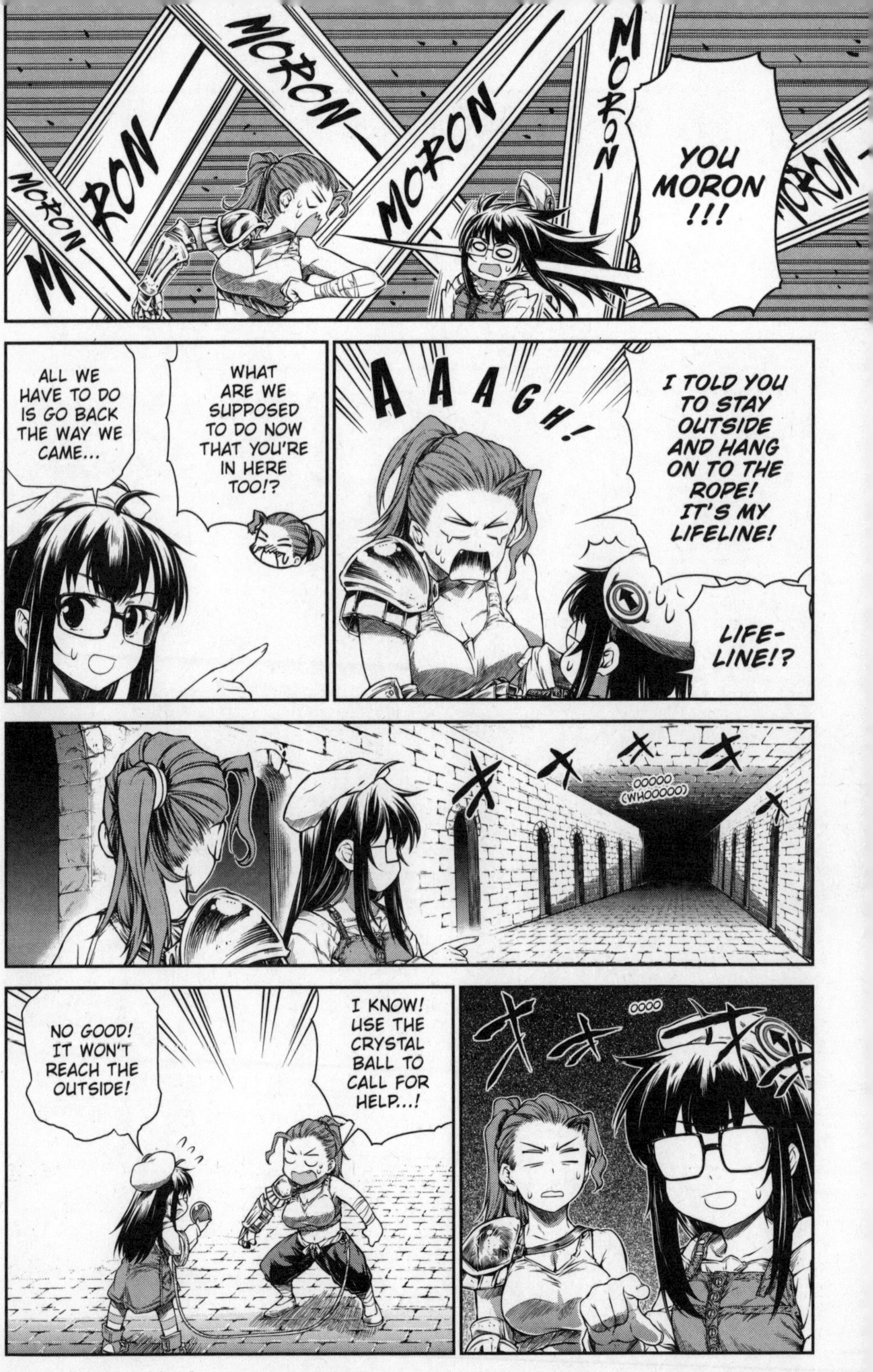
MORON—
YOU MORON !!!
MORON—
MORON—
MORON—
MORON—
MORON—
AAAGH!
I TOLD YOU TO STAY OUTSIDE AND HANG ON TO THE ROPE! IT'S MY LIFELINE!
LIFE-LINE!?
WHAT ARE WE SUPPOSED TO DO NOW THAT YOU'RE IN HERE TOO!?
ALL WE HAVE TO DO IS GO BACK THE WAY WE CAME...
OOOOO (WHOOOOO)
OOOO
I KNOW! USE THE CRYSTAL BALL TO CALL FOR HELP...!
NO GOOD! IT WON'T REACH THE OUTSIDE!

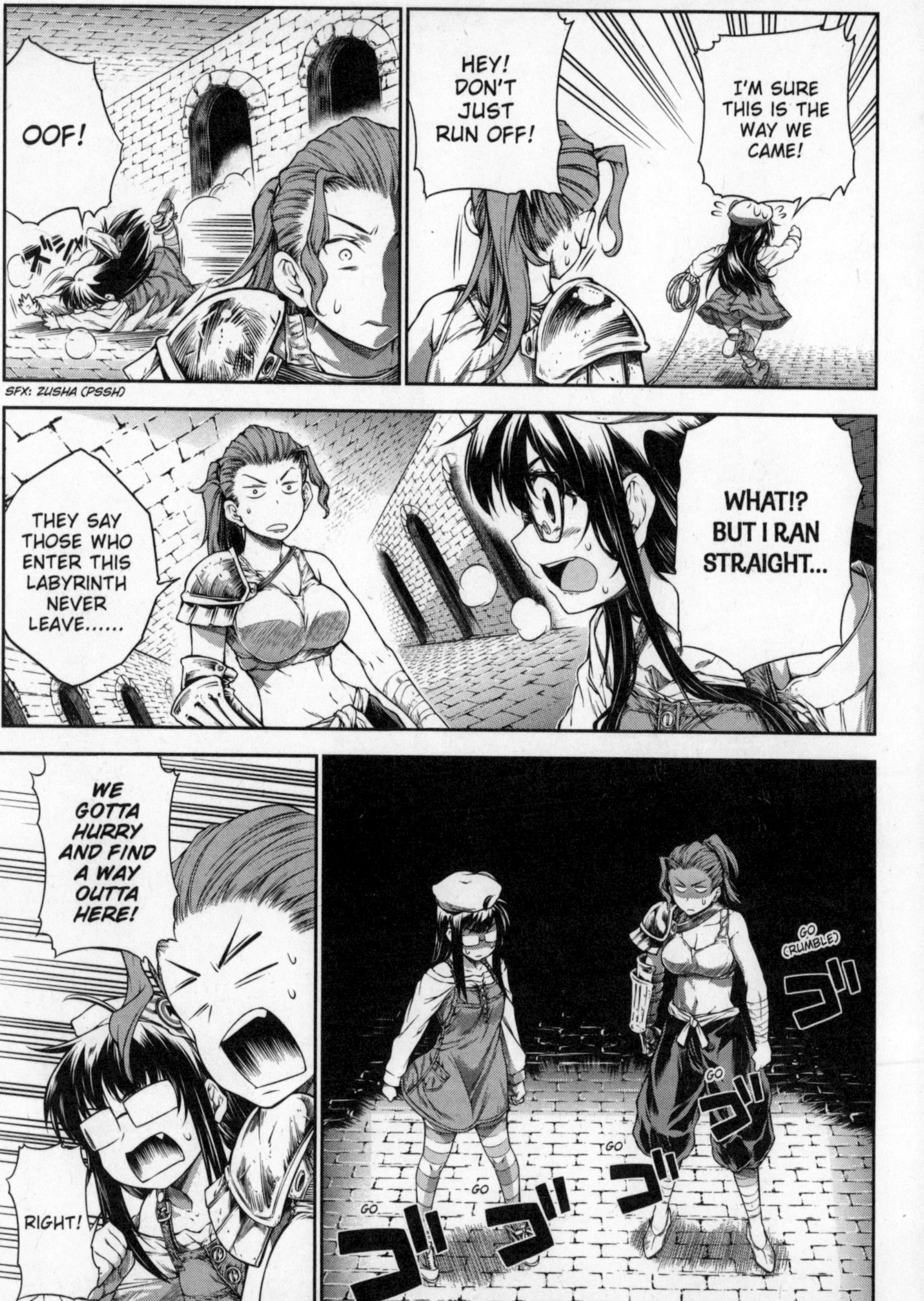
I'M SURE THIS IS THE WAY WE CAME!
HEY! DON'T JUST RUN OFF!
OOF!
SFX: ZUSHA (PSSH)
WHAT!? BUT I RAN STRAIGHT...
THEY SAY THOSE WHO ENTER THIS LABYRINTH NEVER LEAVE......
GO (RUMBLE)
GO
GO
GO
GO
WE GOTTA HURRY AND FIND A WAY OUTTA HERE!
RIGHT!

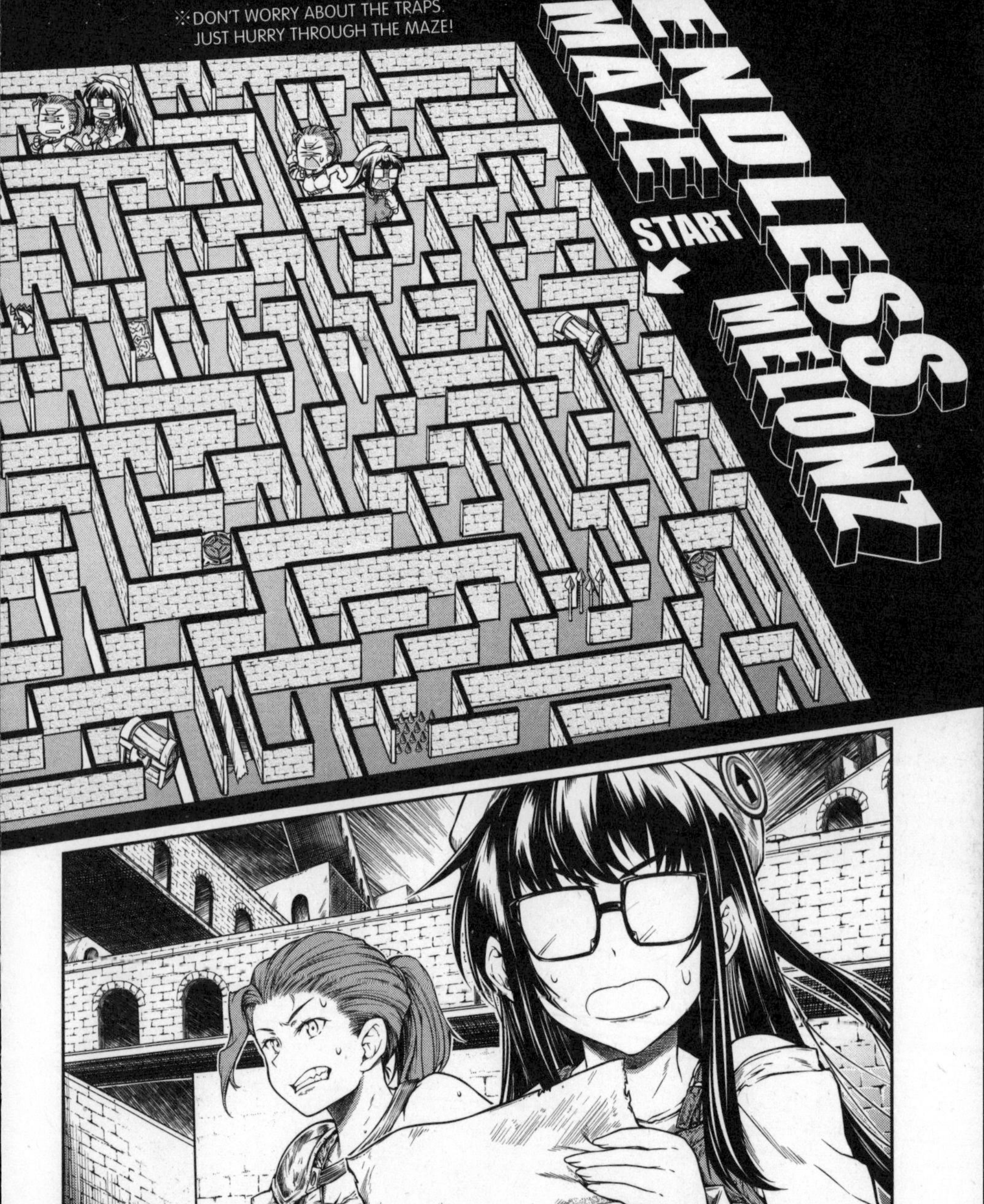
※DON'T WORRY ABOUT THE TRAPS. JUST HURRY THROUGH THE MAZE!
ENDLESS MELONZ MAZE
START

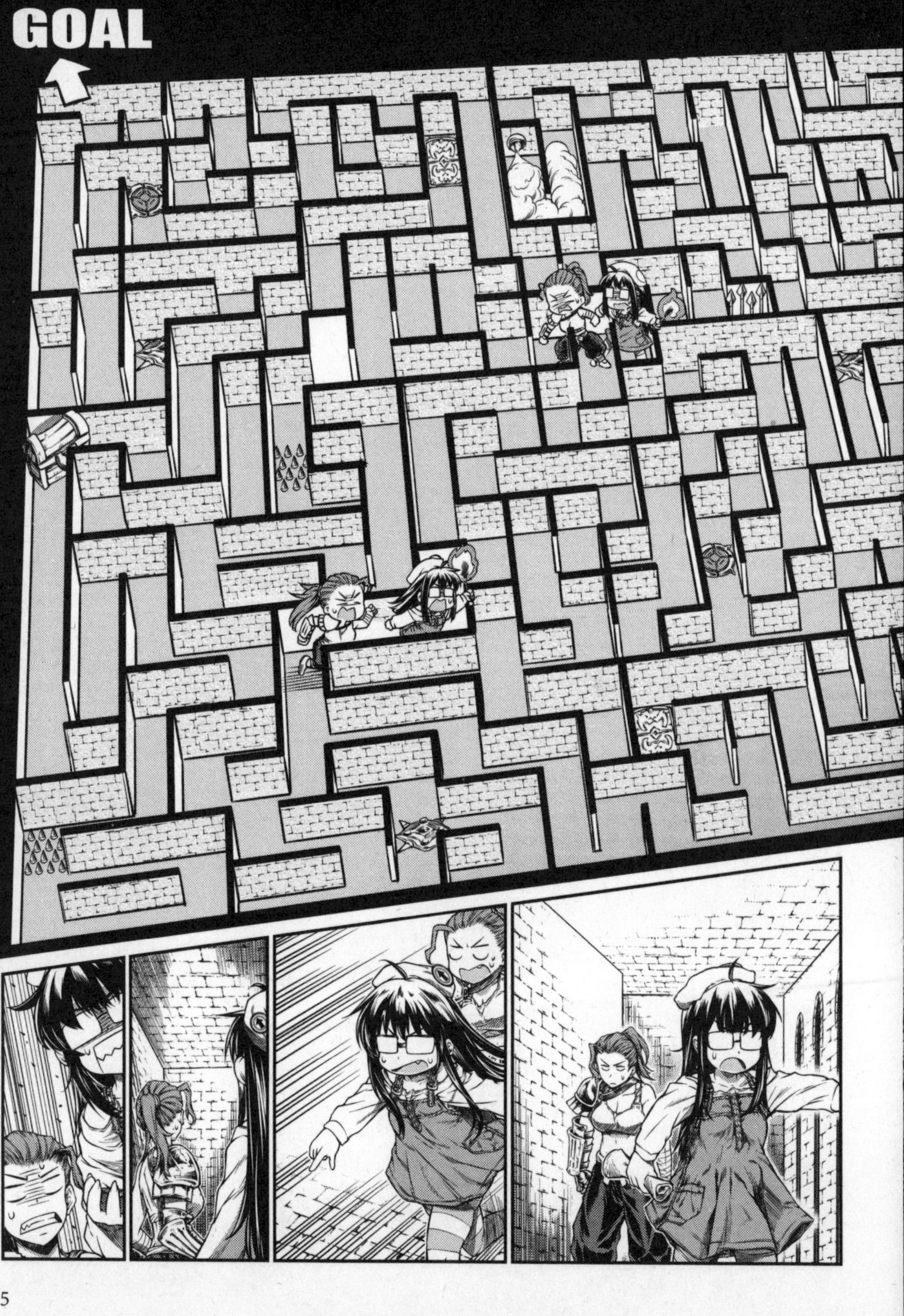
GOAL

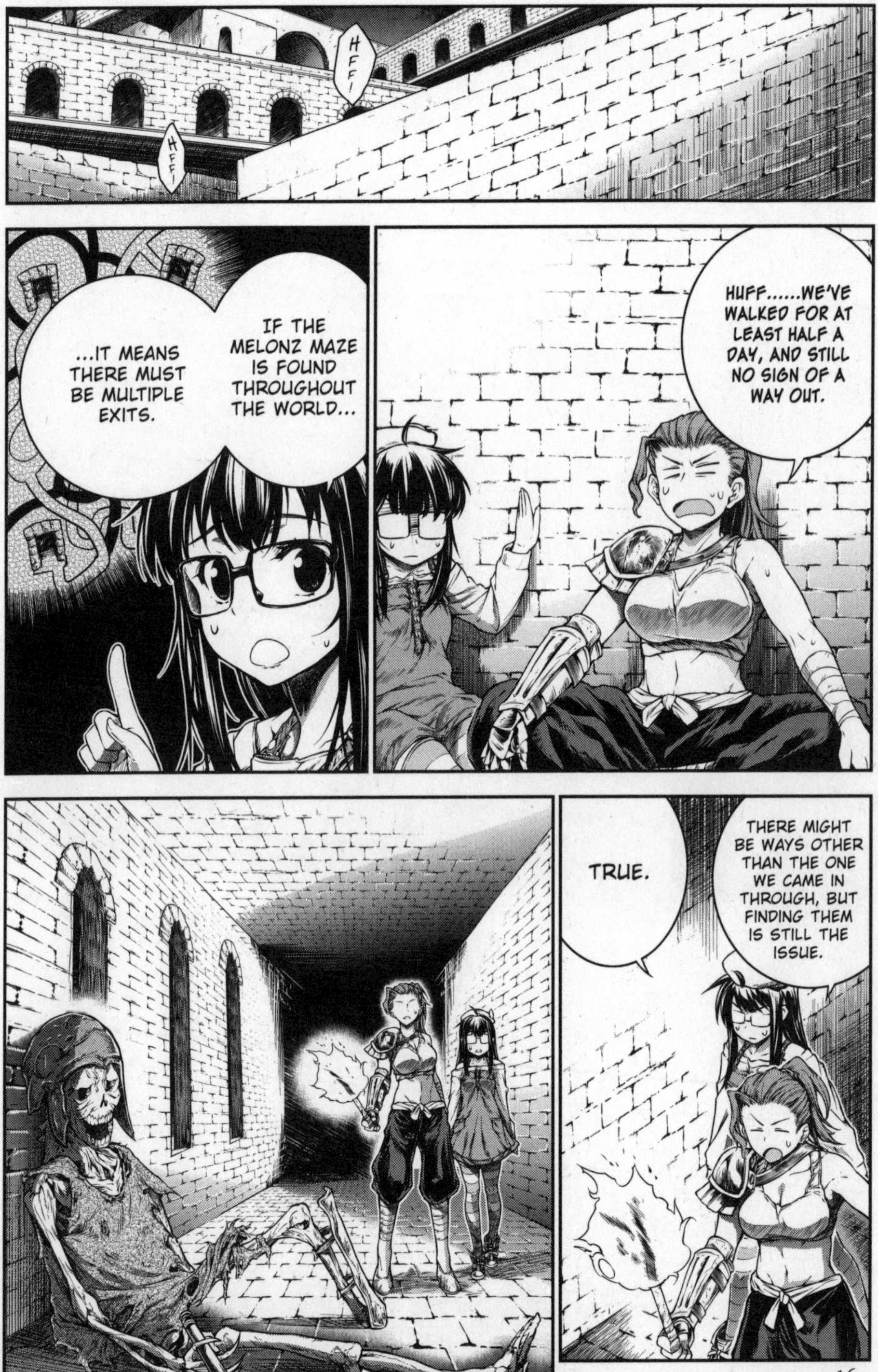
HFF!
HFF!
HUFF......WE'VE WALKED FOR AT LEAST HALF A DAY, AND STILL NO SIGN OF A WAY OUT.
IF THE MELONZ MAZE IS FOUND THROUGHOUT THE WORLD...
...IT MEANS THERE MUST BE MULTIPLE EXITS.
THERE MIGHT BE WAYS OTHER THAN THE ONE WE CAME IN THROUGH, BUT FINDING THEM IS STILL THE ISSUE.
TRUE.

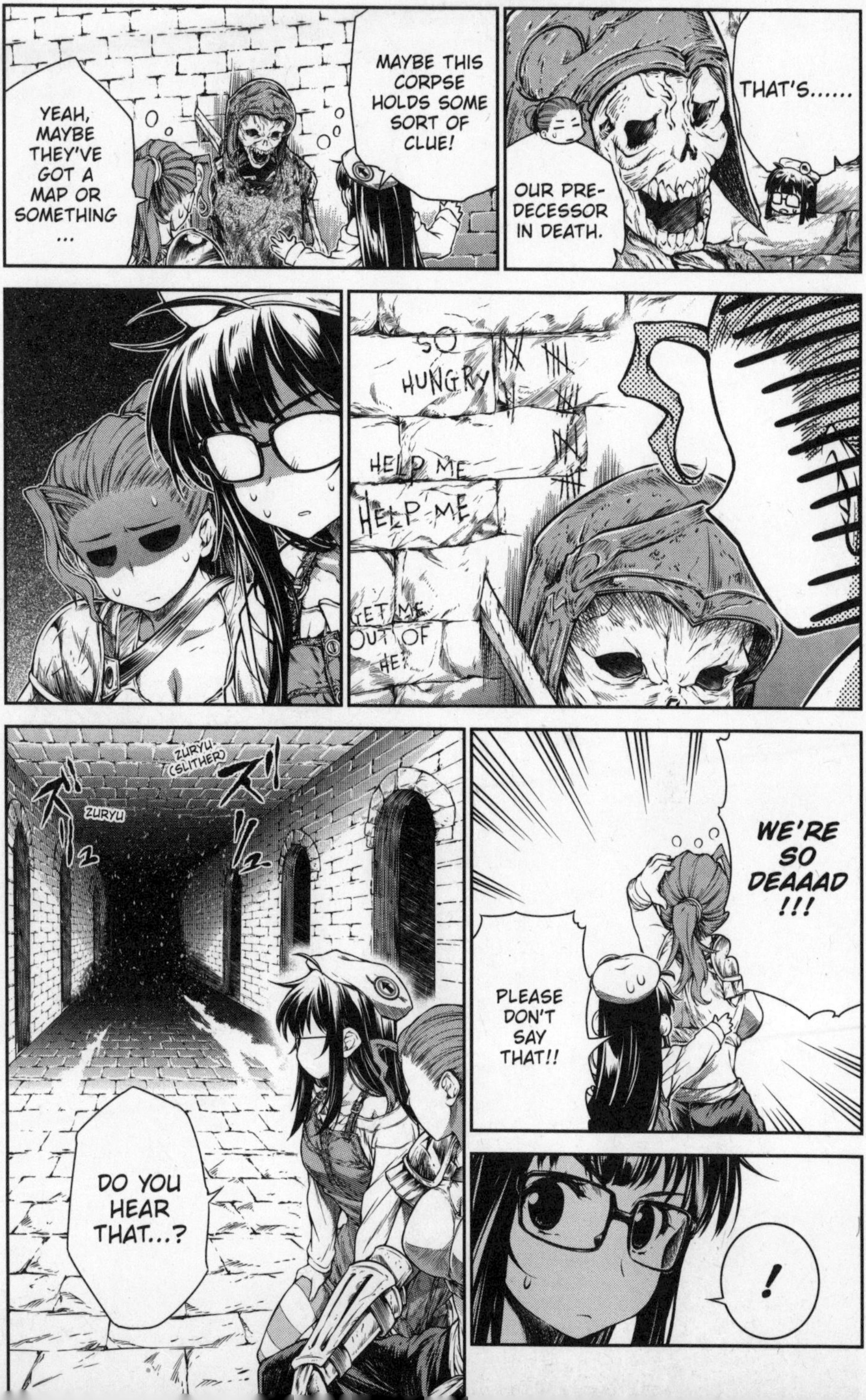
THAT'S......
OUR PRE-
DECESSOR
IN DEATH.
MAYBE THIS CORPSE HOLDS SOME SORT OF CLUE!
YEAH, MAYBE THEY'VE GOT A MAP OR SOMETHING ...
SO HUNGRY
HELP ME
HELP ME
GET ME OUT OF HE
WE'RE SO DEAAAD!!!
PLEASE DON'T SAY THAT!!
!
ZURYU (SLITHER)
ZURYU
DO YOU HEAR THAT...?

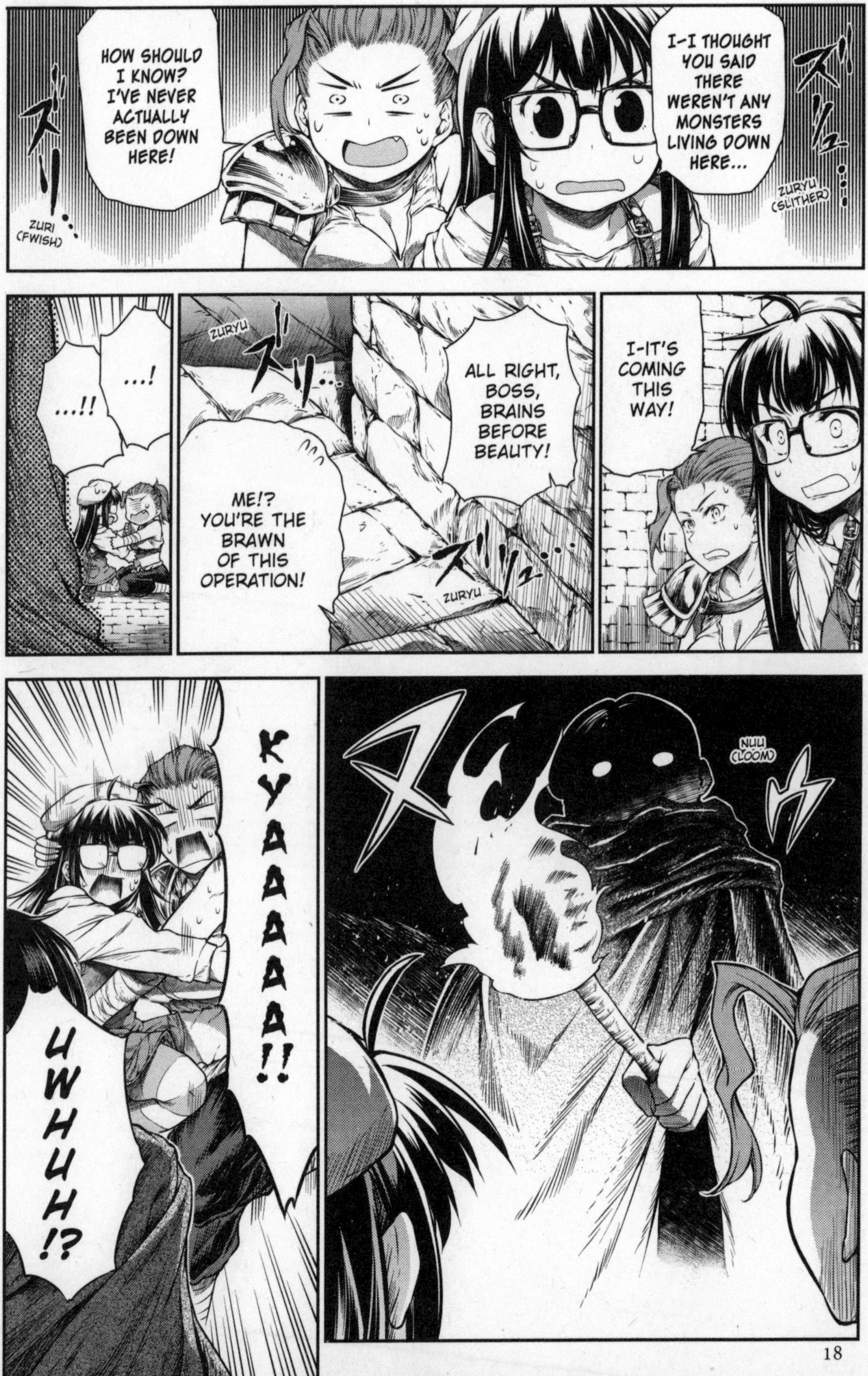
I-I THOUGHT YOU SAID THERE WEREN'T ANY MONSTERS LIVING DOWN HERE...
ZURYU (SLITHER)
HOW SHOULD I KNOW? I'VE NEVER ACTUALLY BEEN DOWN HERE!
ZURI (FWISH)
I-IT'S COMING THIS WAY!
ZURYU
ALL RIGHT, BOSS, BRAINS BEFORE BEAUTY!
ME!? YOU'RE THE BRAWN OF THIS OPERATION!
ZURYU
...!
...!!
NUU (LOOM)
KYAAAAA!!
UWHUH!?

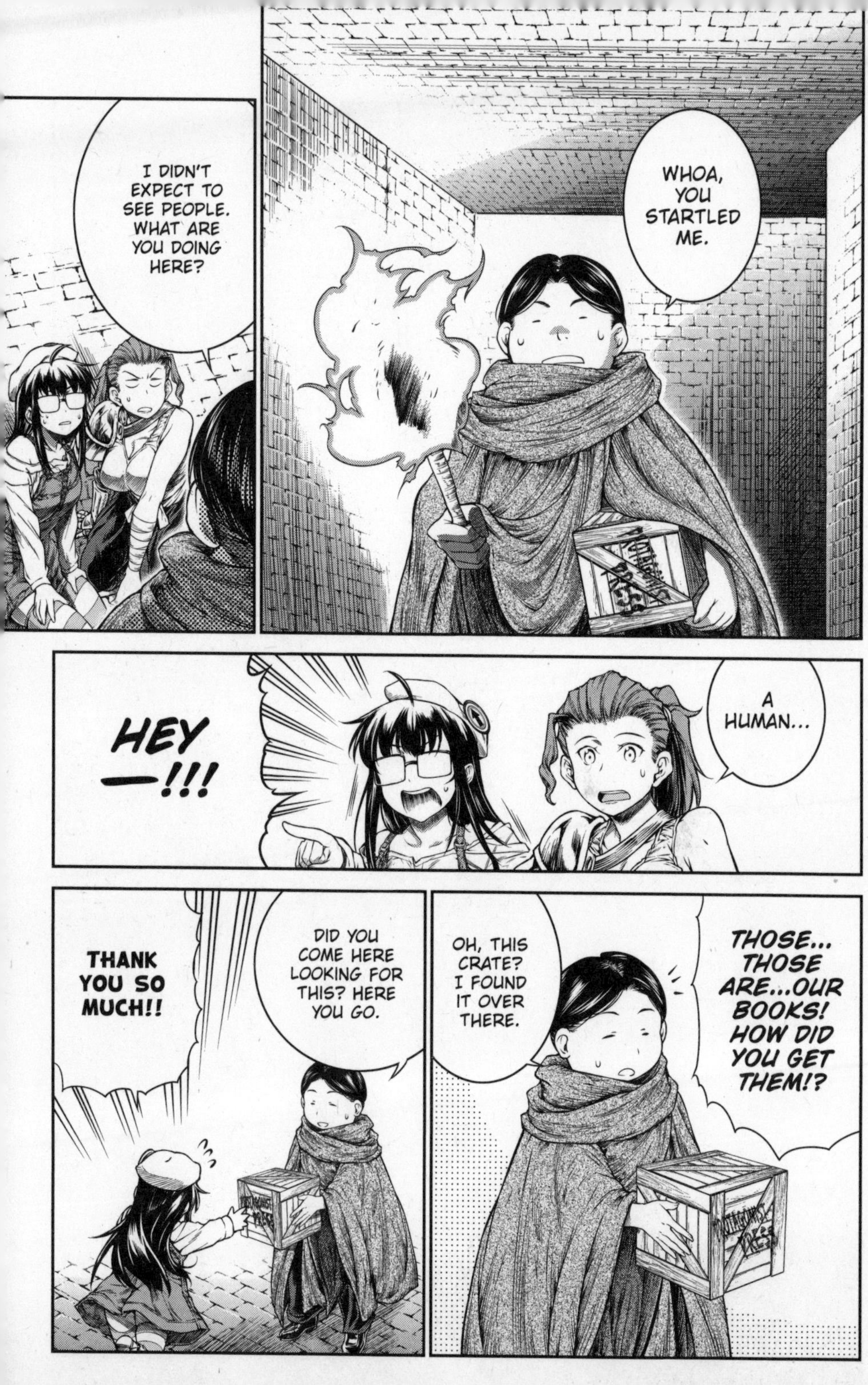
WHOA, YOU STARTLED ME.
I DIDN'T EXPECT TO SEE PEOPLE. WHAT ARE YOU DOING HERE?
A HUMAN...
HEY—!!!
THOSE... THOSE ARE...OUR BOOKS! HOW DID YOU GET THEM!?
OH, THIS CRATE? I FOUND IT OVER THERE.
DID YOU COME HERE LOOKING FOR THIS? HERE YOU GO.
THANK YOU SO MUCH!!

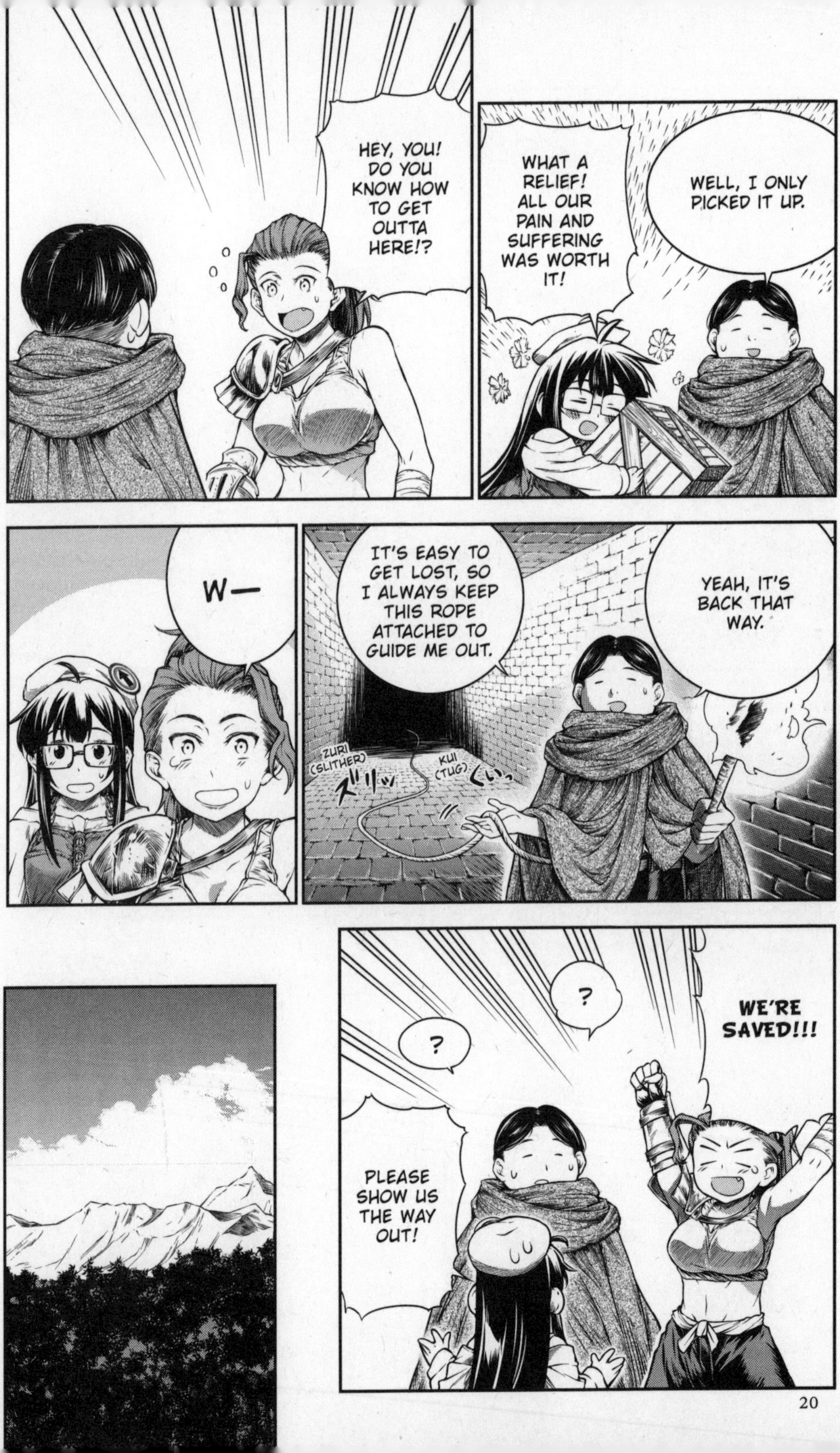
WELL, I ONLY PICKED IT UP.
WHAT A RELIEF! ALL OUR PAIN AND SUFFERING WAS WORTH IT!
HEY, YOU! DO YOU KNOW HOW TO GET OUTTA HERE!?
YEAH, IT'S BACK THAT WAY.
IT'S EASY TO GET LOST, SO I ALWAYS KEEP THIS ROPE ATTACHED TO GUIDE ME OUT.
KUI (TUG)
ZURI (SLITHER)
W—
WE'RE SAVED!!!
?
?
PLEASE SHOW US THE WAY OUT!

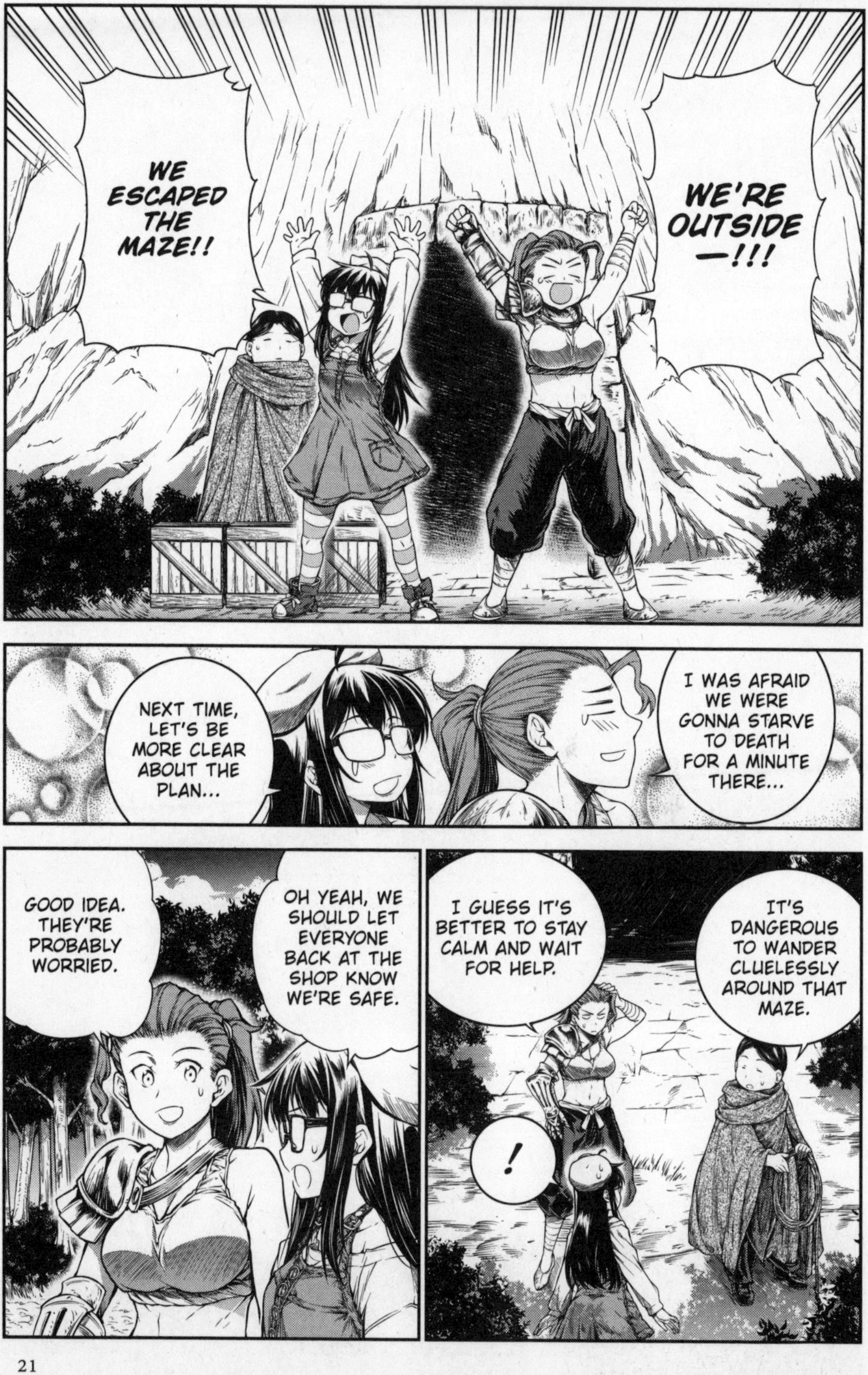
WE'RE OUTSIDE—!!!
WE ESCAPED THE MAZE!!
I WAS AFRAID WE WERE GONNA STARVE TO DEATH FOR A MINUTE THERE...
NEXT TIME, LET'S BE MORE CLEAR ABOUT THE PLAN...
IT'S DANGEROUS TO WANDER CLUELESSLY AROUND THAT MAZE.
I GUESS IT'S BETTER TO STAY CALM AND WAIT FOR HELP.
!
OH YEAH, WE SHOULD LET EVERYONE BACK AT THE SHOP KNOW WE'RE SAFE.
GOOD IDEA. THEY'RE PROBABLY WORRIED.

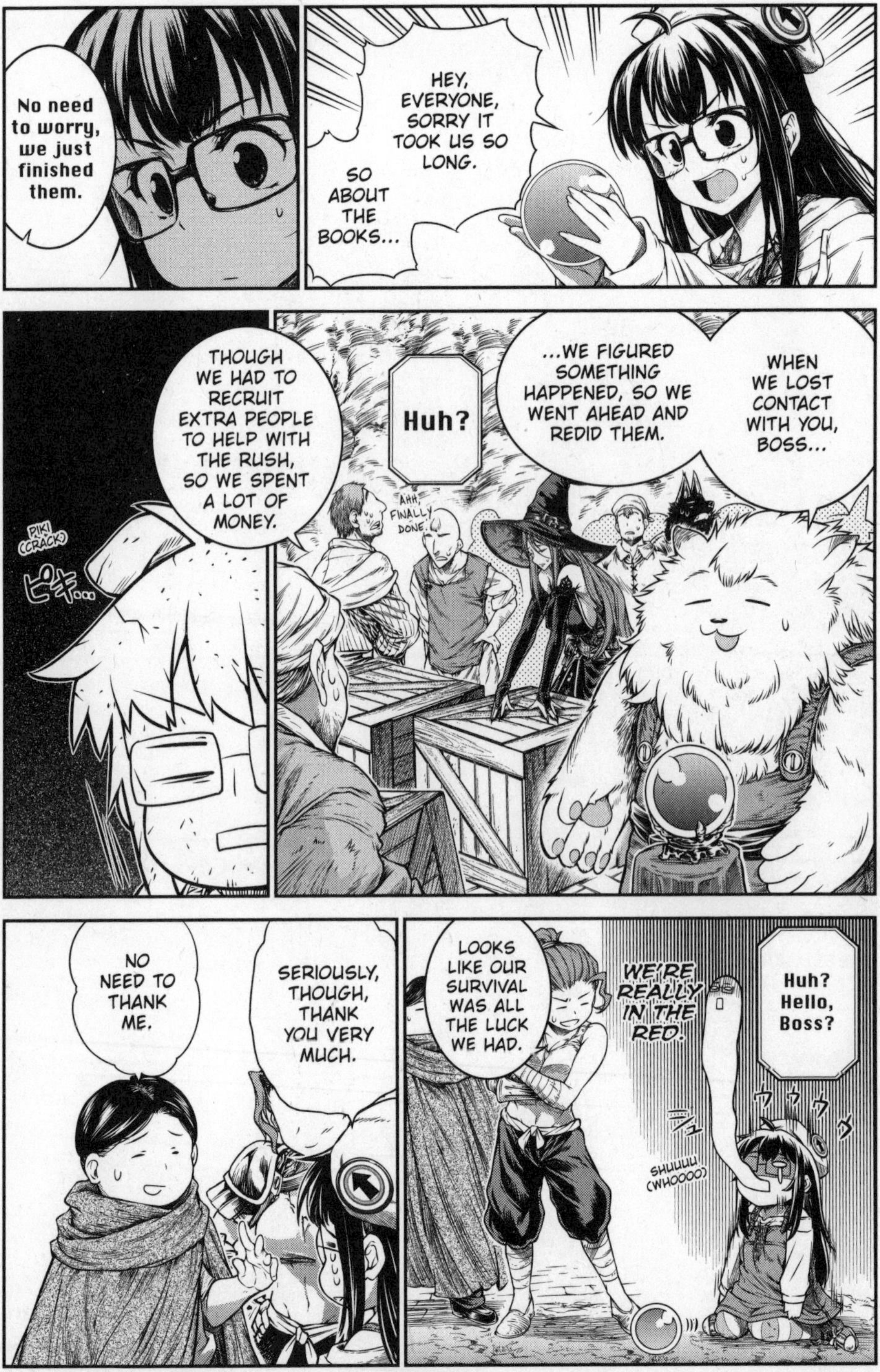
HEY, EVERYONE, SORRY IT TOOK US SO LONG.
SO ABOUT THE BOOKS...
No need to worry, we just finished them.
WHEN WE LOST CONTACT WITH YOU, BOSS...
...WE FIGURED SOMETHING HAPPENED, SO WE WENT AHEAD AND REDID THEM.
Huh?
AHH, FINALLY DONE.
THOUGH WE HAD TO RECRUIT EXTRA PEOPLE TO HELP WITH THE RUSH, SO WE SPENT A LOT OF MONEY.
PIKI (CRACK)
ピキ...
Huh? Hello, Boss?
WE'RE REALLY IN THE RED.
LOOKS LIKE OUR SURVIVAL WAS ALL THE LUCK WE HAD.
SHUUUU (WHOOOO)
SERIOUSLY, THOUGH, THANK YOU VERY MUCH.
NO NEED TO THANK ME.

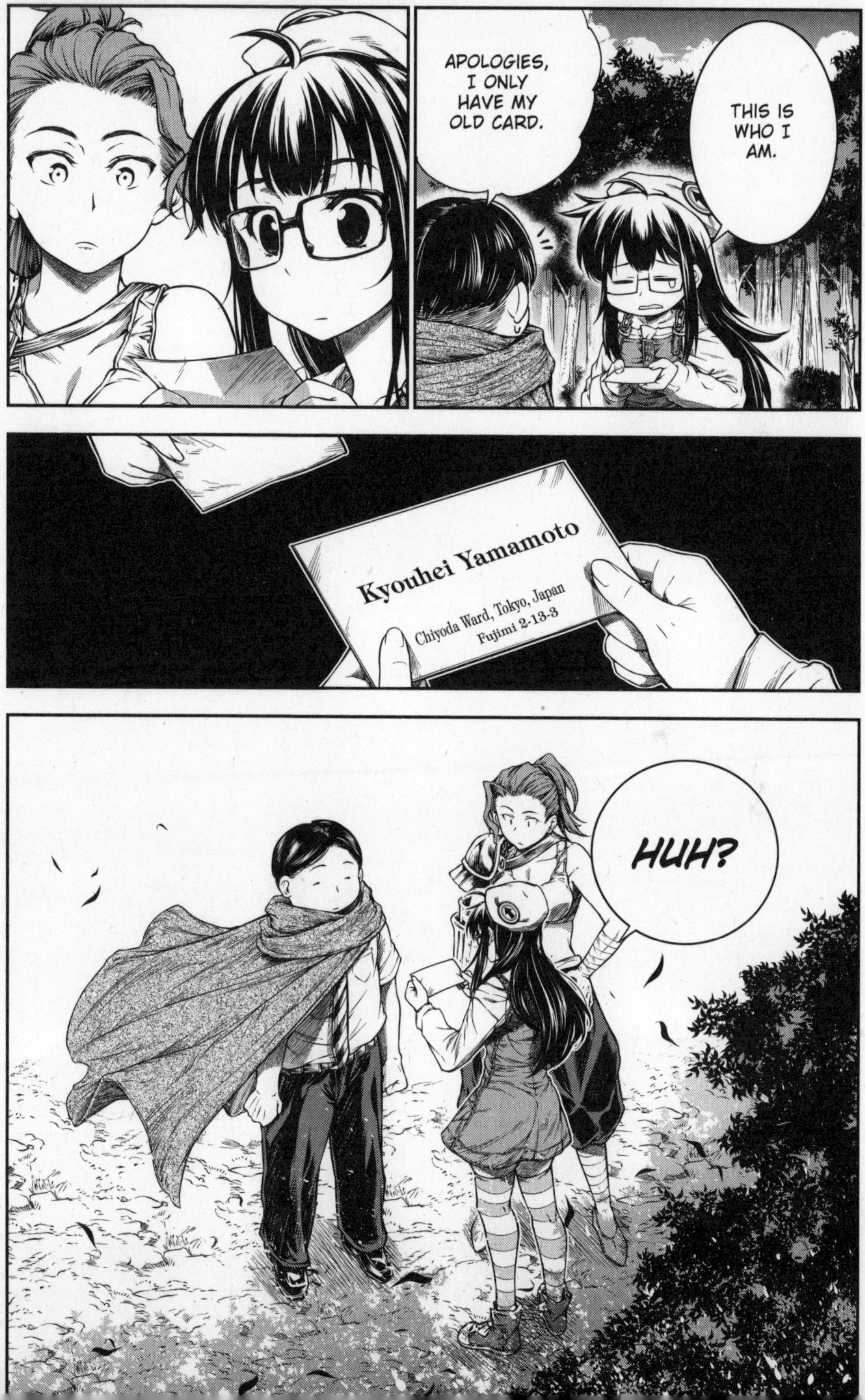
THIS IS WHO I AM.
APOLOGIES, I ONLY HAVE MY OLD CARD.
Kyouhei Yamamoto
Chiyoda Ward, Tokyo, Japan
Fujimi 2-13-3
HUH?

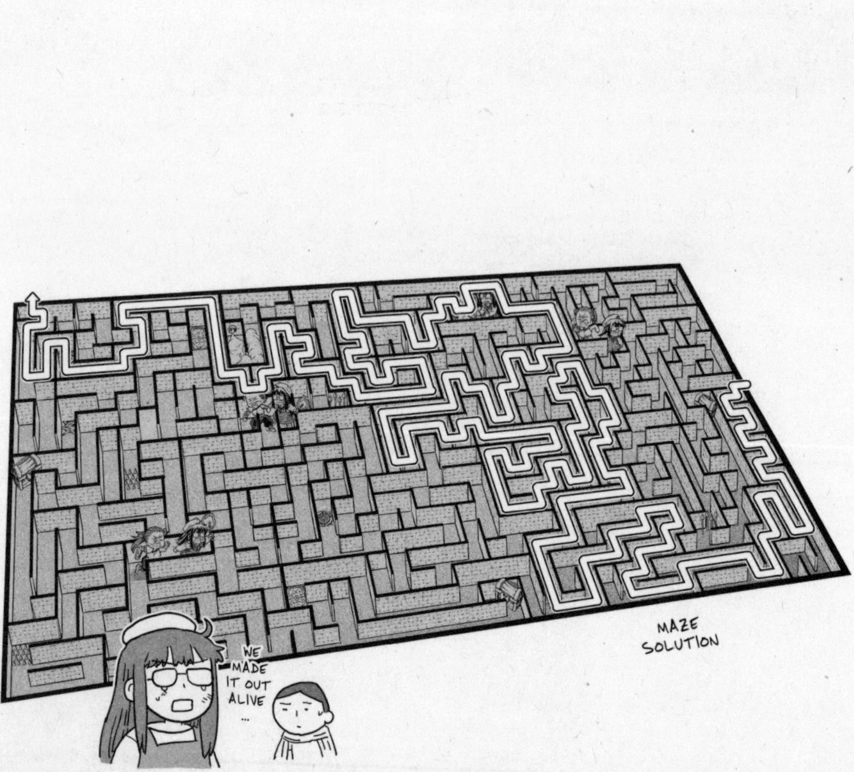
MAZE SOLUTION
WE MADE IT OUT ALIVE ...

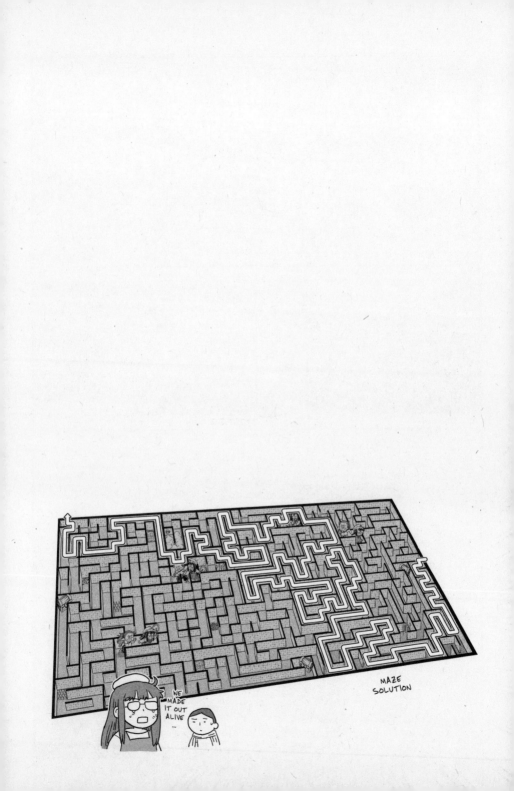

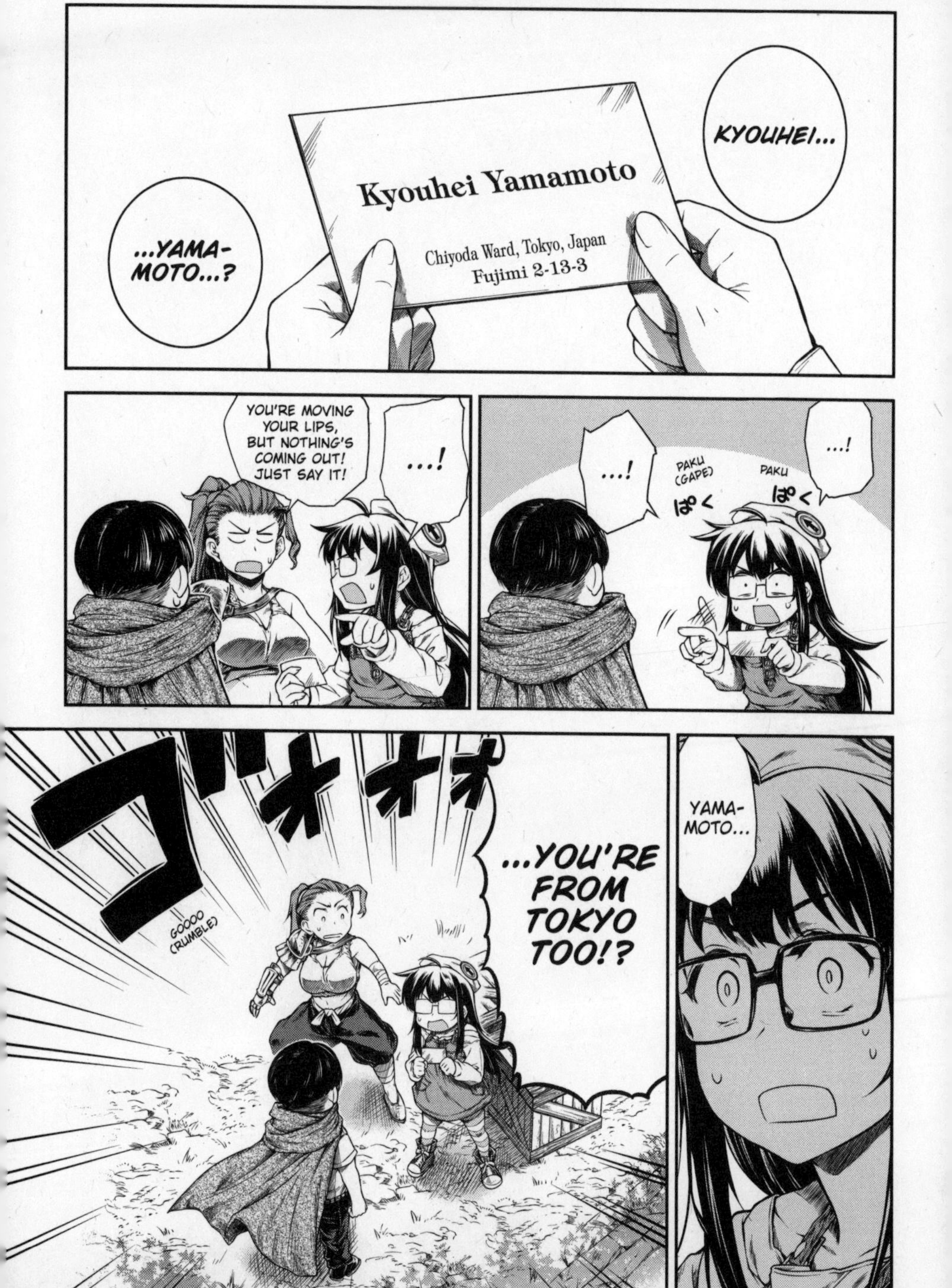

KYOUHEI...
Kyouhei Yamamoto
Chiyoda Ward, Tokyo, Japan
Fujimi 2-13-3
...YAMA-MOTO...?
...!
PAKU ぱく
...!
PAKU (GAPE) ぱく
...!
YOU'RE MOVING YOUR LIPS, BUT NOTHING'S COMING OUT! JUST SAY IT!
YAMA-MOTO...
...YOU'RE FROM TOKYO TOO!?
ゴオオオ
GOOOO (RUMBLE)

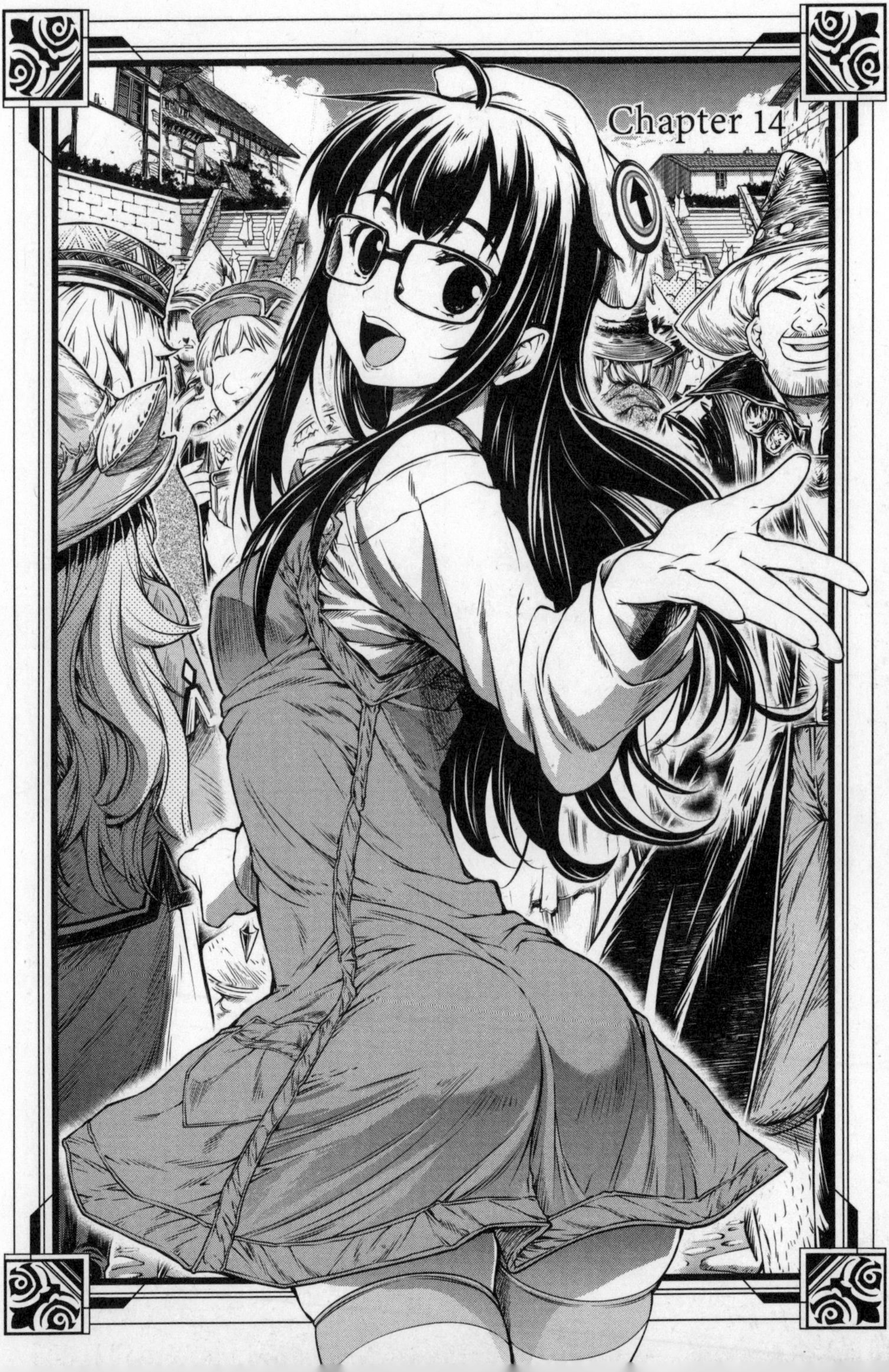
Chapter 14

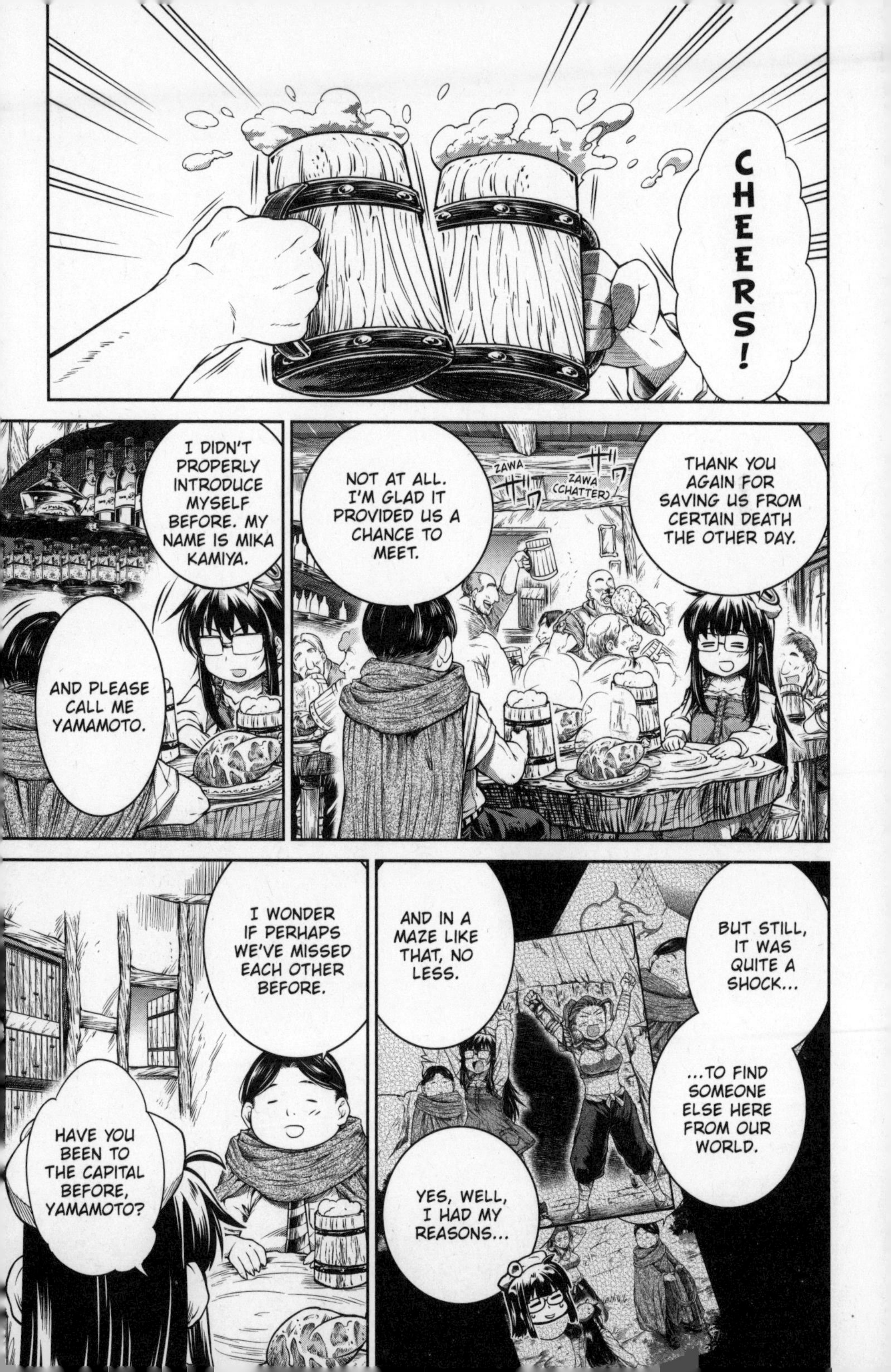
CHEERS!
THANK YOU AGAIN FOR SAVING US FROM CERTAIN DEATH THE OTHER DAY.
ZAWA ZAWA (CHATTER)
NOT AT ALL. I'M GLAD IT PROVIDED US A CHANCE TO MEET.
I DIDN'T PROPERLY INTRODUCE MYSELF BEFORE. MY NAME IS MIKA KAMIYA.
AND PLEASE CALL ME YAMAMOTO.
BUT STILL, IT WAS QUITE A SHOCK...
...TO FIND SOMEONE ELSE HERE FROM OUR WORLD.
AND IN A MAZE LIKE THAT, NO LESS.
YES, WELL, I HAD MY REASONS...
I WONDER IF PERHAPS WE'VE MISSED EACH OTHER BEFORE.
HAVE YOU BEEN TO THE CAPITAL BEFORE, YAMAMOTO?

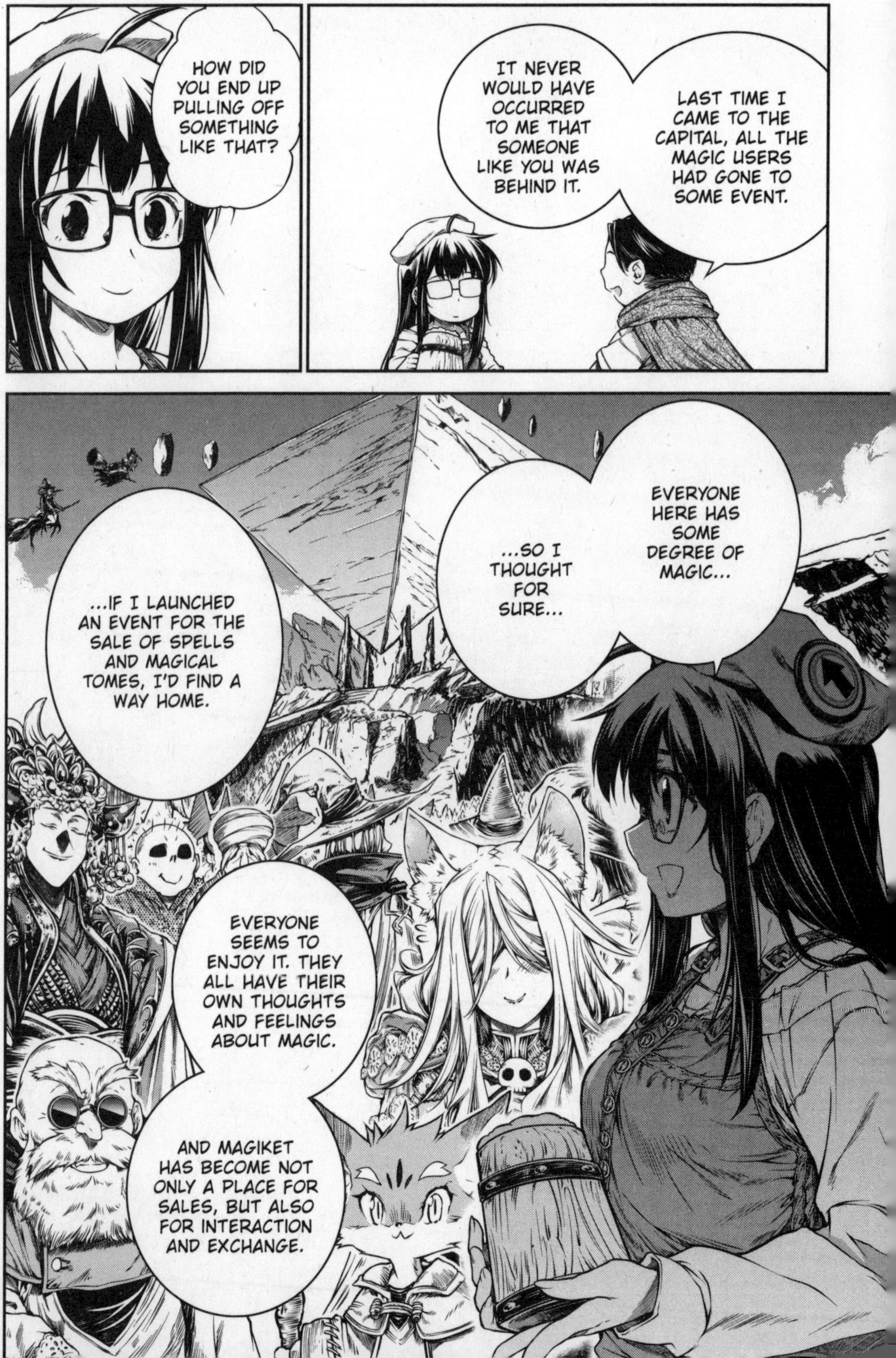
LAST TIME I CAME TO THE CAPITAL, ALL THE MAGIC USERS HAD GONE TO SOME EVENT.
IT NEVER WOULD HAVE OCCURRED TO ME THAT SOMEONE LIKE YOU WAS BEHIND IT.
HOW DID YOU END UP PULLING OFF SOMETHING LIKE THAT?
EVERYONE HERE HAS SOME DEGREE OF MAGIC...
...SO I THOUGHT FOR SURE...
...IF I LAUNCHED AN EVENT FOR THE SALE OF SPELLS AND MAGICAL TOMES, I'D FIND A WAY HOME.
EVERYONE SEEMS TO ENJOY IT. THEY ALL HAVE THEIR OWN THOUGHTS AND FEELINGS ABOUT MAGIC.
AND MAGIKET HAS BECOME NOT ONLY A PLACE FOR SALES, BUT ALSO FOR INTERACTION AND EXCHANGE.

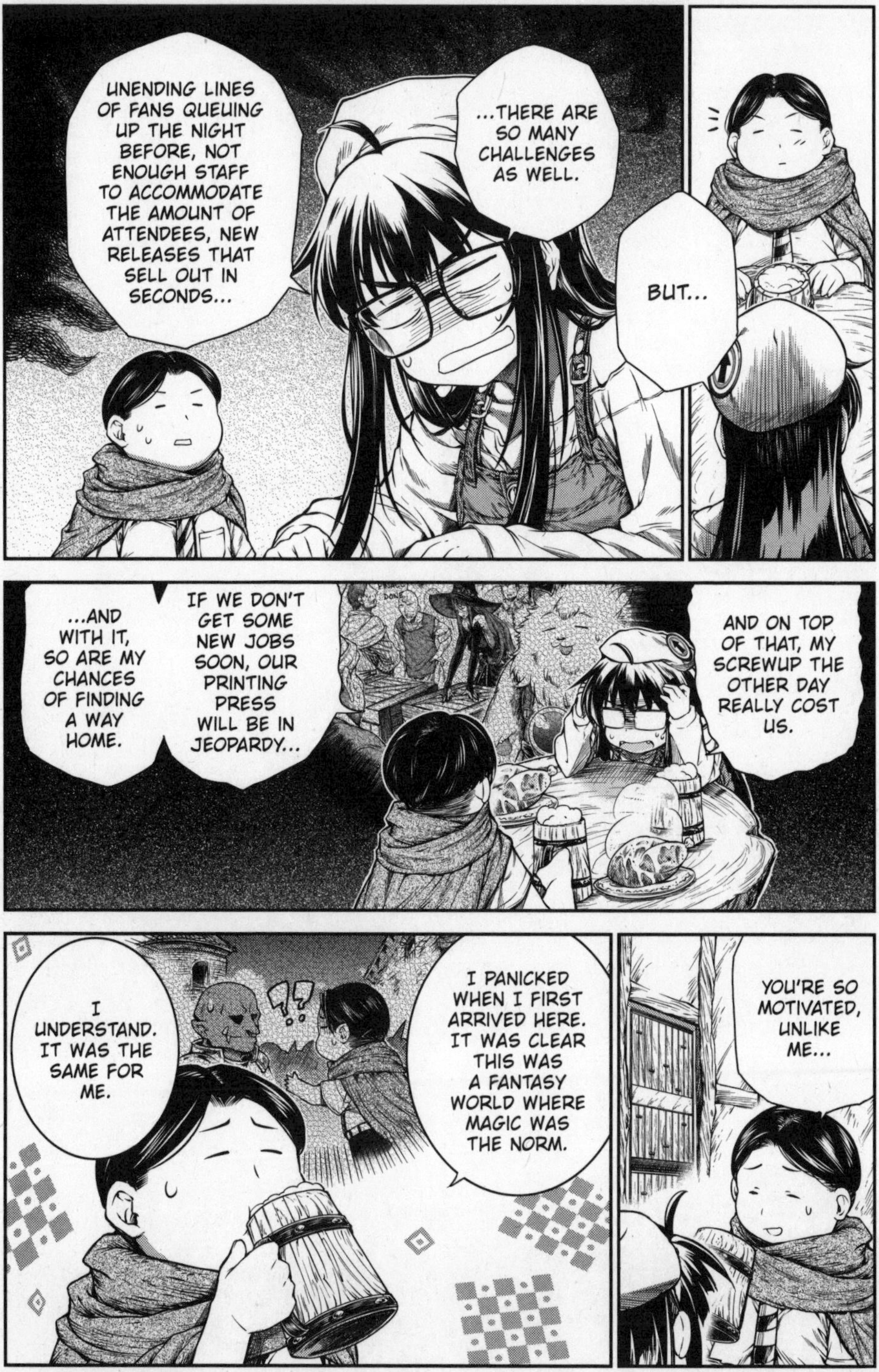
BUT...
...THERE ARE SO MANY CHALLENGES AS WELL.
UNENDING LINES OF FANS QUEUING UP THE NIGHT BEFORE, NOT ENOUGH STAFF TO ACCOMMODATE THE AMOUNT OF ATTENDEES, NEW RELEASES THAT SELL OUT IN SECONDS...
AND ON TOP OF THAT, MY SCREWUP THE OTHER DAY REALLY COST US.
IF WE DON'T GET SOME NEW JOBS SOON, OUR PRINTING PRESS WILL BE IN JEOPARDY...
...AND WITH IT, SO ARE MY CHANCES OF FINDING A WAY HOME.
YOU'RE SO MOTIVATED, UNLIKE ME...
I PANICKED WHEN I FIRST ARRIVED HERE. IT WAS CLEAR THIS WAS A FANTASY WORLD WHERE MAGIC WAS THE NORM.
I UNDERSTAND. IT WAS THE SAME FOR ME.

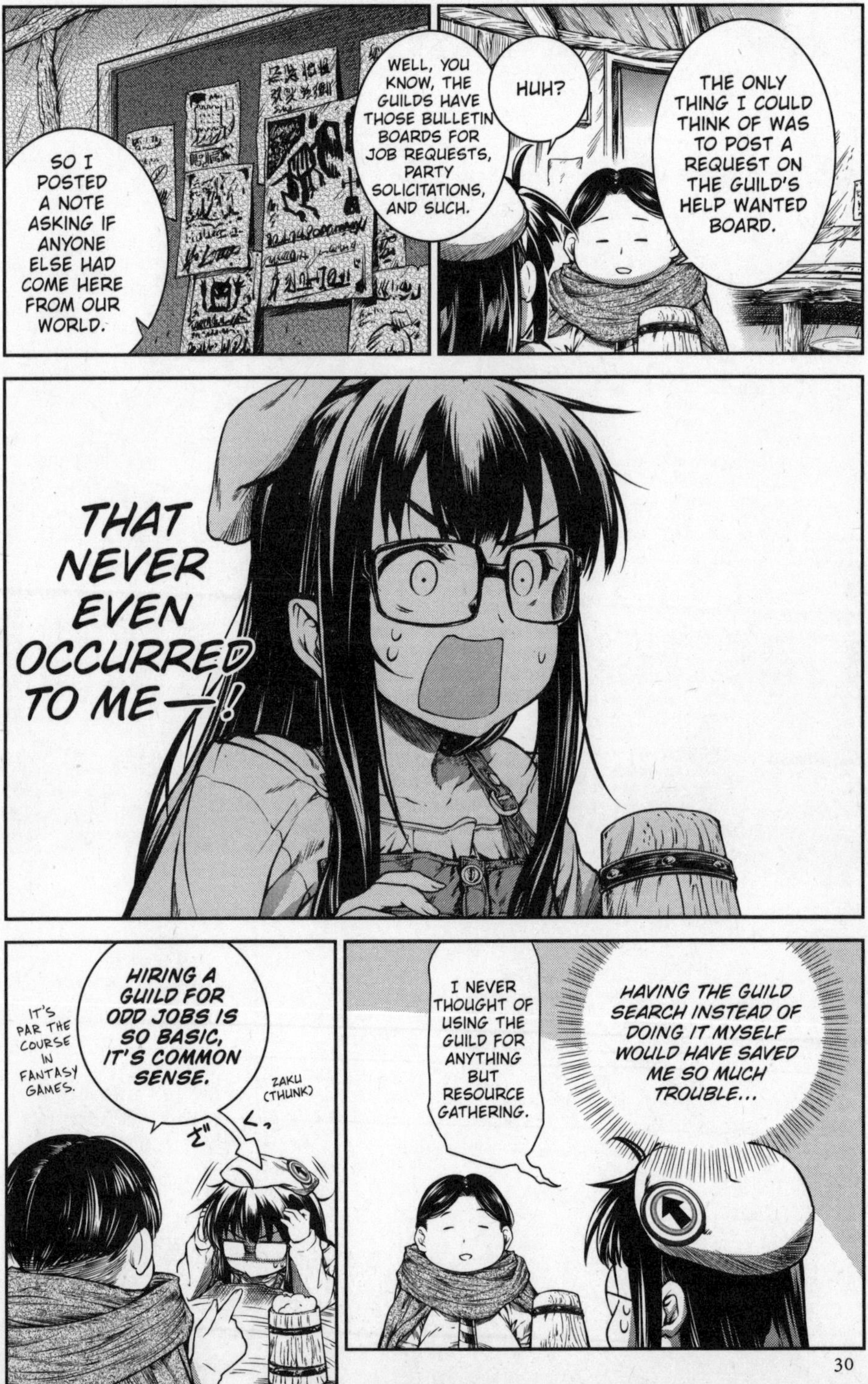
THE ONLY THING I COULD THINK OF WAS TO POST A REQUEST ON THE GUILD'S HELP WANTED BOARD.
HUH?
WELL, YOU KNOW, THE GUILDS HAVE THOSE BULLETIN BOARDS FOR JOB REQUESTS, PARTY SOLICITATIONS, AND SUCH.
SO I POSTED A NOTE ASKING IF ANYONE ELSE HAD COME HERE FROM OUR WORLD.
THAT NEVER EVEN OCCURRED TO ME—!
HAVING THE GUILD SEARCH INSTEAD OF DOING IT MYSELF WOULD HAVE SAVED ME SO MUCH TROUBLE...
I NEVER THOUGHT OF USING THE GUILD FOR ANYTHING BUT RESOURCE GATHERING.
HIRING A GUILD FOR ODD JOBS IS SO BASIC, IT'S COMMON SENSE.
IT'S PAR THE COURSE IN FANTASY GAMES.
ZAKU (THUNK)

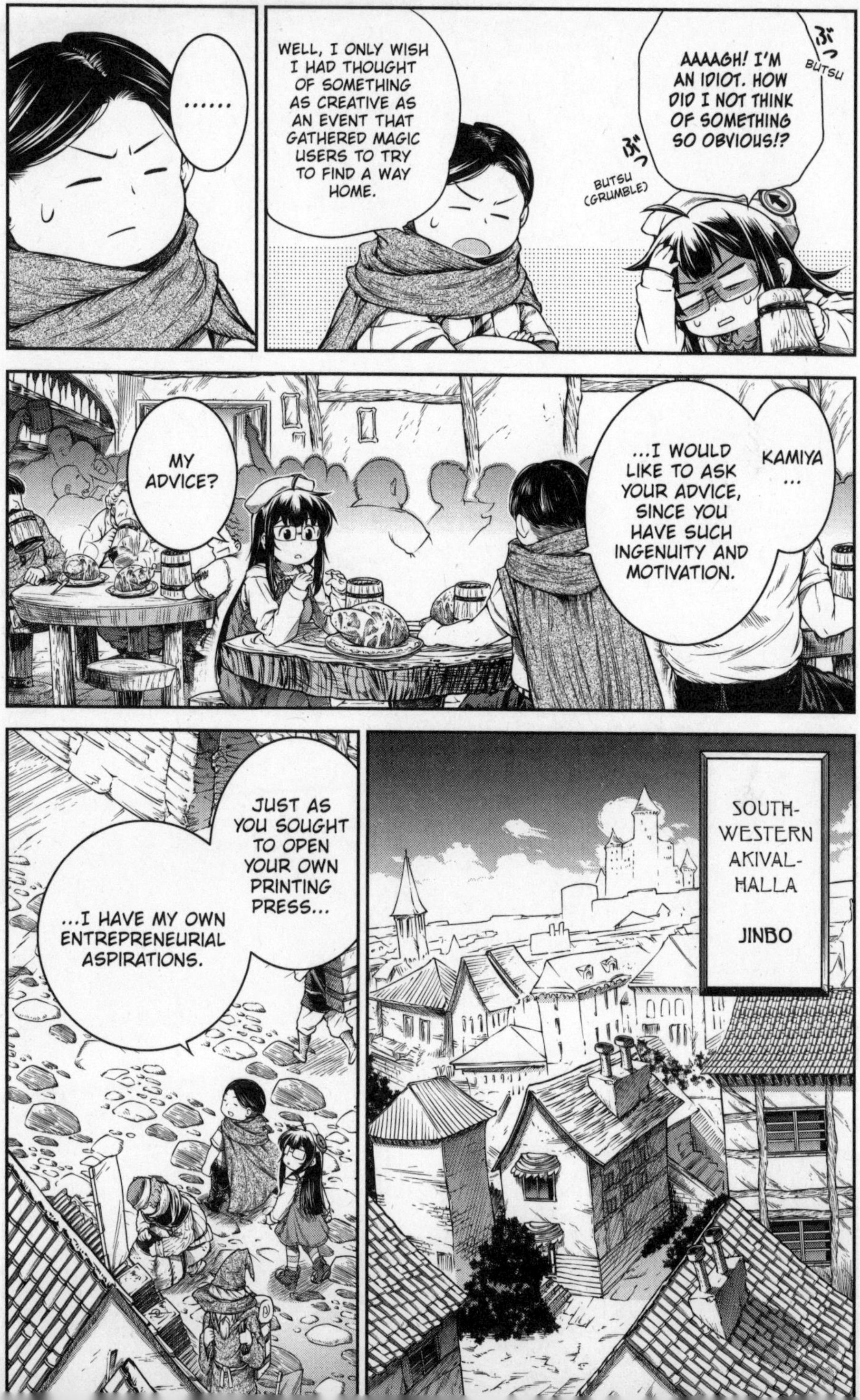
ぶつ
BUTSU
ぶつ
BUTSU (GRUMBLE)
AAAAGH! I'M AN IDIOT. HOW DID I NOT THINK OF SOMETHING SO OBVIOUS!?
WELL, I ONLY WISH I HAD THOUGHT OF SOMETHING AS CREATIVE AS AN EVENT THAT GATHERED MAGIC USERS TO TRY TO FIND A WAY HOME.
......
KAMIYA ...
...I WOULD LIKE TO ASK YOUR ADVICE, SINCE YOU HAVE SUCH INGENUITY AND MOTIVATION.
MY ADVICE?
SOUTH-WESTERN AKIVAL-HALLA
JINBO
JUST AS YOU SOUGHT TO OPEN YOUR OWN PRINTING PRESS...
...I HAVE MY OWN ENTREPRENEURIAL ASPIRATIONS.

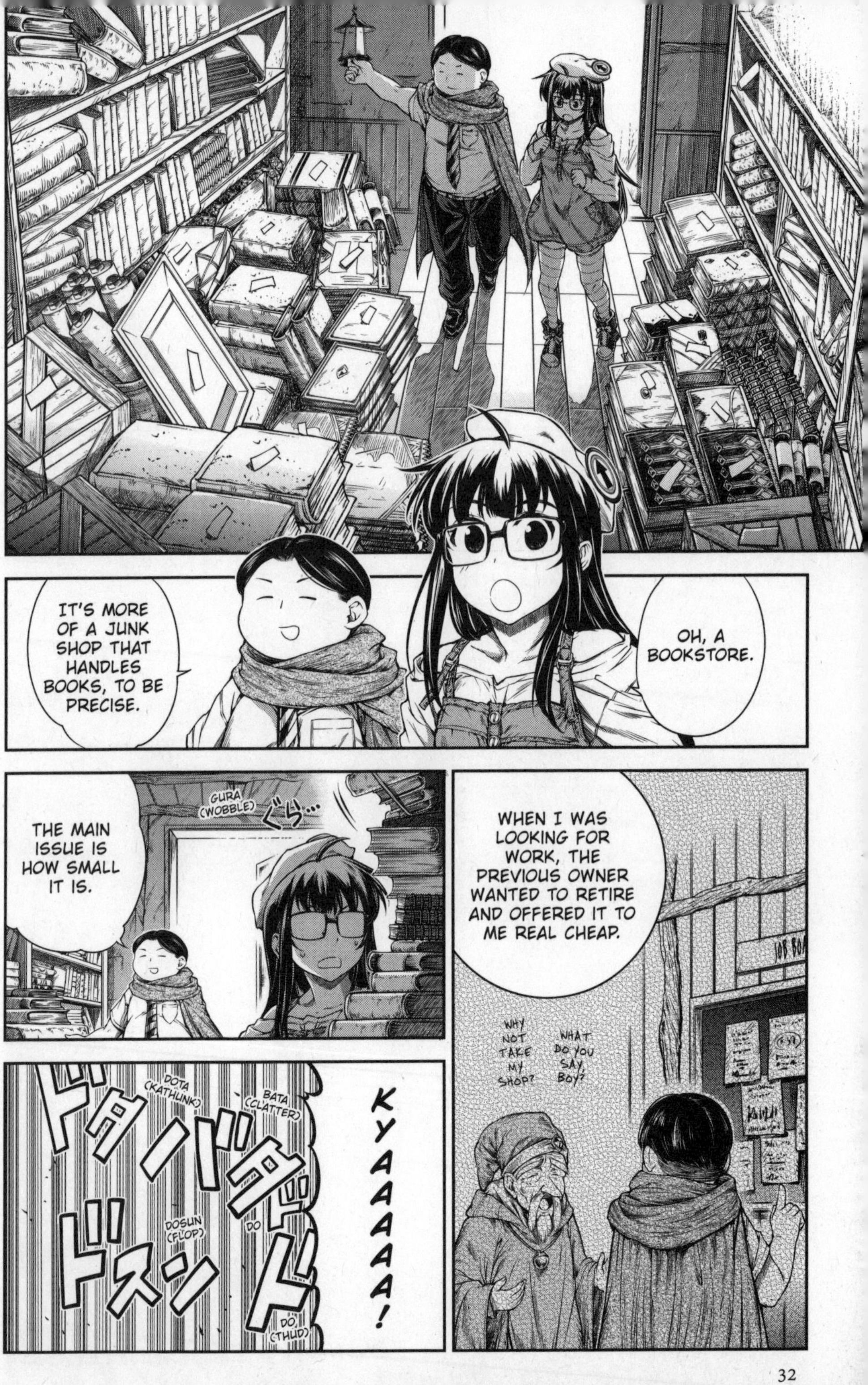
OH, A BOOKSTORE.
IT'S MORE OF A JUNK SHOP THAT HANDLES BOOKS, TO BE PRECISE.
WHEN I WAS LOOKING FOR WORK, THE PREVIOUS OWNER WANTED TO RETIRE AND OFFERED IT TO ME REAL CHEAP.
WHAT DO YOU SAY, BOY?
WHY NOT TAKE MY SHOP?
GURA (WOBBLE) ぐら…
THE MAIN ISSUE IS HOW SMALL IT IS.
KYAAAAAA!
BATA (CLATTER)
DOTA (KATHUNK)
DO
DO (THUD)
DOSUN (FLOP)

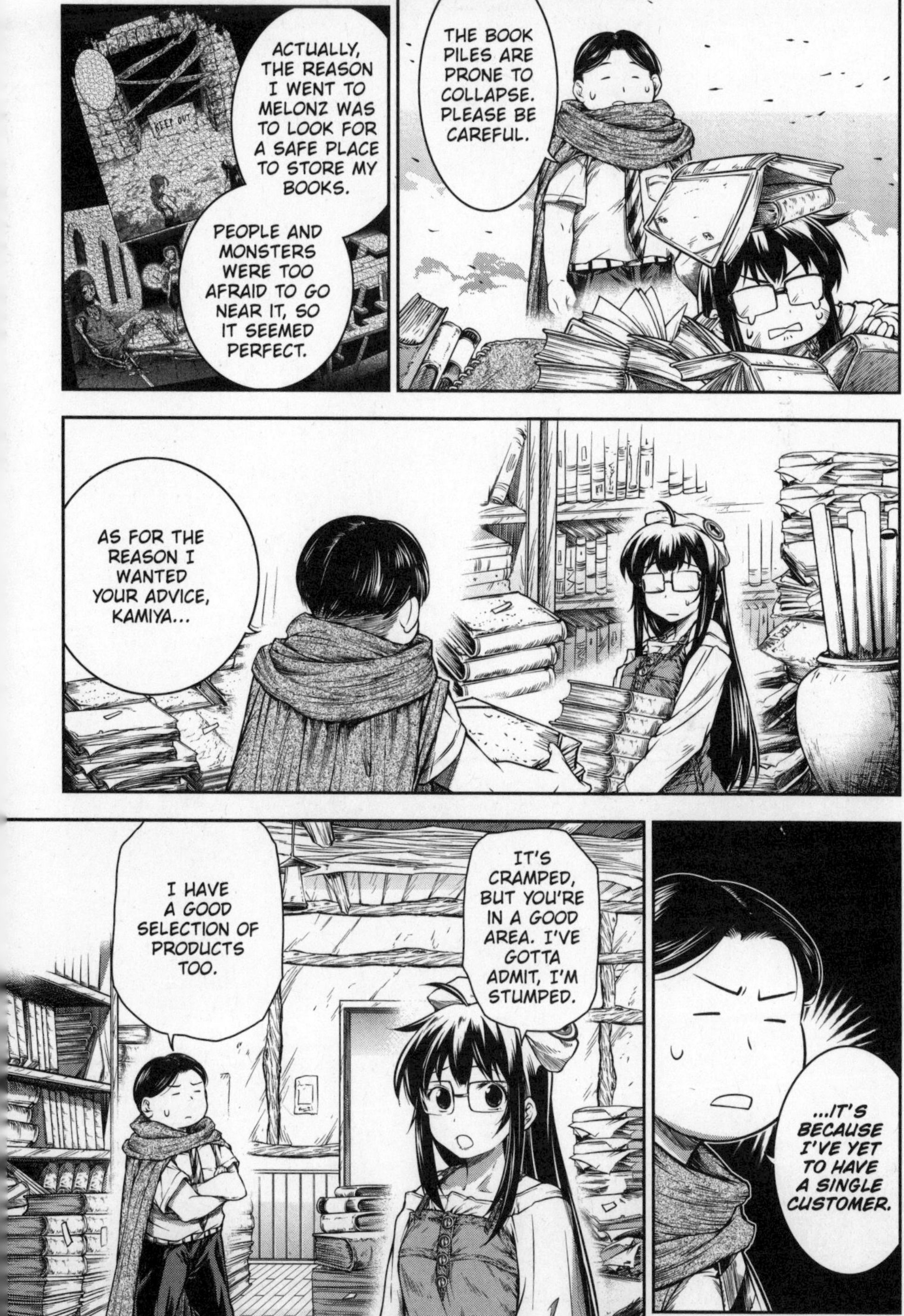
THE BOOK PILES ARE PRONE TO COLLAPSE. PLEASE BE CAREFUL.
ACTUALLY, THE REASON I WENT TO MELONZ WAS TO LOOK FOR A SAFE PLACE TO STORE MY BOOKS.
PEOPLE AND MONSTERS WERE TOO AFRAID TO GO NEAR IT, SO IT SEEMED PERFECT.
AS FOR THE REASON I WANTED YOUR ADVICE, KAMIYA...
...IT'S BECAUSE I'VE YET TO HAVE A SINGLE CUSTOMER.
IT'S CRAMPED, BUT YOU'RE IN A GOOD AREA. I'VE GOTTA ADMIT, I'M STUMPED.
I HAVE A GOOD SELECTION OF PRODUCTS TOO.

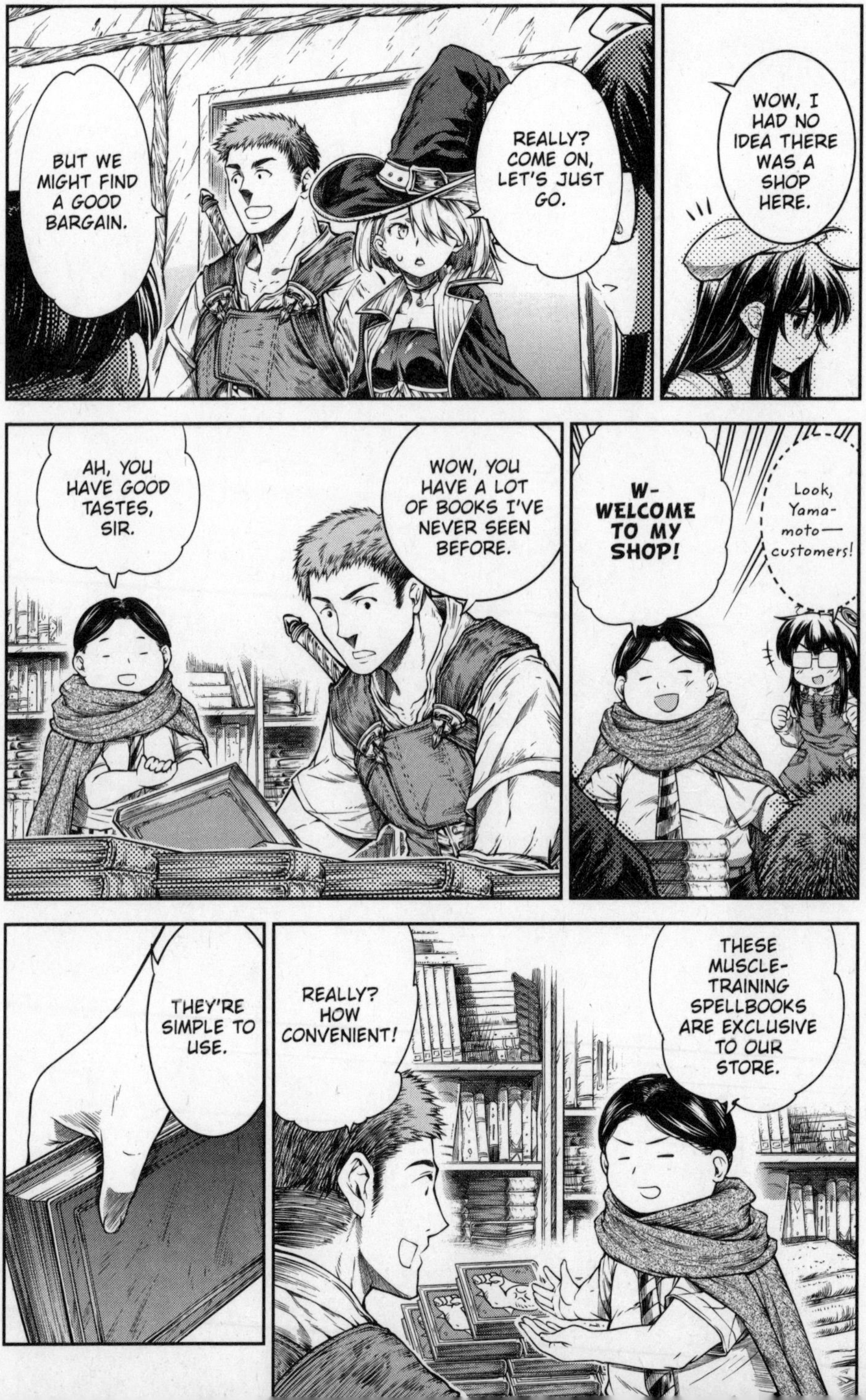
WOW, I HAD NO IDEA THERE WAS A SHOP HERE.
REALLY? COME ON, LET'S JUST GO.
BUT WE MIGHT FIND A GOOD BARGAIN.
Look, Yamamoto—customers!
W-WELCOME TO MY SHOP!
WOW, YOU HAVE A LOT OF BOOKS I'VE NEVER SEEN BEFORE.
AH, YOU HAVE GOOD TASTES, SIR.
THESE MUSCLE-TRAINING SPELLBOOKS ARE EXCLUSIVE TO OUR STORE.
REALLY? HOW CONVENIENT!
THEY'RE SIMPLE TO USE.

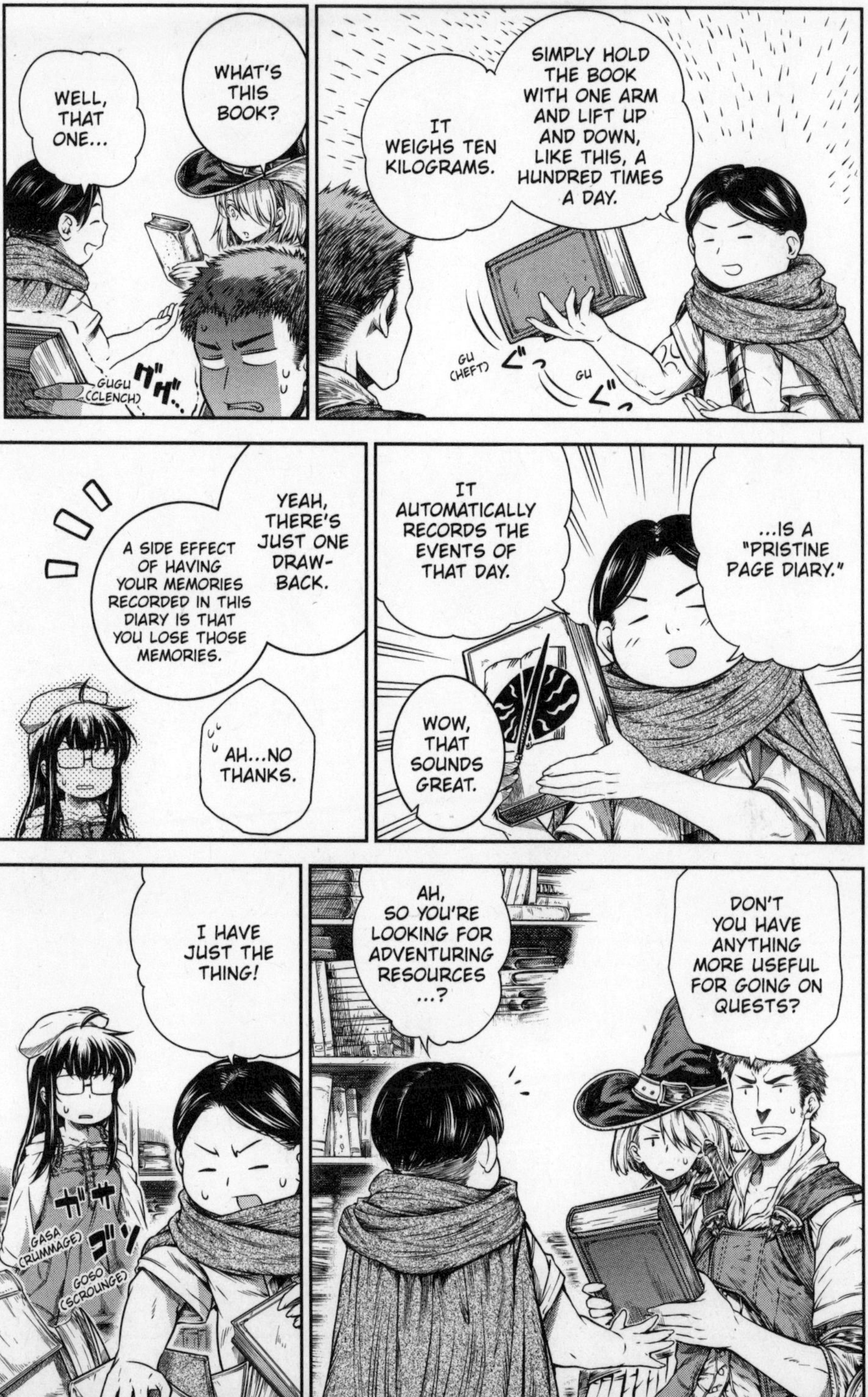
SIMPLY HOLD THE BOOK WITH ONE ARM AND LIFT UP AND DOWN, LIKE THIS, A HUNDRED TIMES A DAY.
IT WEIGHS TEN KILOGRAMS.
GU (HEFT)
GU
WHAT'S THIS BOOK?
WELL, THAT ONE...
GUGU (CLENCH)
...IS A "PRISTINE PAGE DIARY."
IT AUTOMATICALLY RECORDS THE EVENTS OF THAT DAY.
WOW, THAT SOUNDS GREAT.
YEAH, THERE'S JUST ONE DRAW-BACK.
A SIDE EFFECT OF HAVING YOUR MEMORIES RECORDED IN THIS DIARY IS THAT YOU LOSE THOSE MEMORIES.
AH...NO THANKS.
DON'T YOU HAVE ANYTHING MORE USEFUL FOR GOING ON QUESTS?
AH, SO YOU'RE LOOKING FOR ADVENTURING RESOURCES ...?
I HAVE JUST THE THING!
GASA (RUMMAGE)
GOSO (SCROUNGE)

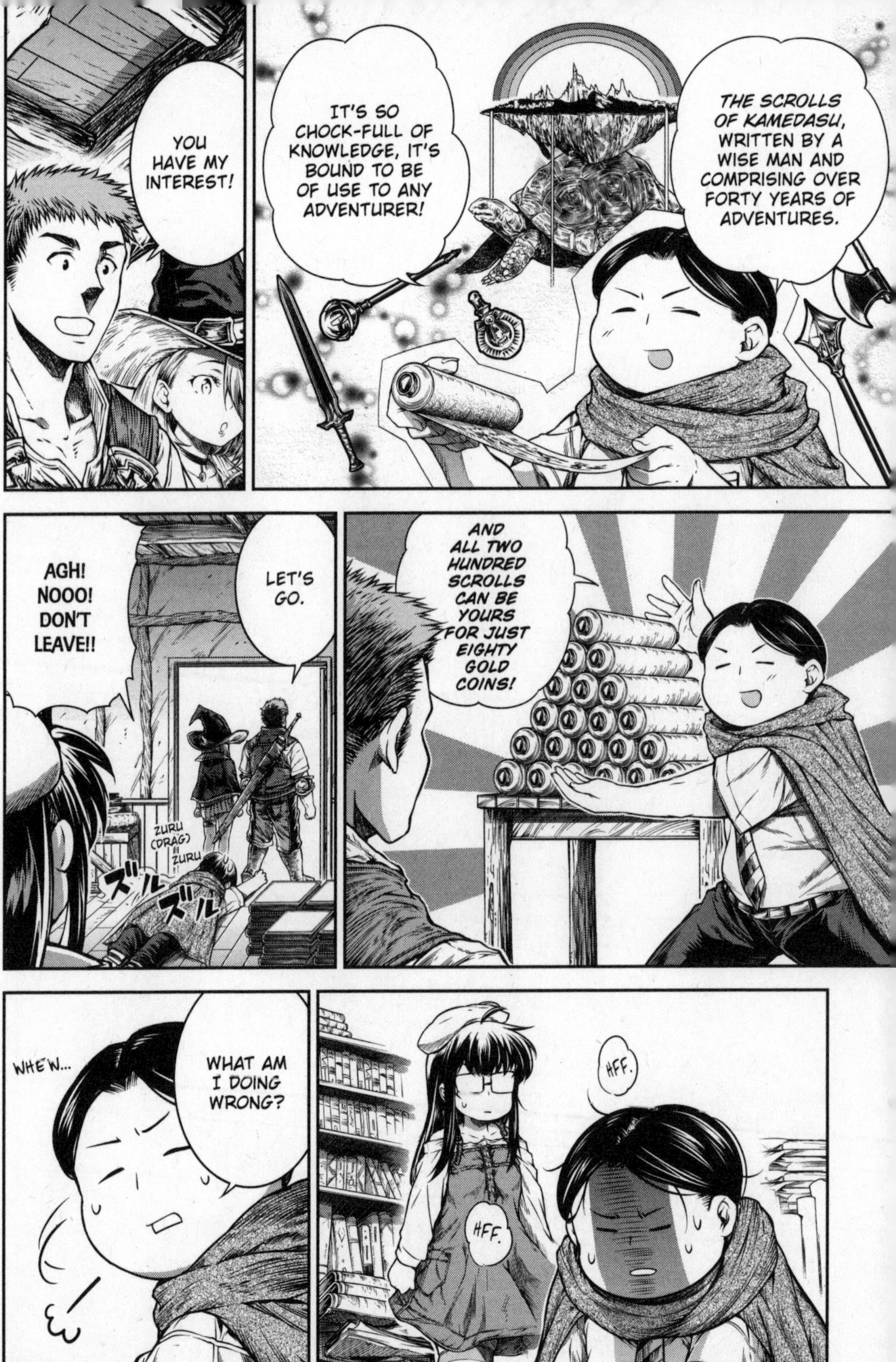
THE SCROLLS OF KAMEDASU, WRITTEN BY A WISE MAN AND COMPRISING OVER FORTY YEARS OF ADVENTURES.
IT'S SO CHOCK-FULL OF KNOWLEDGE, IT'S BOUND TO BE OF USE TO ANY ADVENTURER!
YOU HAVE MY INTEREST!
AND ALL TWO HUNDRED SCROLLS CAN BE YOURS FOR JUST EIGHTY GOLD COINS!
LET'S GO.
AGH! NOOO! DON'T LEAVE!!
ZURU (DRAG) ZURU
HFF.
HFF.
WHAT AM I DOING WRONG?
WHEW...

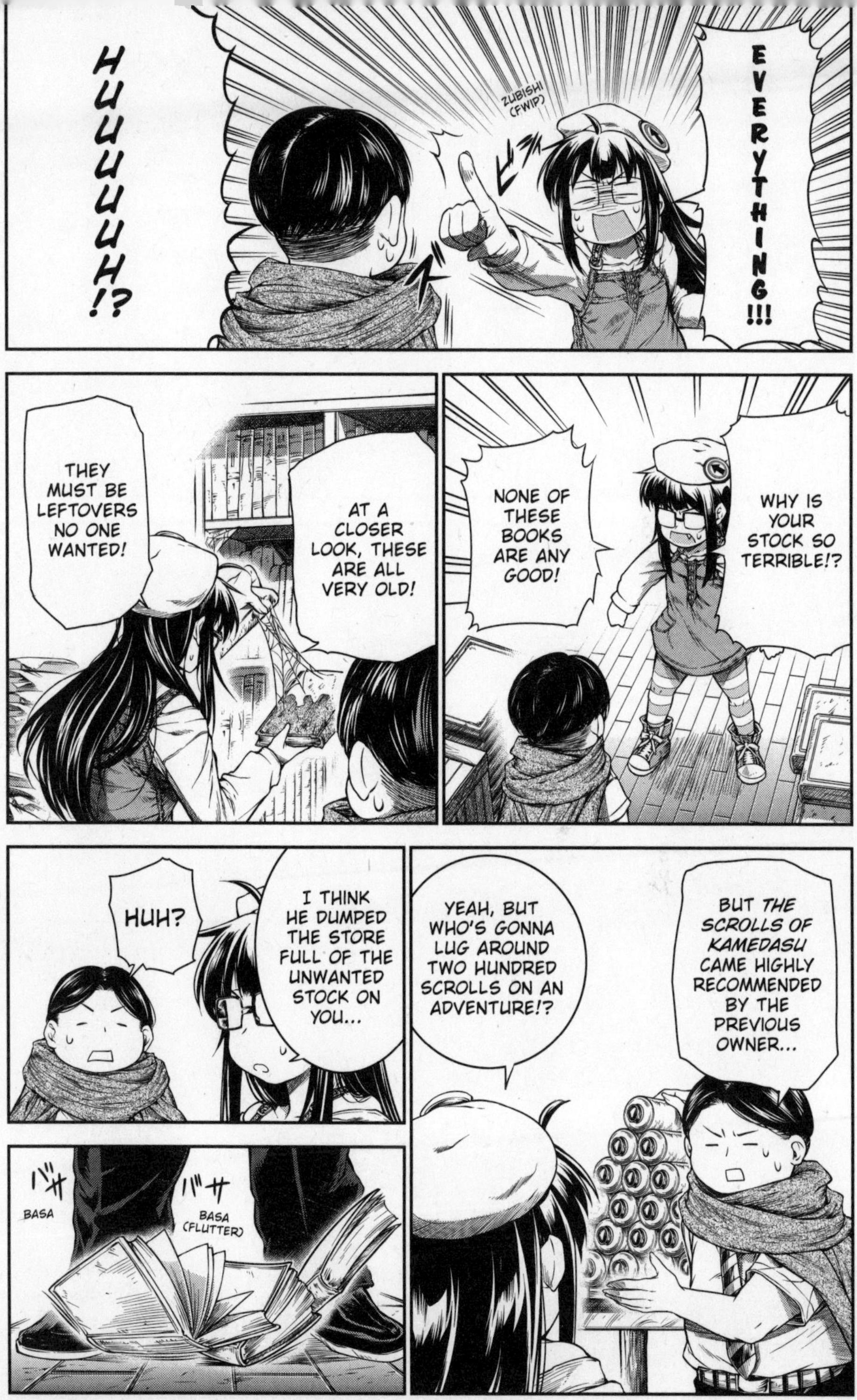
EVERYTHING!!!
ZUBISHI (FWIP)
HUUUUUUH!?
WHY IS YOUR STOCK SO TERRIBLE!?
NONE OF THESE BOOKS ARE ANY GOOD!
AT A CLOSER LOOK, THESE ARE ALL VERY OLD!
THEY MUST BE LEFTOVERS NO ONE WANTED!
BUT *THE SCROLLS OF KAMEDASU* CAME HIGHLY RECOMMENDED BY THE PREVIOUS OWNER...
YEAH, BUT WHO'S GONNA LUG AROUND TWO HUNDRED SCROLLS ON AN ADVENTURE!?
I THINK HE DUMPED THE STORE FULL OF THE UNWANTED STOCK ON YOU...
HUH?
バサ
BASA (FLUTTER)
バサ
BASA

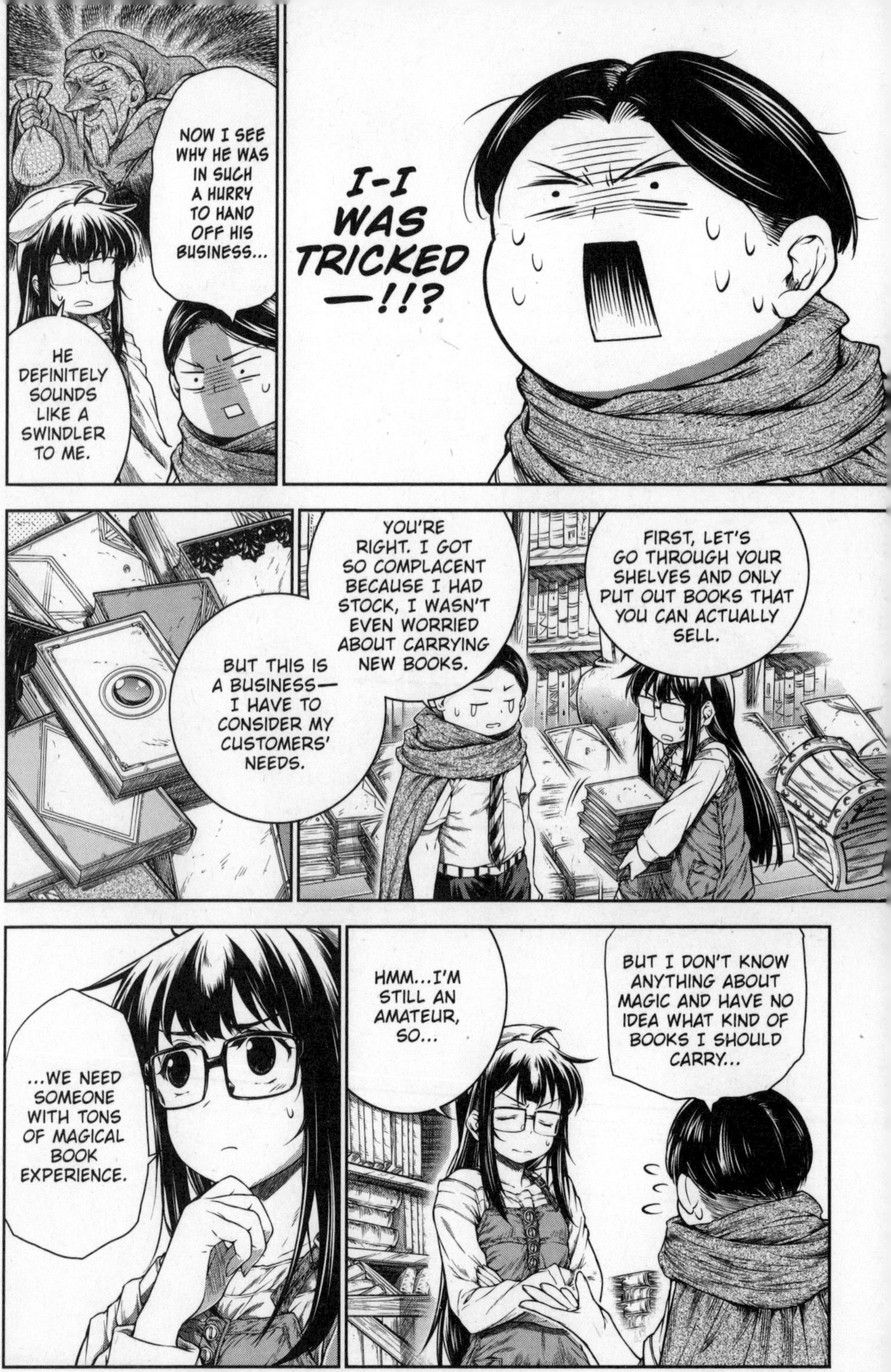
I-I WAS TRICKED—!!?
NOW I SEE WHY HE WAS IN SUCH A HURRY TO HAND OFF HIS BUSINESS...
HE DEFINITELY SOUNDS LIKE A SWINDLER TO ME.
FIRST, LET'S GO THROUGH YOUR SHELVES AND ONLY PUT OUT BOOKS THAT YOU CAN ACTUALLY SELL.
YOU'RE RIGHT. I GOT SO COMPLACENT BECAUSE I HAD STOCK, I WASN'T EVEN WORRIED ABOUT CARRYING NEW BOOKS.
BUT THIS IS A BUSINESS—I HAVE TO CONSIDER MY CUSTOMERS' NEEDS.
BUT I DON'T KNOW ANYTHING ABOUT MAGIC AND HAVE NO IDEA WHAT KIND OF BOOKS I SHOULD CARRY...
HMM...I'M STILL AN AMATEUR, SO...
...WE NEED SOMEONE WITH TONS OF MAGICAL BOOK EXPERIENCE.

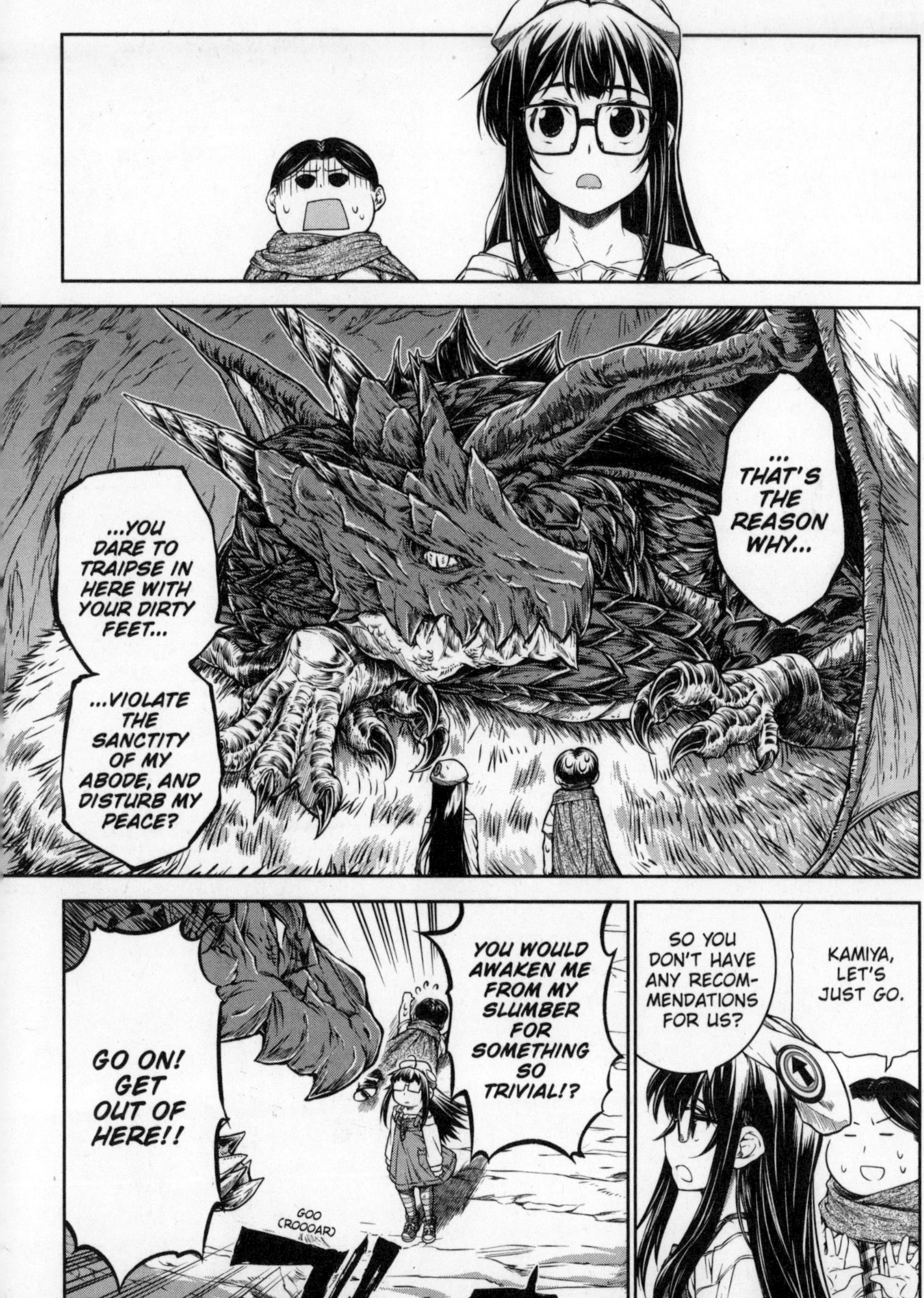
...THAT'S THE REASON WHY...
...YOU DARE TO TRAIPSE IN HERE WITH YOUR DIRTY FEET...
...VIOLATE THE SANCTITY OF MY ABODE, AND DISTURB MY PEACE?
KAMIYA, LET'S JUST GO.
SO YOU DON'T HAVE ANY RECOM-MENDATIONS FOR US?
YOU WOULD AWAKEN ME FROM MY SLUMBER FOR SOMETHING SO TRIVIAL!?
GO ON! GET OUT OF HERE!!
GOO (ROOOAR)

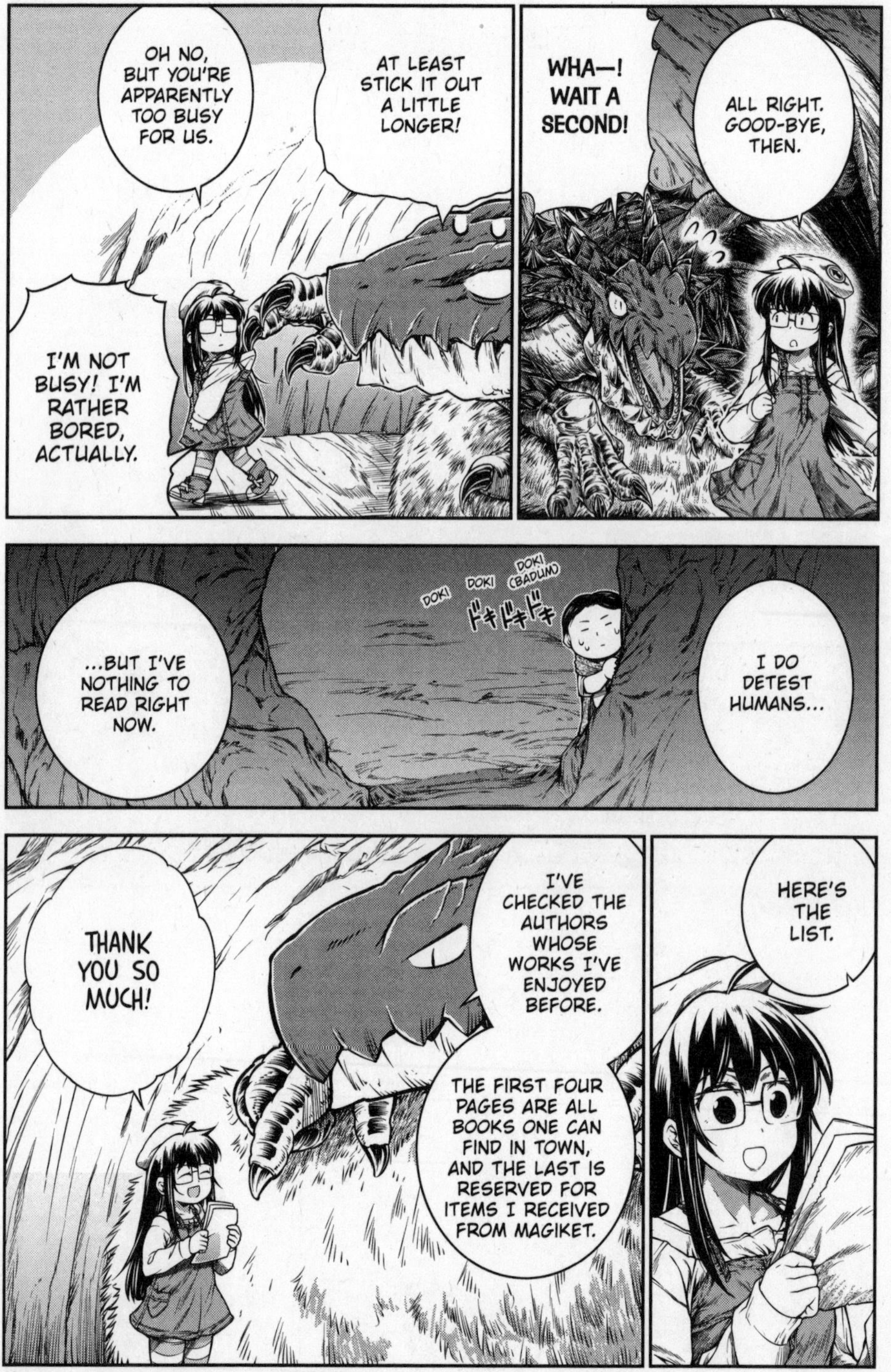
ALL RIGHT. GOOD-BYE, THEN.
WHA—! WAIT A SECOND!
AT LEAST STICK IT OUT A LITTLE LONGER!
OH NO, BUT YOU'RE APPARENTLY TOO BUSY FOR US.
I'M NOT BUSY! I'M RATHER BORED, ACTUALLY.
I DO DETEST HUMANS...
DOKI DOKI DOKI (BADUM)
ドキドキドキ
...BUT I'VE NOTHING TO READ RIGHT NOW.
HERE'S THE LIST.
I'VE CHECKED THE AUTHORS WHOSE WORKS I'VE ENJOYED BEFORE.
THE FIRST FOUR PAGES ARE ALL BOOKS ONE CAN FIND IN TOWN, AND THE LAST IS RESERVED FOR ITEMS I RECEIVED FROM MAGIKET.
THANK YOU SO MUCH!

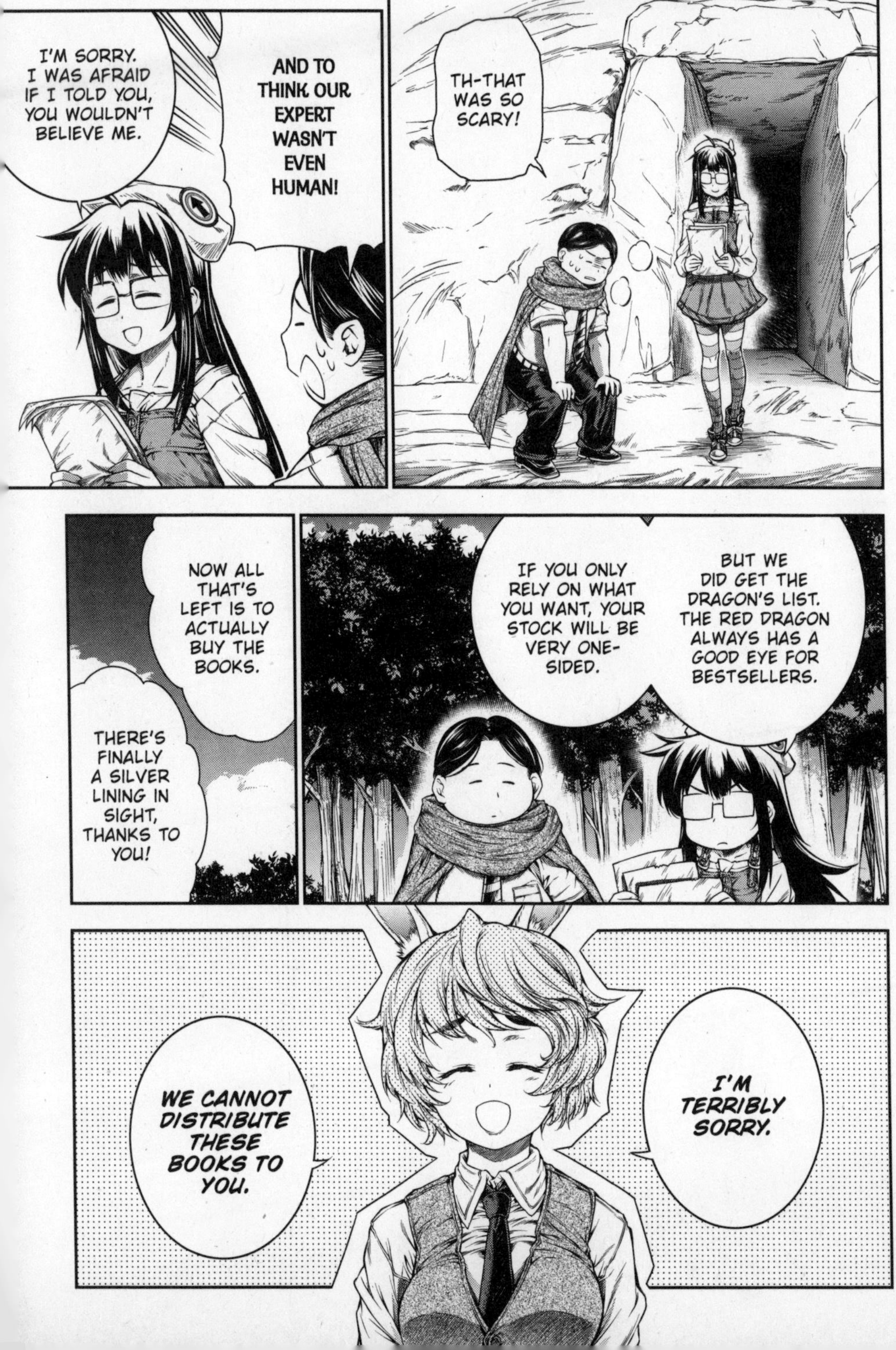
TH-THAT WAS SO SCARY!
AND TO THINK OUR EXPERT WASN'T EVEN HUMAN!
I'M SORRY. I WAS AFRAID IF I TOLD YOU, YOU WOULDN'T BELIEVE ME.
BUT WE DID GET THE DRAGON'S LIST. THE RED DRAGON ALWAYS HAS A GOOD EYE FOR BESTSELLERS.
IF YOU ONLY RELY ON WHAT YOU WANT, YOUR STOCK WILL BE VERY ONE-SIDED.
NOW ALL THAT'S LEFT IS TO ACTUALLY BUY THE BOOKS.
THERE'S FINALLY A SILVER LINING IN SIGHT, THANKS TO YOU!
I'M TERRIBLY SORRY.
WE CANNOT DISTRIBUTE THESE BOOKS TO YOU.

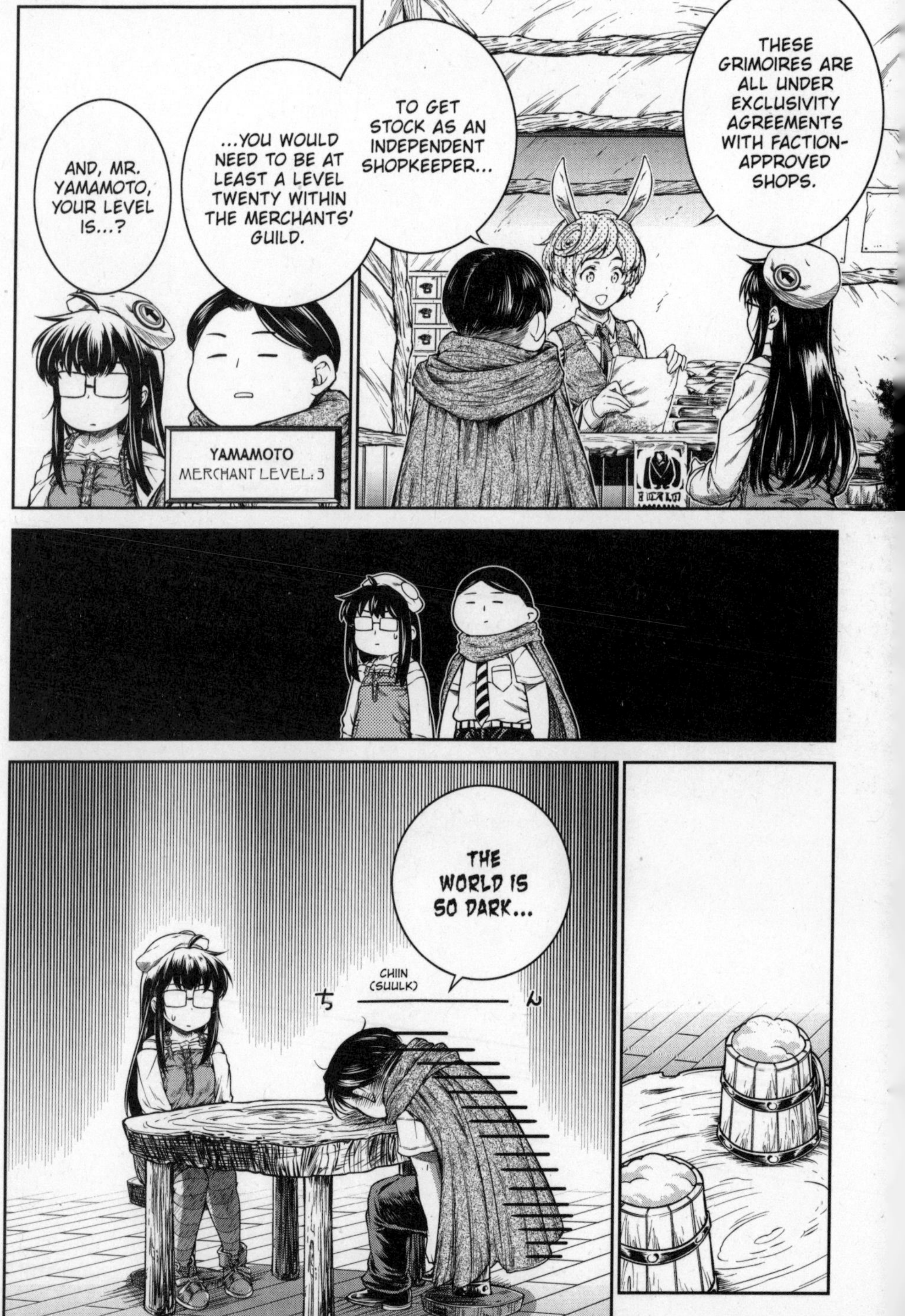
THESE GRIMOIRES ARE ALL UNDER EXCLUSIVITY AGREEMENTS WITH FACTION-APPROVED SHOPS.
TO GET STOCK AS AN INDEPENDENT SHOPKEEPER...
...YOU WOULD NEED TO BE AT LEAST A LEVEL TWENTY WITHIN THE MERCHANTS' GUILD.
AND, MR. YAMAMOTO, YOUR LEVEL IS...?
YAMAMOTO
MERCHANT LEVEL: 3
THE WORLD IS SO DARK...
CHIIN (SUULK)
ち ん

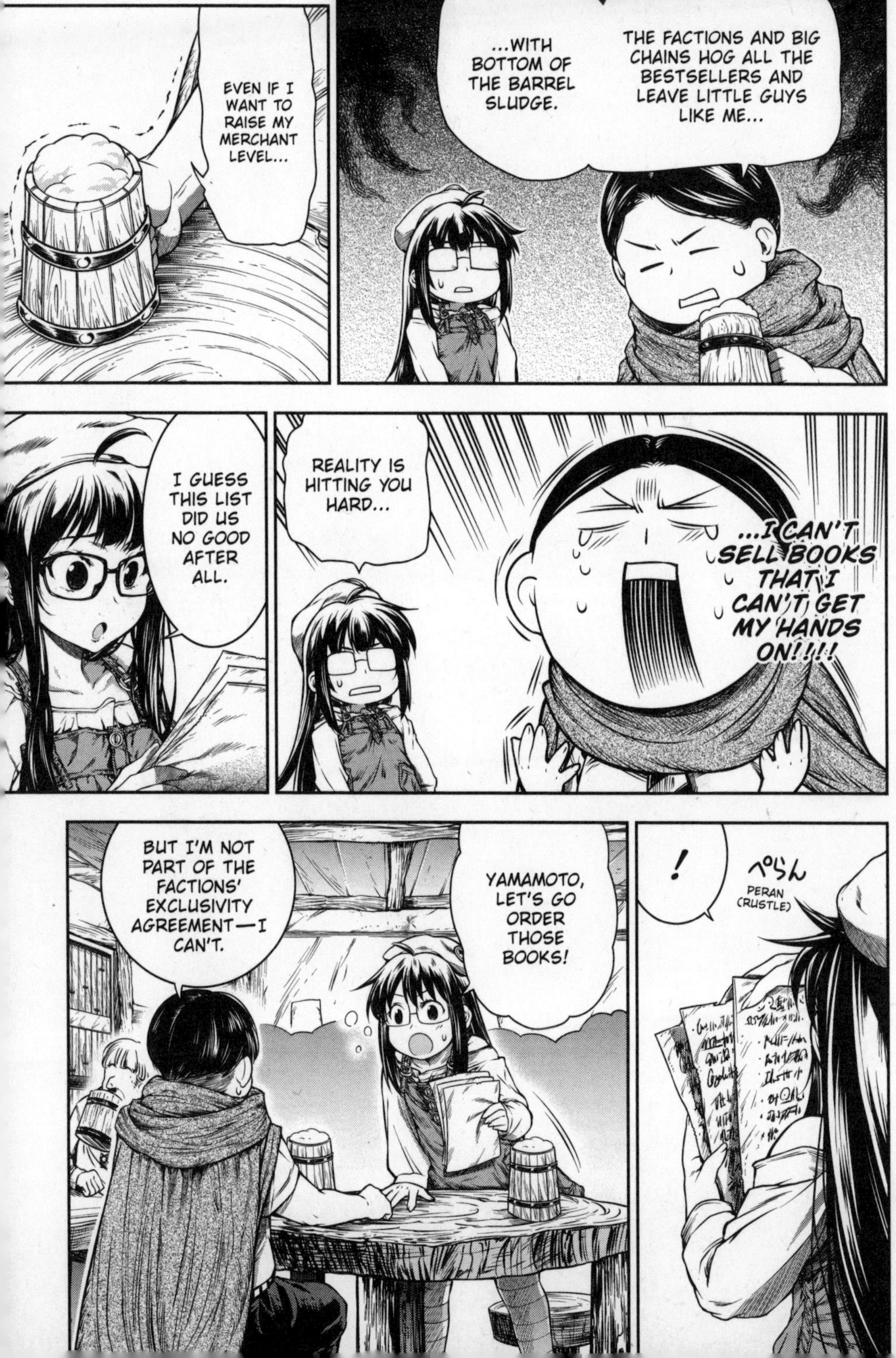
THE FACTIONS AND BIG CHAINS HOG ALL THE BESTSELLERS AND LEAVE LITTLE GUYS LIKE ME...
...WITH BOTTOM OF THE BARREL SLUDGE.
EVEN IF I WANT TO RAISE MY MERCHANT LEVEL...
...I CAN'T SELL BOOKS THAT I CAN'T GET MY HANDS ON!!!!
REALITY IS HITTING YOU HARD...
I GUESS THIS LIST DID US NO GOOD AFTER ALL.
!
ぺらん
PERAN (RUSTLE)
YAMAMOTO, LET'S GO ORDER THOSE BOOKS!
BUT I'M NOT PART OF THE FACTIONS' EXCLUSIVITY AGREEMENT—I CAN'T.

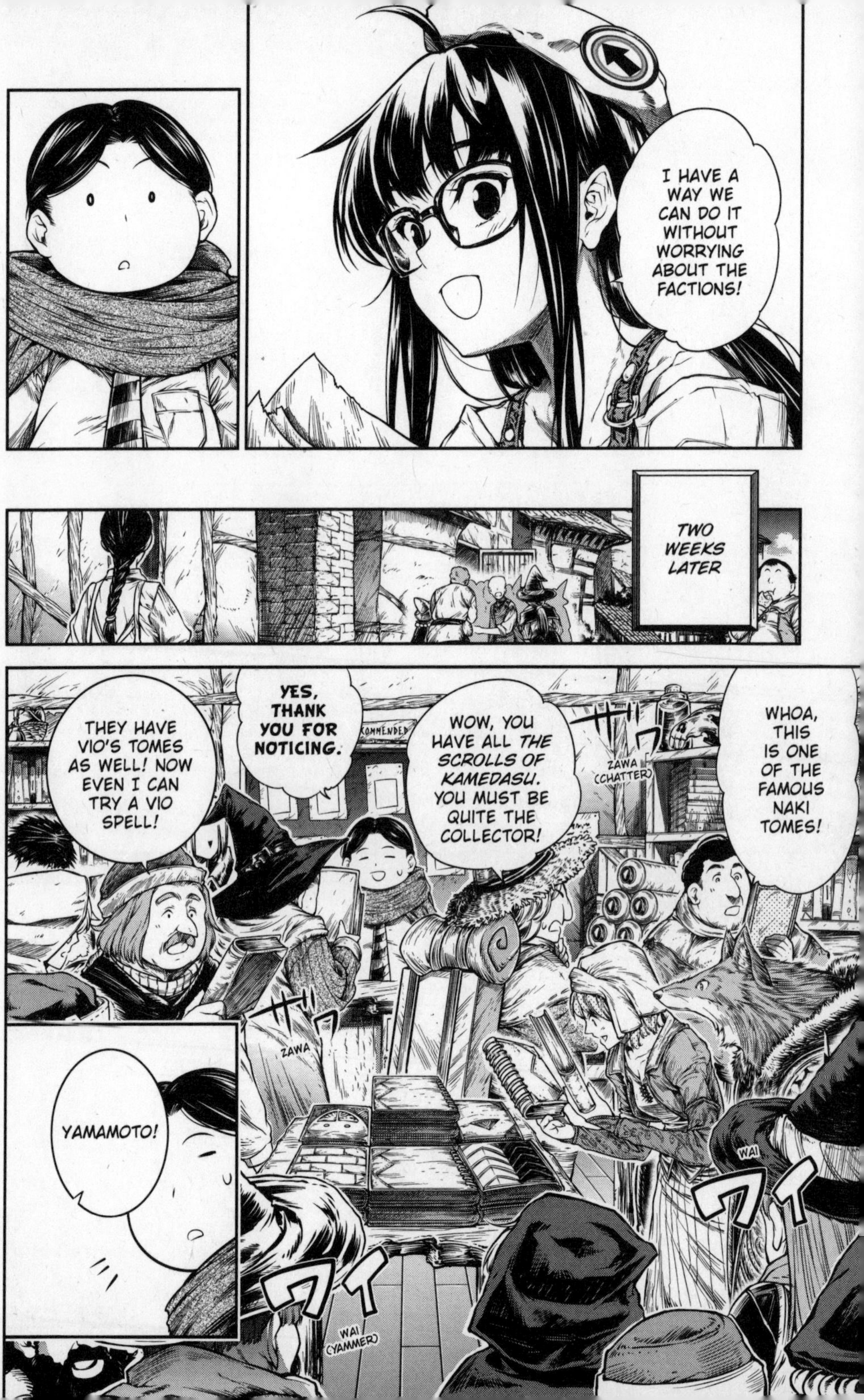

I HAVE A WAY WE CAN DO IT WITHOUT WORRYING ABOUT THE FACTIONS!
TWO WEEKS LATER
WHOA, THIS IS ONE OF THE FAMOUS NAKI TOMES!
ZAWA (CHATTER)
WOW, YOU HAVE ALL *THE SCROLLS OF KAMEDASU*. YOU MUST BE QUITE THE COLLECTOR!
YES, THANK YOU FOR NOTICING.
THEY HAVE VIO'S TOMES AS WELL! NOW EVEN I CAN TRY A VIO SPELL!
ZAWA
WAI
WAI (YAMMER)
YAMAMOTO!

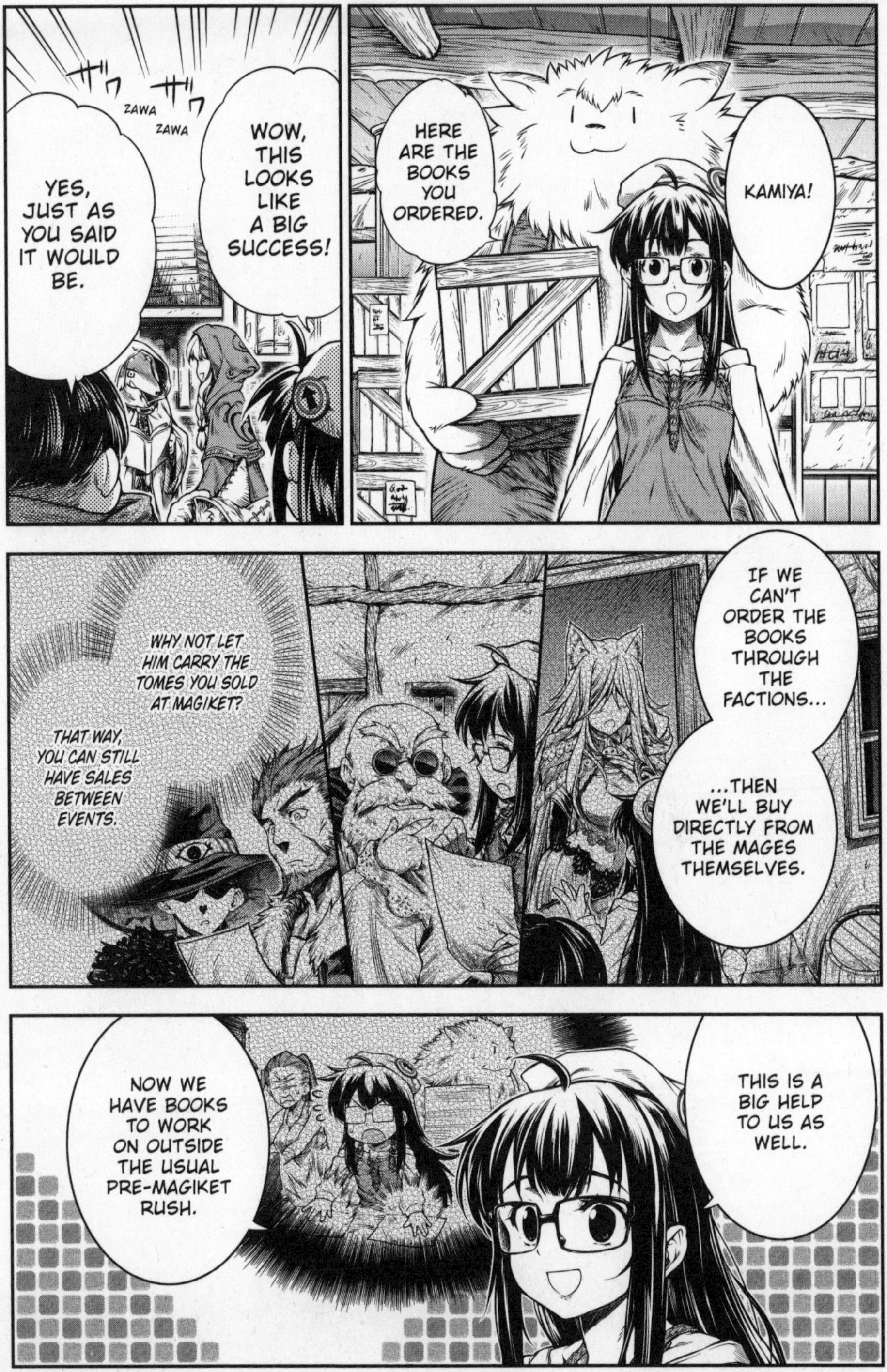
KAMIYA!
HERE ARE THE BOOKS YOU ORDERED.
WOW, THIS LOOKS LIKE A BIG SUCCESS!
ザワ ザワ
ZAWA ZAWA
YES, JUST AS YOU SAID IT WOULD BE.
IF WE CAN'T ORDER THE BOOKS THROUGH THE FACTIONS...
...THEN WE'LL BUY DIRECTLY FROM THE MAGES THEMSELVES.
WHY NOT LET HIM CARRY THE TOMES YOU SOLD AT MAGIKET?
THAT WAY, YOU CAN STILL HAVE SALES BETWEEN EVENTS.
THIS IS A BIG HELP TO US AS WELL.
NOW WE HAVE BOOKS TO WORK ON OUTSIDE THE USUAL PRE-MAGIKET RUSH.

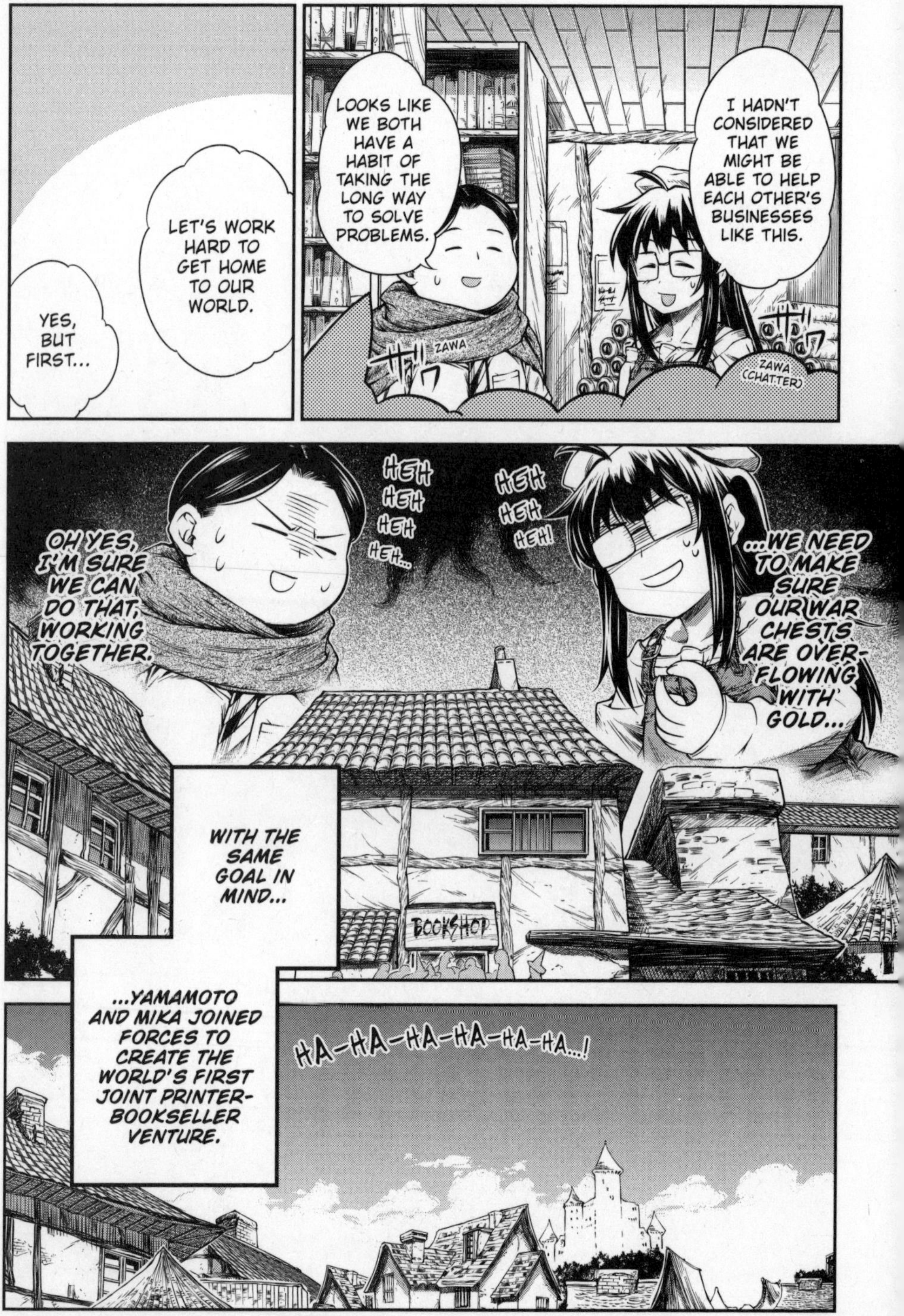
I HADN'T CONSIDERED THAT WE MIGHT BE ABLE TO HELP EACH OTHER'S BUSINESSES LIKE THIS.
LOOKS LIKE WE BOTH HAVE A HABIT OF TAKING THE LONG WAY TO SOLVE PROBLEMS.
ZAWA (CHATTER)
ZAWA
LET'S WORK HARD TO GET HOME TO OUR WORLD.
YES, BUT FIRST...
...WE NEED TO MAKE SURE OUR WAR CHESTS ARE OVER-FLOWING WITH GOLD...
HEH HEH HEH!
HEH HEH HEH HEH...
OH YES, I'M SURE WE CAN DO THAT, WORKING TOGETHER.
BOOKSHOP
WITH THE SAME GOAL IN MIND...
...YAMAMOTO AND MIKA JOINED FORCES TO CREATE THE WORLD'S FIRST JOINT PRINTER-BOOKSELLER VENTURE.
HA-HA-HA-HA-HA-HA-HA...!

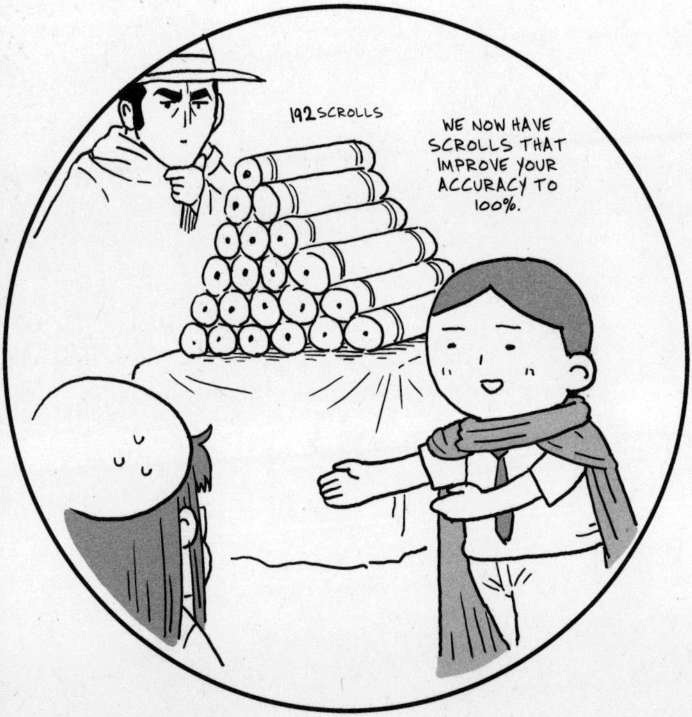
192 SCROLLS
WE NOW HAVE SCROLLS THAT IMPROVE YOUR ACCURACY TO 100%.

TRANSLATION NOTES

Page 7 – The Endless Maze
The Endless Maze Melonz is a callout to Melonbooks, a bookstore chain known specifically for selling *doujinshi*, or fan-made works. Their stores are often packed with books and hard to navigate. Yamamoto's little bookstore, packed as it is with oddball titles and fan favorites, is apparently this world's equivalent.

Page 31 – Jinbo
The town of Jinbo is a play on *Jinbouchou,* an area of Tokyo known for its used-book stores and publishing houses.

Page 49
Fans of *Girls und Panzer* will probably find quite a few references to the girls in battling tanks anime throughout this chapter. From the names of the teams used in Mihon's magical chant, to the name of their town being a play on Ooarai Girls Academy, see how many references you can catch!

Page 58 – Witches of the Black Forest
One of the prominent schools in *Girls und Panzer* is Kuromorimine Girls Academy, in which the *Kuromori* can be read as "Black Forest."

Page 76 – Zolken, King of Magic
The villain of this chapter is a reference to one from the *Fate/Grand Order* franchise, known there as the "King of Mages."

Page 99 – Jupps & the Suei Faction
The Suei faction depicted in this chapter is a parody of the real-world publisher, Shueisha. Jupps's name is a play on the word "Jump," as in *Shonen Jump.* As with many situations in this series, their operations are a parody of the real-world manga publishing. The "spell consultant" fulfills the function of a real-world editor.

Page 104 – Best works
Continuing the parody of Shueisha, some of the publisher's top titles are shadowed in the background: (from left to right) *JoJo's Bizarre Adventure, One Piece, Ultimate Muscle, Dragon Ball, Fist of the North Star.*

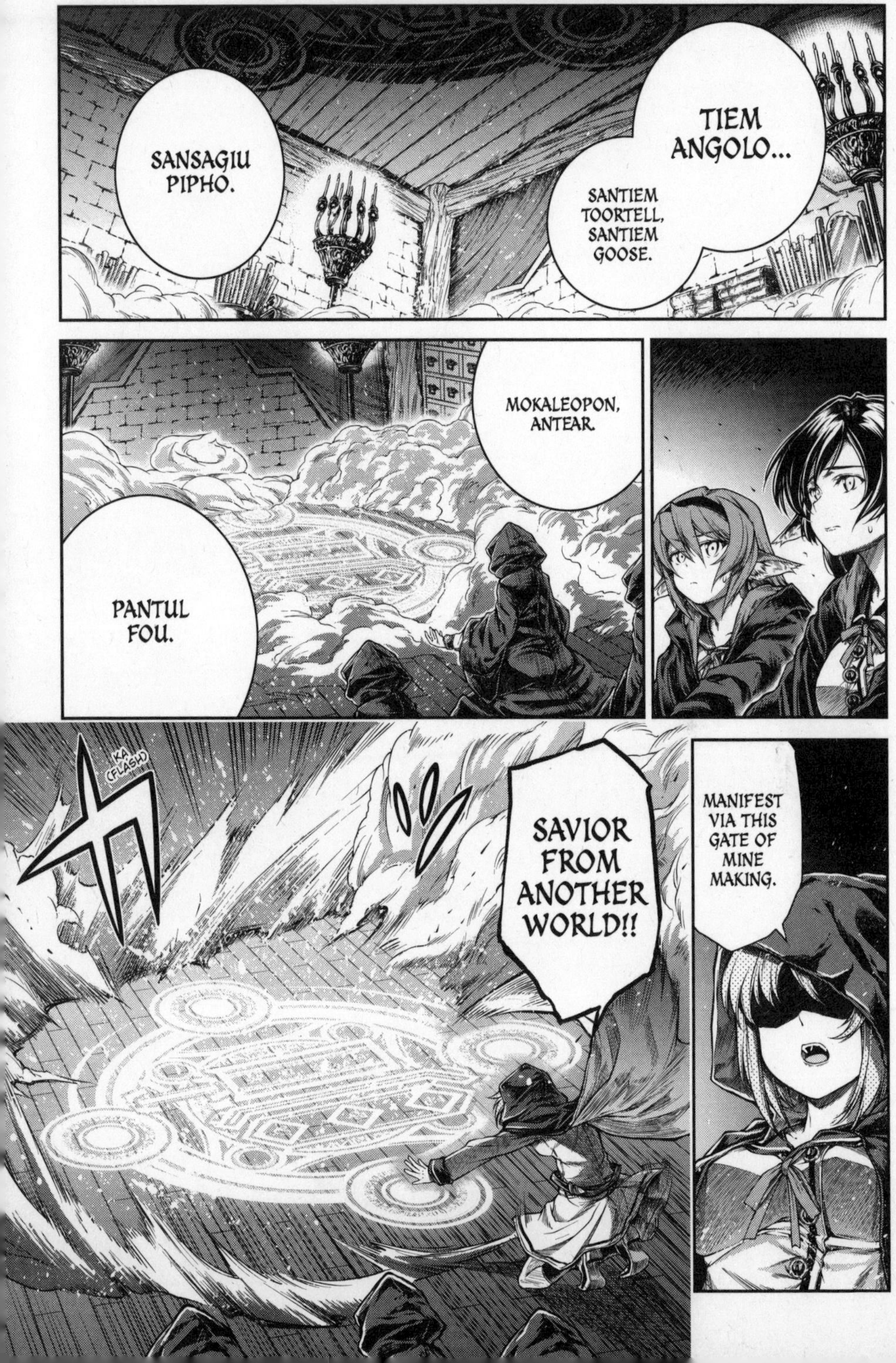
TIEM ANGOLO...
SANTIEM TOORTELL, SANTIEM GOOSE.
SANSAGIU PIPHO.
MOKALEOPON, ANTEAR.
PANTUL FOU.
MANIFEST VIA THIS GATE OF MINE MAKING.
SAVIOR FROM ANOTHER WORLD!!
KA (FLASH)

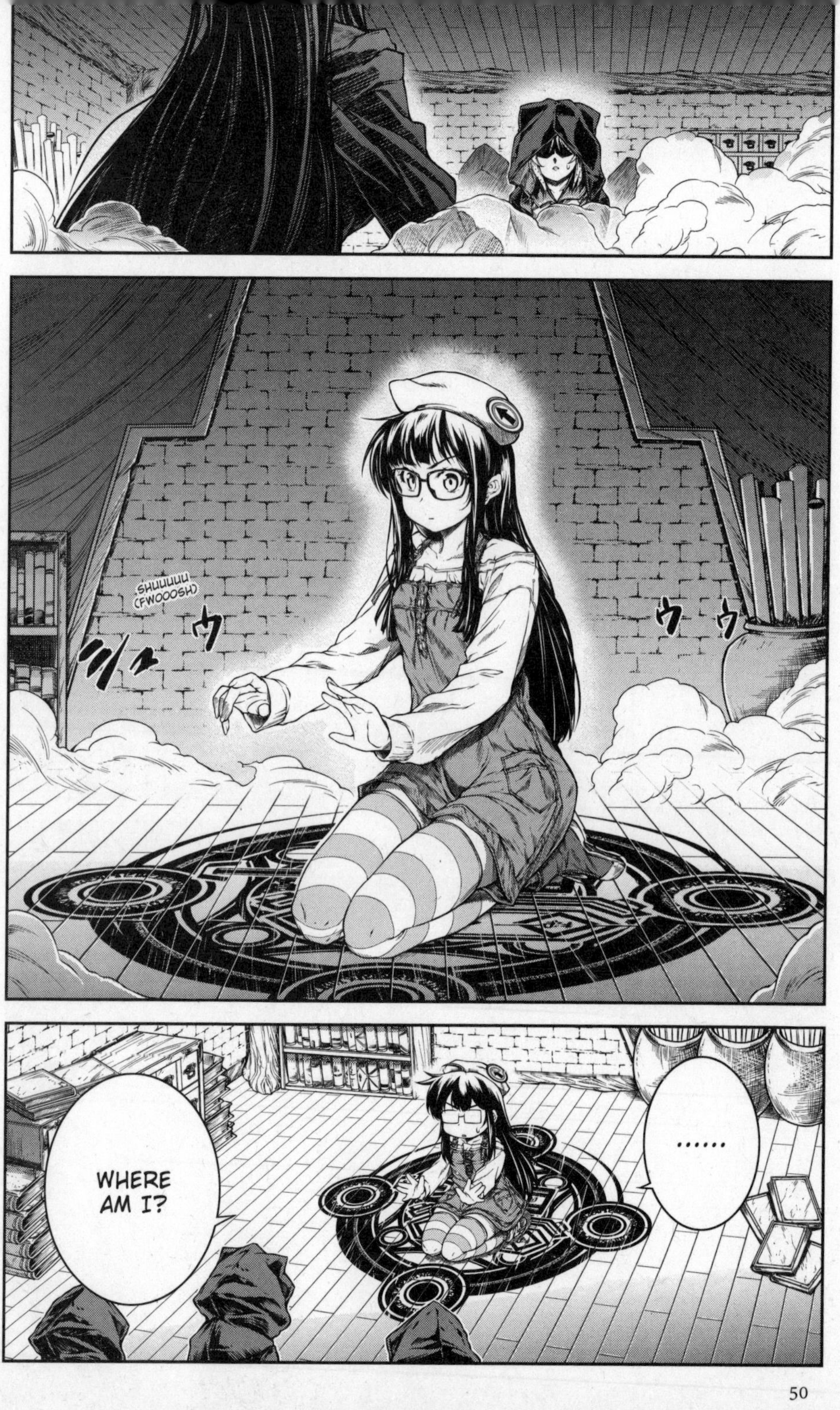
SHUUUUU (FWOOOSH)
......
WHERE AM I?

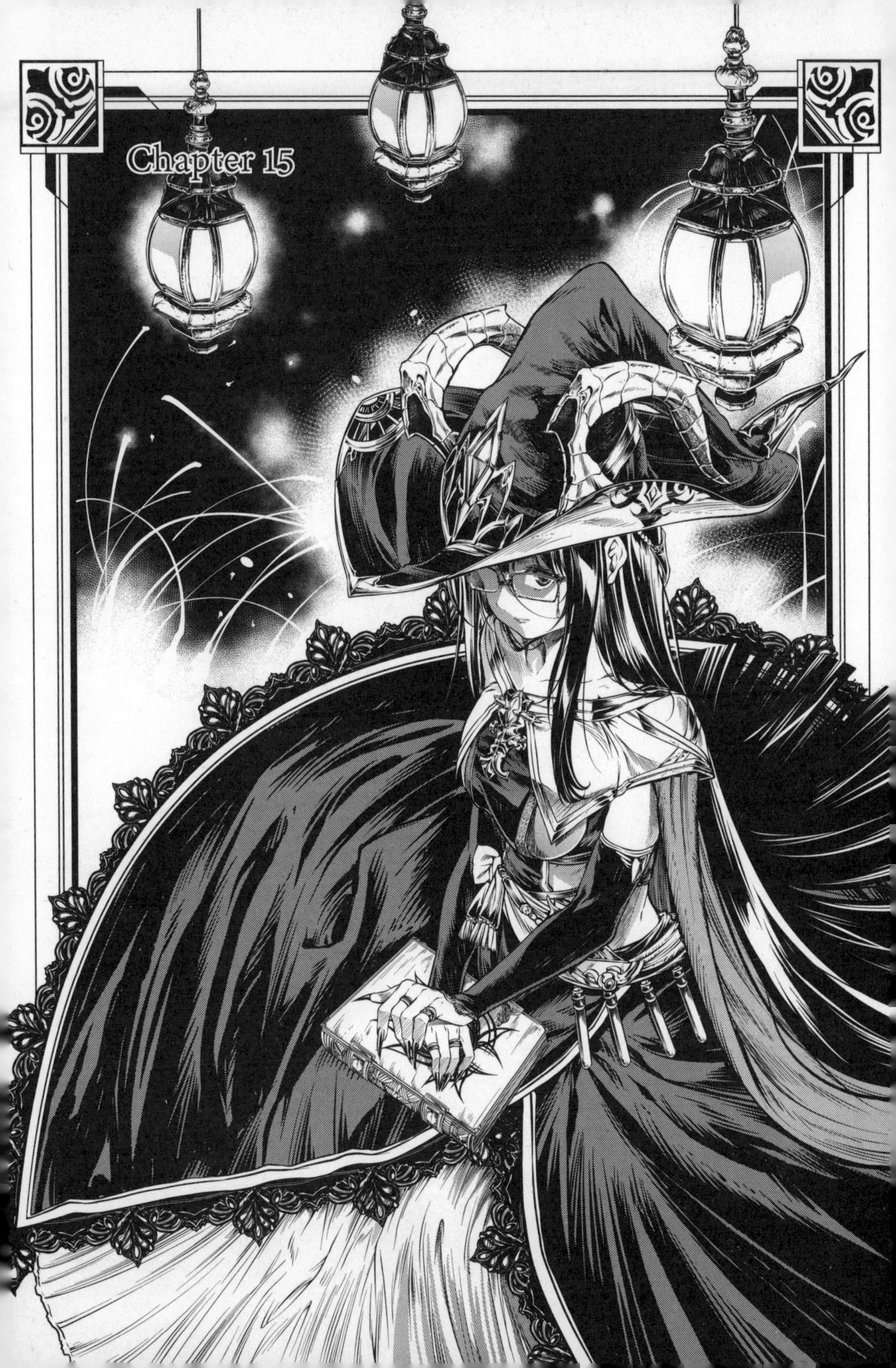
Chapter 15

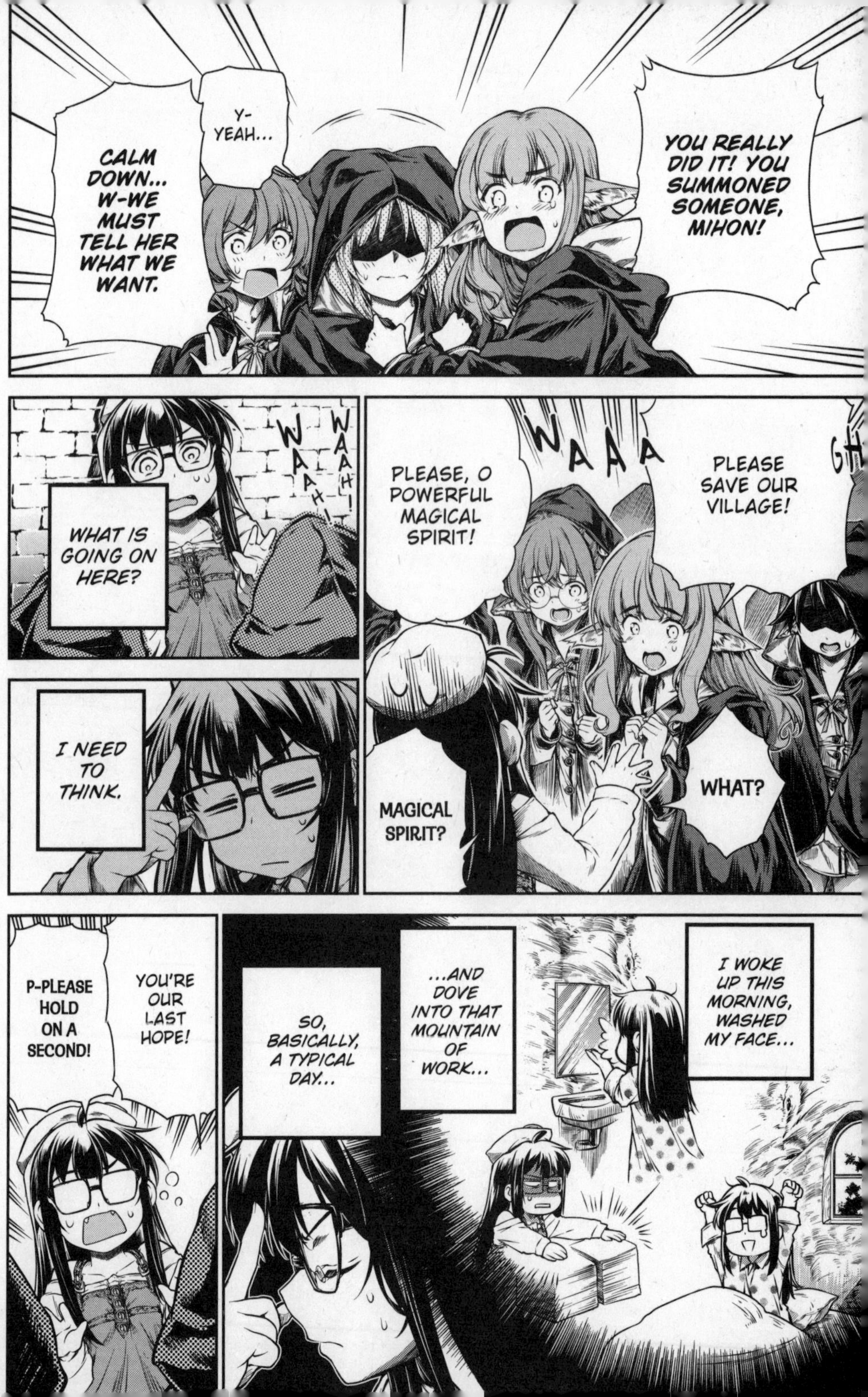
YOU REALLY DID IT! YOU SUMMONED SOMEONE, MIHON!
Y-YEAH...
CALM DOWN... W-WE MUST TELL HER WHAT WE WANT.
PLEASE SAVE OUR VILLAGE!
WAAA
PLEASE, O POWERFUL MAGICAL SPIRIT!
WHAT?
MAGICAL SPIRIT?
WAAH! WAAH!
WHAT IS GOING ON HERE?
I NEED TO THINK.
I WOKE UP THIS MORNING, WASHED MY FACE...
...AND DOVE INTO THAT MOUNTAIN OF WORK...
SO, BASICALLY, A TYPICAL DAY...
YOU'RE OUR LAST HOPE!
P-PLEASE HOLD ON A SECOND!

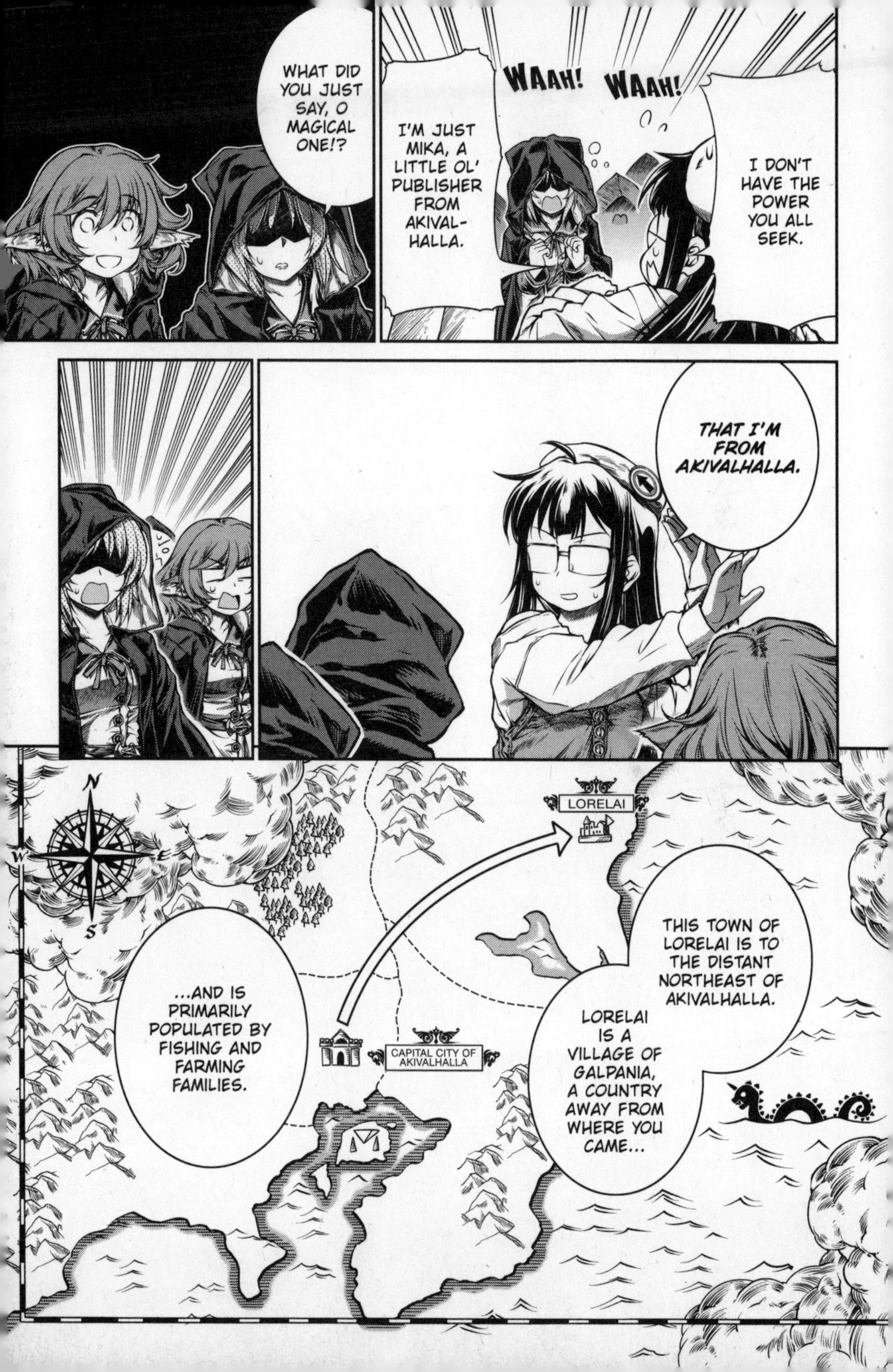

WAAH!
WAAH!
I DON'T HAVE THE POWER YOU ALL SEEK.
I'M JUST MIKA, A LITTLE OL' PUBLISHER FROM AKIVAL-HALLA.
WHAT DID YOU JUST SAY, O MAGICAL ONE!?
THAT I'M FROM AKIVALHALLA.
LORELAI
THIS TOWN OF LORELAI IS TO THE DISTANT NORTHEAST OF AKIVALHALLA.
LORELAI IS A VILLAGE OF GALPANIA, A COUNTRY AWAY FROM WHERE YOU CAME...
CAPITAL CITY OF AKIVALHALLA
...AND IS PRIMARILY POPULATED BY FISHING AND FARMING FAMILIES.
N
W
E
S

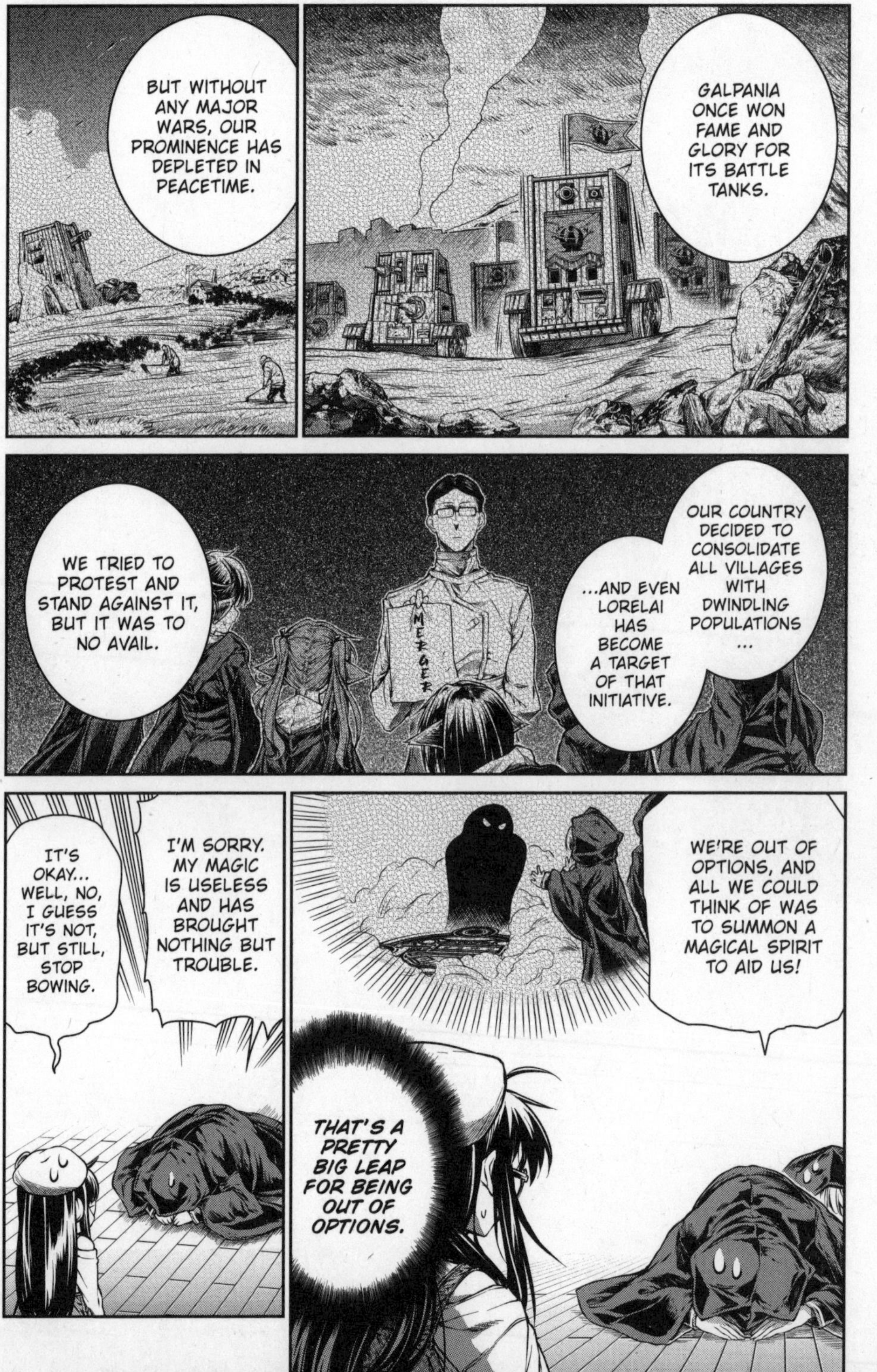
GALPANIA ONCE WON FAME AND GLORY FOR ITS BATTLE TANKS.
BUT WITHOUT ANY MAJOR WARS, OUR PROMINENCE HAS DEPLETED IN PEACETIME.
OUR COUNTRY DECIDED TO CONSOLIDATE ALL VILLAGES WITH DWINDLING POPULATIONS...
...AND EVEN LORELAI HAS BECOME A TARGET OF THAT INITIATIVE.
MERGER
WE TRIED TO PROTEST AND STAND AGAINST IT, BUT IT WAS TO NO AVAIL.
WE'RE OUT OF OPTIONS, AND ALL WE COULD THINK OF WAS TO SUMMON A MAGICAL SPIRIT TO AID US!
THAT'S A PRETTY BIG LEAP FOR BEING OUT OF OPTIONS.
I'M SORRY. MY MAGIC IS USELESS AND HAS BROUGHT NOTHING BUT TROUBLE.
IT'S OKAY... WELL, NO, I GUESS IT'S NOT, BUT STILL, STOP BOWING.

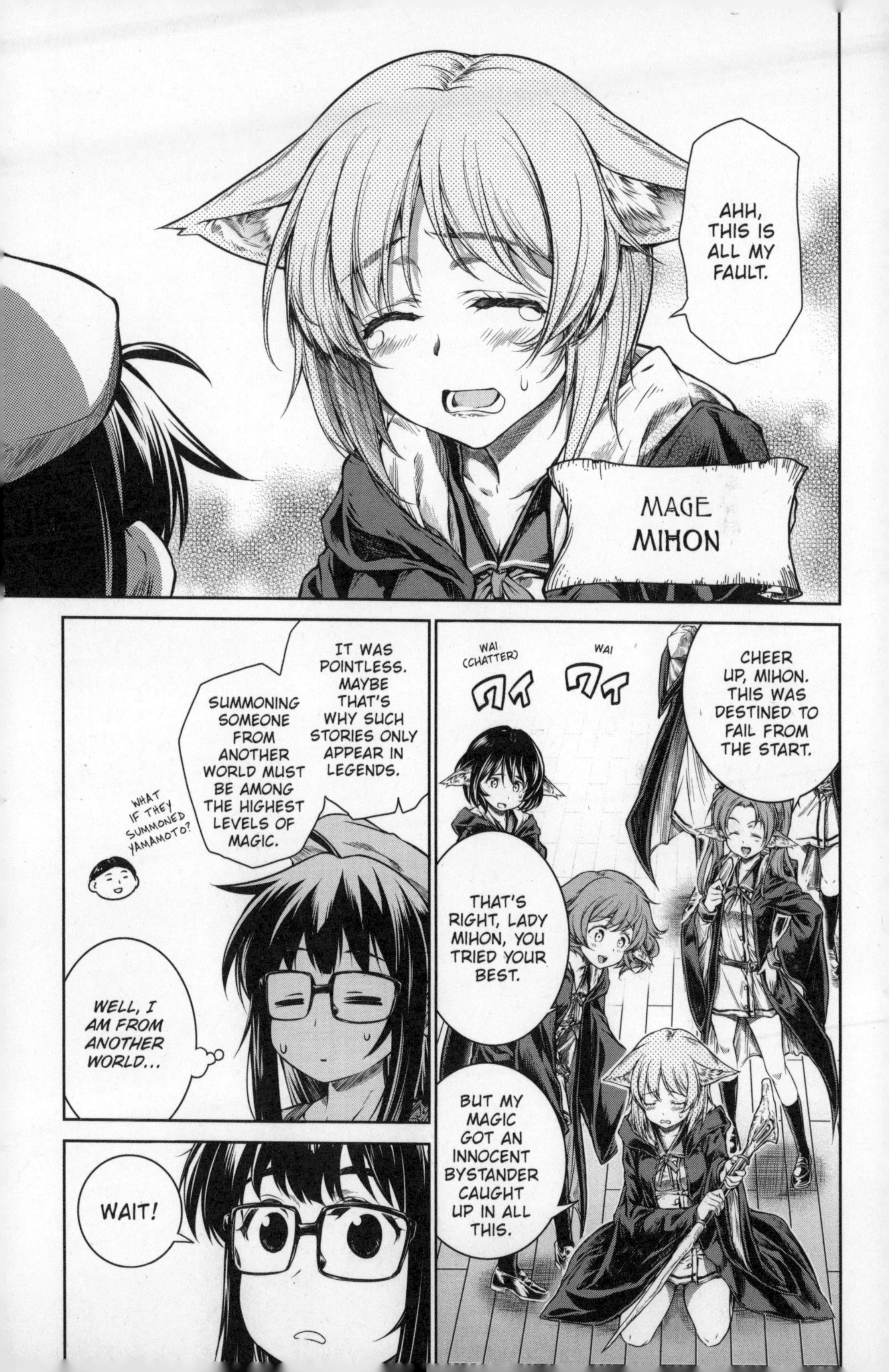
AHH, THIS IS ALL MY FAULT.
MAGE MIHON
CHEER UP, MIHON. THIS WAS DESTINED TO FAIL FROM THE START.
WAI
WAI (CHATTER)
THAT'S RIGHT, LADY MIHON, YOU TRIED YOUR BEST.
BUT MY MAGIC GOT AN INNOCENT BYSTANDER CAUGHT UP IN ALL THIS.
IT WAS POINTLESS. MAYBE THAT'S WHY SUCH STORIES ONLY APPEAR IN LEGENDS.
SUMMONING SOMEONE FROM ANOTHER WORLD MUST BE AMONG THE HIGHEST LEVELS OF MAGIC.
WHAT IF THEY SUMMONED YAMAMOTO?
WELL, I AM FROM ANOTHER WORLD...
WAIT!

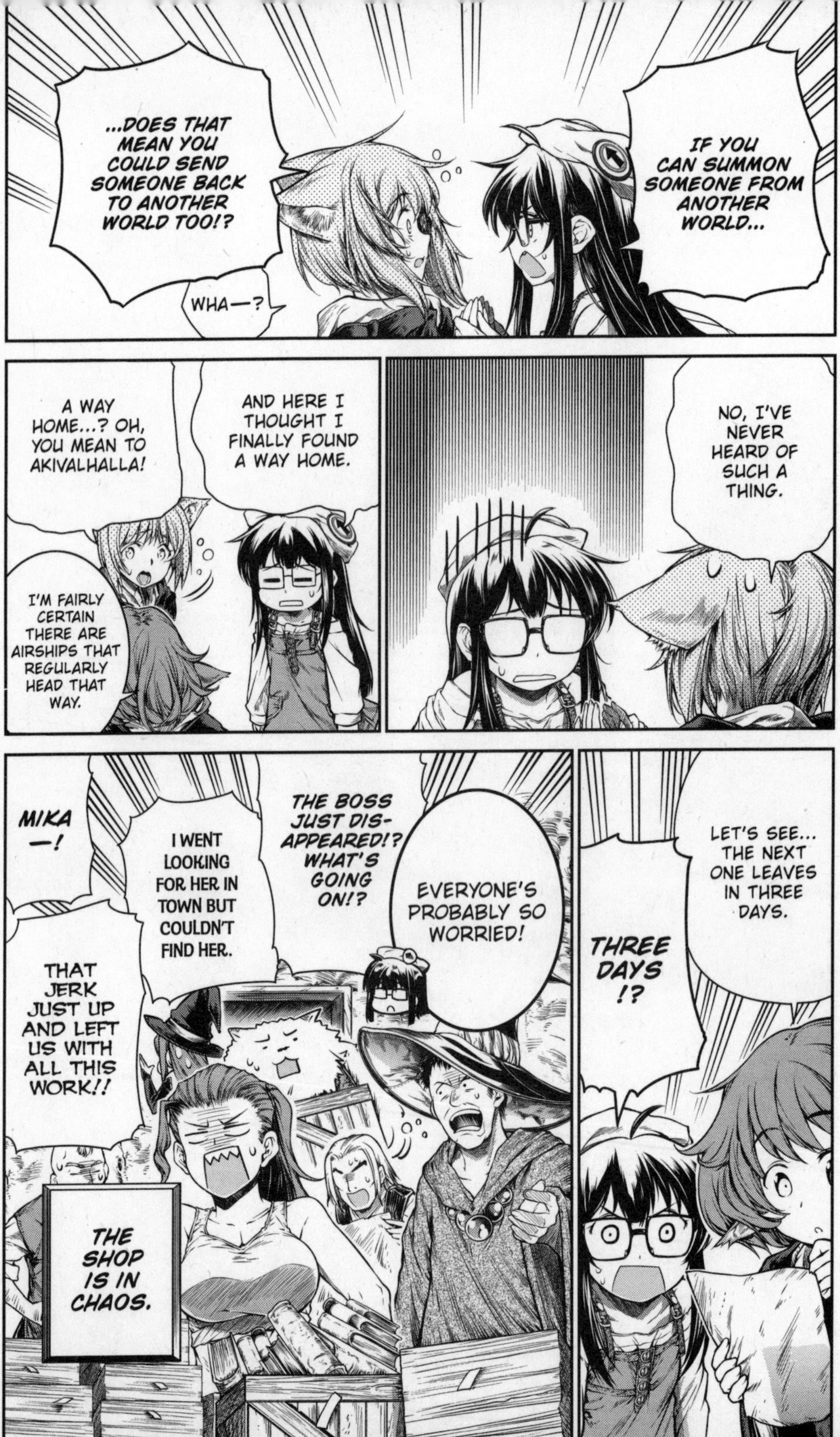
IF YOU CAN SUMMON SOMEONE FROM ANOTHER WORLD...
...DOES THAT MEAN YOU COULD SEND SOMEONE BACK TO ANOTHER WORLD TOO!?
WHA—?
NO, I'VE NEVER HEARD OF SUCH A THING.
AND HERE I THOUGHT I FINALLY FOUND A WAY HOME.
A WAY HOME...? OH, YOU MEAN TO AKIVALHALLA!
I'M FAIRLY CERTAIN THERE ARE AIRSHIPS THAT REGULARLY HEAD THAT WAY.
LET'S SEE... THE NEXT ONE LEAVES IN THREE DAYS.
THREE DAYS!?
EVERYONE'S PROBABLY SO WORRIED!
THE BOSS JUST DISAPPEARED!? WHAT'S GOING ON!?
MIKA—!
I WENT LOOKING FOR HER IN TOWN BUT COULDN'T FIND HER.
THAT JERK JUST UP AND LEFT US WITH ALL THIS WORK!!
THE SHOP IS IN CHAOS.

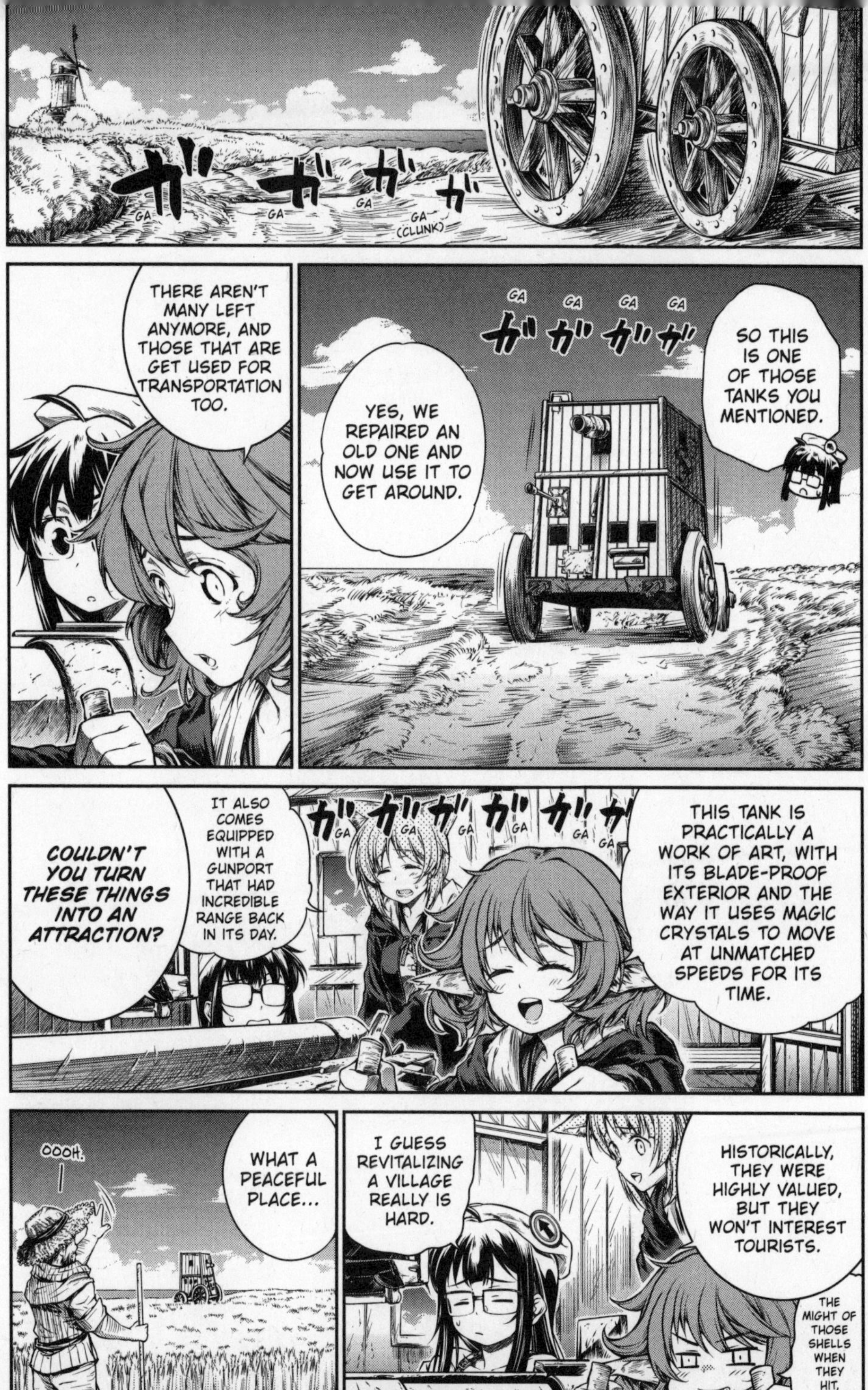
GA
GA
GA
GA (CLUNK)
SO THIS IS ONE OF THOSE TANKS YOU MENTIONED.
GA GA GA GA
YES, WE REPAIRED AN OLD ONE AND NOW USE IT TO GET AROUND.
THERE AREN'T MANY LEFT ANYMORE, AND THOSE THAT ARE GET USED FOR TRANSPORTATION TOO.
GA GA GA GA GA GA
THIS TANK IS PRACTICALLY A WORK OF ART, WITH ITS BLADE-PROOF EXTERIOR AND THE WAY IT USES MAGIC CRYSTALS TO MOVE AT UNMATCHED SPEEDS FOR ITS TIME.
IT ALSO COMES EQUIPPED WITH A GUNPORT THAT HAD INCREDIBLE RANGE BACK IN ITS DAY.
COULDN'T YOU TURN THESE THINGS INTO AN ATTRACTION?
HISTORICALLY, THEY WERE HIGHLY VALUED, BUT THEY WON'T INTEREST TOURISTS.
THE MIGHT OF THOSE SHELLS WHEN THEY HIT, THOUGH...
I GUESS REVITALIZING A VILLAGE REALLY IS HARD.
WHAT A PEACEFUL PLACE...
OOOH.

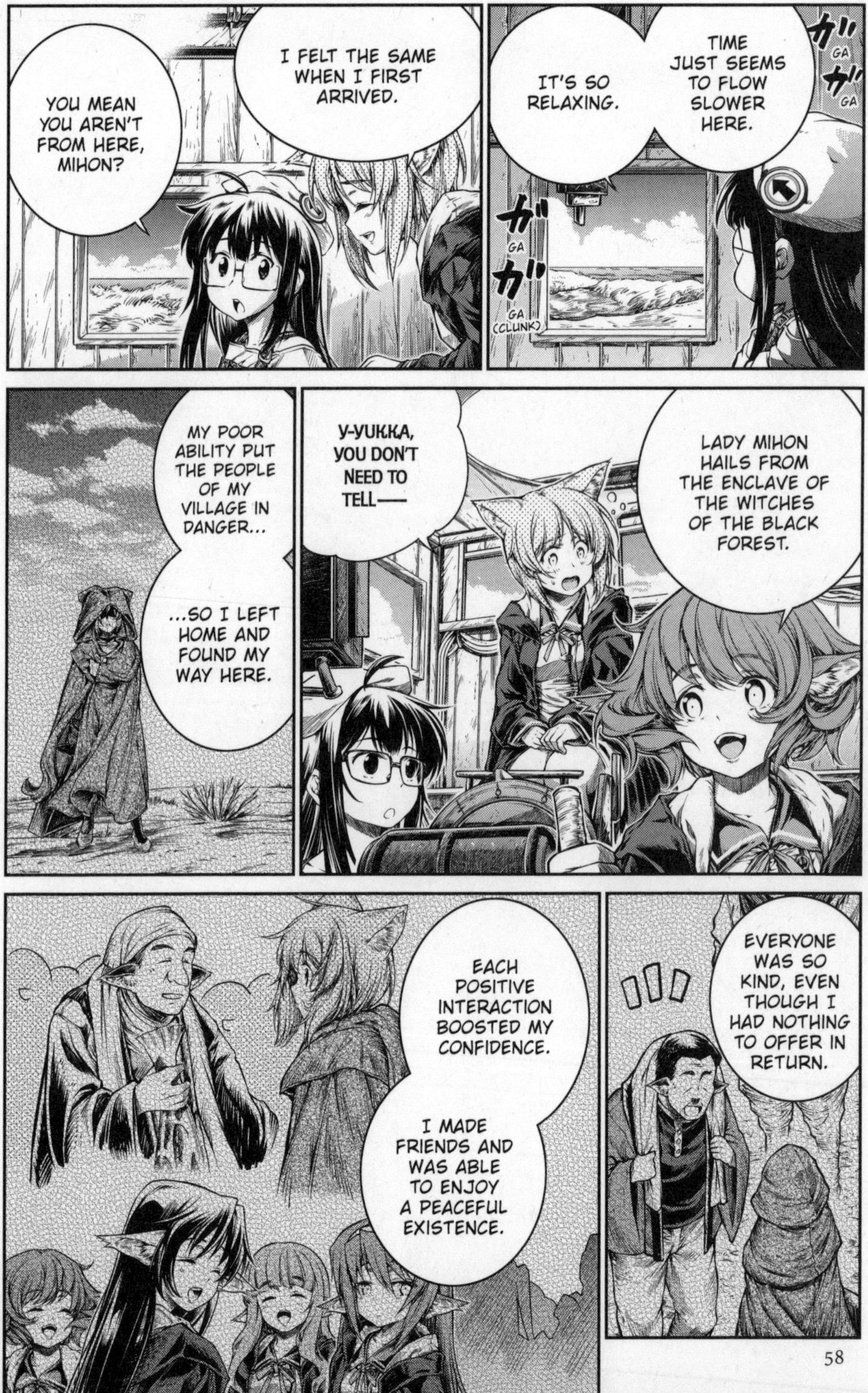
ガ GA
ガ GA
TIME JUST SEEMS TO FLOW SLOWER HERE.
IT'S SO RELAXING.
ガ GA
ガ GA (CLUNK)
I FELT THE SAME WHEN I FIRST ARRIVED.
YOU MEAN YOU AREN'T FROM HERE, MIHON?
LADY MIHON HAILS FROM THE ENCLAVE OF THE WITCHES OF THE BLACK FOREST.
Y-YUKKA, YOU DON'T NEED TO TELL—
MY POOR ABILITY PUT THE PEOPLE OF MY VILLAGE IN DANGER...
...SO I LEFT HOME AND FOUND MY WAY HERE.
EVERYONE WAS SO KIND, EVEN THOUGH I HAD NOTHING TO OFFER IN RETURN.
EACH POSITIVE INTERACTION BOOSTED MY CONFIDENCE.
I MADE FRIENDS AND WAS ABLE TO ENJOY A PEACEFUL EXISTENCE.

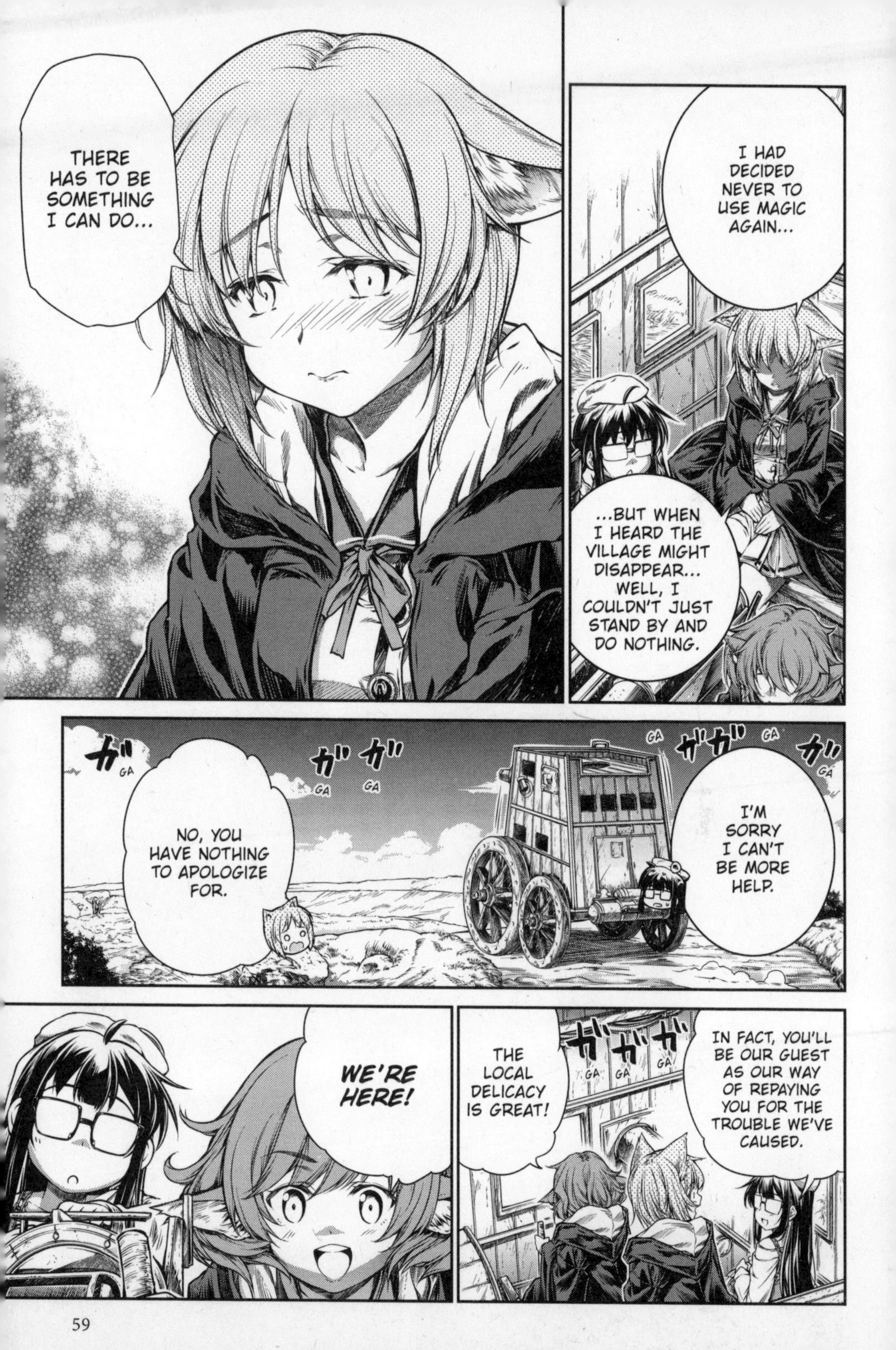
I HAD DECIDED NEVER TO USE MAGIC AGAIN...
...BUT WHEN I HEARD THE VILLAGE MIGHT DISAPPEAR... WELL, I COULDN'T JUST STAND BY AND DO NOTHING.
THERE HAS TO BE SOMETHING I CAN DO...
ガ GA ガガ GA ガ GA
I'M SORRY I CAN'T BE MORE HELP.
ガガ GA GA ガ GA
NO, YOU HAVE NOTHING TO APOLOGIZE FOR.
IN FACT, YOU'LL BE OUR GUEST AS OUR WAY OF REPAYING YOU FOR THE TROUBLE WE'VE CAUSED.
ガガガ GA GA GA
THE LOCAL DELICACY IS GREAT!
WE'RE HERE!

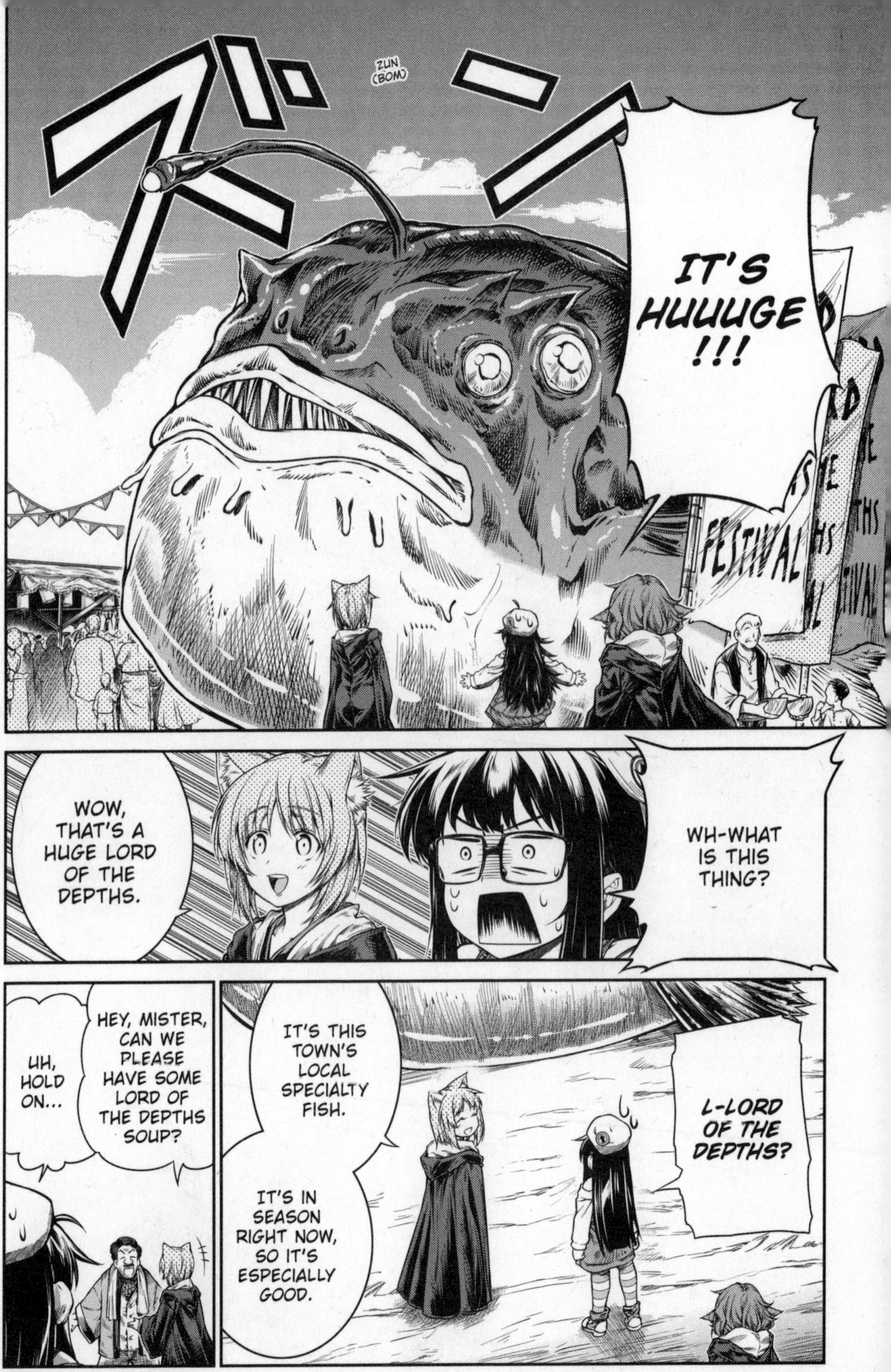
ZUN (BOM)
IT'S HUUUGE!!!
FESTIVAL
WH-WHAT IS THIS THING?
WOW, THAT'S A HUGE LORD OF THE DEPTHS.
L-LORD OF THE DEPTHS?
IT'S THIS TOWN'S LOCAL SPECIALTY FISH.
IT'S IN SEASON RIGHT NOW, SO IT'S ESPECIALLY GOOD.
HEY, MISTER, CAN WE PLEASE HAVE SOME LORD OF THE DEPTHS SOUP?
UH, HOLD ON...

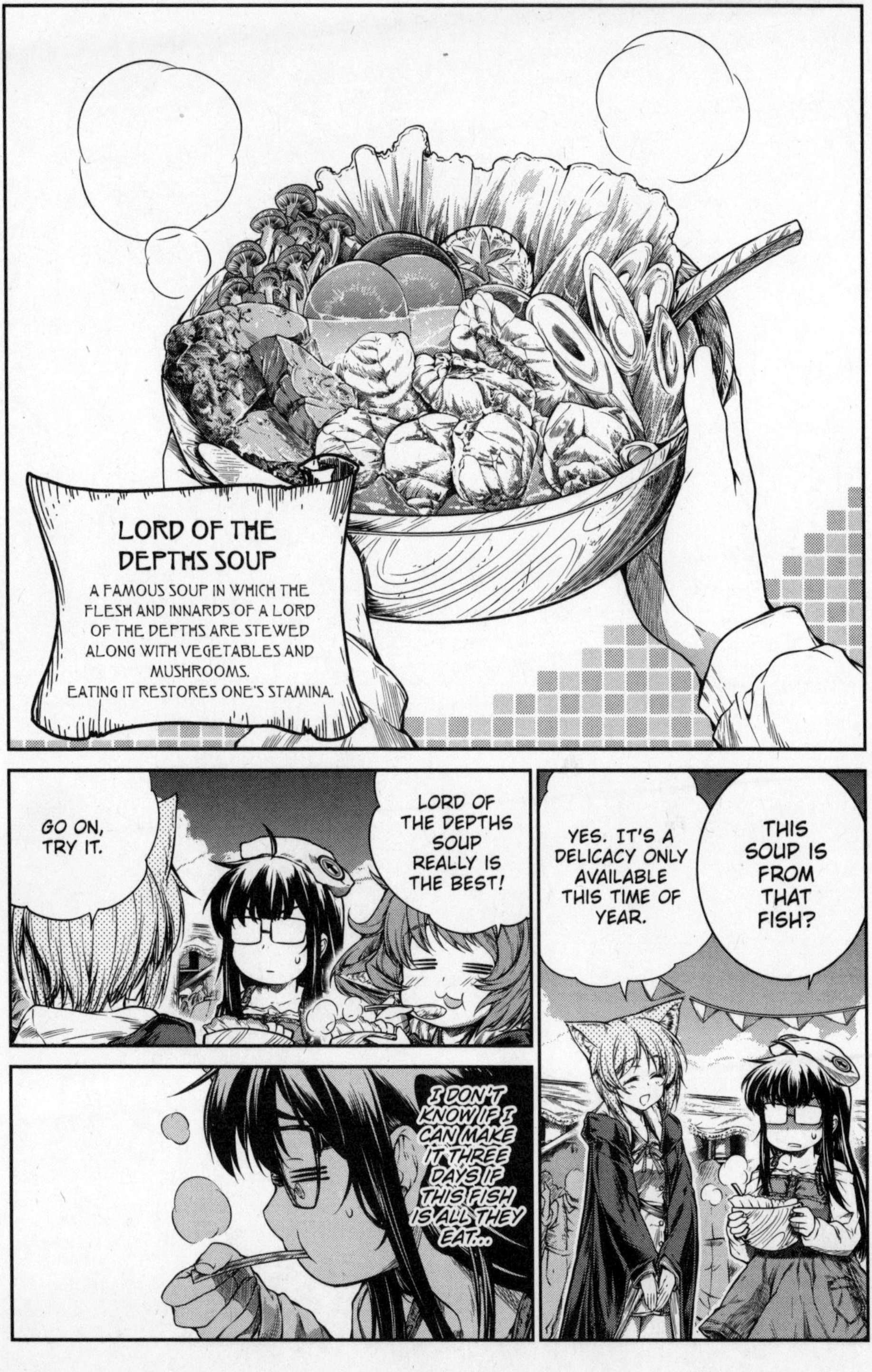
LORD OF THE DEPTHS SOUP
A FAMOUS SOUP IN WHICH THE FLESH AND INNARDS OF A LORD OF THE DEPTHS ARE STEWED ALONG WITH VEGETABLES AND MUSHROOMS.
EATING IT RESTORES ONE'S STAMINA.
THIS SOUP IS FROM THAT FISH?
YES. IT'S A DELICACY ONLY AVAILABLE THIS TIME OF YEAR.
LORD OF THE DEPTHS SOUP REALLY IS THE BEST!
GO ON, TRY IT.
I DON'T KNOW IF I CAN MAKE IT THREE DAYS IF THIS FISH IS ALL THEY EAT...

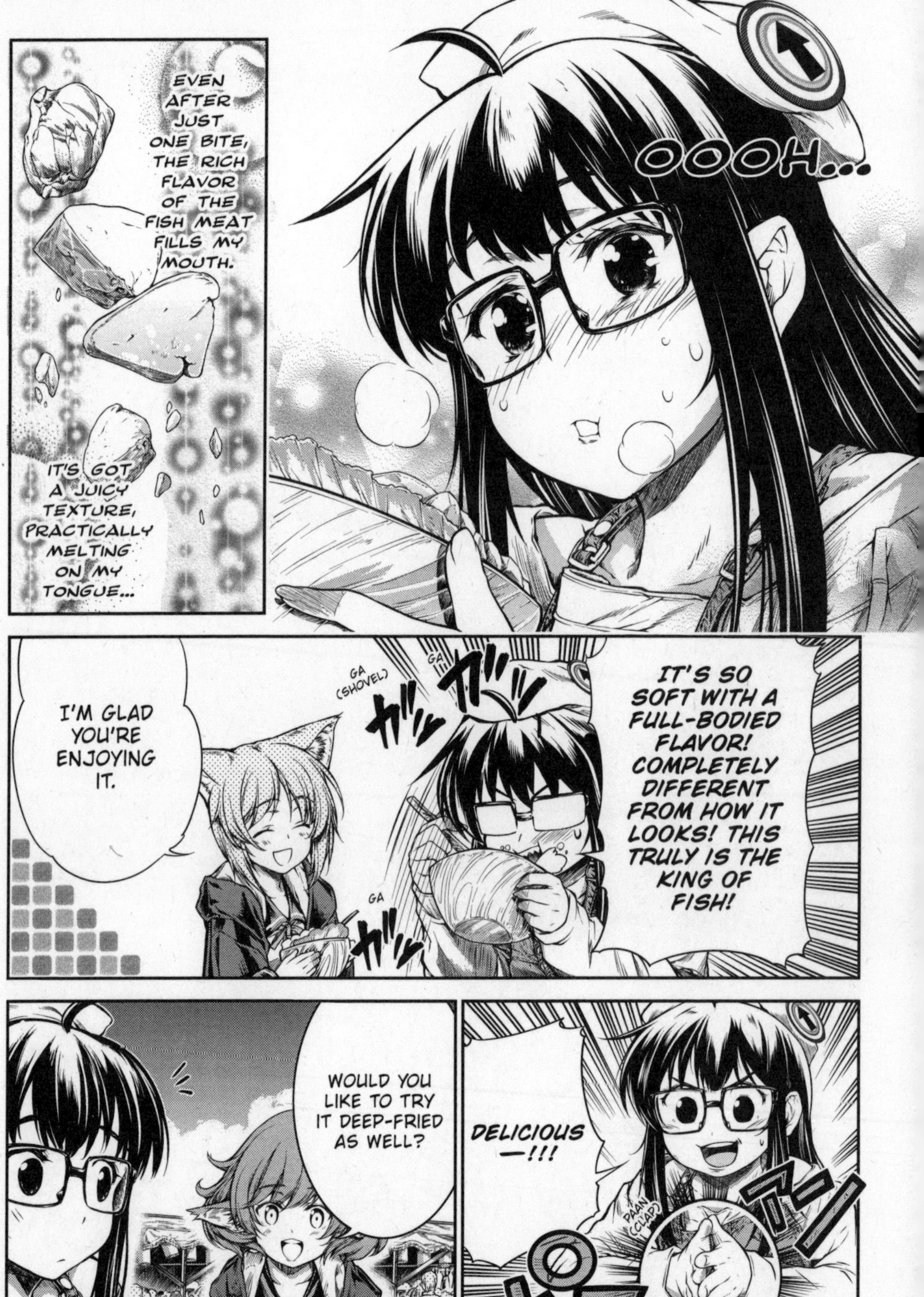
OOOH...
EVEN AFTER JUST ONE BITE, THE RICH FLAVOR OF THE FISH MEAT FILLS MY MOUTH.
IT'S GOT A JUICY TEXTURE, PRACTICALLY MELTING ON MY TONGUE...
IT'S SO SOFT WITH A FULL-BODIED FLAVOR! COMPLETELY DIFFERENT FROM HOW IT LOOKS! THIS TRULY IS THE KING OF FISH!
GA
GA (SHOVEL)
GA
I'M GLAD YOU'RE ENJOYING IT.
DELICIOUS—!!!
PAAN (CLAP)
WOULD YOU LIKE TO TRY IT DEEP-FRIED AS WELL?

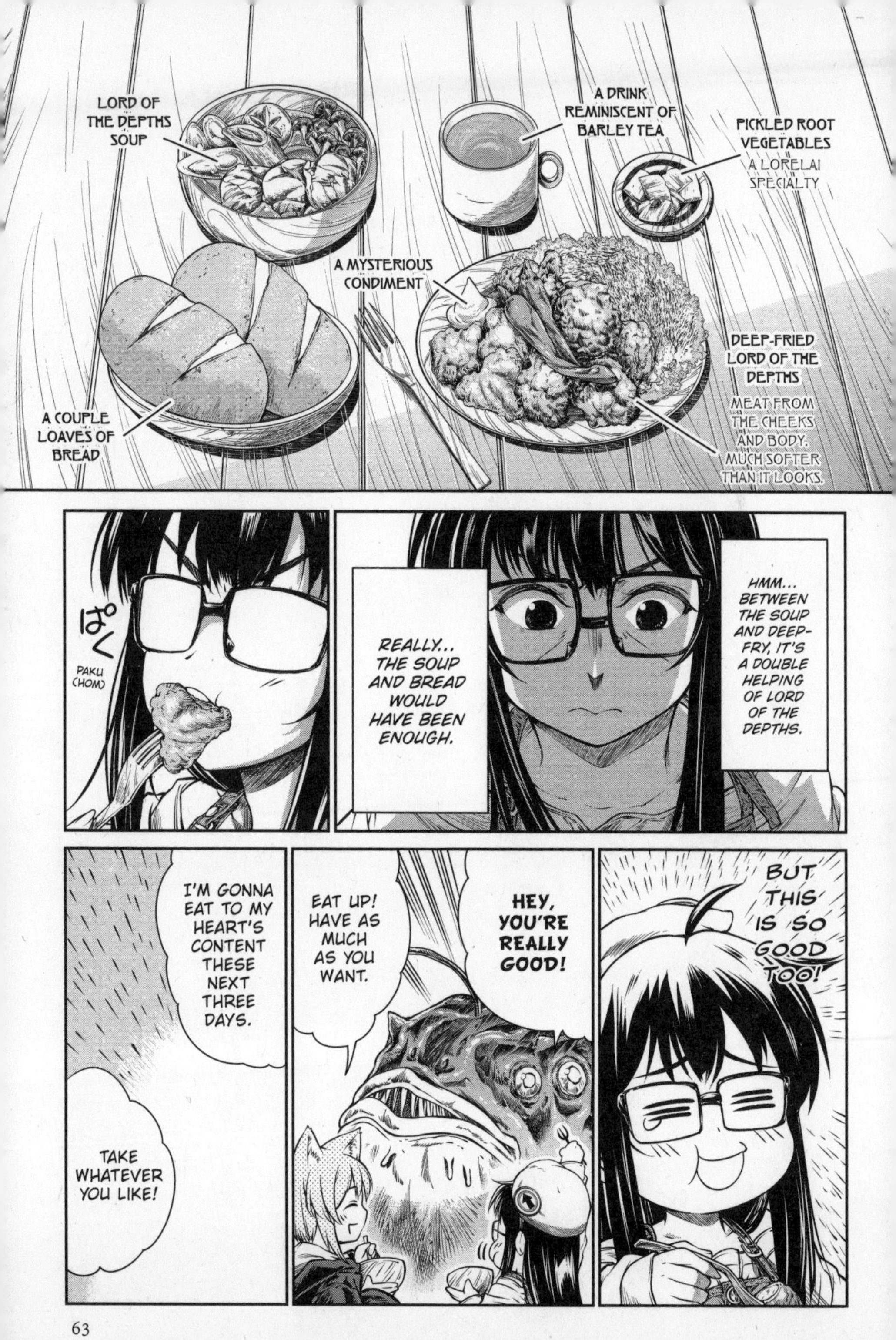
PICKLED ROOT VEGETABLES
A LORELAI SPECIALTY
A DRINK REMINISCENT OF BARLEY TEA
LORD OF THE DEPTHS SOUP
DEEP-FRIED LORD OF THE DEPTHS
MEAT FROM THE CHEEKS AND BODY. MUCH SOFTER THAN IT LOOKS.
A MYSTERIOUS CONDIMENT
A COUPLE LOAVES OF BREAD
HMM... BETWEEN THE SOUP AND DEEP-FRY, IT'S A DOUBLE HELPING OF LORD OF THE DEPTHS.
REALLY... THE SOUP AND BREAD WOULD HAVE BEEN ENOUGH.
ぱく
PAKU (HOM)
BUT THIS IS SO GOOD TOO!
HEY, YOU'RE REALLY GOOD!
EAT UP! HAVE AS MUCH AS YOU WANT.
I'M GONNA EAT TO MY HEART'S CONTENT THESE NEXT THREE DAYS.
TAKE WHATEVER YOU LIKE!

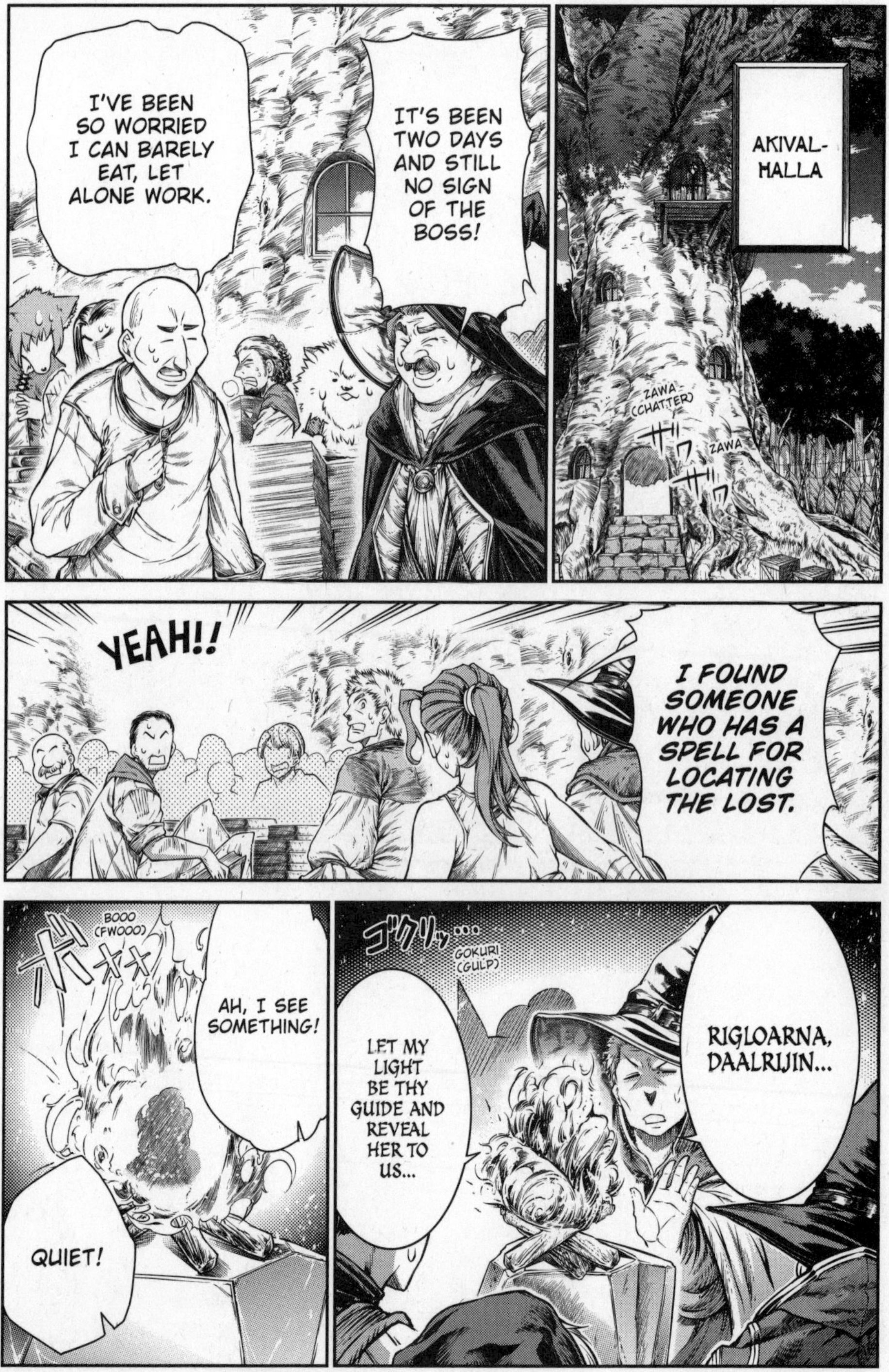
AKIVAL-HALLA
ZAWA (CHATTER)
ZAWA
IT'S BEEN TWO DAYS AND STILL NO SIGN OF THE BOSS!
I'VE BEEN SO WORRIED I CAN BARELY EAT, LET ALONE WORK.
I FOUND SOMEONE WHO HAS A SPELL FOR LOCATING THE LOST.
YEAH!!
RIGLOARNA, DAALRIJIN...
LET MY LIGHT BE THY GUIDE AND REVEAL HER TO US...
GOKURI (GULP)
AH, I SEE SOMETHING!
BOOO (FWOOO)
QUIET!

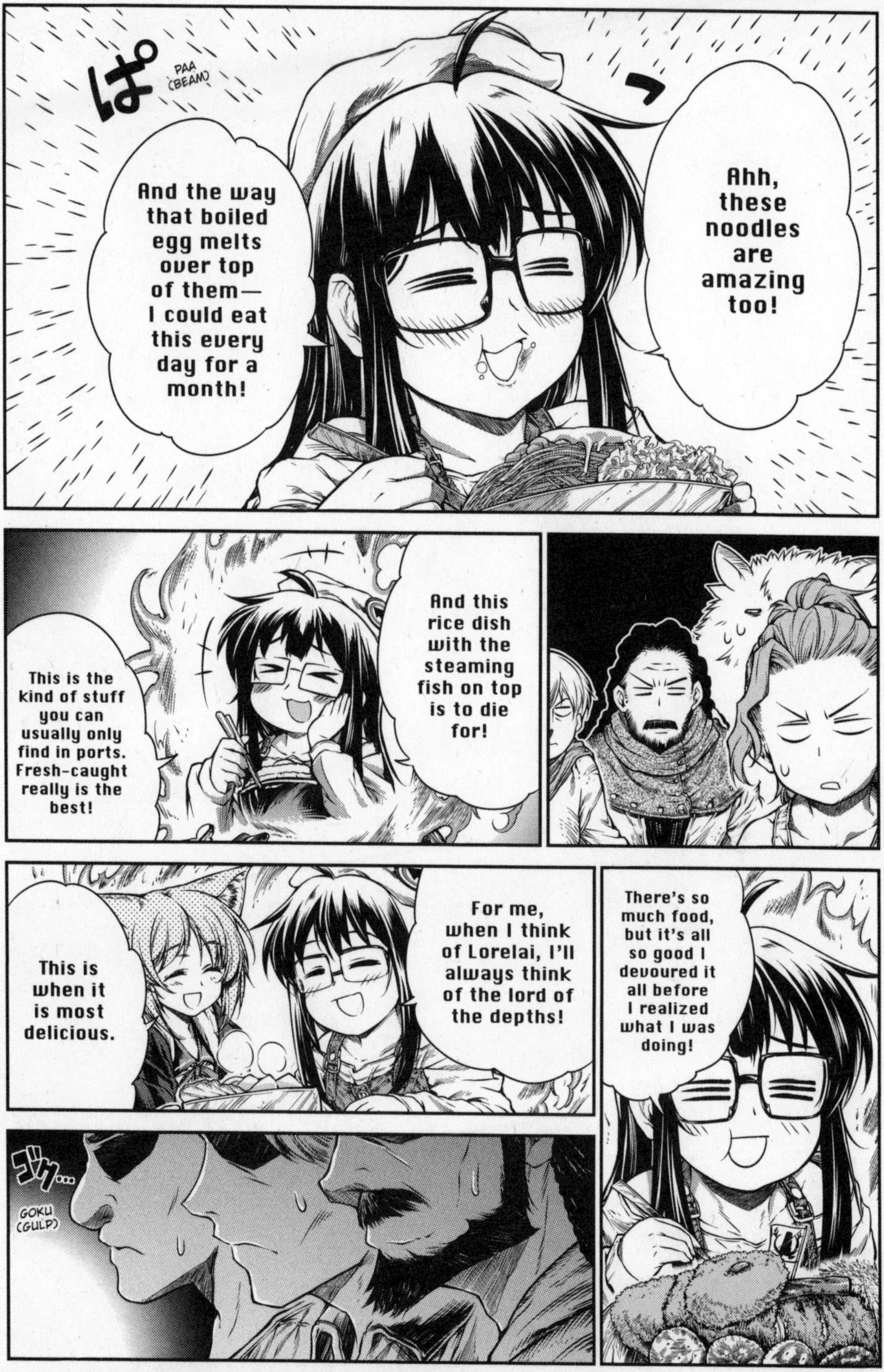
ぱっ
PAA (BEAM)
Ahh, these noodles are amazing too!
And the way that boiled egg melts over top of them— I could eat this every day for a month!
And this rice dish with the steaming fish on top is to die for!
This is the kind of stuff you can usually only find in ports. Fresh-caught really is the best!
There's so much food, but it's all so good I devoured it all before I realized what I was doing!
For me, when I think of Lorelai, I'll always think of the lord of the depths!
This is when it is most delicious.
ゴク…
GOKU (GULP)

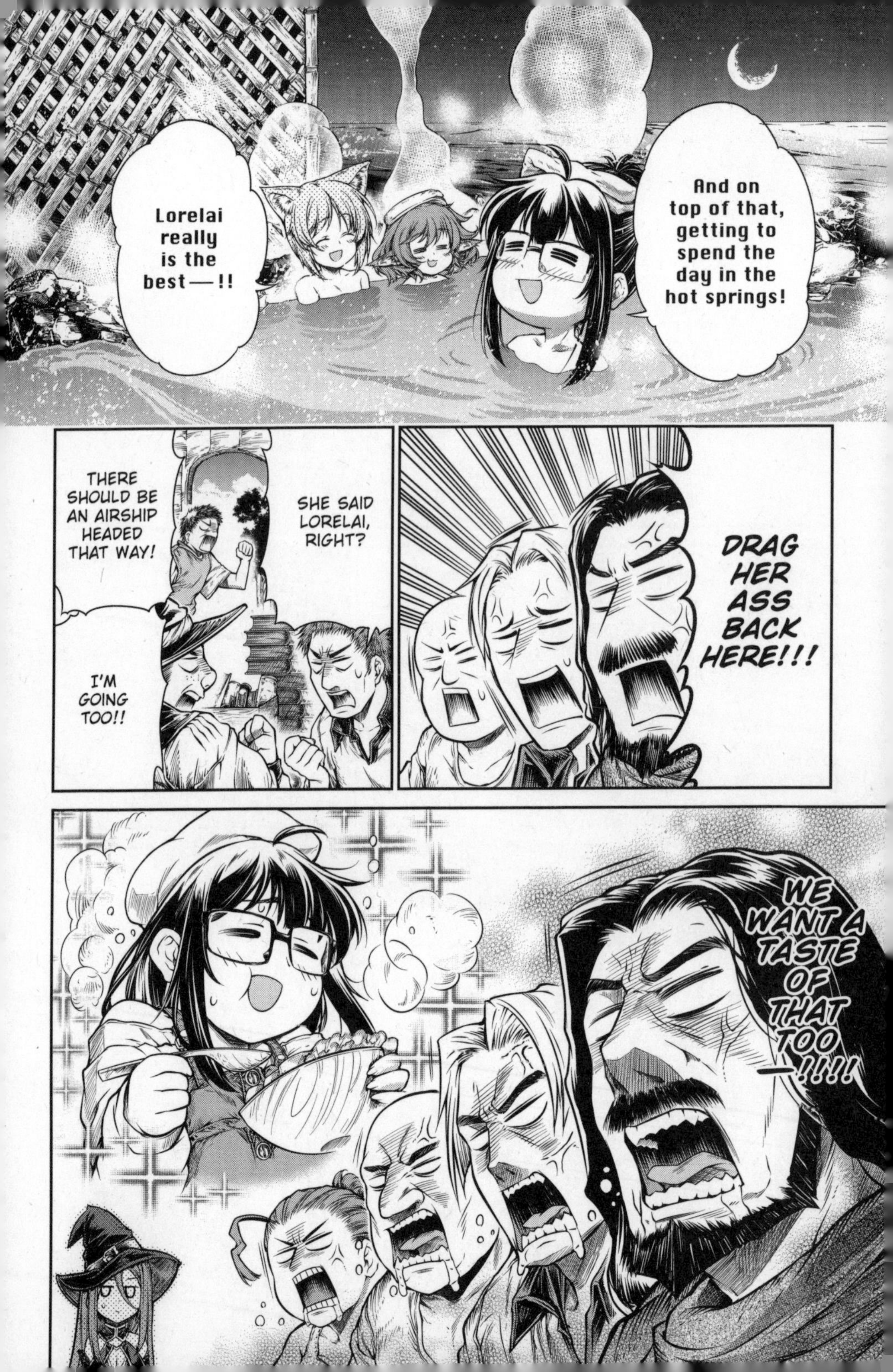

And on top of that, getting to spend the day in the hot springs!
Lorelai really is the best—!!
DRAG HER ASS BACK HERE!!!
SHE SAID LORELAI, RIGHT?
THERE SHOULD BE AN AIRSHIP HEADED THAT WAY!
I'M GOING TOO!!
WE WANT A TASTE OF THAT TOO—!!!!

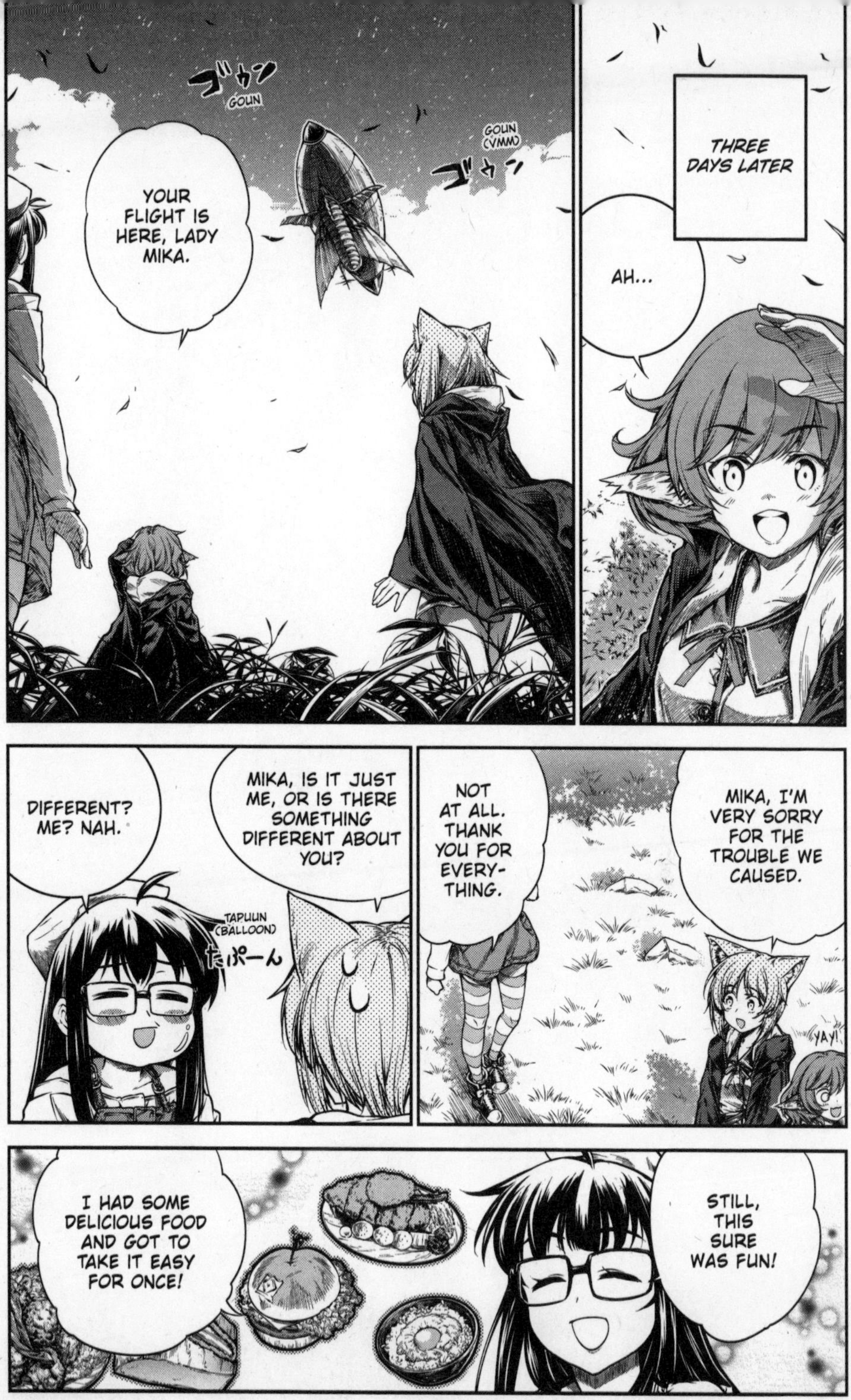
THREE DAYS LATER
AH...
ゴゥン
GOUN
GOUN (VMM)
ゴゥン
YOUR FLIGHT IS HERE, LADY MIKA.
MIKA, I'M VERY SORRY FOR THE TROUBLE WE CAUSED.
YAY!
NOT AT ALL. THANK YOU FOR EVERY-THING.
MIKA, IS IT JUST ME, OR IS THERE SOMETHING DIFFERENT ABOUT YOU?
TAPUUN (BALLOON)
たぷーん
DIFFERENT? ME? NAH.
STILL, THIS SURE WAS FUN!
I HAD SOME DELICIOUS FOOD AND GOT TO TAKE IT EASY FOR ONCE!

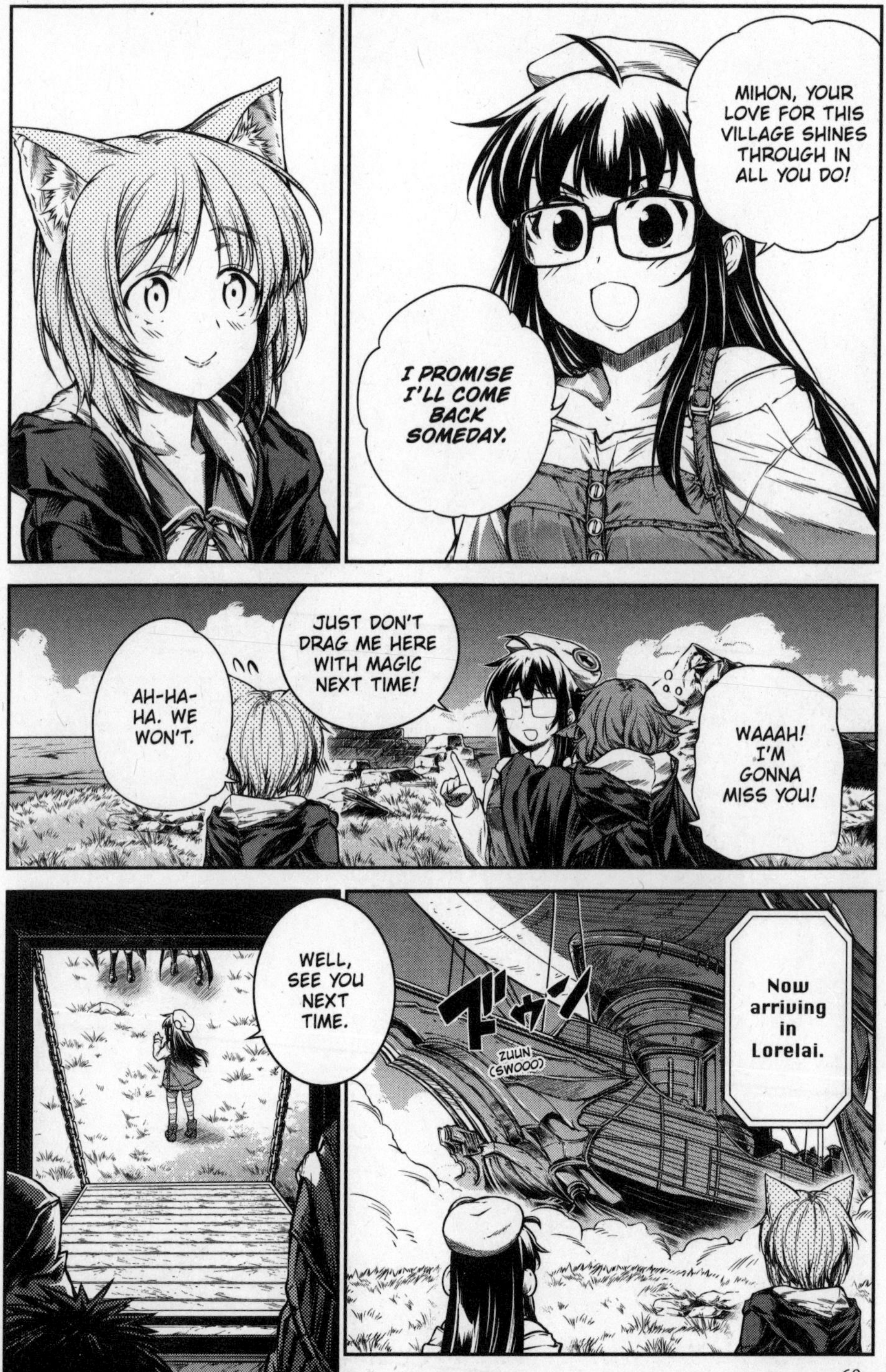
MIHON, YOUR LOVE FOR THIS VILLAGE SHINES THROUGH IN ALL YOU DO!
I PROMISE I'LL COME BACK SOMEDAY.
WAAAH! I'M GONNA MISS YOU!
JUST DON'T DRAG ME HERE WITH MAGIC NEXT TIME!
AH-HA-HA. WE WON'T.
Now arriving in Lorelai.
ZUUN (SWOOO)
WELL, SEE YOU NEXT TIME.

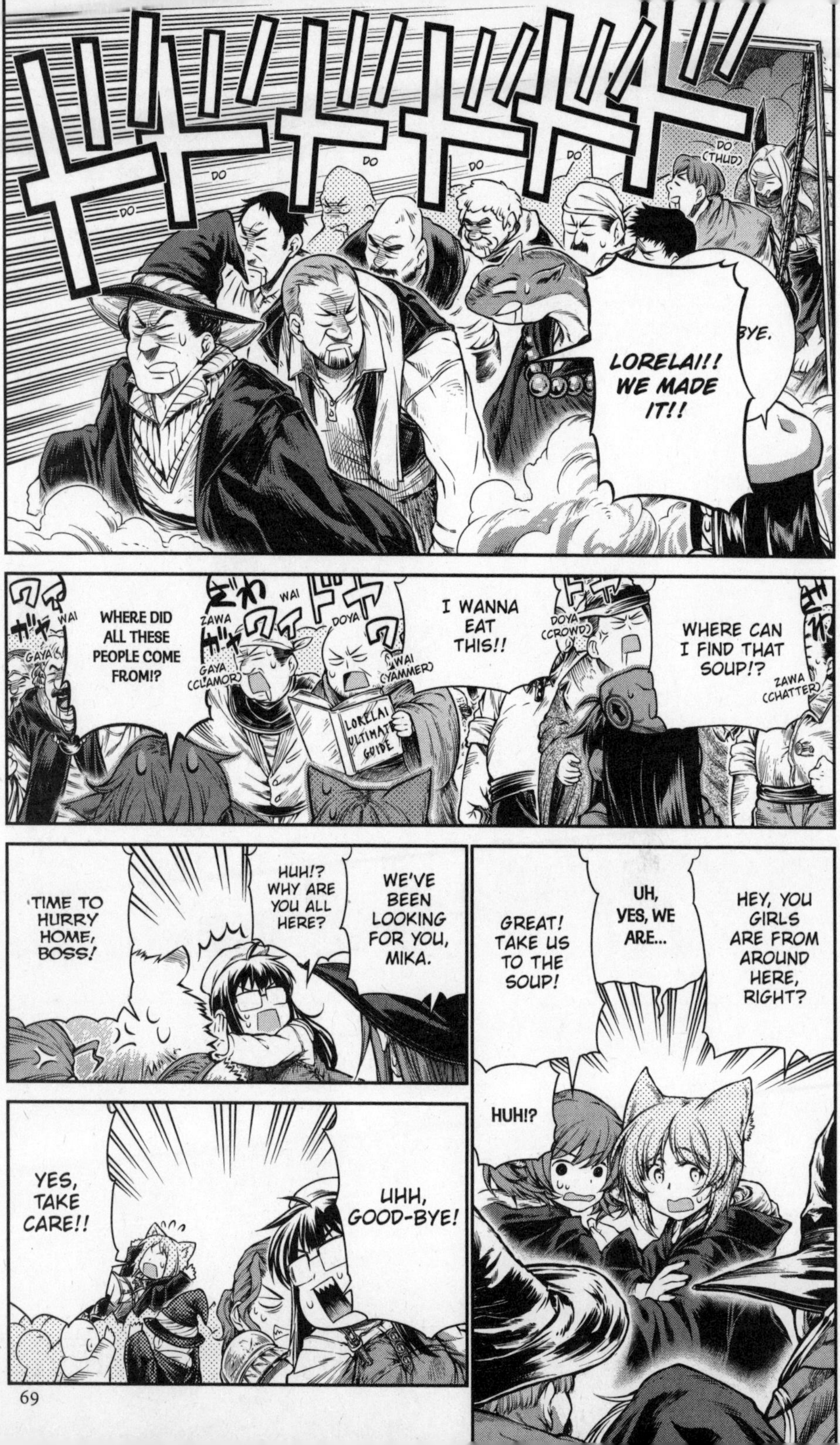
DO
DO
DO
DO
DO (THUD)
BYE.
LORELAI!! WE MADE IT!!
WHERE CAN I FIND THAT SOUP!?
ZAWA (CHATTER)
DOYA (CROWD)
I WANNA EAT THIS!!
WAI (YAMMER)
DOYA
WAI
LORELAI ULTIMATE GUIDE
ZAWA
GAYA (CLAMOR)
WHERE DID ALL THESE PEOPLE COME FROM!?
WAI
GAYA
HEY, YOU GIRLS ARE FROM AROUND HERE, RIGHT?
UH, YES, WE ARE...
GREAT! TAKE US TO THE SOUP!
HUH!?
WE'VE BEEN LOOKING FOR YOU, MIKA.
HUH!? WHY ARE YOU ALL HERE?
TIME TO HURRY HOME, BOSS!
UHH, GOOD-BYE!
YES, TAKE CARE!!

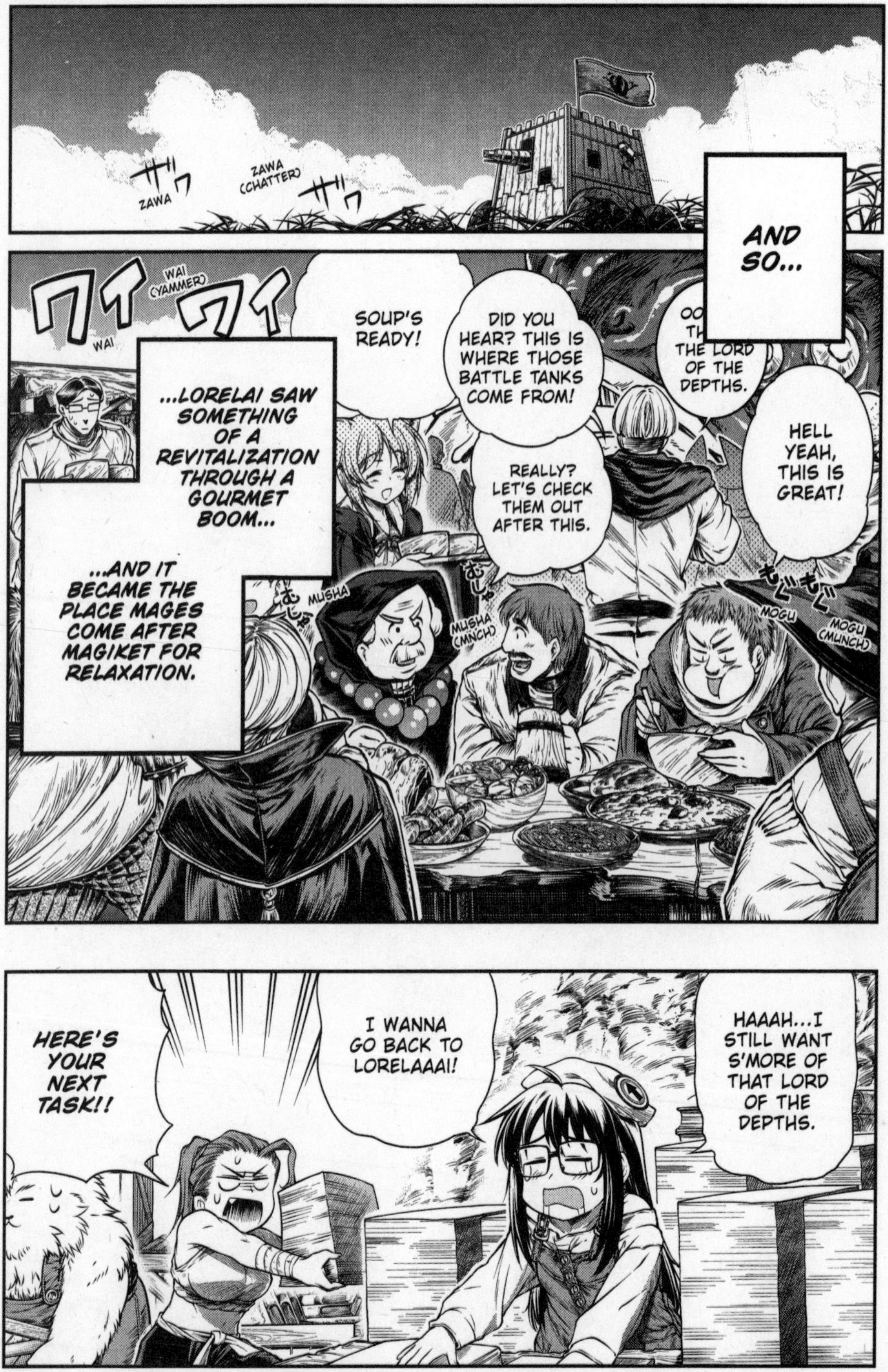
ZAWA (CHATTER)
ZAWA
AND SO...
THE LORD OF THE DEPTHS.
HELL YEAH, THIS IS GREAT!
MOGU (MUNCH)
MOGU
DID YOU HEAR? THIS IS WHERE THOSE BATTLE TANKS COME FROM!
REALLY? LET'S CHECK THEM OUT AFTER THIS.
MUSHA (MNCH)
MUSHA
SOUP'S READY!
WAI (YAMMER)
WAI
...LORELAI SAW SOMETHING OF A REVITALIZATION THROUGH A GOURMET BOOM...
...AND IT BECAME THE PLACE MAGES COME AFTER MAGIKET FOR RELAXATION.
HAAAH...I STILL WANT S'MORE OF THAT LORD OF THE DEPTHS.
I WANNA GO BACK TO LORELAAAI!
HERE'S YOUR NEXT TASK!!

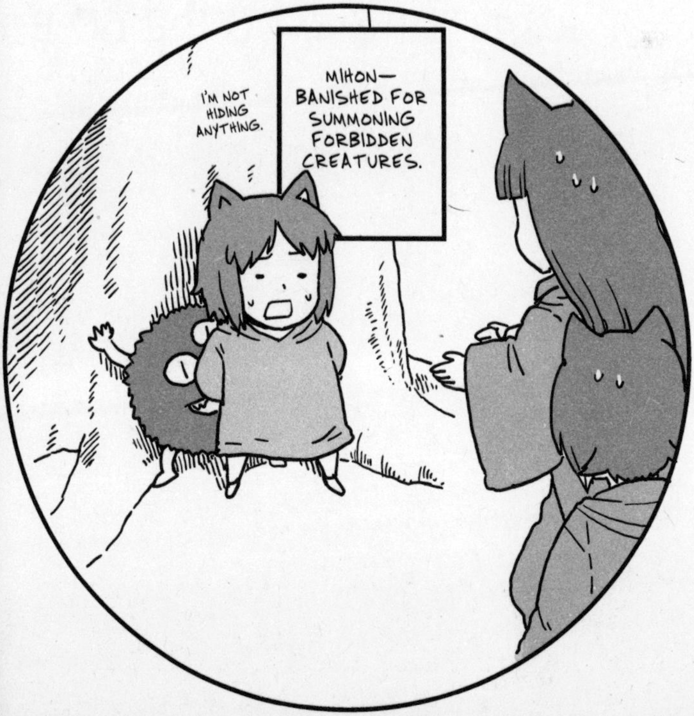
MIHON—BANISHED FOR SUMMONING FORBIDDEN CREATURES.
I'M NOT HIDING ANYTHING.

A WITCH'S PRINTING OFFICE

Chapter 16

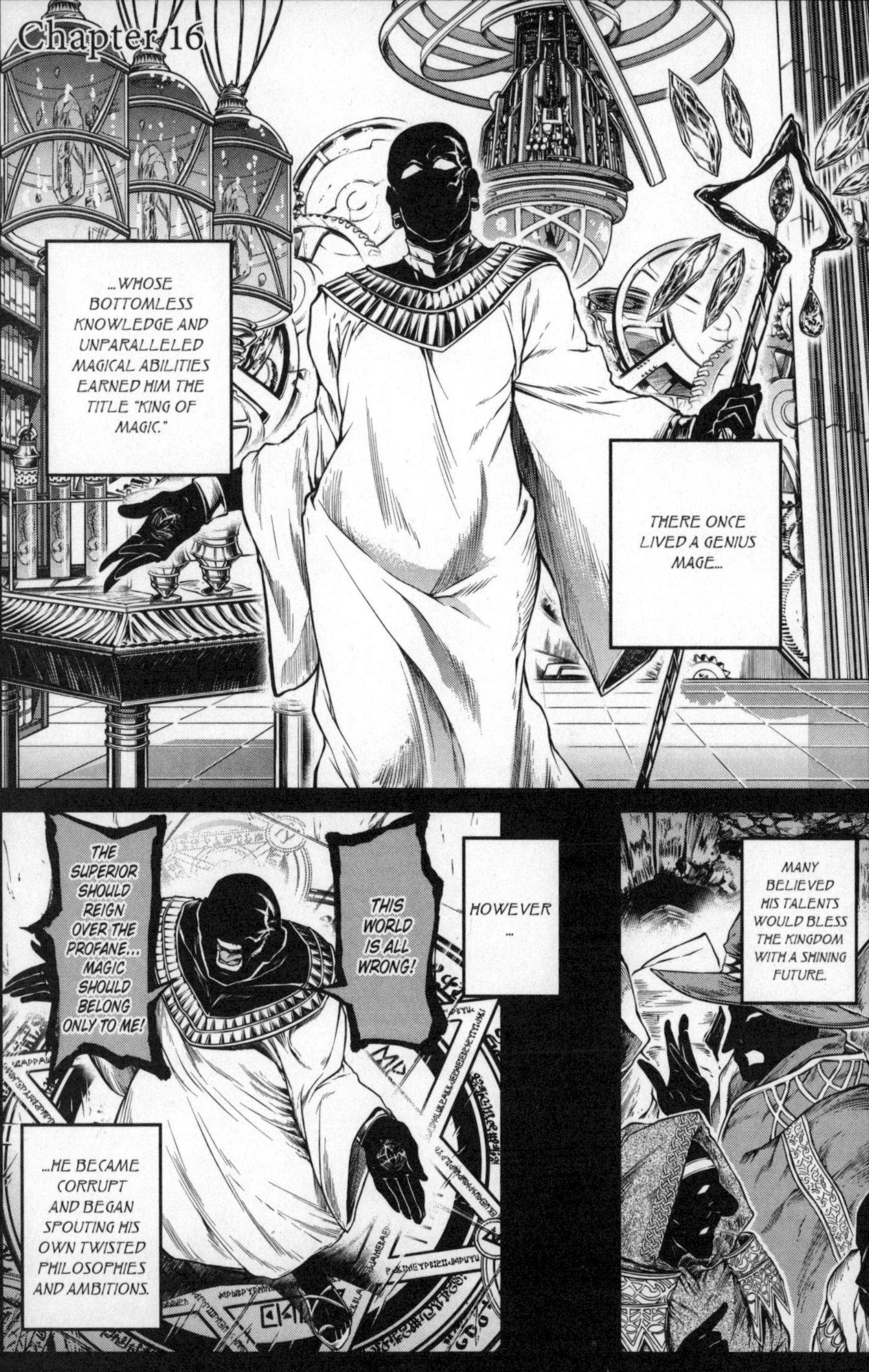
THERE ONCE LIVED A GENIUS MAGE...
...WHOSE BOTTOMLESS KNOWLEDGE AND UNPARALLELED MAGICAL ABILITIES EARNED HIM THE TITLE "KING OF MAGIC."
MANY BELIEVED HIS TALENTS WOULD BLESS THE KINGDOM WITH A SHINING FUTURE.
HOWEVER...
THIS WORLD IS ALL WRONG!
THE SUPERIOR SHOULD REIGN OVER THE PROFANE... MAGIC SHOULD BELONG ONLY TO ME!
...HE BECAME CORRUPT AND BEGAN SPOUTING HIS OWN TWISTED PHILOSOPHIES AND AMBITIONS.

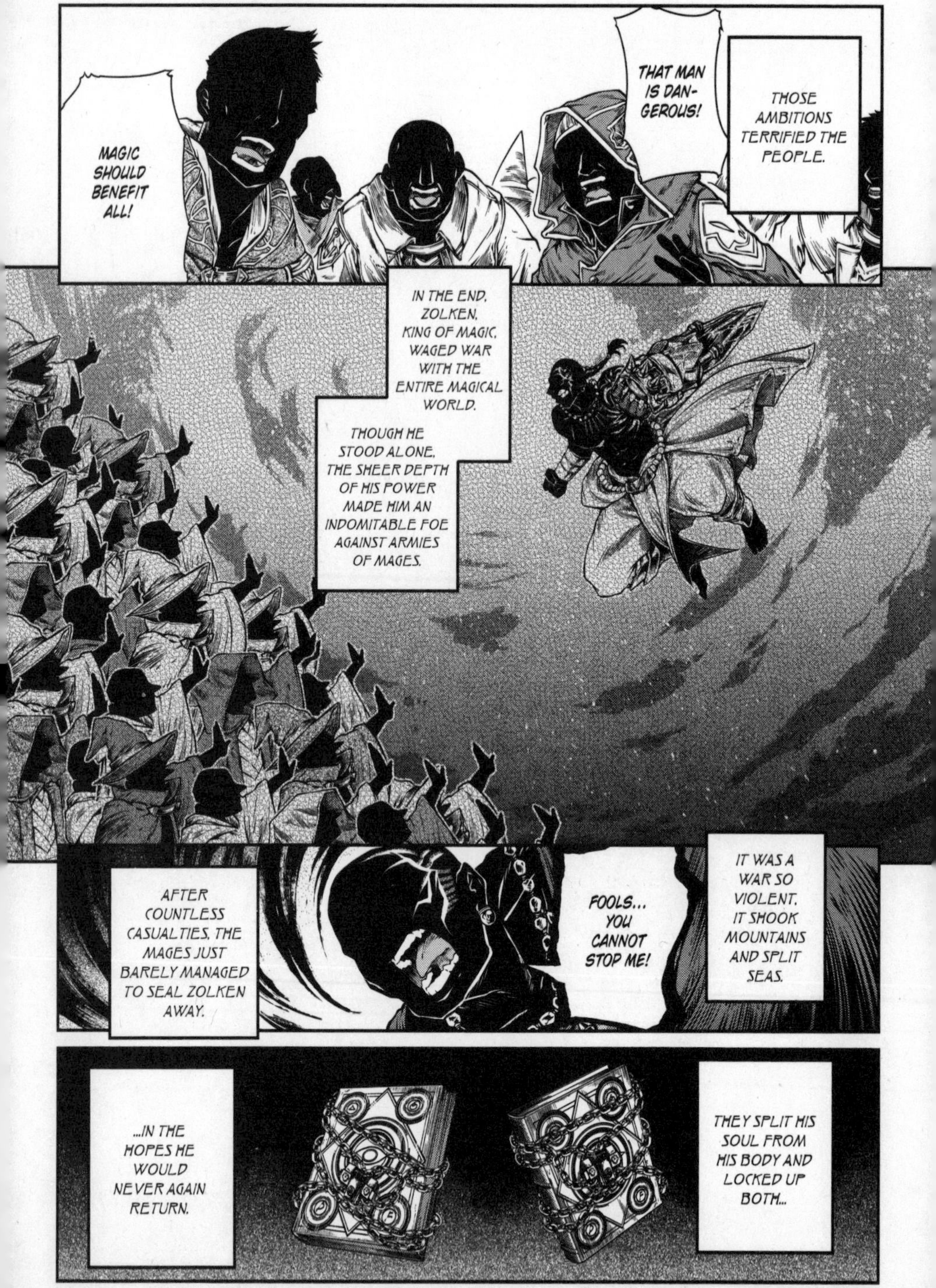
THOSE AMBITIONS TERRIFIED THE PEOPLE.
THAT MAN IS DAN-GEROUS!
MAGIC SHOULD BENEFIT ALL!
IN THE END, ZOLKEN, KING OF MAGIC, WAGED WAR WITH THE ENTIRE MAGICAL WORLD.
THOUGH HE STOOD ALONE, THE SHEER DEPTH OF HIS POWER MADE HIM AN INDOMITABLE FOE AGAINST ARMIES OF MAGES.
IT WAS A WAR SO VIOLENT, IT SHOOK MOUNTAINS AND SPLIT SEAS.
FOOLS... YOU CANNOT STOP ME!
AFTER COUNTLESS CASUALTIES, THE MAGES JUST BARELY MANAGED TO SEAL ZOLKEN AWAY.
THEY SPLIT HIS SOUL FROM HIS BODY AND LOCKED UP BOTH...
...IN THE HOPES HE WOULD NEVER AGAIN RETURN.

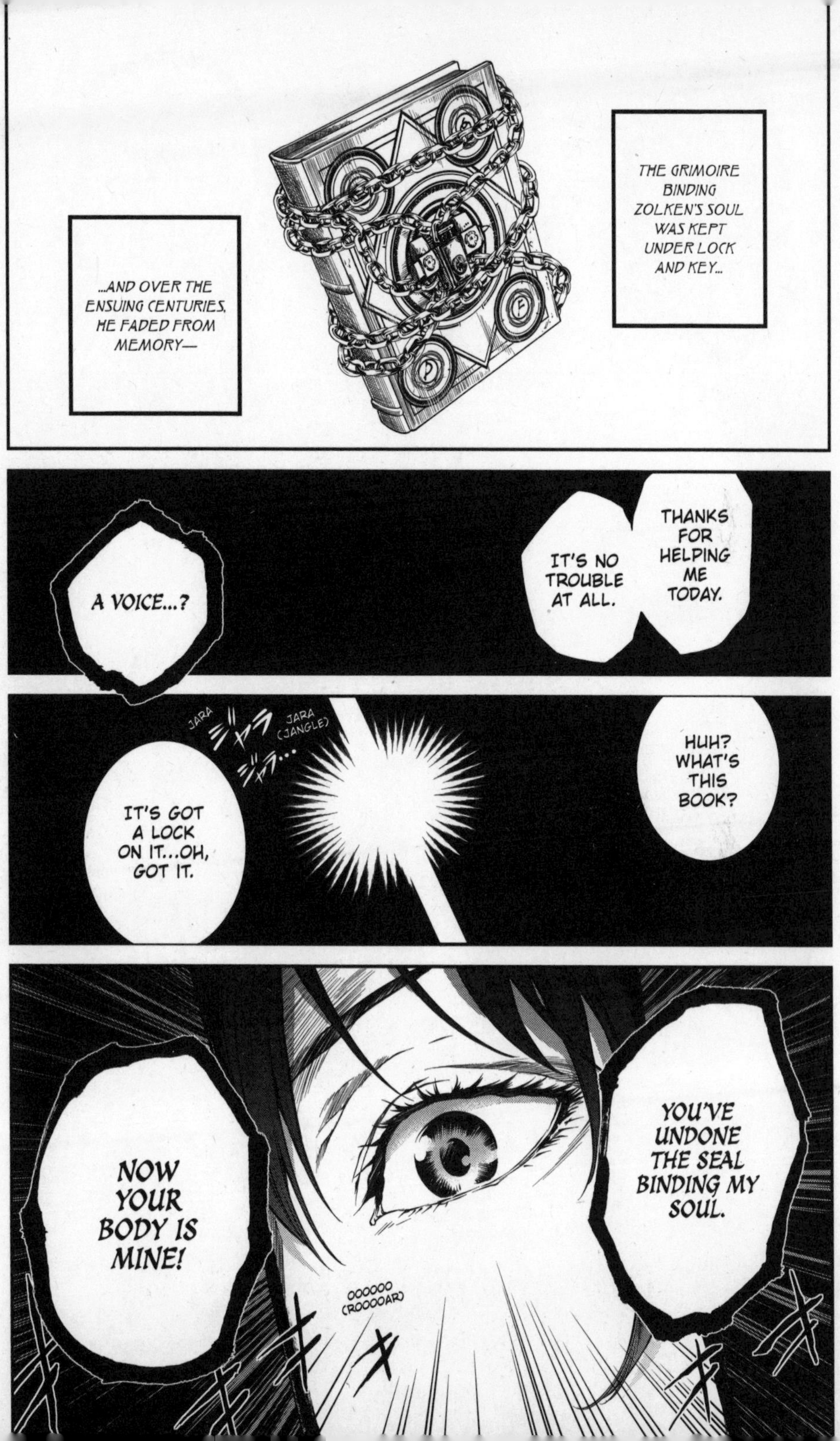

THE GRIMOIRE BINDING ZOLKEN'S SOUL WAS KEPT UNDER LOCK AND KEY...
...AND OVER THE ENSUING CENTURIES, HE FADED FROM MEMORY—
THANKS FOR HELPING ME TODAY.
IT'S NO TROUBLE AT ALL.
A VOICE...?
HUH? WHAT'S THIS BOOK?
JARA (JANGLE)
ジャラ
JARA
ジャラ...
IT'S GOT A LOCK ON IT...OH, GOT IT.
YOU'VE UNDONE THE SEAL BINDING MY SOUL.
NOW YOUR BODY IS MINE!
OOOOOO (ROOOOAR)

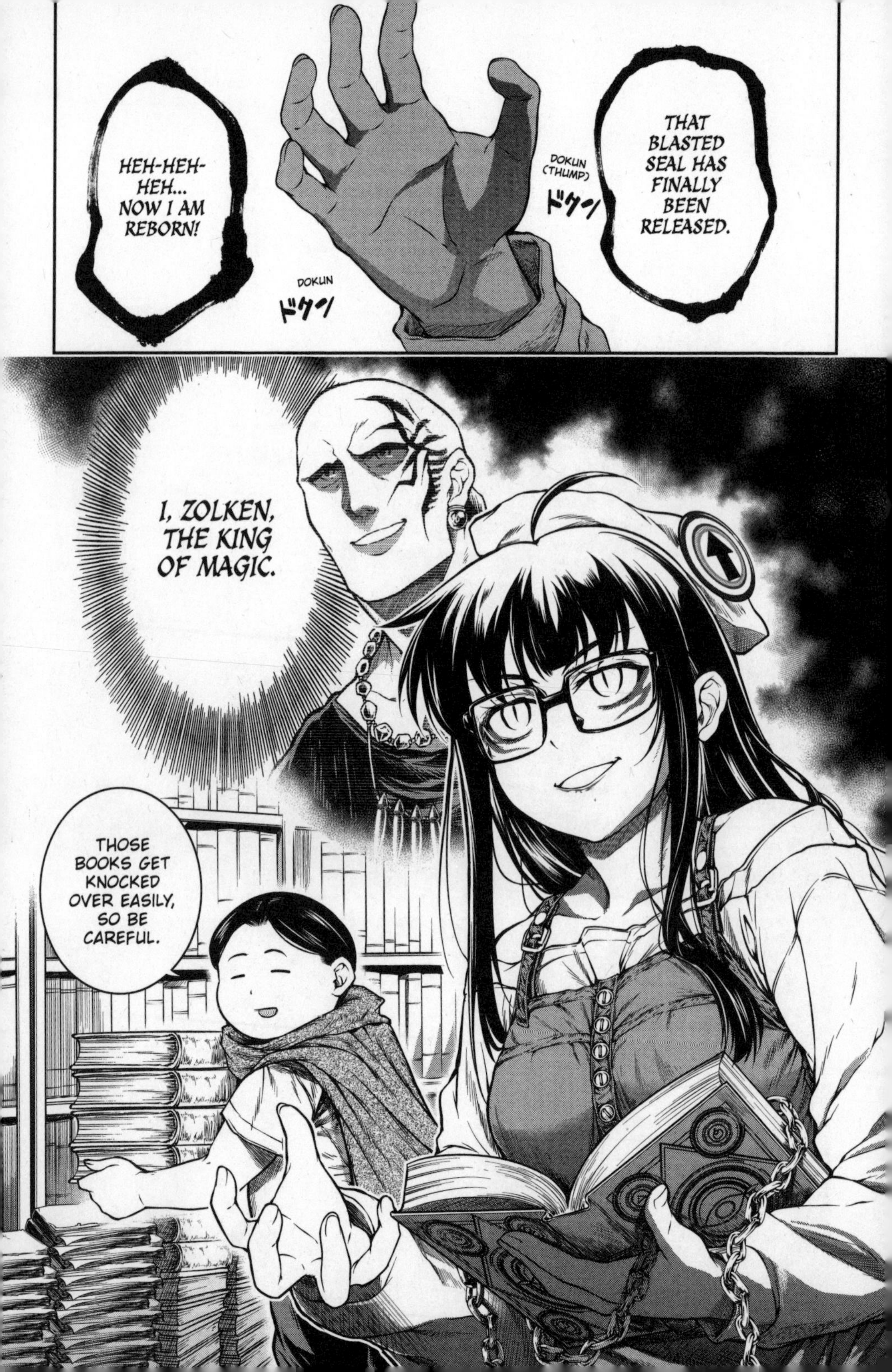
THAT BLASTED SEAL HAS FINALLY BEEN RELEASED.
DOKUN (THUMP)
ドクン
DOKUN
ドクン
HEH-HEH-HEH... NOW I AM REBORN!
I, ZOLKEN, THE KING OF MAGIC.
THOSE BOOKS GET KNOCKED OVER EASILY, SO BE CAREFUL.

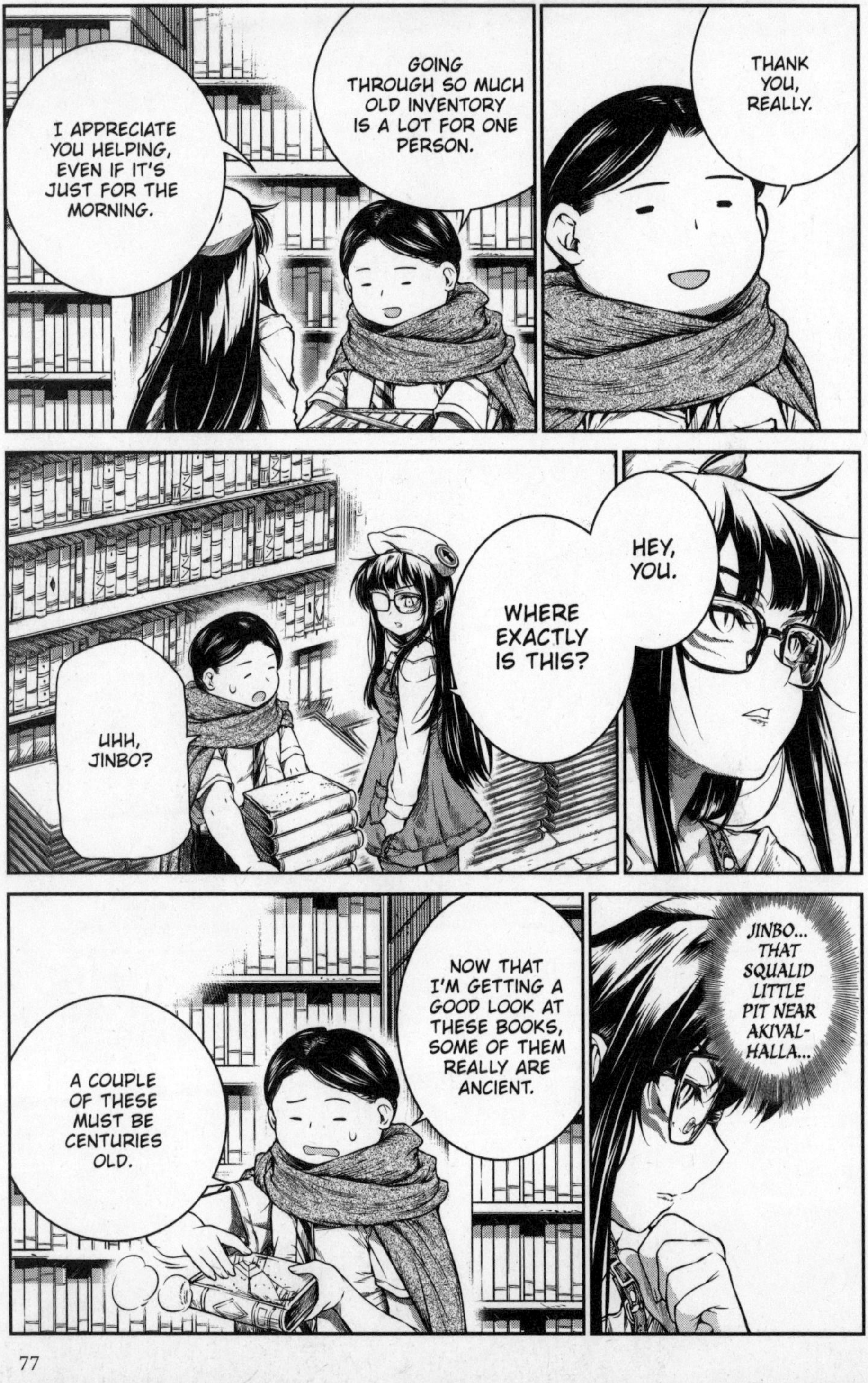

THANK YOU, REALLY.
GOING THROUGH SO MUCH OLD INVENTORY IS A LOT FOR ONE PERSON.
I APPRECIATE YOU HELPING, EVEN IF IT'S JUST FOR THE MORNING.
HEY, YOU.
WHERE EXACTLY IS THIS?
UHH, JINBO?
JINBO... THAT SQUALID LITTLE PIT NEAR AKIVAL-HALLA...
NOW THAT I'M GETTING A GOOD LOOK AT THESE BOOKS, SOME OF THEM REALLY ARE ANCIENT.
A COUPLE OF THESE MUST BE CENTURIES OLD.

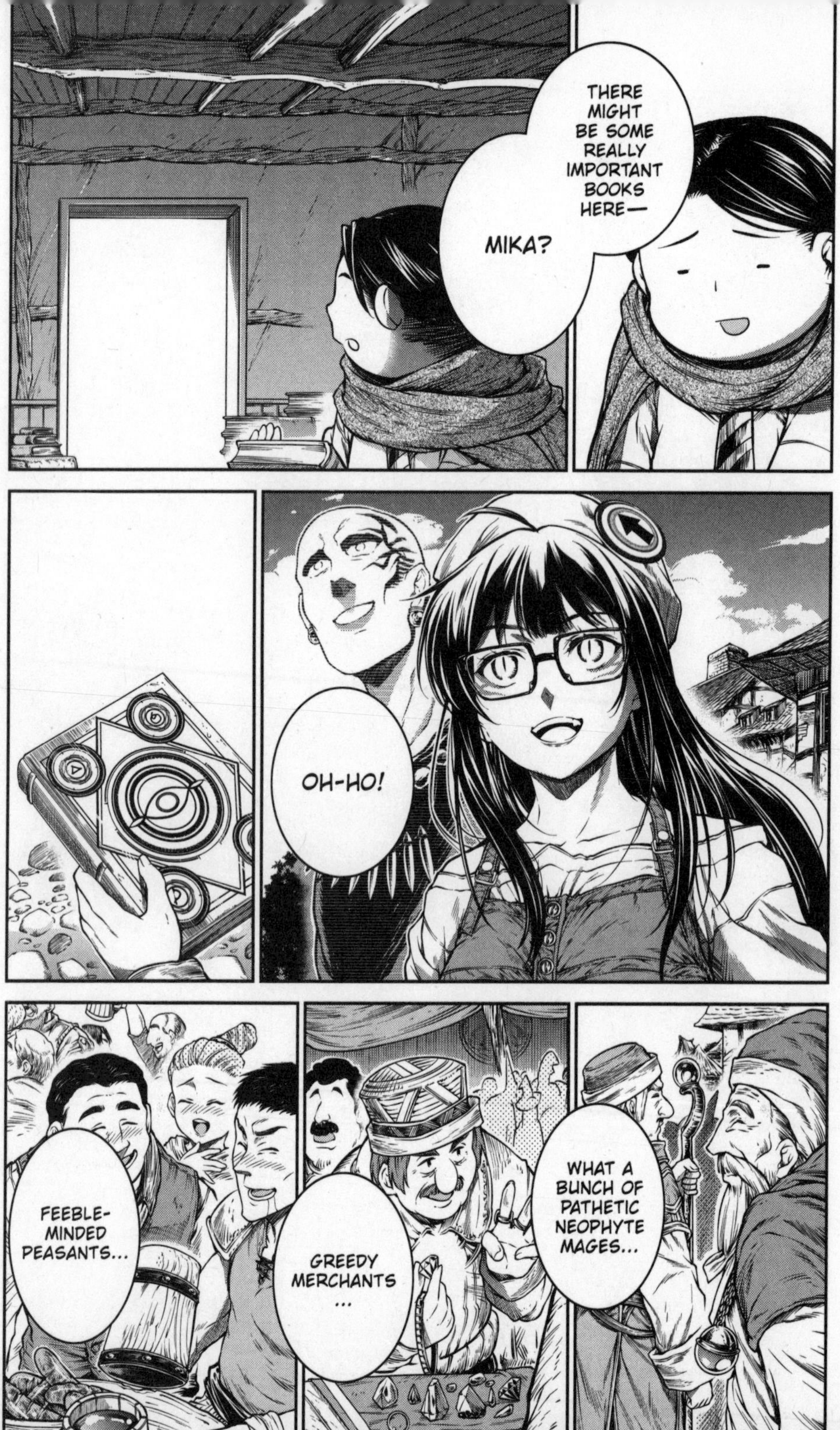
THERE MIGHT BE SOME REALLY IMPORTANT BOOKS HERE—
MIKA?
OH-HO!
WHAT A BUNCH OF PATHETIC NEOPHYTE MAGES...
GREEDY MERCHANTS...
FEEBLE-MINDED PEASANTS...

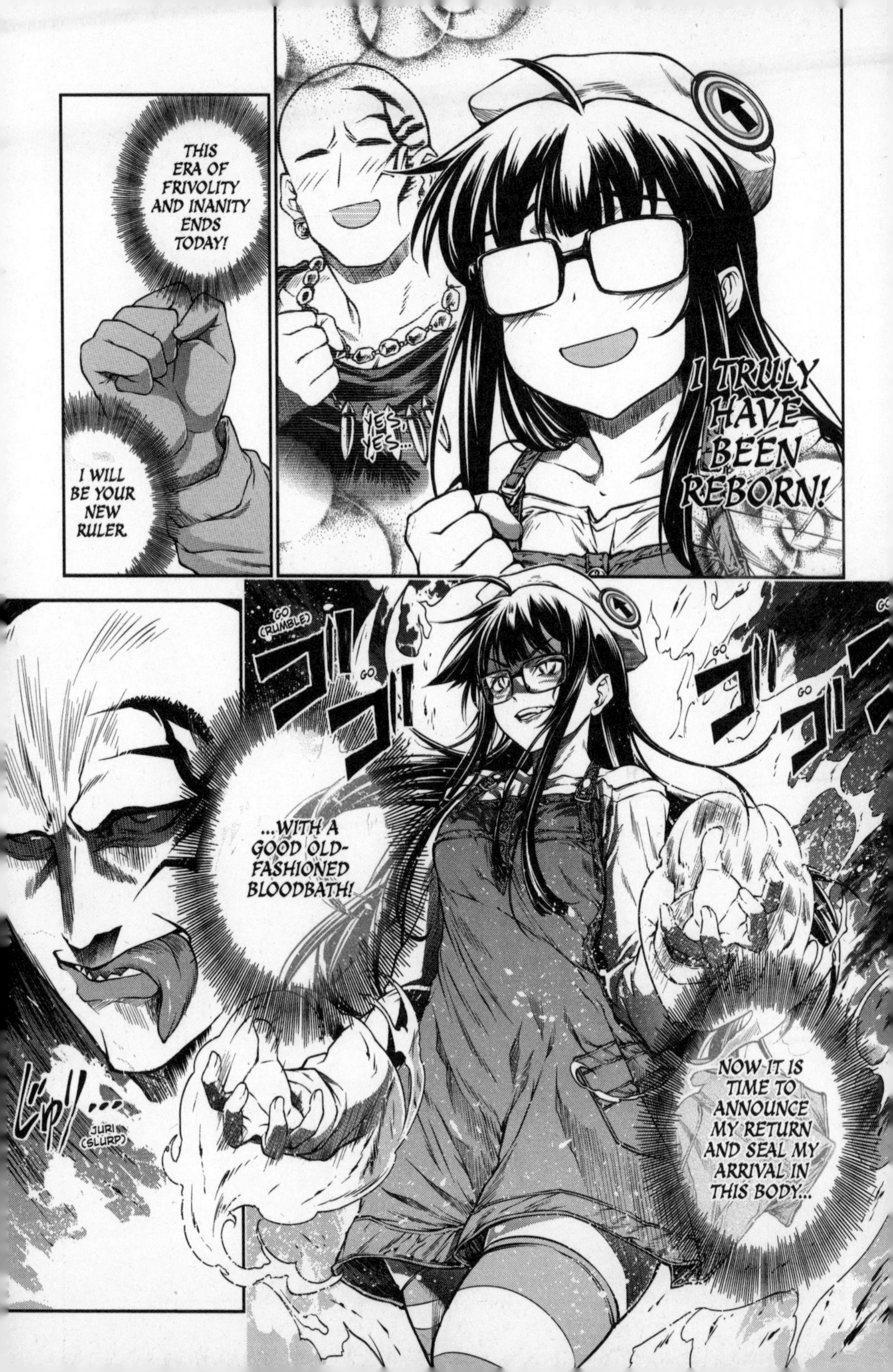

I TRULY HAVE BEEN REBORN!
YES, YES...
THIS ERA OF FRIVOLITY AND INANITY ENDS TODAY!
I WILL BE YOUR NEW RULER.
GO (RUMBLE)
GO
GO
GO
GO
NOW IT IS TIME TO ANNOUNCE MY RETURN AND SEAL MY ARRIVAL IN THIS BODY...
...WITH A GOOD OLD-FASHIONED BLOODBATH!
JURI (SLURP)

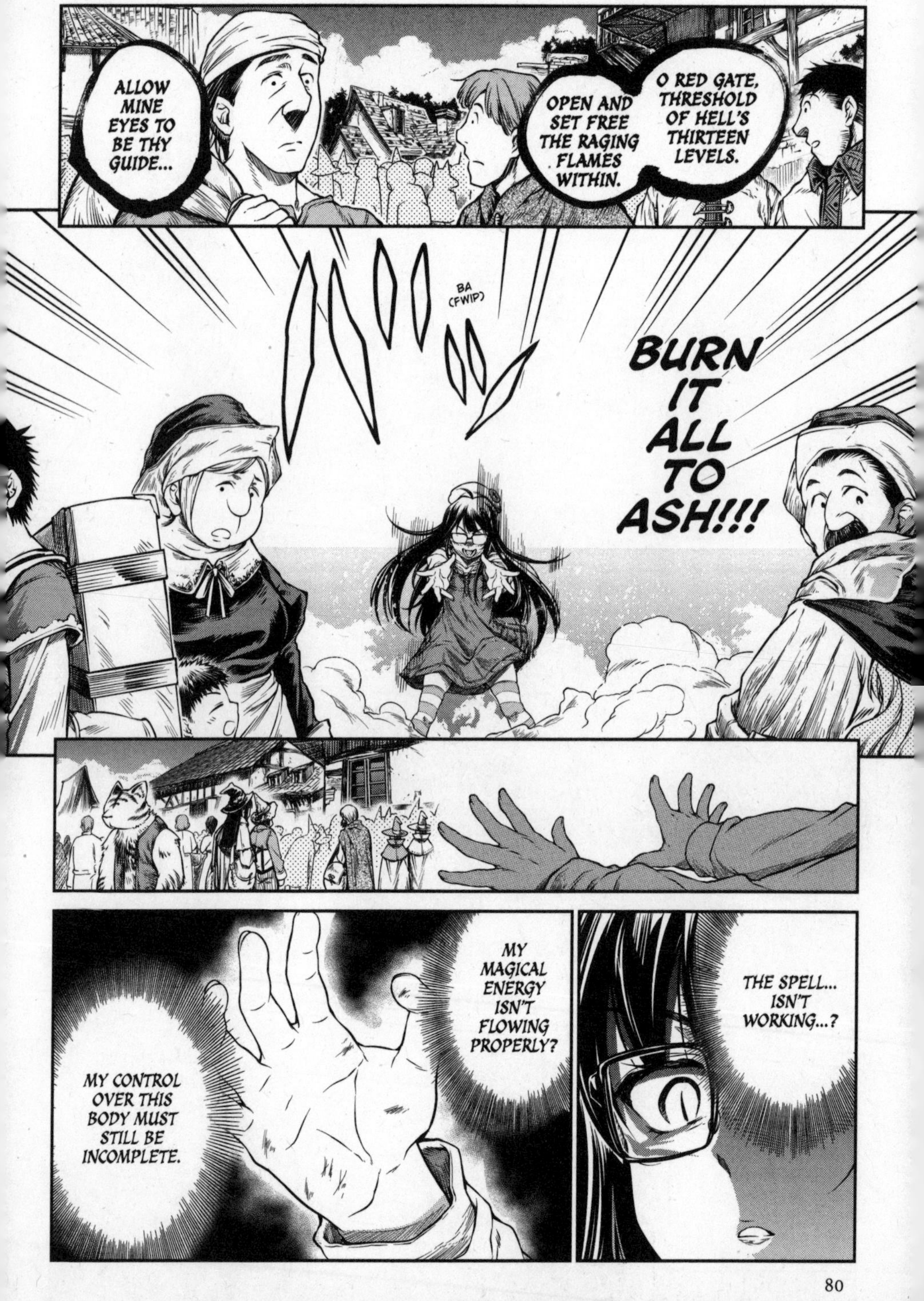
O RED GATE, THRESHOLD OF HELL'S THIRTEEN LEVELS.
OPEN AND SET FREE THE RAGING FLAMES WITHIN.
ALLOW MINE EYES TO BE THY GUIDE...
BURN IT ALL TO ASH!!!
BA (FWIP)
THE SPELL... ISN'T WORKING...?
MY MAGICAL ENERGY ISN'T FLOWING PROPERLY?
MY CONTROL OVER THIS BODY MUST STILL BE INCOMPLETE.

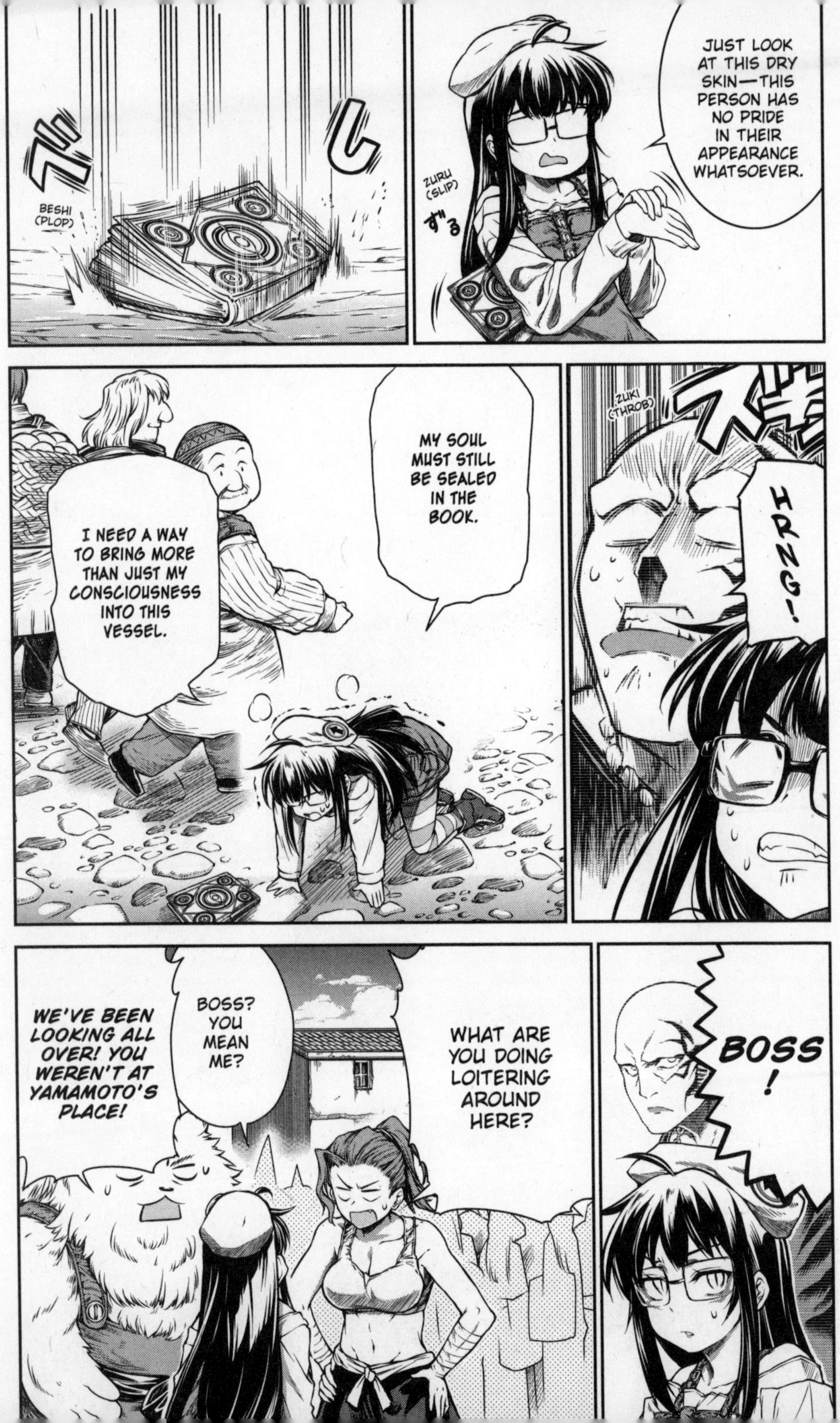
JUST LOOK AT THIS DRY SKIN—THIS PERSON HAS NO PRIDE IN THEIR APPEARANCE WHATSOEVER.
ZURU (SLIP)
ずる
BESHI (PLOP)
ZUKI (THROB)
HRNG!
MY SOUL MUST STILL BE SEALED IN THE BOOK.
I NEED A WAY TO BRING MORE THAN JUST MY CONSCIOUSNESS INTO THIS VESSEL.
BOSS!
WHAT ARE YOU DOING LOITERING AROUND HERE?
BOSS? YOU MEAN ME?
WE'VE BEEN LOOKING ALL OVER! YOU WEREN'T AT YAMAMOTO'S PLACE!

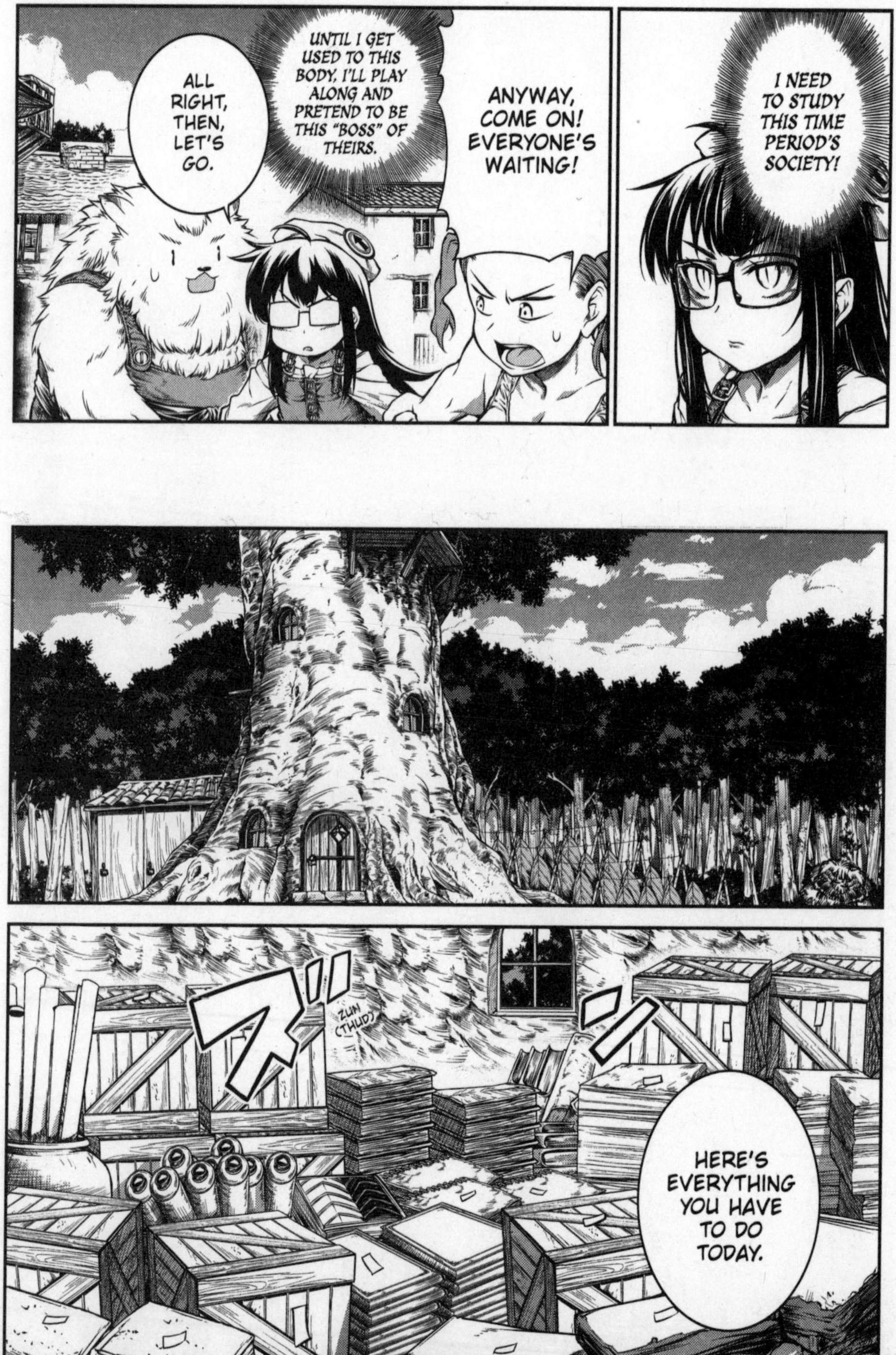
I NEED TO STUDY THIS TIME PERIOD'S SOCIETY!
ANYWAY, COME ON! EVERYONE'S WAITING!
UNTIL I GET USED TO THIS BODY, I'LL PLAY ALONG AND PRETEND TO BE THIS "BOSS" OF THEIRS.
ALL RIGHT, THEN, LET'S GO.
ZUN (THUD)
HERE'S EVERYTHING YOU HAVE TO DO TODAY.

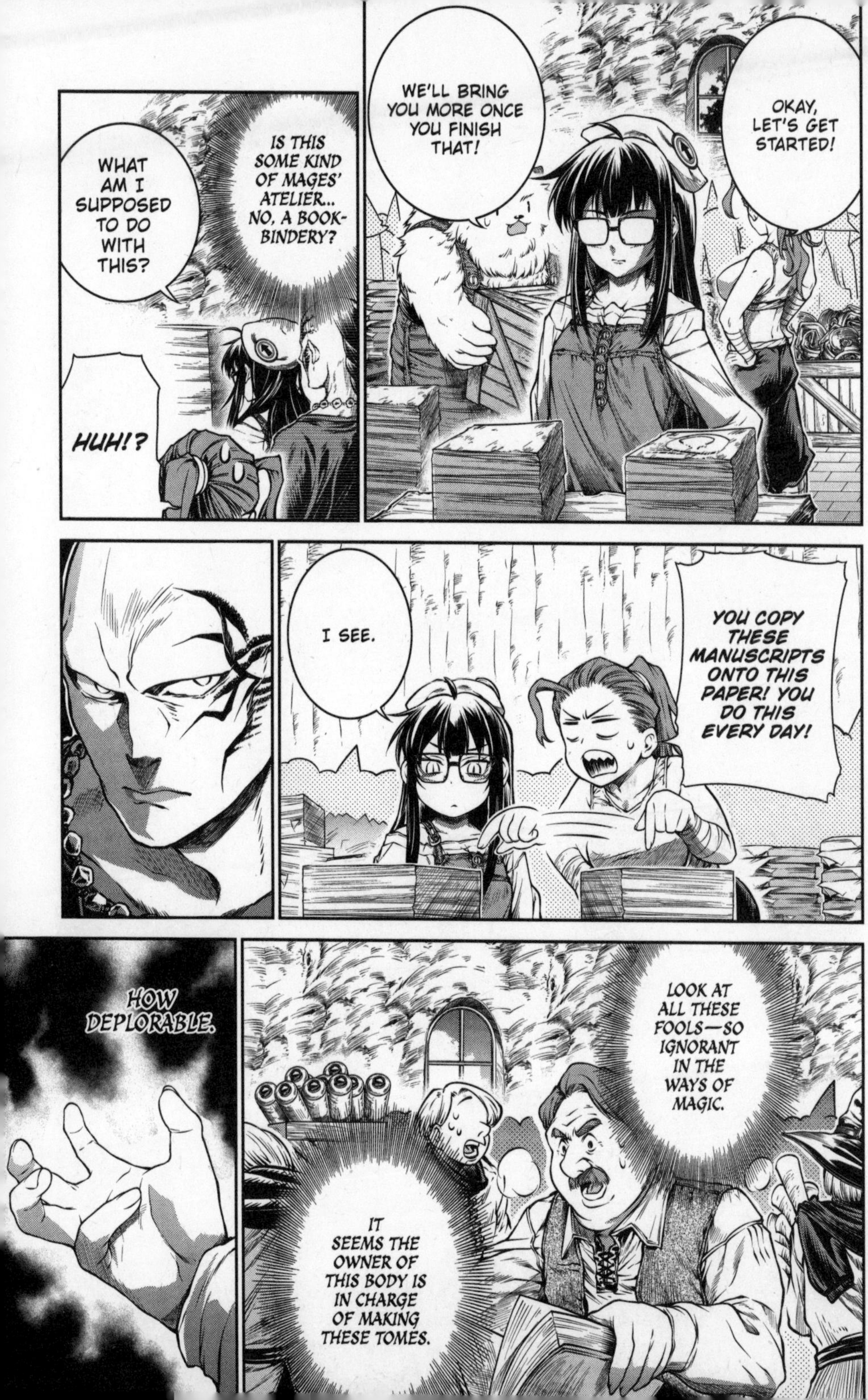
OKAY, LET'S GET STARTED!
WE'LL BRING YOU MORE ONCE YOU FINISH THAT!
IS THIS SOME KIND OF MAGES' ATELIER... NO, A BOOK-BINDERY?
WHAT AM I SUPPOSED TO DO WITH THIS?
HUH!?
YOU COPY THESE MANUSCRIPTS ONTO THIS PAPER! YOU DO THIS EVERY DAY!
I SEE.
LOOK AT ALL THESE FOOLS—SO IGNORANT IN THE WAYS OF MAGIC.
IT SEEMS THE OWNER OF THIS BODY IS IN CHARGE OF MAKING THESE TOMES.
HOW DEPLORABLE.

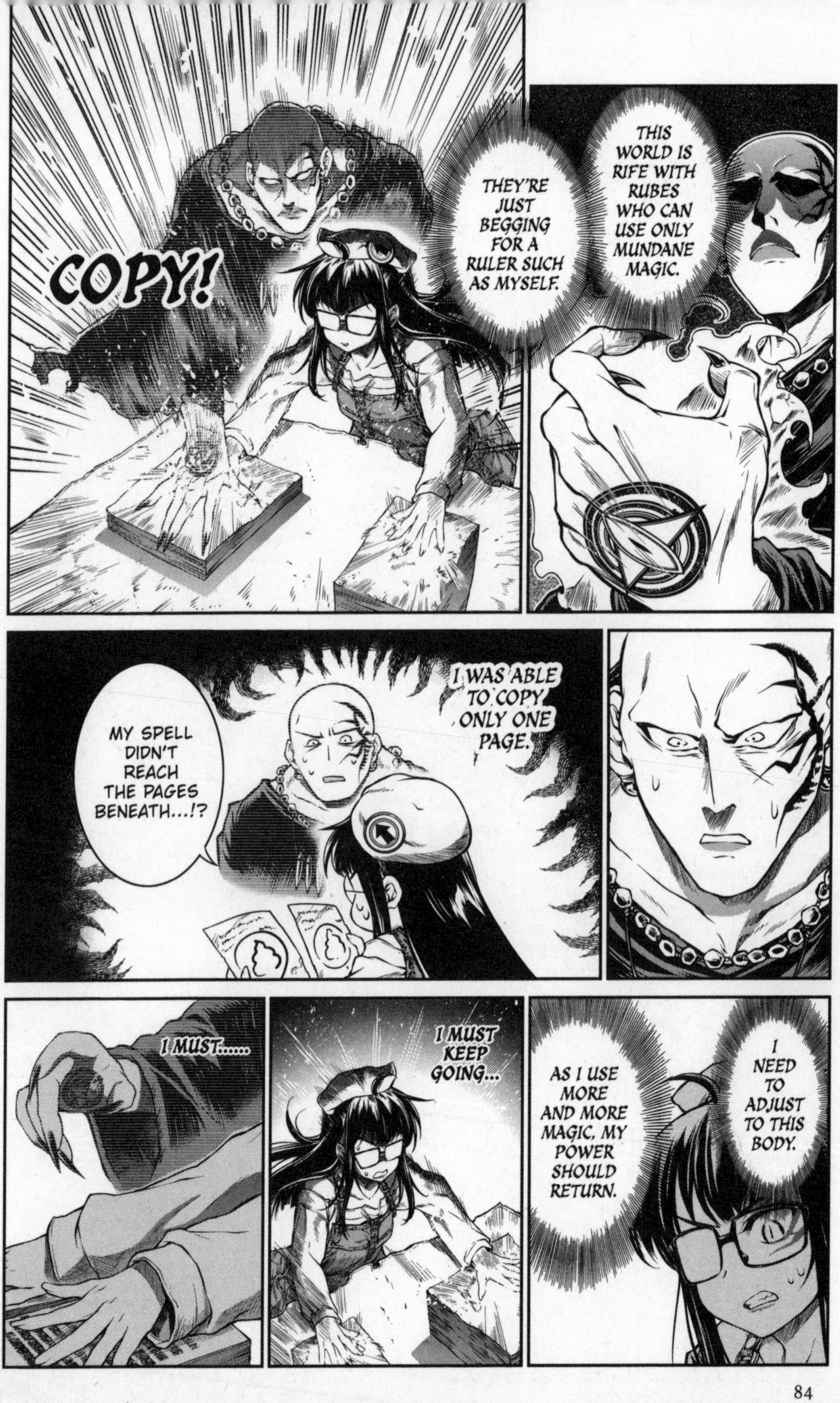
THIS WORLD IS RIFE WITH RUBES WHO CAN USE ONLY MUNDANE MAGIC.
THEY'RE JUST BEGGING FOR A RULER SUCH AS MYSELF.
COPY!
I WAS ABLE TO COPY ONLY ONE PAGE.
MY SPELL DIDN'T REACH THE PAGES BENEATH...!?
I NEED TO ADJUST TO THIS BODY.
AS I USE MORE AND MORE MAGIC, MY POWER SHOULD RETURN.
I MUST KEEP GOING...
I MUST......

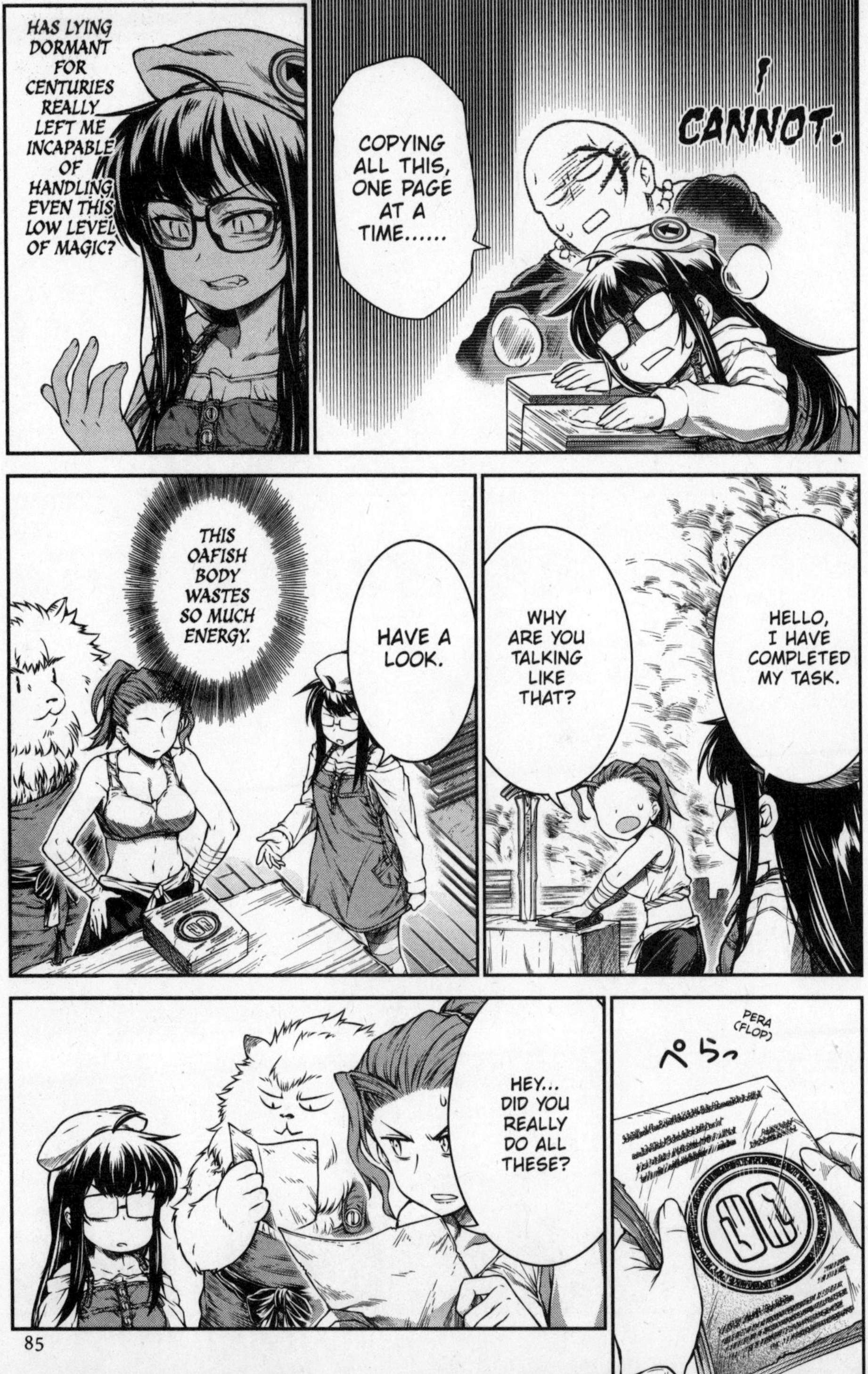
I CANNOT.
COPYING ALL THIS, ONE PAGE AT A TIME......
HAS LYING DORMANT FOR CENTURIES REALLY LEFT ME INCAPABLE OF HANDLING EVEN THIS LOW LEVEL OF MAGIC?
HELLO, I HAVE COMPLETED MY TASK.
WHY ARE YOU TALKING LIKE THAT?
HAVE A LOOK.
THIS OAFISH BODY WASTES SO MUCH ENERGY.
PERA (FLOP)
ぺらっ
HEY... DID YOU REALLY DO ALL THESE?

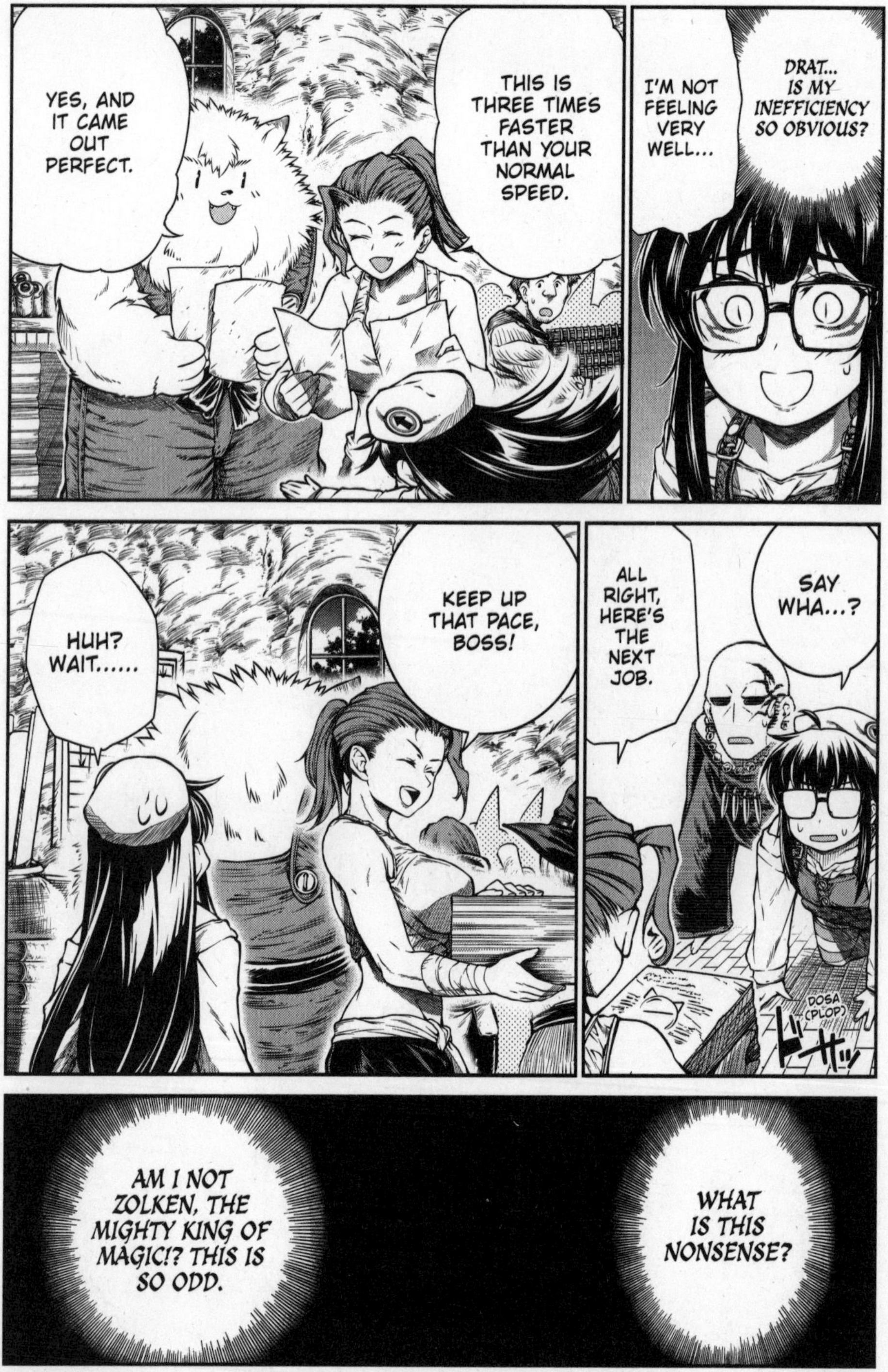
DRAT... IS MY INEFFICIENCY SO OBVIOUS?
I'M NOT FEELING VERY WELL...
THIS IS THREE TIMES FASTER THAN YOUR NORMAL SPEED.
YES, AND IT CAME OUT PERFECT.
SAY WHA...?
ALL RIGHT, HERE'S THE NEXT JOB.
DOSA (PLOP)
KEEP UP THAT PACE, BOSS!
HUH? WAIT......
WHAT IS THIS NONSENSE?
AM I NOT ZOLKEN, THE MIGHTY KING OF MAGIC!? THIS IS SO ODD.

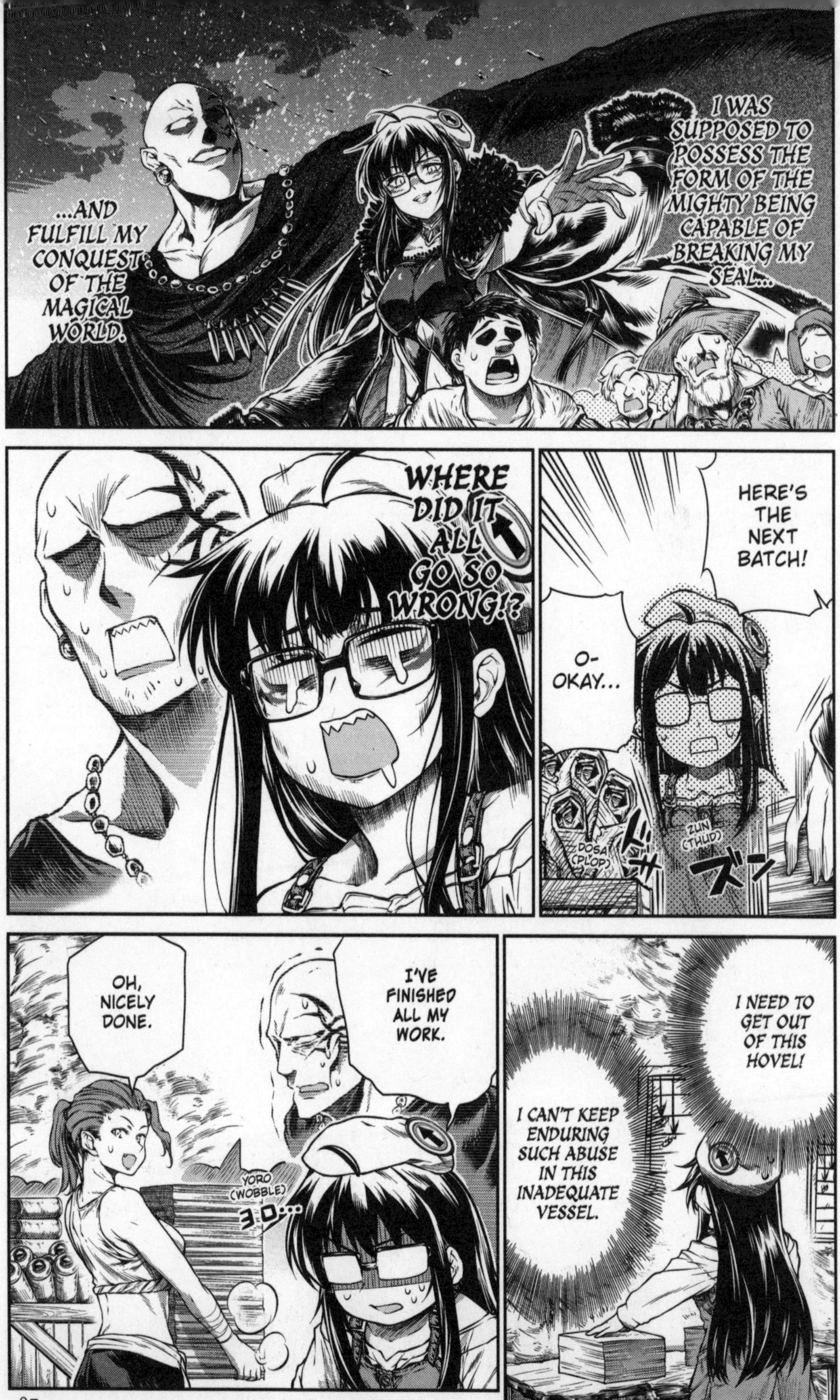
I WAS SUPPOSED TO POSSESS THE FORM OF THE MIGHTY BEING CAPABLE OF BREAKING MY SEAL...
...AND FULFILL MY CONQUEST OF THE MAGICAL WORLD.
HERE'S THE NEXT BATCH!
O- OKAY...
ZUN (THUD)
DOSA (PLOP)
WHERE DID IT ALL GO SO WRONG!?
I NEED TO GET OUT OF THIS HOVEL!
I CAN'T KEEP ENDURING SUCH ABUSE IN THIS INADEQUATE VESSEL.
I'VE FINISHED ALL MY WORK.
OH, NICELY DONE.
YORO (WOBBLE)

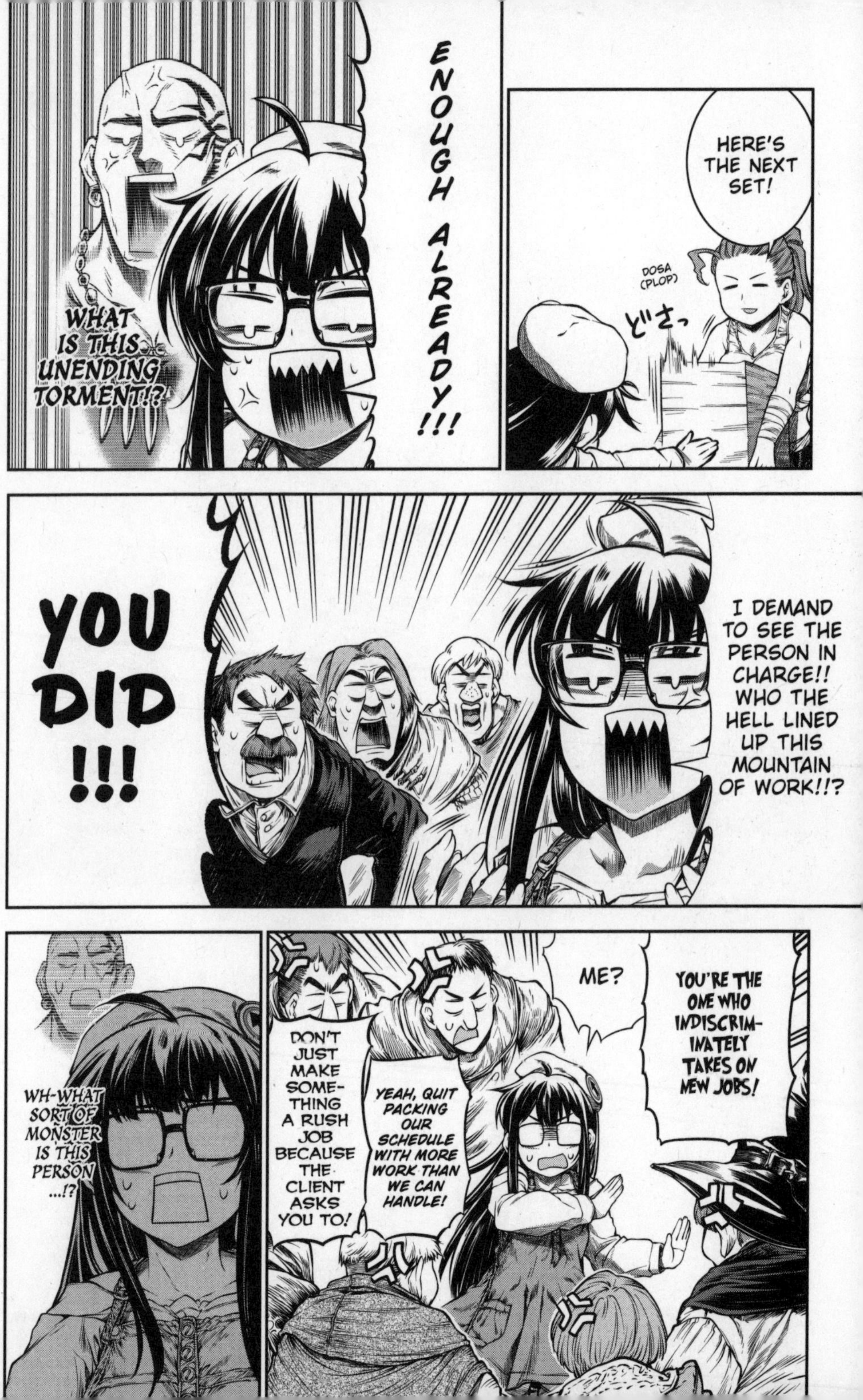
HERE'S THE NEXT SET!
DOSA (PLOP)
どさっ
ENOUGH ALREADY!!!
WHAT IS THIS UNENDING TORMENT!?
I DEMAND TO SEE THE PERSON IN CHARGE!! WHO THE HELL LINED UP THIS MOUNTAIN OF WORK!!?
YOU DID!!!
ME?
YOU'RE THE ONE WHO INDISCRIM-INATELY TAKES ON NEW JOBS!
YEAH, QUIT PACKING OUR SCHEDULE WITH MORE WORK THAN WE CAN HANDLE!
DON'T JUST MAKE SOME-THING A RUSH JOB BECAUSE THE CLIENT ASKS YOU TO!
WH-WHAT SORT OF MONSTER IS THIS PERSON ...!?

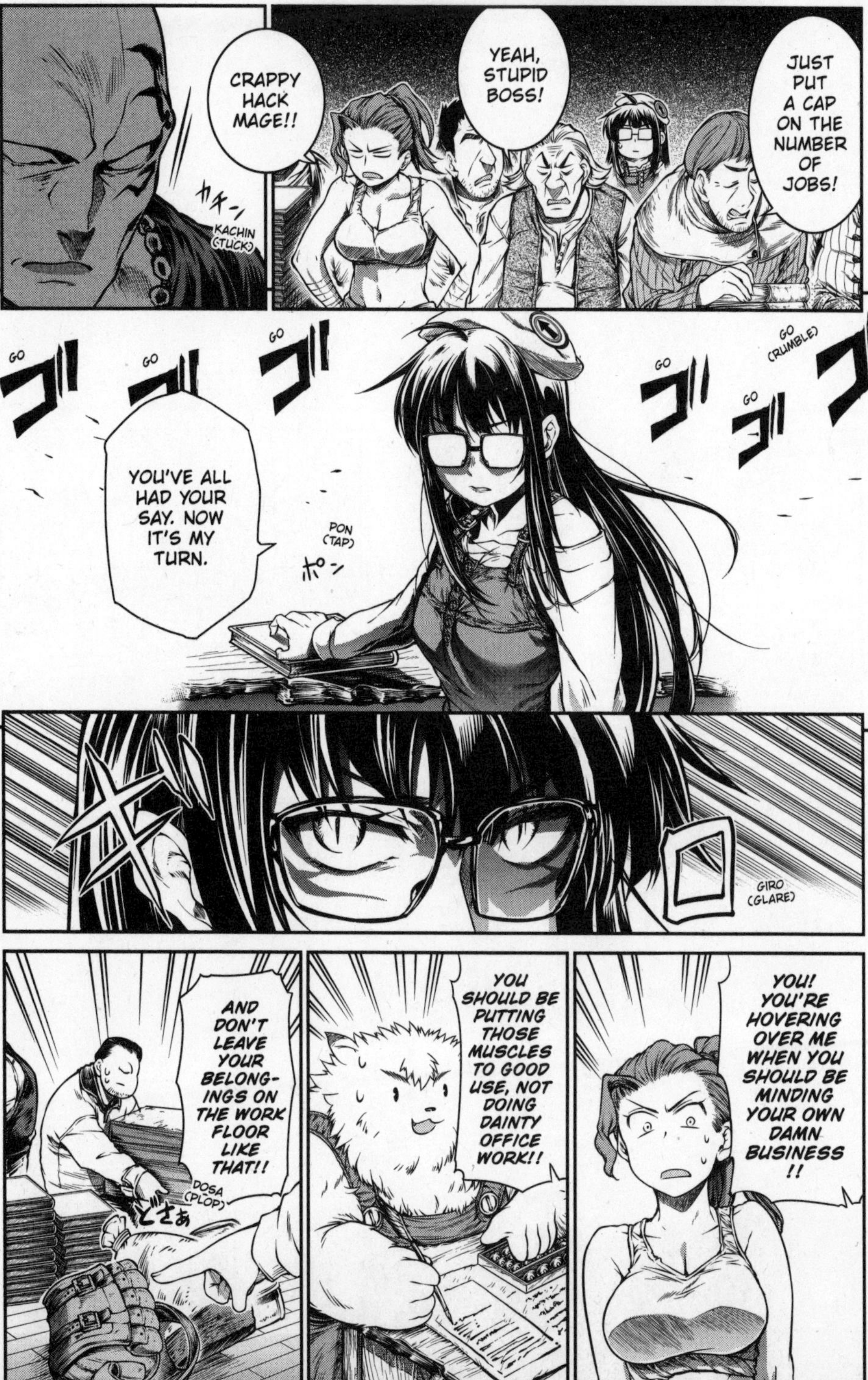
JUST PUT A CAP ON THE NUMBER OF JOBS!
YEAH, STUPID BOSS!
CRAPPY HACK MAGE!!
KACHIN (TUCK)
GO (RUMBLE)
GO
GO
GO
GO
GO
YOU'VE ALL HAD YOUR SAY. NOW IT'S MY TURN.
PON (TAP)
GIRO (GLARE)
YOU! YOU'RE HOVERING OVER ME WHEN YOU SHOULD BE MINDING YOUR OWN DAMN BUSINESS!!
YOU SHOULD BE PUTTING THOSE MUSCLES TO GOOD USE, NOT DOING DAINTY OFFICE WORK!!
AND DON'T LEAVE YOUR BELONGINGS ON THE WORK FLOOR LIKE THAT!!
DOSA (PLOP)

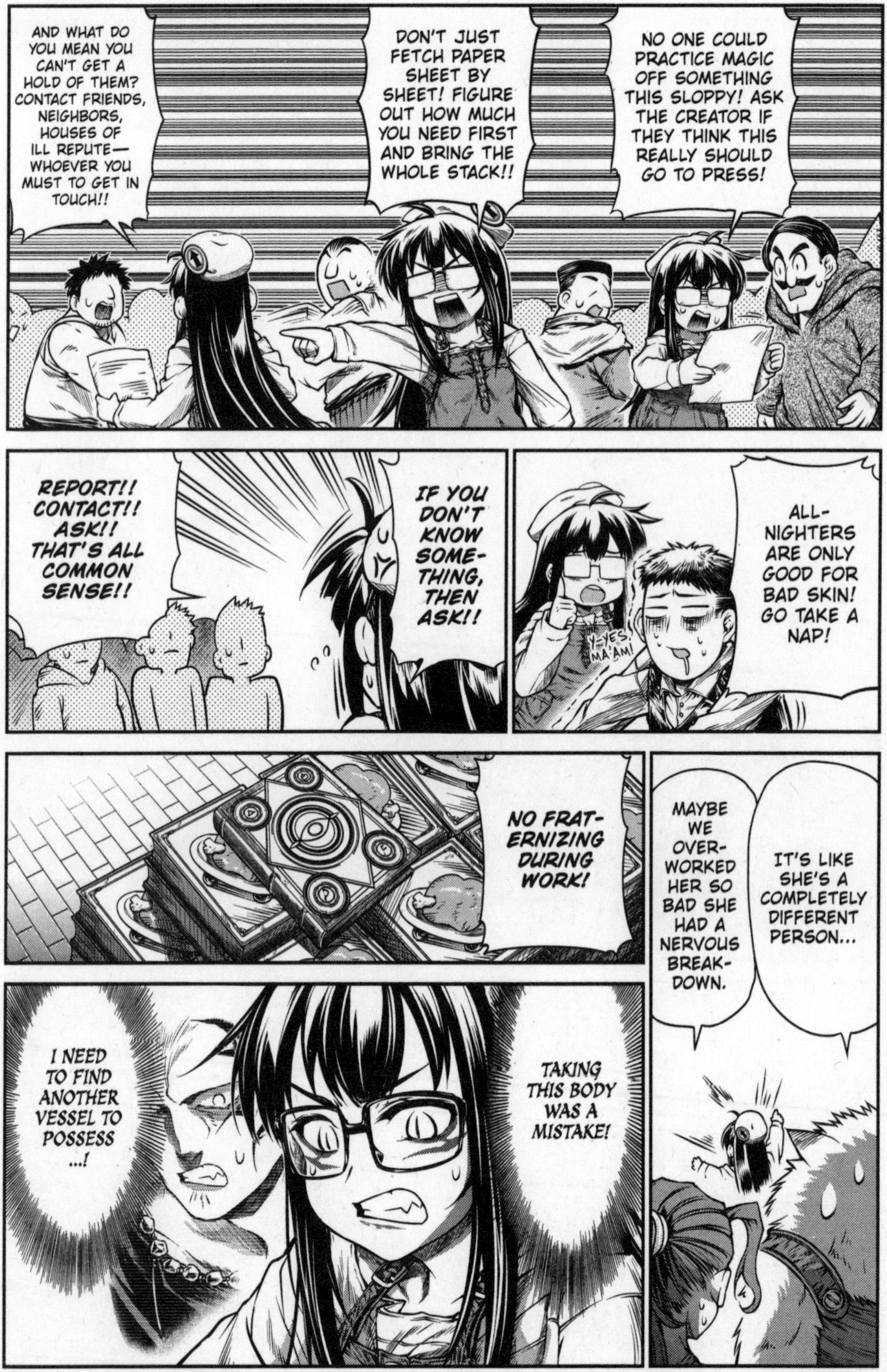
NO ONE COULD PRACTICE MAGIC OFF SOMETHING THIS SLOPPY! ASK THE CREATOR IF THEY THINK THIS REALLY SHOULD GO TO PRESS!
DON'T JUST FETCH PAPER SHEET BY SHEET! FIGURE OUT HOW MUCH YOU NEED FIRST AND BRING THE WHOLE STACK!!
AND WHAT DO YOU MEAN YOU CAN'T GET A HOLD OF THEM? CONTACT FRIENDS, NEIGHBORS, HOUSES OF ILL REPUTE—WHOEVER YOU MUST TO GET IN TOUCH!!
ALL-NIGHTERS ARE ONLY GOOD FOR BAD SKIN! GO TAKE A NAP!
Y-YES, MA'AM!
IF YOU DON'T KNOW SOME-THING, THEN ASK!!
REPORT!! CONTACT!! ASK!! THAT'S ALL COMMON SENSE!!
IT'S LIKE SHE'S A COMPLETELY DIFFERENT PERSON...
MAYBE WE OVER-WORKED HER SO BAD SHE HAD A NERVOUS BREAK-DOWN.
NO FRAT-ERNIZING DURING WORK!
TAKING THIS BODY WAS A MISTAKE!
I NEED TO FIND ANOTHER VESSEL TO POSSESS ...!

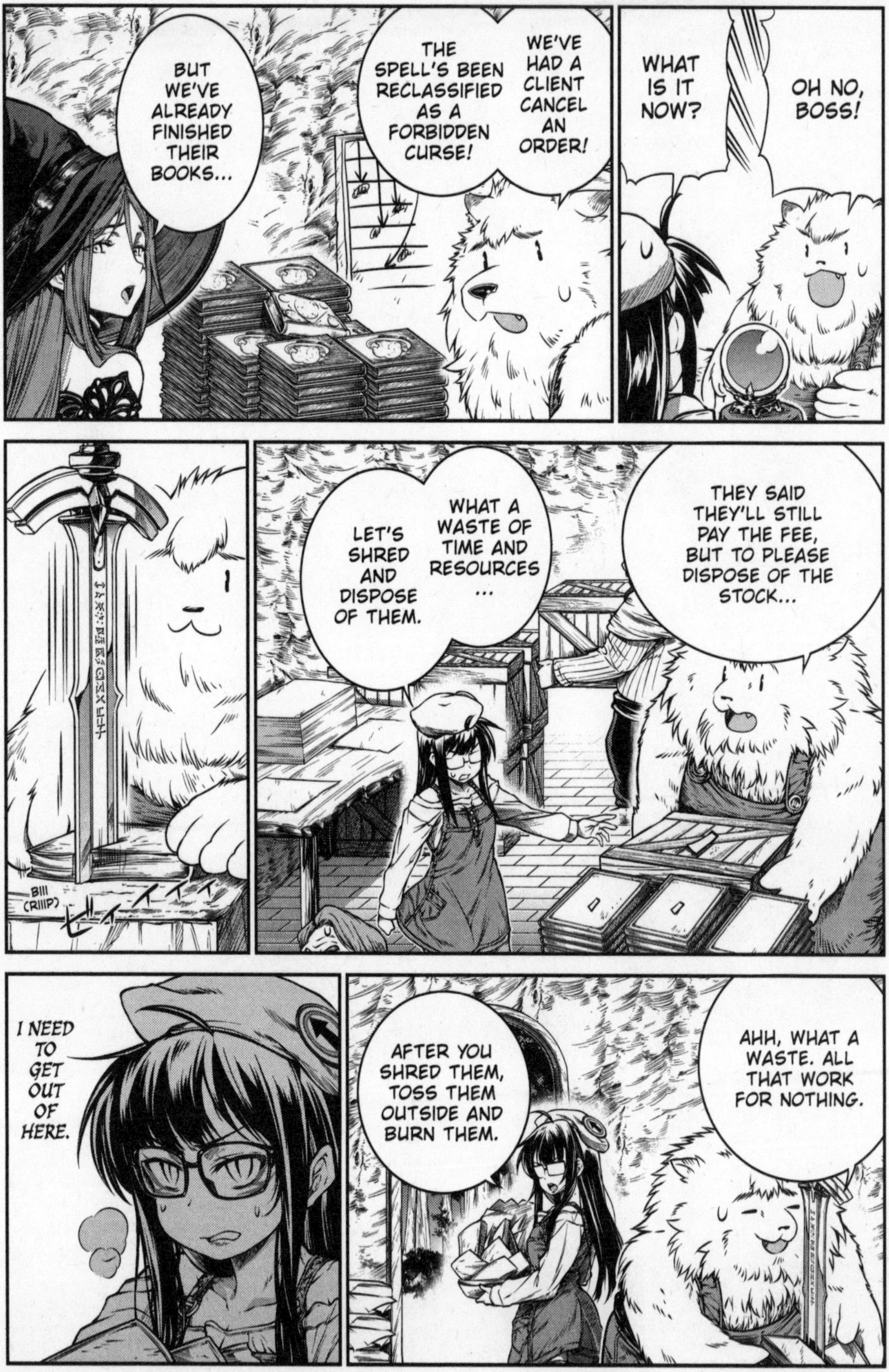
OH NO, BOSS!
WHAT IS IT NOW?
WE'VE HAD A CLIENT CANCEL AN ORDER!
THE SPELL'S BEEN RECLASSIFIED AS A FORBIDDEN CURSE!
BUT WE'VE ALREADY FINISHED THEIR BOOKS...
THEY SAID THEY'LL STILL PAY THE FEE, BUT TO PLEASE DISPOSE OF THE STOCK...
WHAT A WASTE OF TIME AND RESOURCES...
LET'S SHRED AND DISPOSE OF THEM.
BIII (RIIIP)
AHH, WHAT A WASTE. ALL THAT WORK FOR NOTHING.
AFTER YOU SHRED THEM, TOSS THEM OUTSIDE AND BURN THEM.
I NEED TO GET OUT OF HERE.

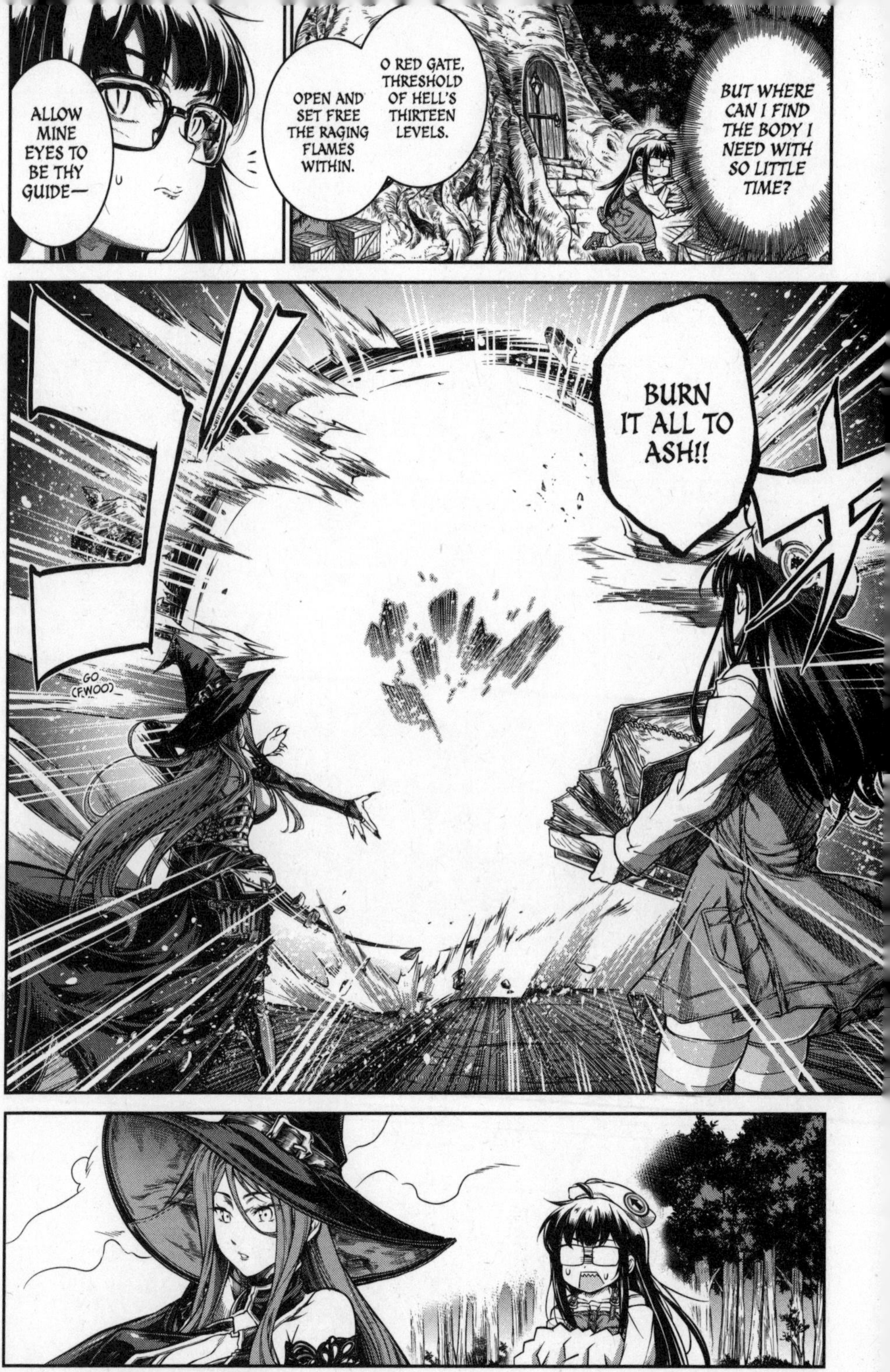
BUT WHERE CAN I FIND THE BODY I NEED WITH SO LITTLE TIME?
O RED GATE, THRESHOLD OF HELL'S THIRTEEN LEVELS.
OPEN AND SET FREE THE RAGING FLAMES WITHIN.
ALLOW MINE EYES TO BE THY GUIDE—
BURN IT ALL TO ASH!!
GO (FWOO)

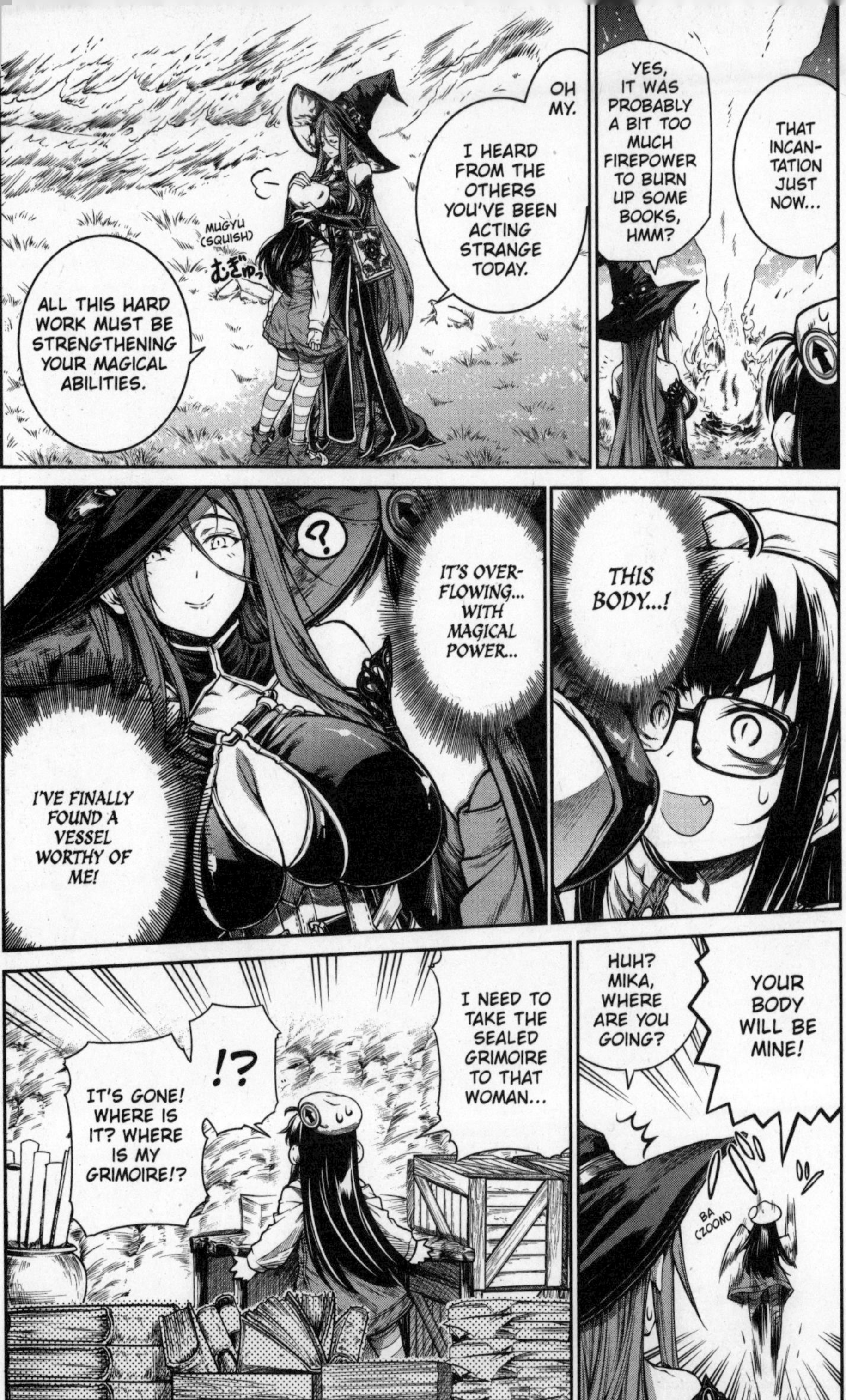
THAT INCANTATION JUST NOW...
YES, IT WAS PROBABLY A BIT TOO MUCH FIREPOWER TO BURN UP SOME BOOKS, HMM?
OH MY.
I HEARD FROM THE OTHERS YOU'VE BEEN ACTING STRANGE TODAY.
MUGYU (SQUISH)
むぎゅっ
ALL THIS HARD WORK MUST BE STRENGTHENING YOUR MAGICAL ABILITIES.
THIS BODY...!
IT'S OVER-FLOWING... WITH MAGICAL POWER...
I'VE FINALLY FOUND A VESSEL WORTHY OF ME!
YOUR BODY WILL BE MINE!
HUH? MIKA, WHERE ARE YOU GOING?
BA (ZOOM)
I NEED TO TAKE THE SEALED GRIMOIRE TO THAT WOMAN...
!?
IT'S GONE! WHERE IS IT? WHERE IS MY GRIMOIRE!?

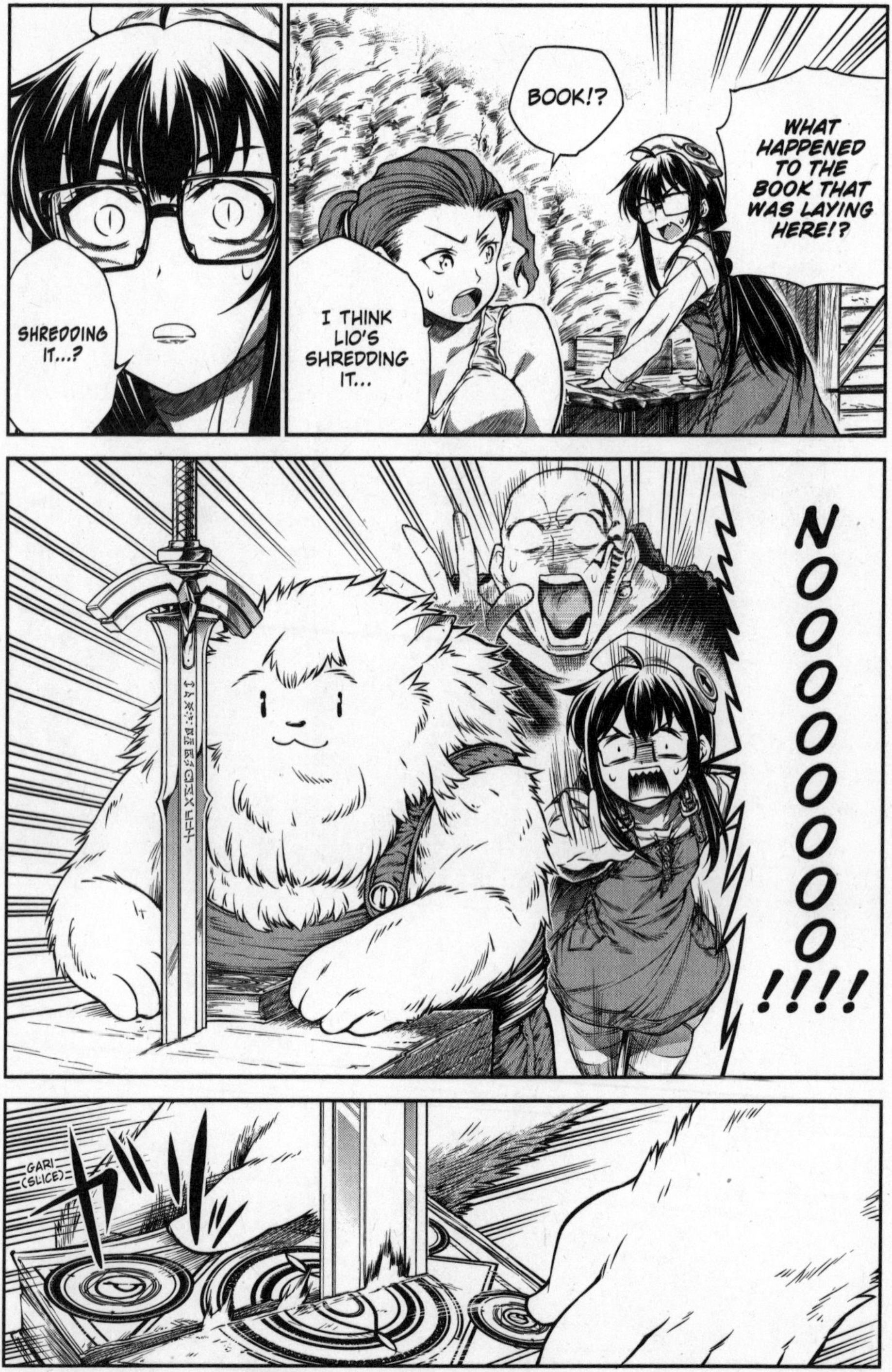
WHAT HAPPENED TO THE BOOK THAT WAS LAYING HERE!?
BOOK!?
I THINK LIO'S SHREDDING IT...
SHREDDING IT...?
NOOOOOOOO!!!!
GARI (SLICE)

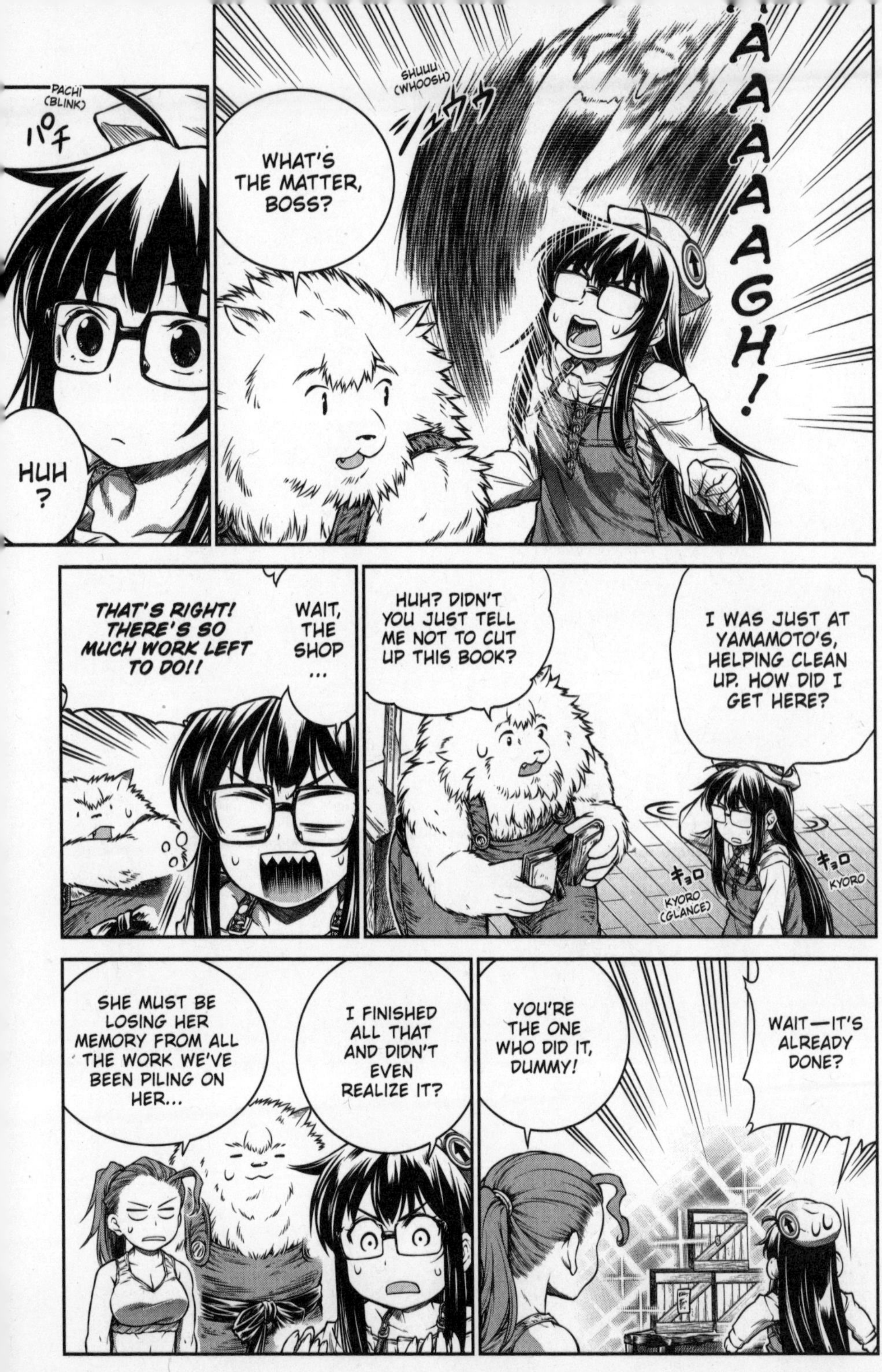
AAAAAAGH!
シュウウ
SHUUU (WHOOSH)
WHAT'S THE MATTER, BOSS?
パチ
PACHI (BLINK)
HUH ?
I WAS JUST AT YAMAMOTO'S, HELPING CLEAN UP. HOW DID I GET HERE?
キョロ
KYORO
キョロ
KYORO (GLANCE)
HUH? DIDN'T YOU JUST TELL ME NOT TO CUT UP THIS BOOK?
WAIT, THE SHOP ...
THAT'S RIGHT! THERE'S SO MUCH WORK LEFT TO DO!!
WAIT—IT'S ALREADY DONE?
YOU'RE THE ONE WHO DID IT, DUMMY!
I FINISHED ALL THAT AND DIDN'T EVEN REALIZE IT?
SHE MUST BE LOSING HER MEMORY FROM ALL THE WORK WE'VE BEEN PILING ON HER...

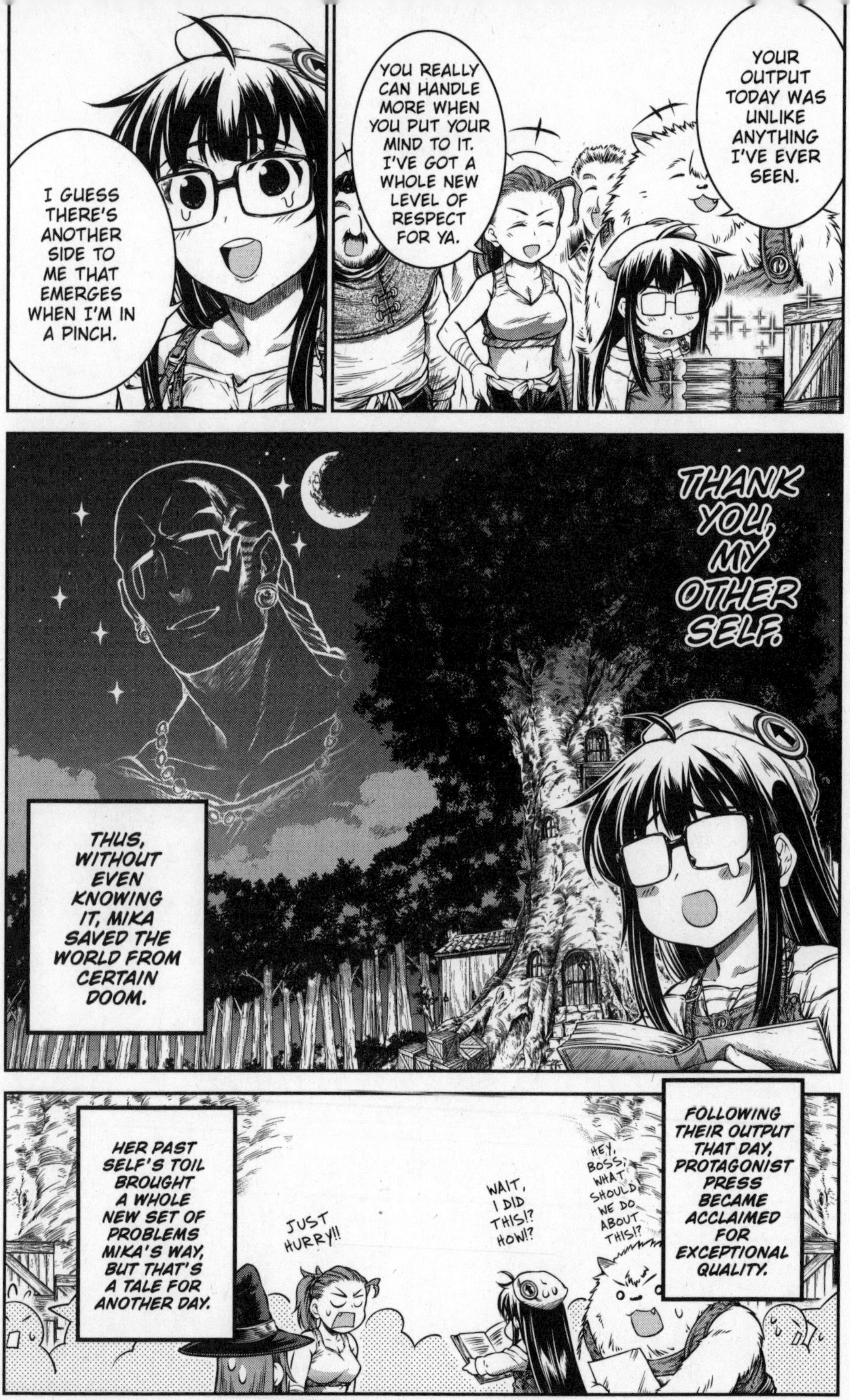
YOUR OUTPUT TODAY WAS UNLIKE ANYTHING I'VE EVER SEEN.
YOU REALLY CAN HANDLE MORE WHEN YOU PUT YOUR MIND TO IT. I'VE GOT A WHOLE NEW LEVEL OF RESPECT FOR YA.
I GUESS THERE'S ANOTHER SIDE TO ME THAT EMERGES WHEN I'M IN A PINCH.
THANK YOU, MY OTHER SELF.
THUS, WITHOUT EVEN KNOWING IT, MIKA SAVED THE WORLD FROM CERTAIN DOOM.
FOLLOWING THEIR OUTPUT THAT DAY, PROTAGONIST PRESS BECAME ACCLAIMED FOR EXCEPTIONAL QUALITY.
HEY, BOSS, WHAT SHOULD WE DO ABOUT THIS!?
WAIT, I DID THIS!? HOW!?
JUST HURRY!!
HER PAST SELF'S TOIL BROUGHT A WHOLE NEW SET OF PROBLEMS MIKA'S WAY, BUT THAT'S A TALE FOR ANOTHER DAY.

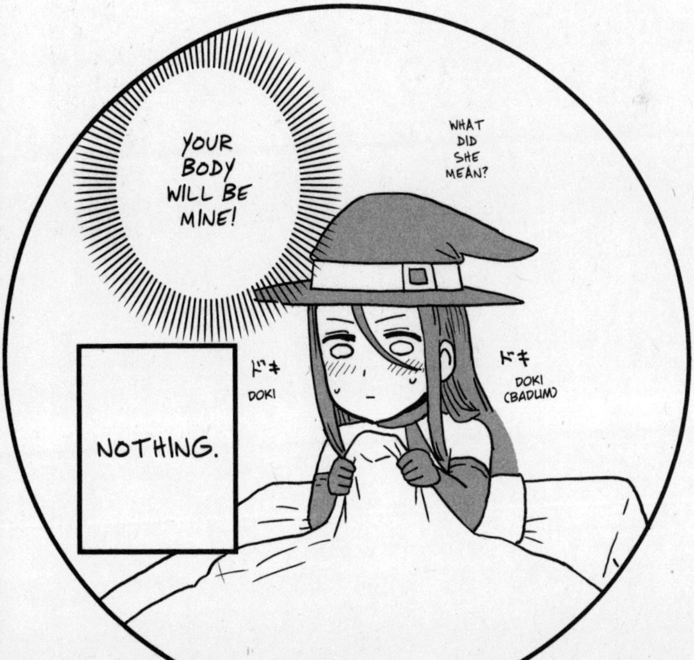
WHAT DID SHE MEAN?
YOUR BODY WILL BE MINE!
ドキ
DOKI (BADUM)
ドキ
DOKI
NOTHING.

A WITCH'S PRINTING OFFICE

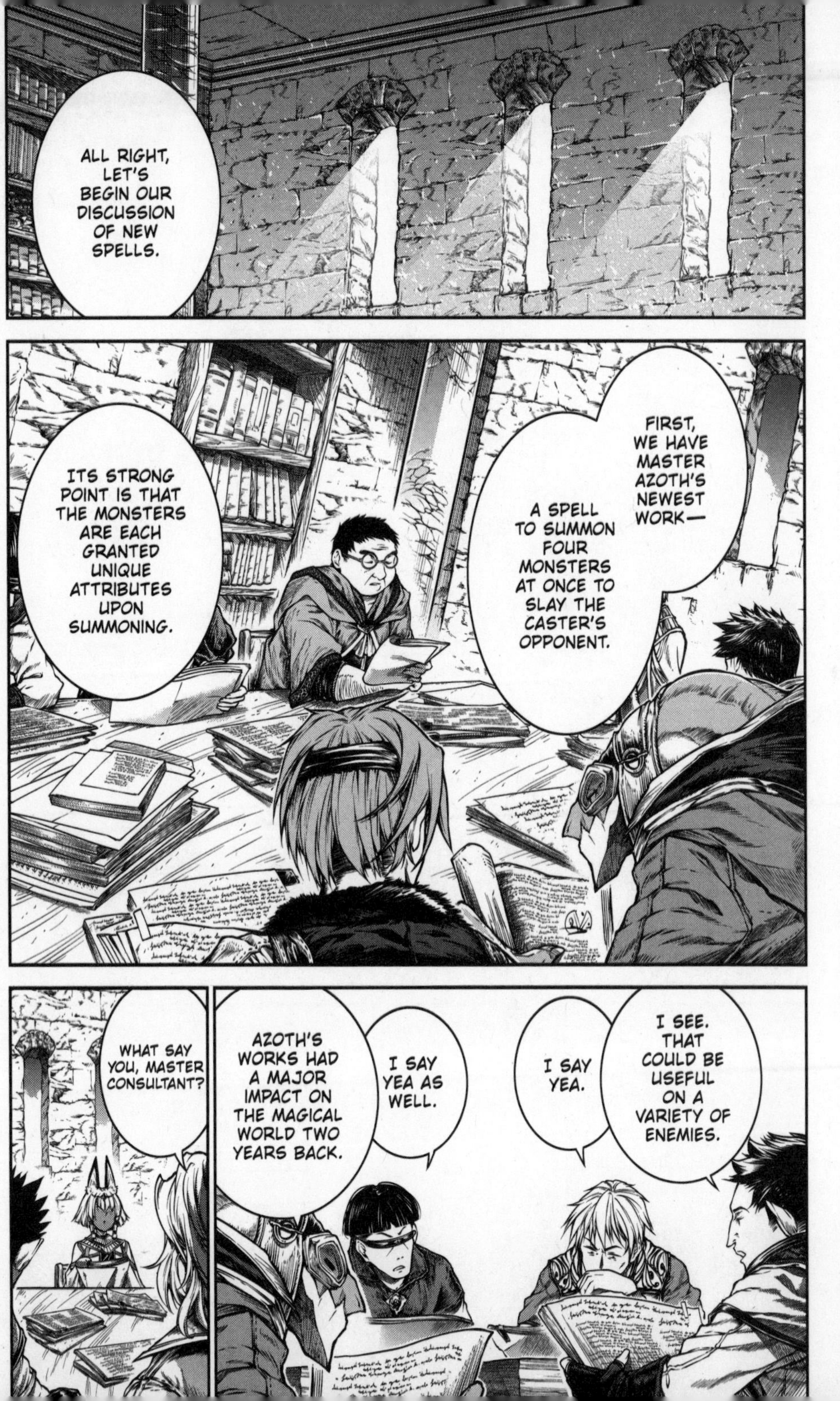
ALL RIGHT, LET'S BEGIN OUR DISCUSSION OF NEW SPELLS.
FIRST, WE HAVE MASTER AZOTH'S NEWEST WORK—
A SPELL TO SUMMON FOUR MONSTERS AT ONCE TO SLAY THE CASTER'S OPPONENT.
ITS STRONG POINT IS THAT THE MONSTERS ARE EACH GRANTED UNIQUE ATTRIBUTES UPON SUMMONING.
I SEE. THAT COULD BE USEFUL ON A VARIETY OF ENEMIES.
I SAY YEA.
I SAY YEA AS WELL.
AZOTH'S WORKS HAD A MAJOR IMPACT ON THE MAGICAL WORLD TWO YEARS BACK.
WHAT SAY YOU, MASTER CONSULTANT?

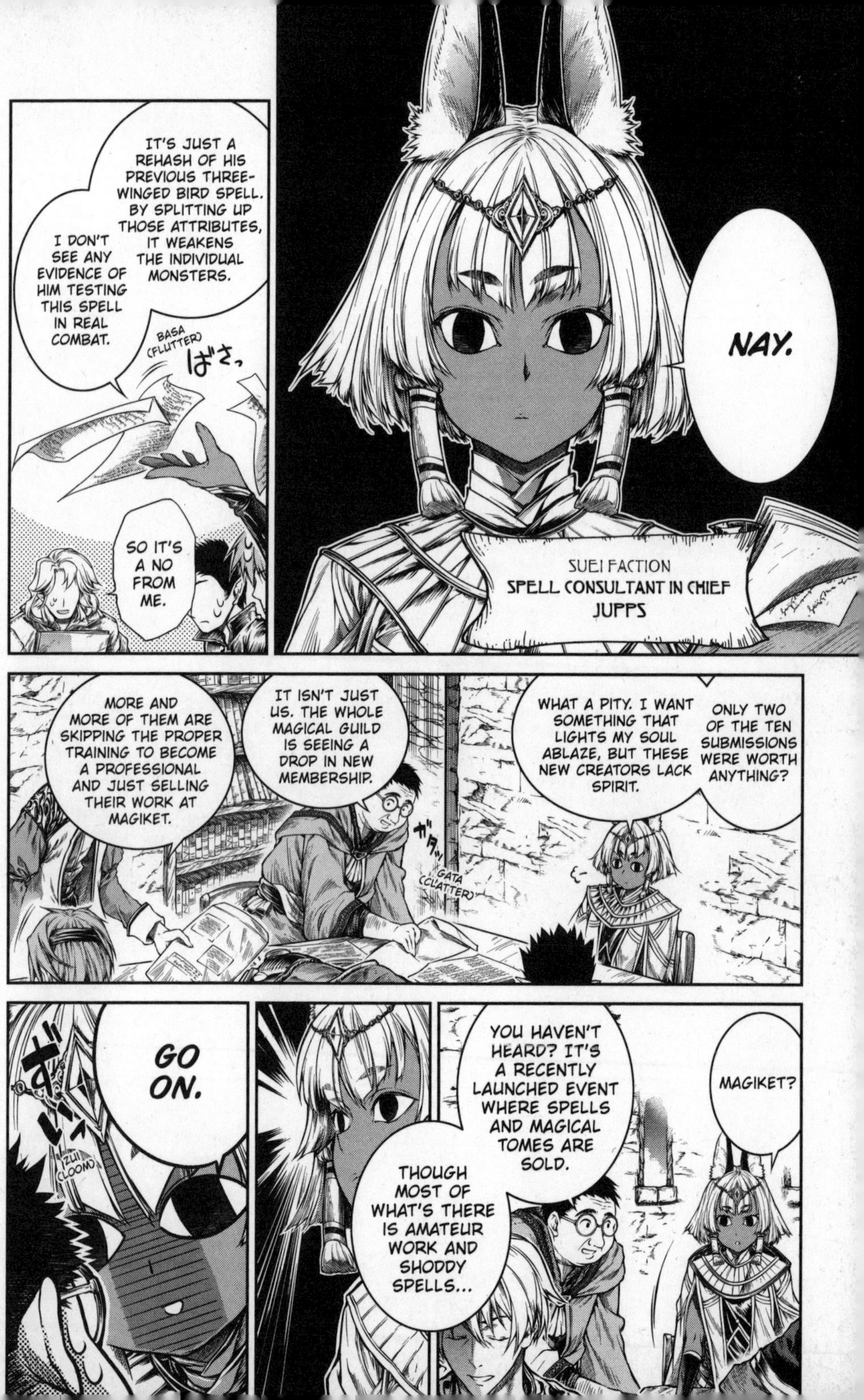
NAY.
SUEI FACTION
SPELL CONSULTANT IN CHIEF
JUPPS
IT'S JUST A REHASH OF HIS PREVIOUS THREE-WINGED BIRD SPELL. BY SPLITTING UP THOSE ATTRIBUTES, IT WEAKENS THE INDIVIDUAL MONSTERS.
I DON'T SEE ANY EVIDENCE OF HIM TESTING THIS SPELL IN REAL COMBAT.
ばさっ
BASA (FLUTTER)
SO IT'S A NO FROM ME.
WHAT A PITY. I WANT SOMETHING THAT LIGHTS MY SOUL ABLAZE, BUT THESE NEW CREATORS LACK SPIRIT.
ONLY TWO OF THE TEN SUBMISSIONS WERE WORTH ANYTHING?
ガタッ
GATA (CLATTER)
IT ISN'T JUST US. THE WHOLE MAGICAL GUILD IS SEEING A DROP IN NEW MEMBERSHIP.
MORE AND MORE OF THEM ARE SKIPPING THE PROPER TRAINING TO BECOME A PROFESSIONAL AND JUST SELLING THEIR WORK AT MAGIKET.
MAGIKET?
YOU HAVEN'T HEARD? IT'S A RECENTLY LAUNCHED EVENT WHERE SPELLS AND MAGICAL TOMES ARE SOLD.
THOUGH MOST OF WHAT'S THERE IS AMATEUR WORK AND SHODDY SPELLS...
GO ON.
ずいっ
ZUI (LOOM)

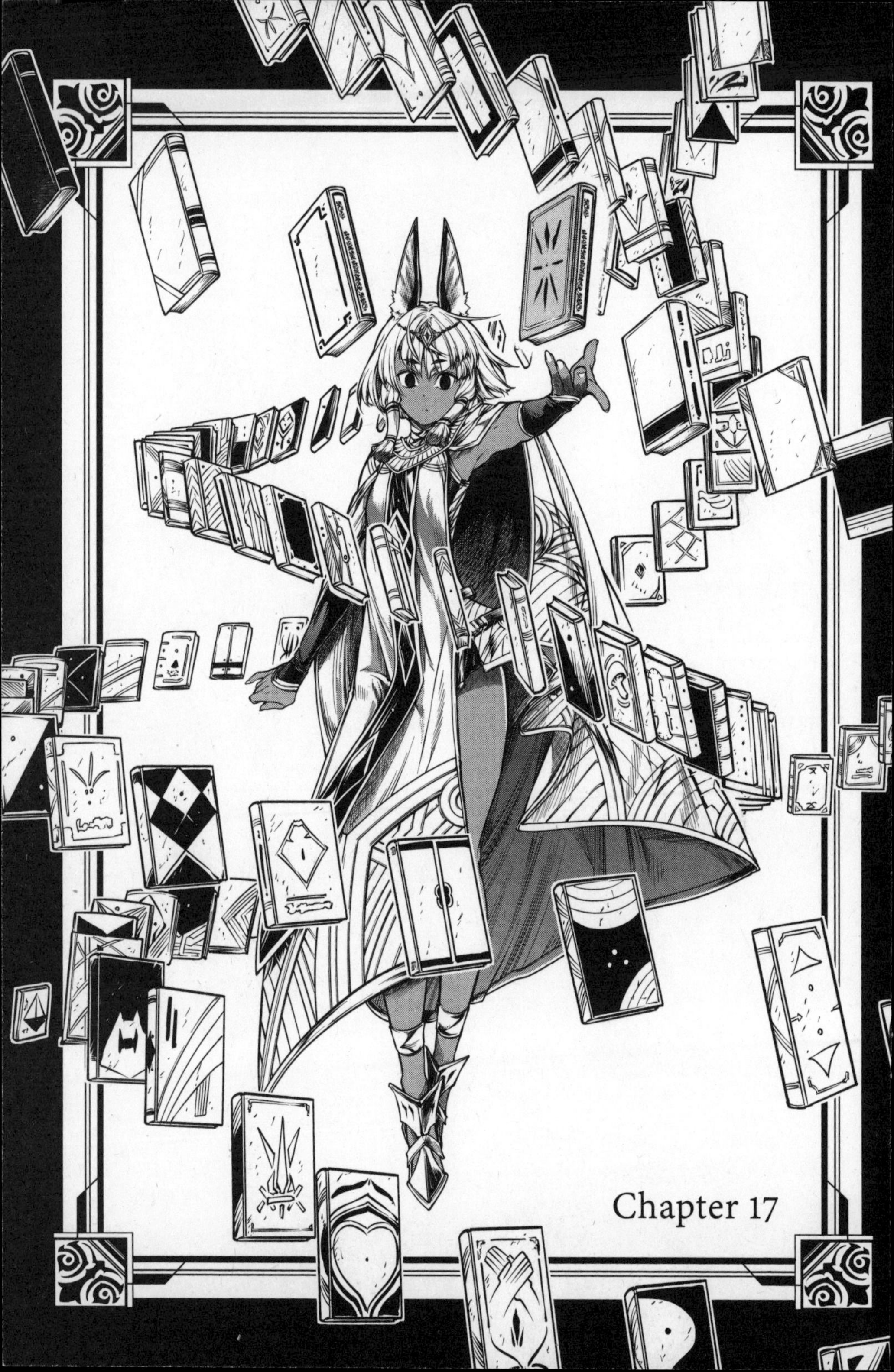

Chapter 17

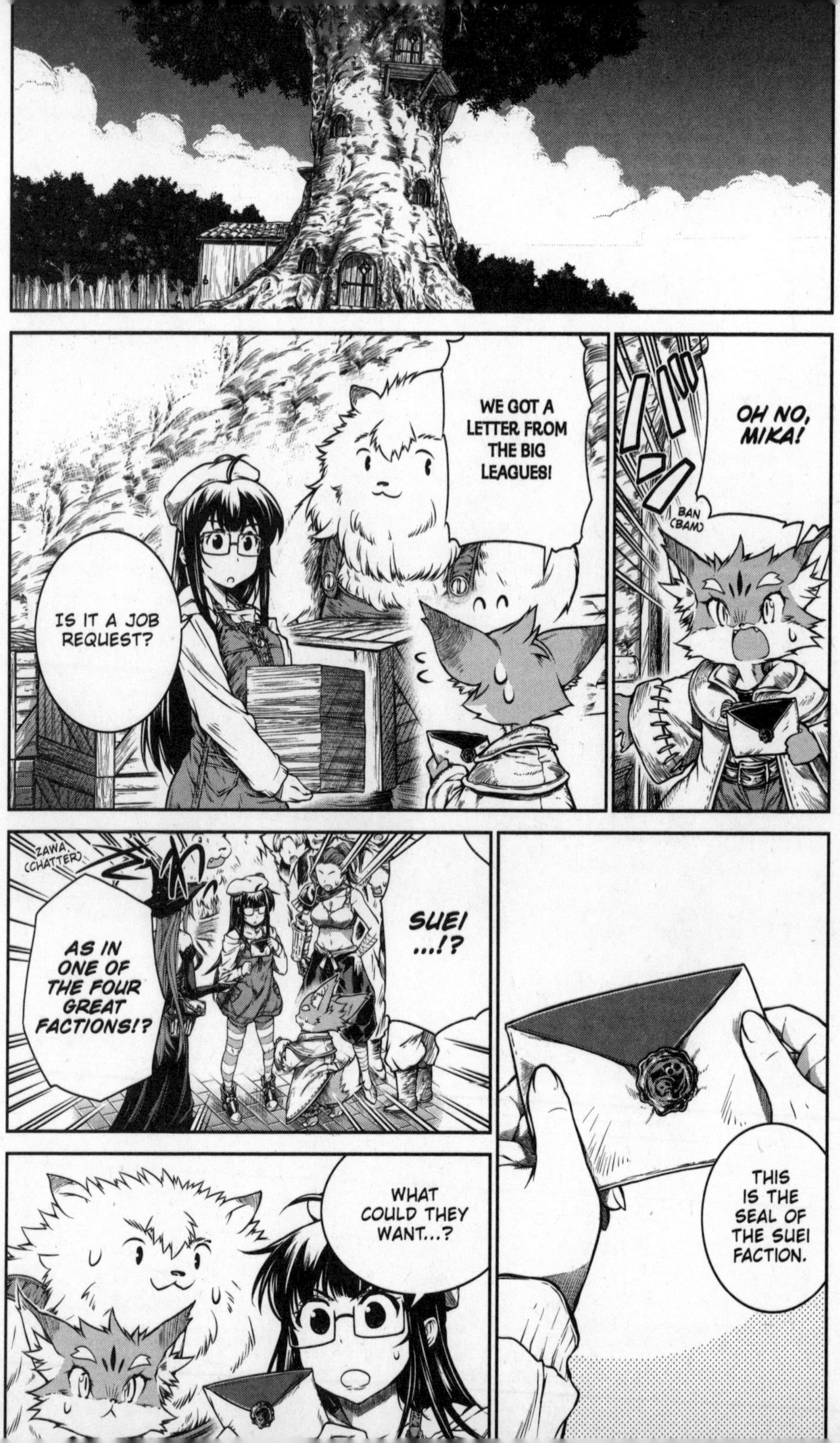
OH NO, MIKA!
BAN (BAM)
WE GOT A LETTER FROM THE BIG LEAGUES!
IS IT A JOB REQUEST?
THIS IS THE SEAL OF THE SUEI FACTION.
SUEI ...!?
ZAWA (CHATTER)
AS IN ONE OF THE FOUR GREAT FACTIONS!?
WHAT COULD THEY WANT...?

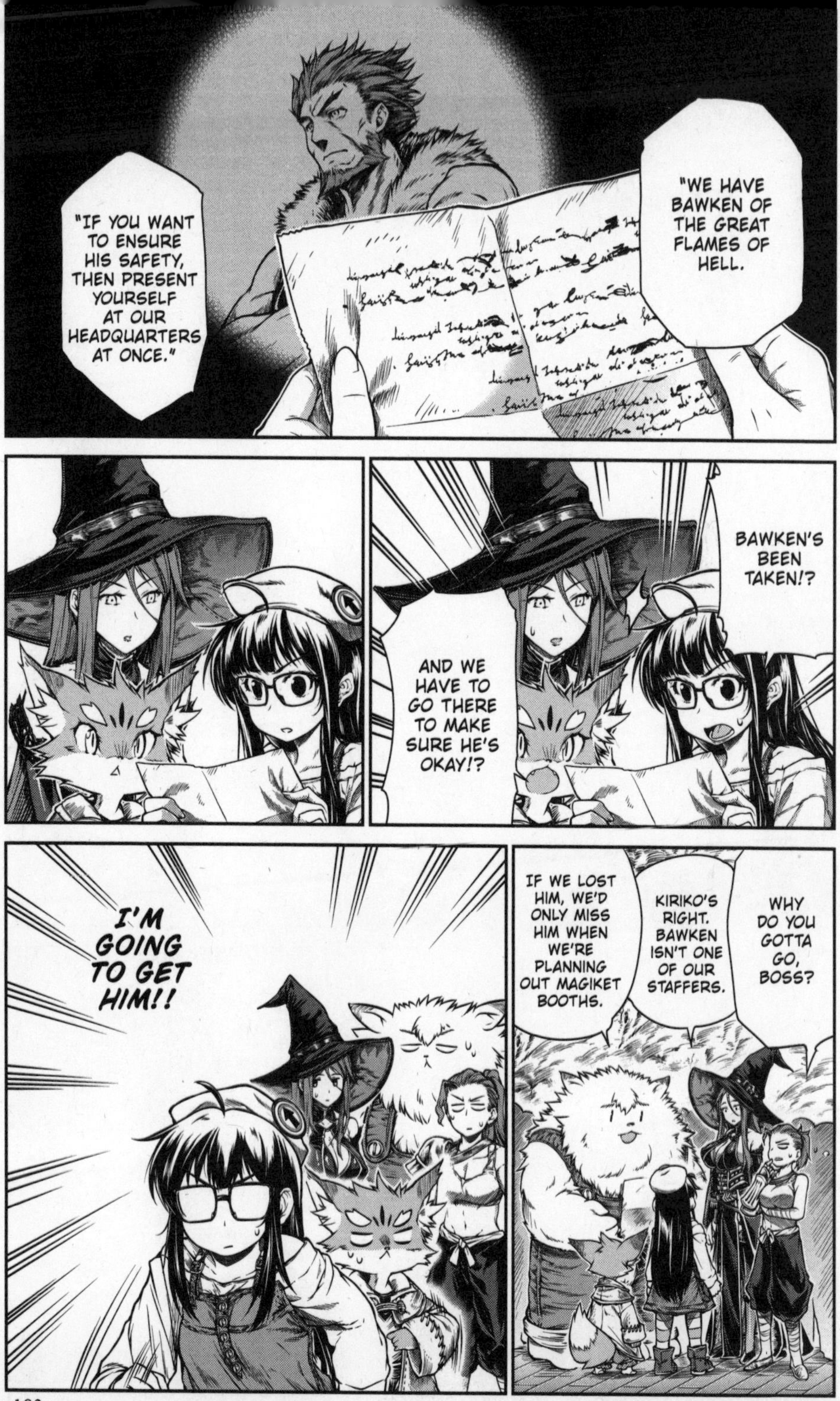
"WE HAVE BAWKEN OF THE GREAT FLAMES OF HELL.
"IF YOU WANT TO ENSURE HIS SAFETY, THEN PRESENT YOURSELF AT OUR HEADQUARTERS AT ONCE."
BAWKEN'S BEEN TAKEN!?
AND WE HAVE TO GO THERE TO MAKE SURE HE'S OKAY!?
WHY DO YOU GOTTA GO, BOSS?
KIRIKO'S RIGHT. BAWKEN ISN'T ONE OF OUR STAFFERS.
IF WE LOST HIM, WE'D ONLY MISS HIM WHEN WE'RE PLANNING OUT MAGIKET BOOTHS.
I'M GOING TO GET HIM!!

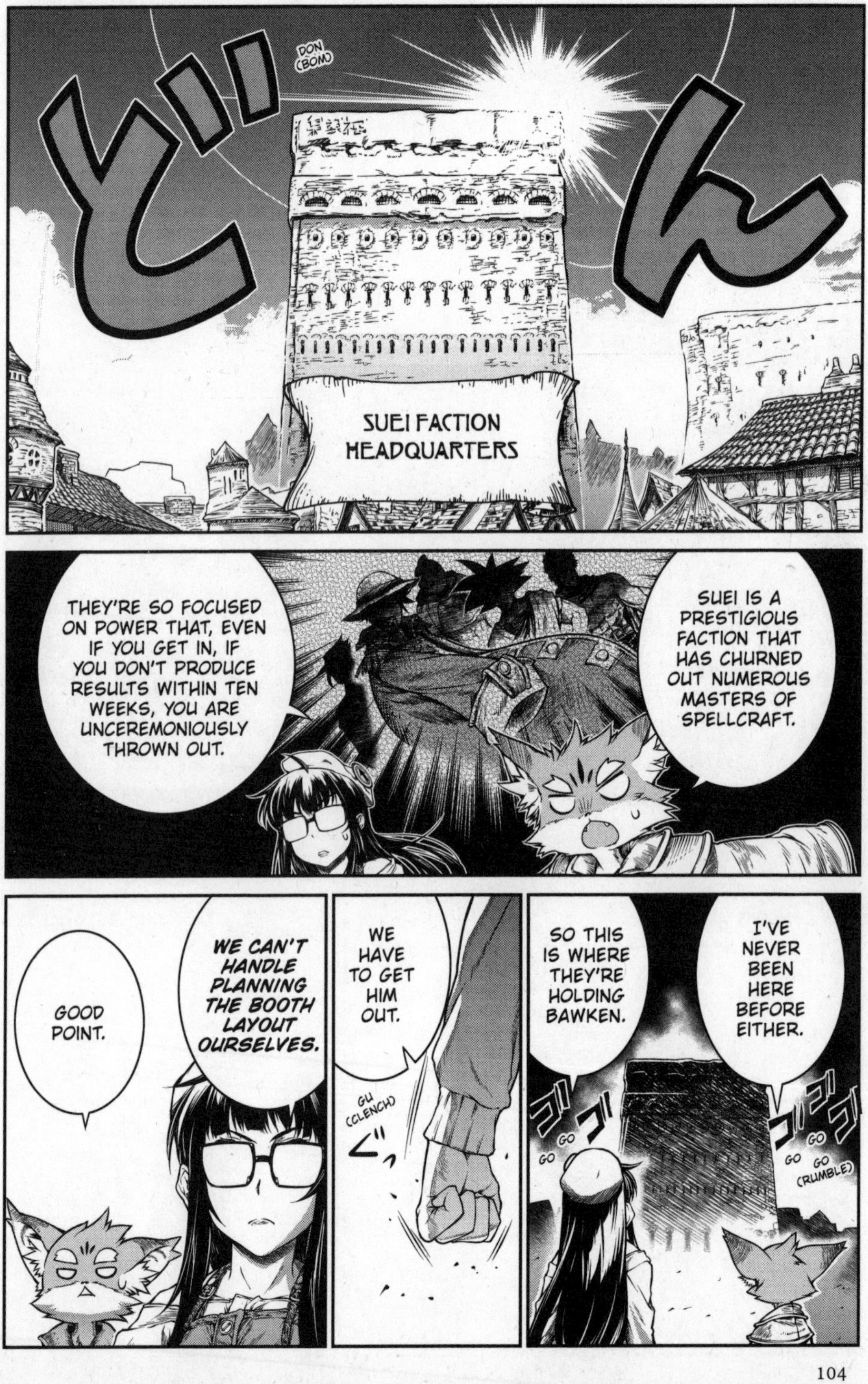
DON (BOM)
SUEI FACTION HEADQUARTERS
SUEI IS A PRESTIGIOUS FACTION THAT HAS CHURNED OUT NUMEROUS MASTERS OF SPELLCRAFT.
THEY'RE SO FOCUSED ON POWER THAT, EVEN IF YOU GET IN, IF YOU DON'T PRODUCE RESULTS WITHIN TEN WEEKS, YOU ARE UNCEREMONIOUSLY THROWN OUT.
I'VE NEVER BEEN HERE BEFORE EITHER.
SO THIS IS WHERE THEY'RE HOLDING BAWKEN.
GO GO GO GO (RUMBLE)
GO GO
WE HAVE TO GET HIM OUT.
GU (CLENCH)
WE CAN'T HANDLE PLANNING THE BOOTH LAYOUT OURSELVES.
GOOD POINT.

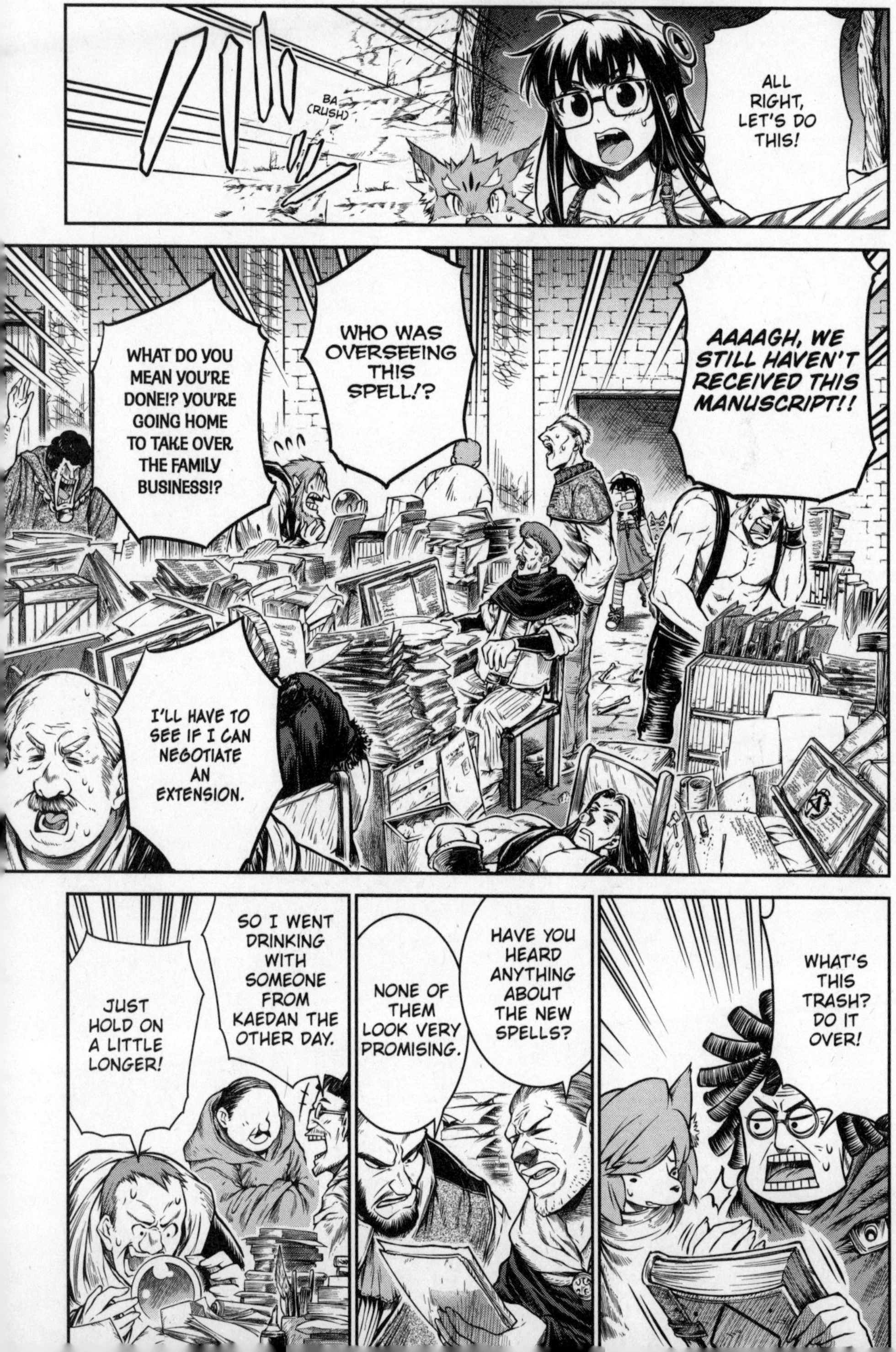
ALL RIGHT, LET'S DO THIS!
BA (RUSH)
AAAAGH, WE STILL HAVEN'T RECEIVED THIS MANUSCRIPT!!
WHO WAS OVERSEEING THIS SPELL!?
WHAT DO YOU MEAN YOU'RE DONE!? YOU'RE GOING HOME TO TAKE OVER THE FAMILY BUSINESS!?
I'LL HAVE TO SEE IF I CAN NEGOTIATE AN EXTENSION.
WHAT'S THIS TRASH? DO IT OVER!
HAVE YOU HEARD ANYTHING ABOUT THE NEW SPELLS?
NONE OF THEM LOOK VERY PROMISING.
SO I WENT DRINKING WITH SOMEONE FROM KAEDAN THE OTHER DAY.
JUST HOLD ON A LITTLE LONGER!

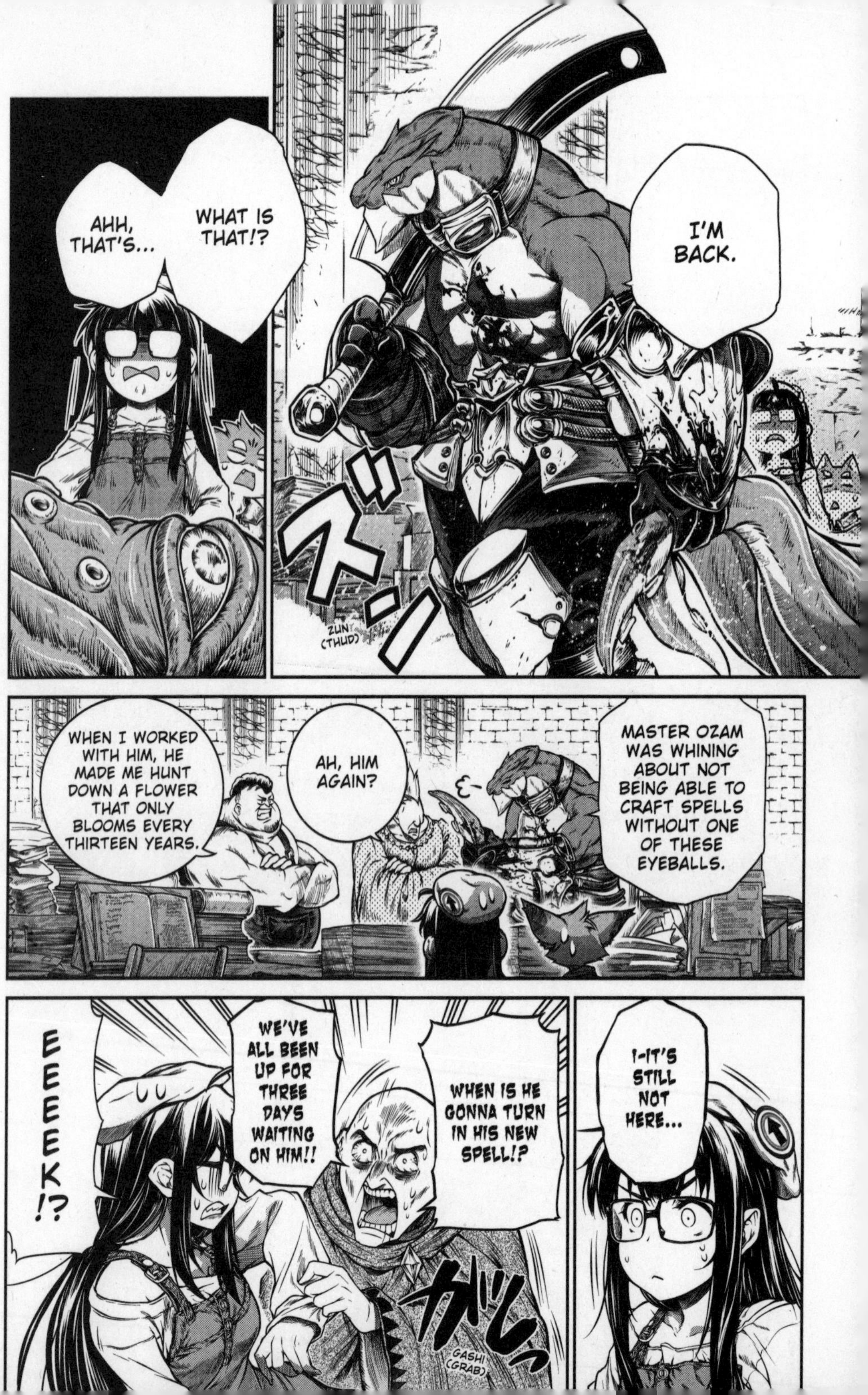
I'M BACK.
ZUN (THUD)
WHAT IS THAT!?
AHH, THAT'S...
MASTER OZAM WAS WHINING ABOUT NOT BEING ABLE TO CRAFT SPELLS WITHOUT ONE OF THESE EYEBALLS.
AH, HIM AGAIN?
WHEN I WORKED WITH HIM, HE MADE ME HUNT DOWN A FLOWER THAT ONLY BLOOMS EVERY THIRTEEN YEARS.
I-IT'S STILL NOT HERE...
WHEN IS HE GONNA TURN IN HIS NEW SPELL!?
WE'VE ALL BEEN UP FOR THREE DAYS WAITING ON HIM!!
EEEEEK!?
GASHI (GRAB)

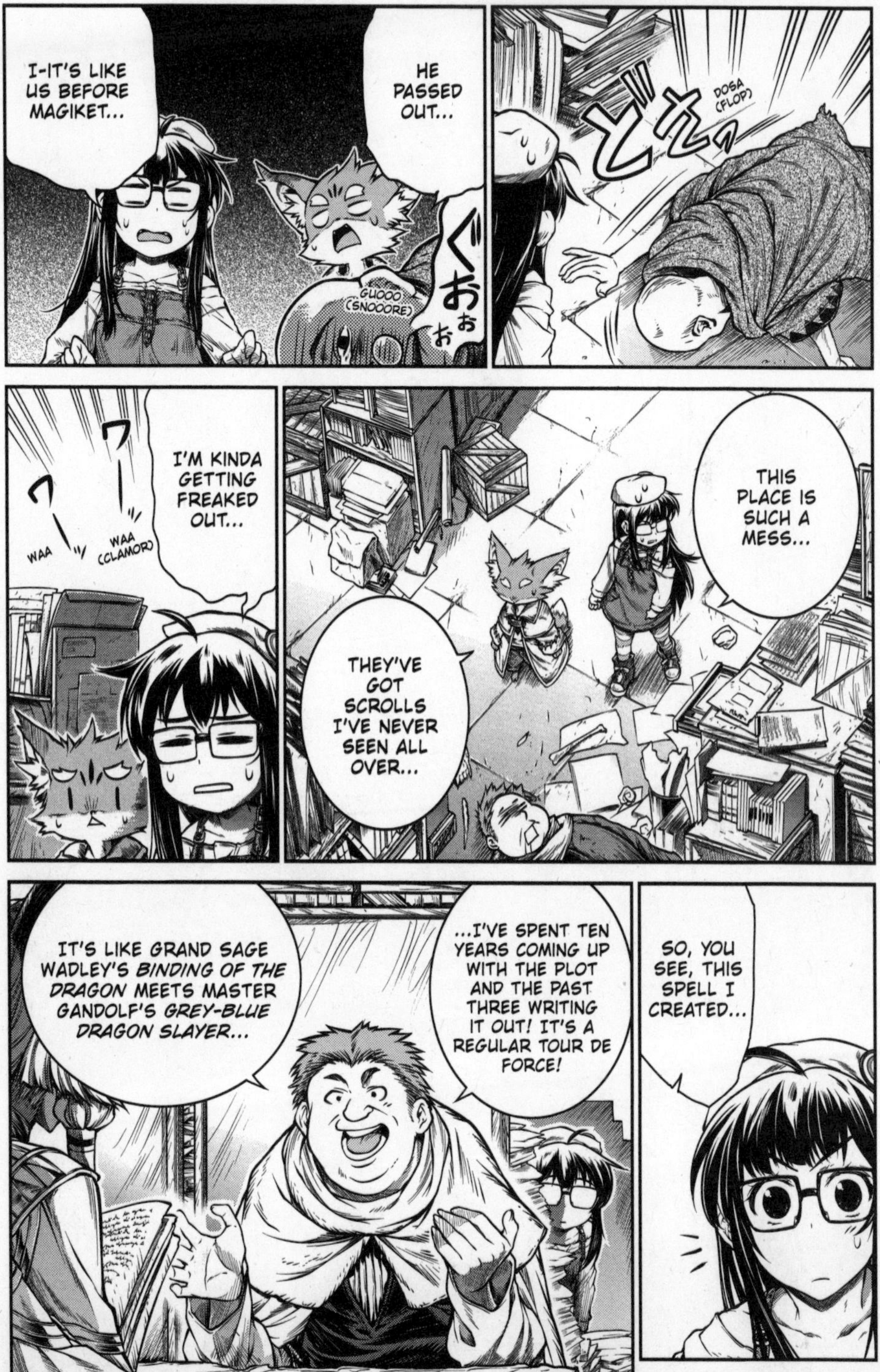
どさっ
DOSA (FLOP)
HE PASSED OUT...
I-IT'S LIKE US BEFORE MAGIKET...
ぐおぉぉ
GUOOO (SNOOORE)
THIS PLACE IS SUCH A MESS...
THEY'VE GOT SCROLLS I'VE NEVER SEEN ALL OVER...
I'M KINDA GETTING FREAKED OUT...
ワー
WAA (CLAMOR)
ワー
WAA
SO, YOU SEE, THIS SPELL I CREATED...
...I'VE SPENT TEN YEARS COMING UP WITH THE PLOT AND THE PAST THREE WRITING IT OUT! IT'S A REGULAR TOUR DE FORCE!
IT'S LIKE GRAND SAGE WADLEY'S *BINDING OF THE DRAGON* MEETS MASTER GANDOLF'S *GREY-BLUE DRAGON SLAYER*...

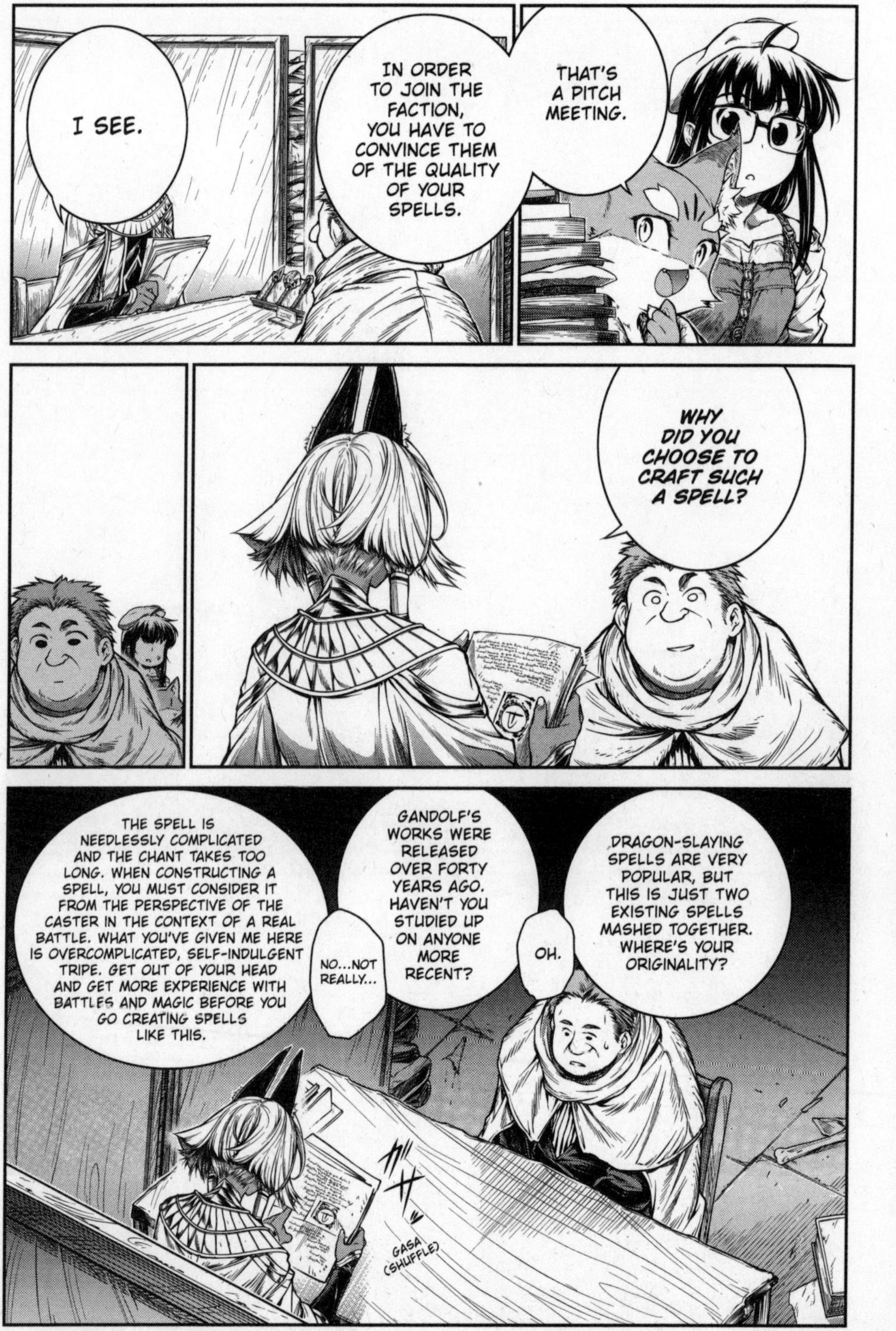
THAT'S A PITCH MEETING.
IN ORDER TO JOIN THE FACTION, YOU HAVE TO CONVINCE THEM OF THE QUALITY OF YOUR SPELLS.
I SEE.
WHY DID YOU CHOOSE TO CRAFT SUCH A SPELL?
DRAGON-SLAYING SPELLS ARE VERY POPULAR, BUT THIS IS JUST TWO EXISTING SPELLS MASHED TOGETHER. WHERE'S YOUR ORIGINALITY?
OH.
GANDOLF'S WORKS WERE RELEASED OVER FORTY YEARS AGO. HAVEN'T YOU STUDIED UP ON ANYONE MORE RECENT?
NO...NOT REALLY...
THE SPELL IS NEEDLESSLY COMPLICATED AND THE CHANT TAKES TOO LONG. WHEN CONSTRUCTING A SPELL, YOU MUST CONSIDER IT FROM THE PERSPECTIVE OF THE CASTER IN THE CONTEXT OF A REAL BATTLE. WHAT YOU'VE GIVEN ME HERE IS OVERCOMPLICATED, SELF-INDULGENT TRIPE. GET OUT OF YOUR HEAD AND GET MORE EXPERIENCE WITH BATTLES AND MAGIC BEFORE YOU GO CREATING SPELLS LIKE THIS.
GASA (SHUFFLE)

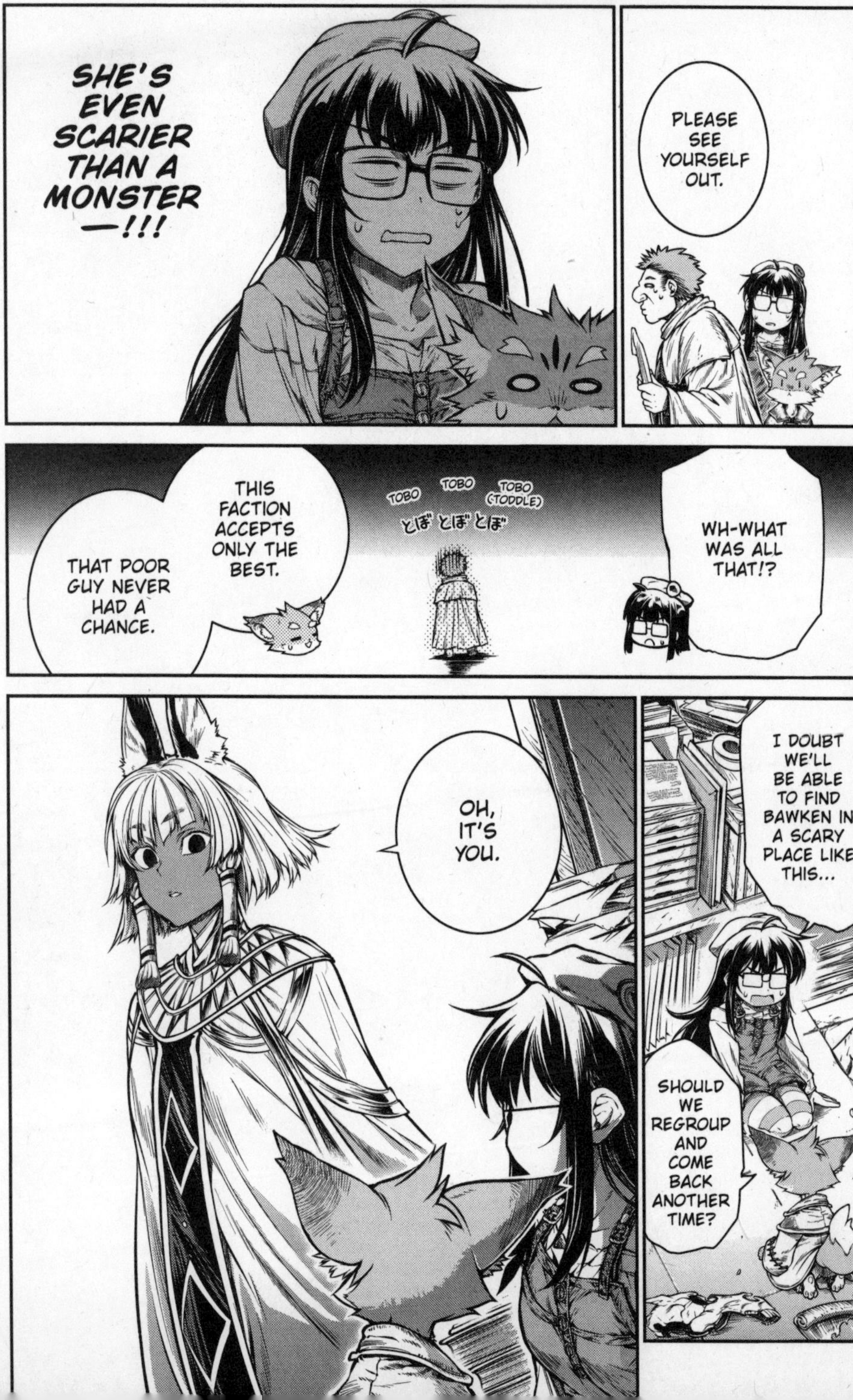
PLEASE SEE YOURSELF OUT.
SHE'S EVEN SCARIER THAN A MONSTER—!!!
WH-WHAT WAS ALL THAT!?
TOBO TOBO TOBO (TODDLE)
とぼとぼとぼ
THIS FACTION ACCEPTS ONLY THE BEST.
THAT POOR GUY NEVER HAD A CHANCE.
I DOUBT WE'LL BE ABLE TO FIND BAWKEN IN A SCARY PLACE LIKE THIS...
SHOULD WE REGROUP AND COME BACK ANOTHER TIME?
OH, IT'S YOU.

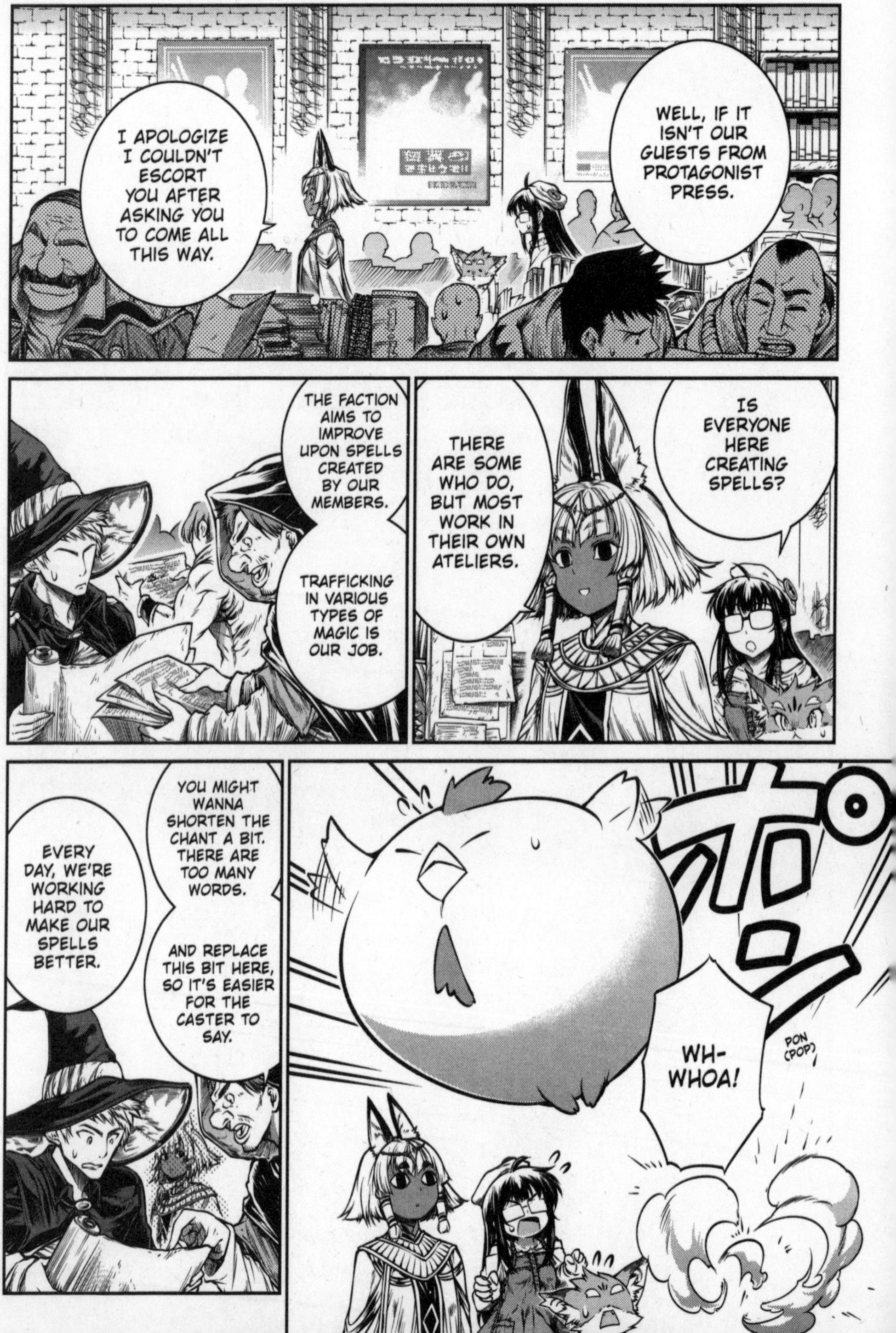
WELL, IF IT ISN'T OUR GUESTS FROM PROTAGONIST PRESS.
I APOLOGIZE I COULDN'T ESCORT YOU AFTER ASKING YOU TO COME ALL THIS WAY.
IS EVERYONE HERE CREATING SPELLS?
THERE ARE SOME WHO DO, BUT MOST WORK IN THEIR OWN ATELIERS.
THE FACTION AIMS TO IMPROVE UPON SPELLS CREATED BY OUR MEMBERS.
TRAFFICKING IN VARIOUS TYPES OF MAGIC IS OUR JOB.
PON (POP)
WH- WHOA!
YOU MIGHT WANNA SHORTEN THE CHANT A BIT. THERE ARE TOO MANY WORDS.
AND REPLACE THIS BIT HERE, SO IT'S EASIER FOR THE CASTER TO SAY.
EVERY DAY, WE'RE WORKING HARD TO MAKE OUR SPELLS BETTER.

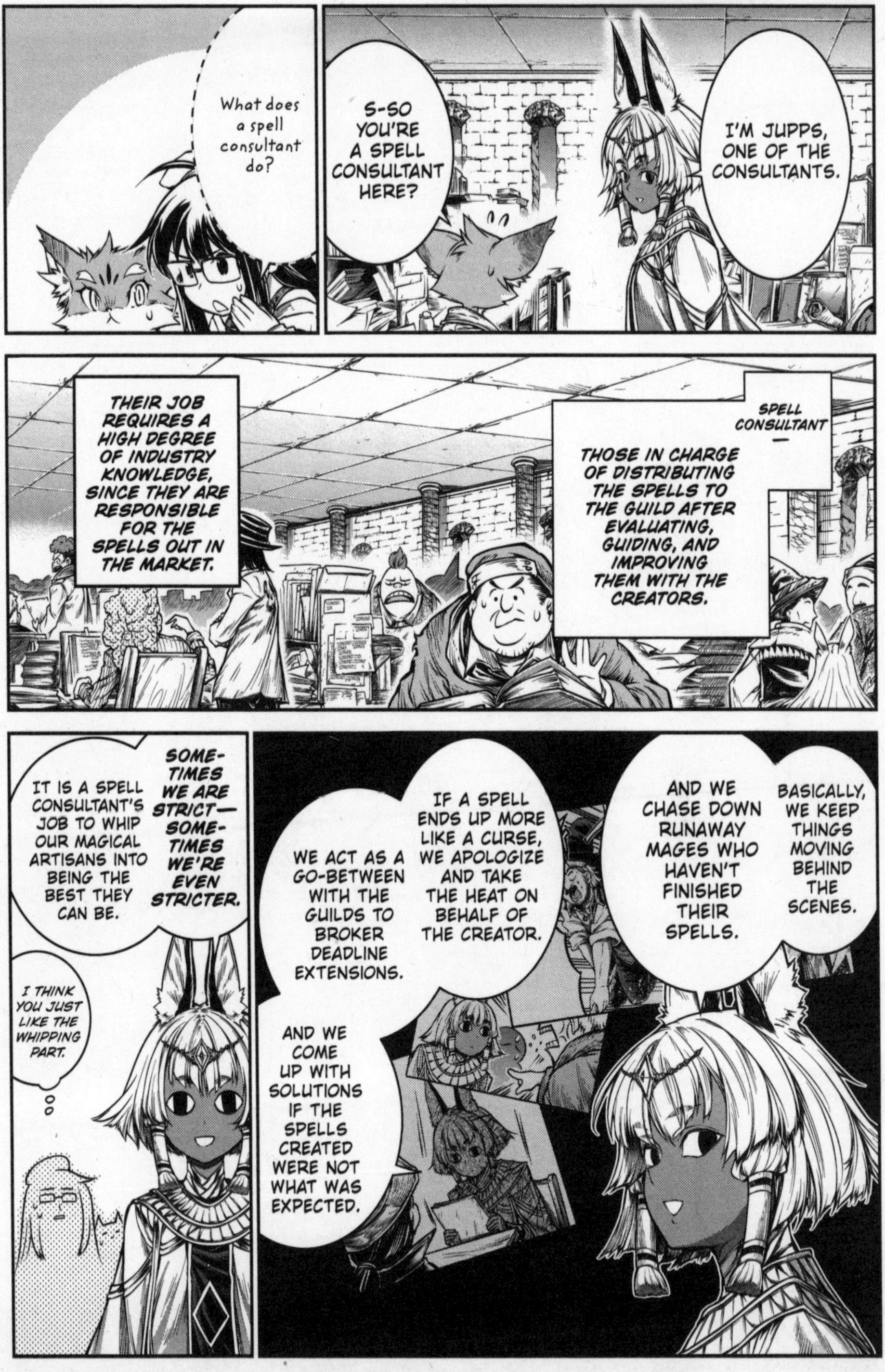
I'M JUPPS, ONE OF THE CONSULTANTS.
S-SO YOU'RE A SPELL CONSULTANT HERE?
What does a spell consultant do?
SPELL CONSULTANT — THOSE IN CHARGE OF DISTRIBUTING THE SPELLS TO THE GUILD AFTER EVALUATING, GUIDING, AND IMPROVING THEM WITH THE CREATORS.
THEIR JOB REQUIRES A HIGH DEGREE OF INDUSTRY KNOWLEDGE, SINCE THEY ARE RESPONSIBLE FOR THE SPELLS OUT IN THE MARKET.
BASICALLY, WE KEEP THINGS MOVING BEHIND THE SCENES.
AND WE CHASE DOWN RUNAWAY MAGES WHO HAVEN'T FINISHED THEIR SPELLS.
IF A SPELL ENDS UP MORE LIKE A CURSE, WE APOLOGIZE AND TAKE THE HEAT ON BEHALF OF THE CREATOR.
WE ACT AS A GO-BETWEEN WITH THE GUILDS TO BROKER DEADLINE EXTENSIONS.
AND WE COME UP WITH SOLUTIONS IF THE SPELLS CREATED WERE NOT WHAT WAS EXPECTED.
SOME-TIMES WE ARE STRICT— SOME-TIMES WE'RE EVEN STRICTER.
IT IS A SPELL CONSULTANT'S JOB TO WHIP OUR MAGICAL ARTISANS INTO BEING THE BEST THEY CAN BE.
I THINK YOU JUST LIKE THE WHIPPING PART.

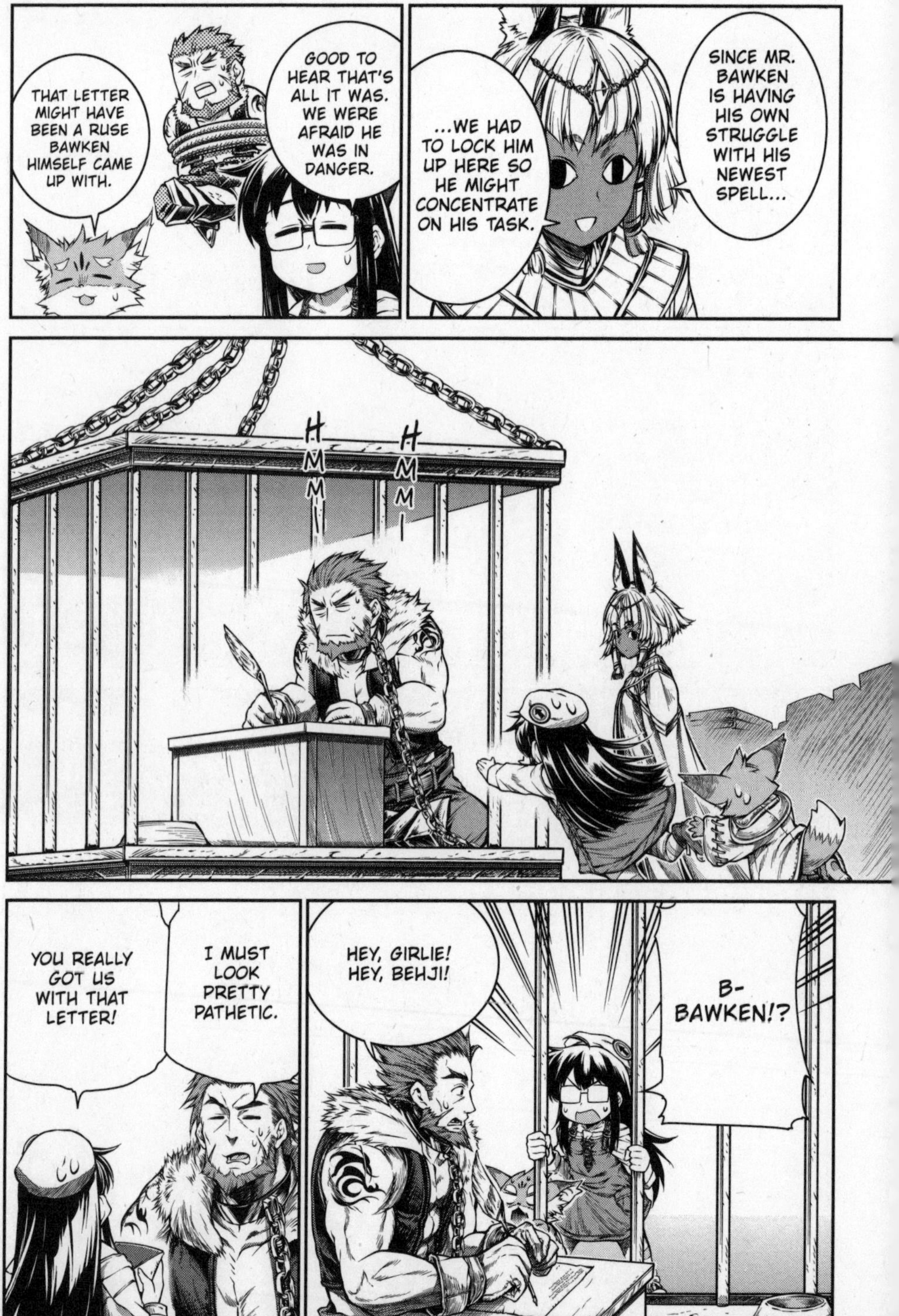
SINCE MR. BAWKEN IS HAVING HIS OWN STRUGGLE WITH HIS NEWEST SPELL...
...WE HAD TO LOCK HIM UP HERE SO HE MIGHT CONCENTRATE ON HIS TASK.
GOOD TO HEAR THAT'S ALL IT WAS. WE WERE AFRAID HE WAS IN DANGER.
THAT LETTER MIGHT HAVE BEEN A RUSE BAWKEN HIMSELF CAME UP WITH.
HMMM
HMMM
B-BAWKEN!?
HEY, GIRLIE! HEY, BEHJI!
POOCH
I MUST LOOK PRETTY PATHETIC.
YOU REALLY GOT US WITH THAT LETTER!

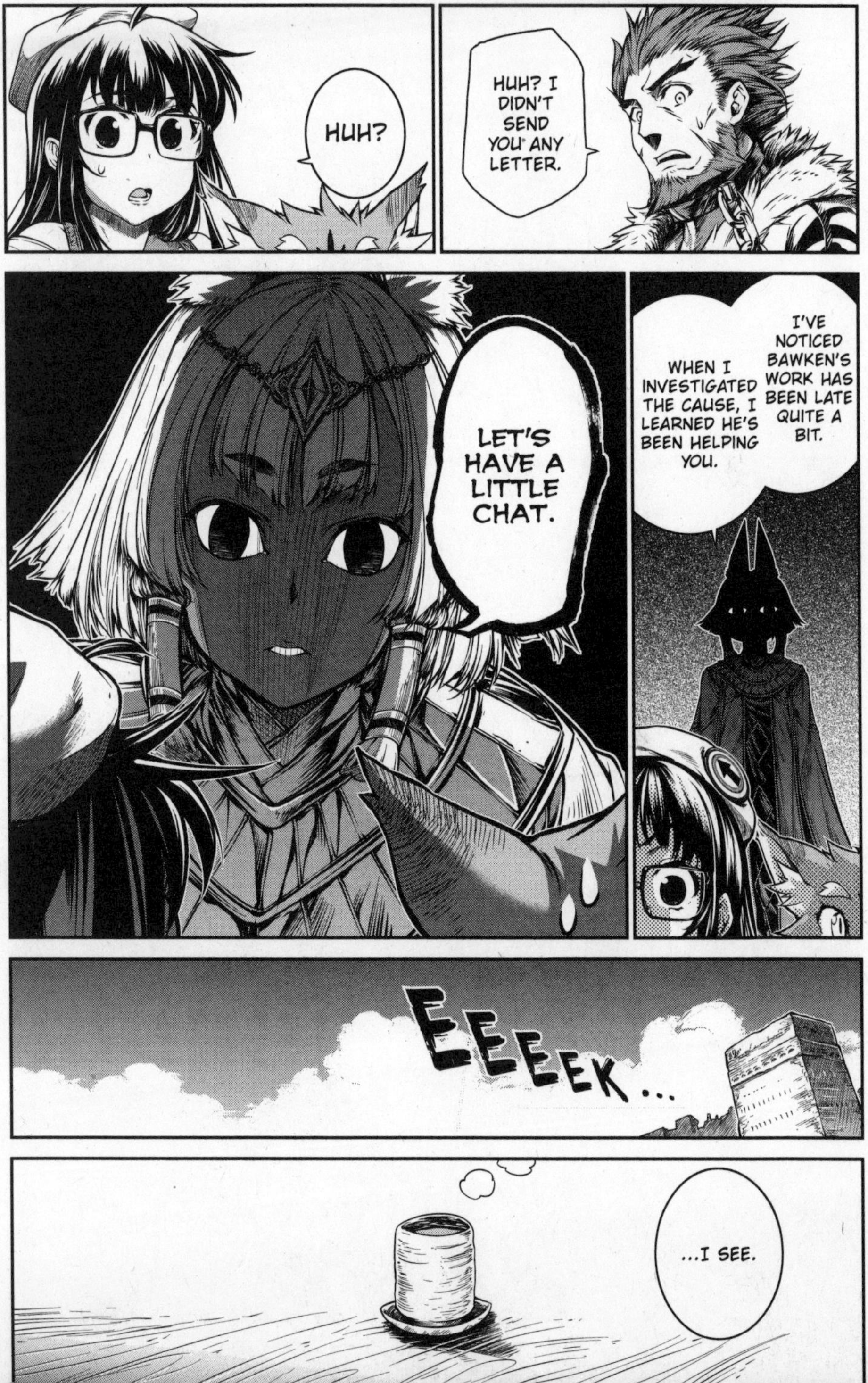
HUH? I DIDN'T SEND YOU ANY LETTER.
HUH?
I'VE NOTICED BAWKEN'S WORK HAS BEEN LATE QUITE A BIT.
WHEN I INVESTIGATED THE CAUSE, I LEARNED HE'S BEEN HELPING YOU.
LET'S HAVE A LITTLE CHAT.
EEEEEK...
...I SEE.

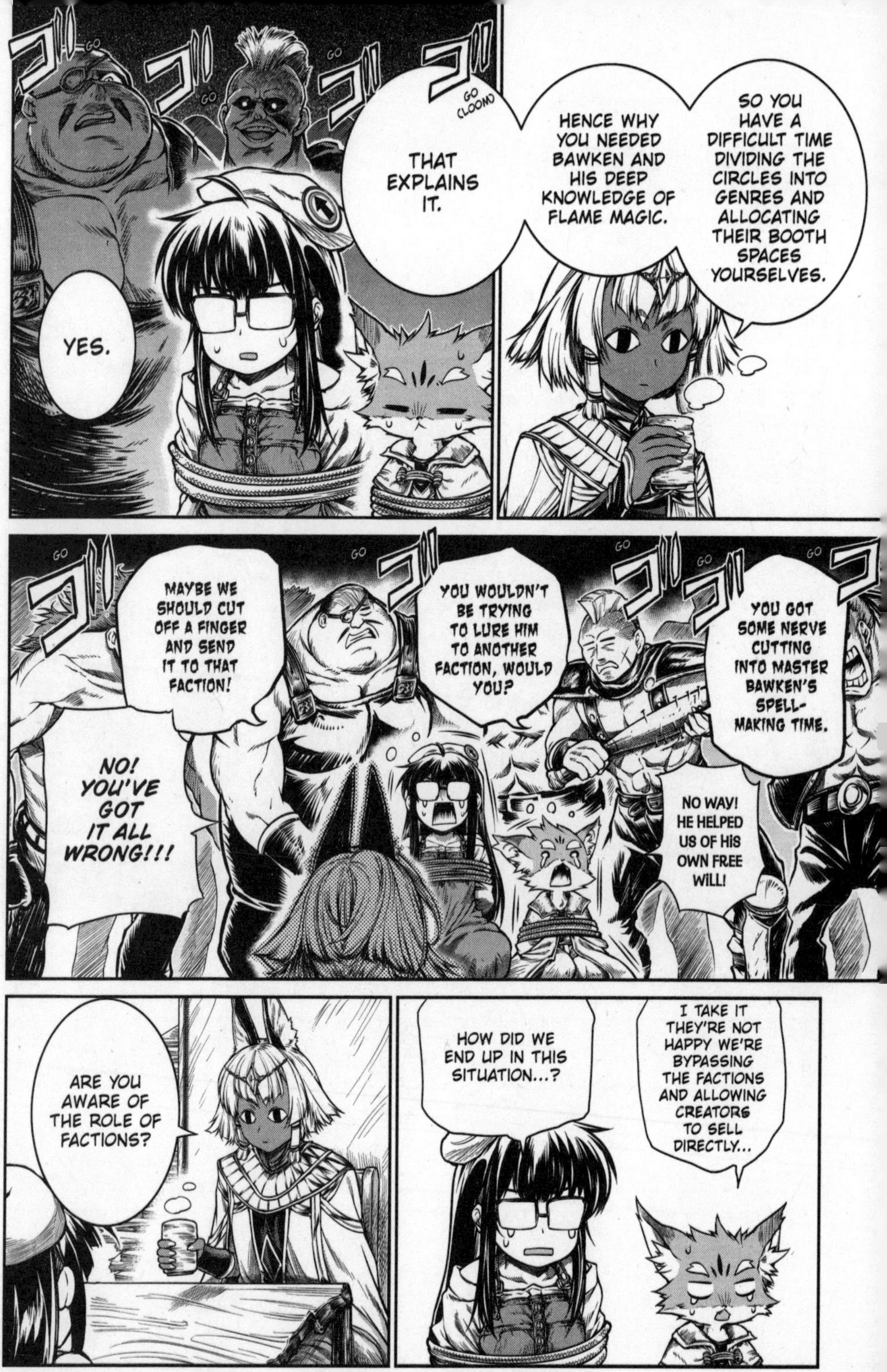
SO YOU HAVE A DIFFICULT TIME DIVIDING THE CIRCLES INTO GENRES AND ALLOCATING THEIR BOOTH SPACES YOURSELVES.
HENCE WHY YOU NEEDED BAWKEN AND HIS DEEP KNOWLEDGE OF FLAME MAGIC.
GO (LOOM)
GO
GO
GO
THAT EXPLAINS IT.
YES.
GO
GO
GO
GO
YOU GOT SOME NERVE CUTTING INTO MASTER BAWKEN'S SPELL-MAKING TIME.
YOU WOULDN'T BE TRYING TO LURE HIM TO ANOTHER FACTION, WOULD YOU?
MAYBE WE SHOULD CUT OFF A FINGER AND SEND IT TO THAT FACTION!
NO WAY! HE HELPED US OF HIS OWN FREE WILL!
NO! YOU'VE GOT IT ALL WRONG!!!
I TAKE IT THEY'RE NOT HAPPY WE'RE BYPASSING THE FACTIONS AND ALLOWING CREATORS TO SELL DIRECTLY...
HOW DID WE END UP IN THIS SITUATION...?
ARE YOU AWARE OF THE ROLE OF FACTIONS?

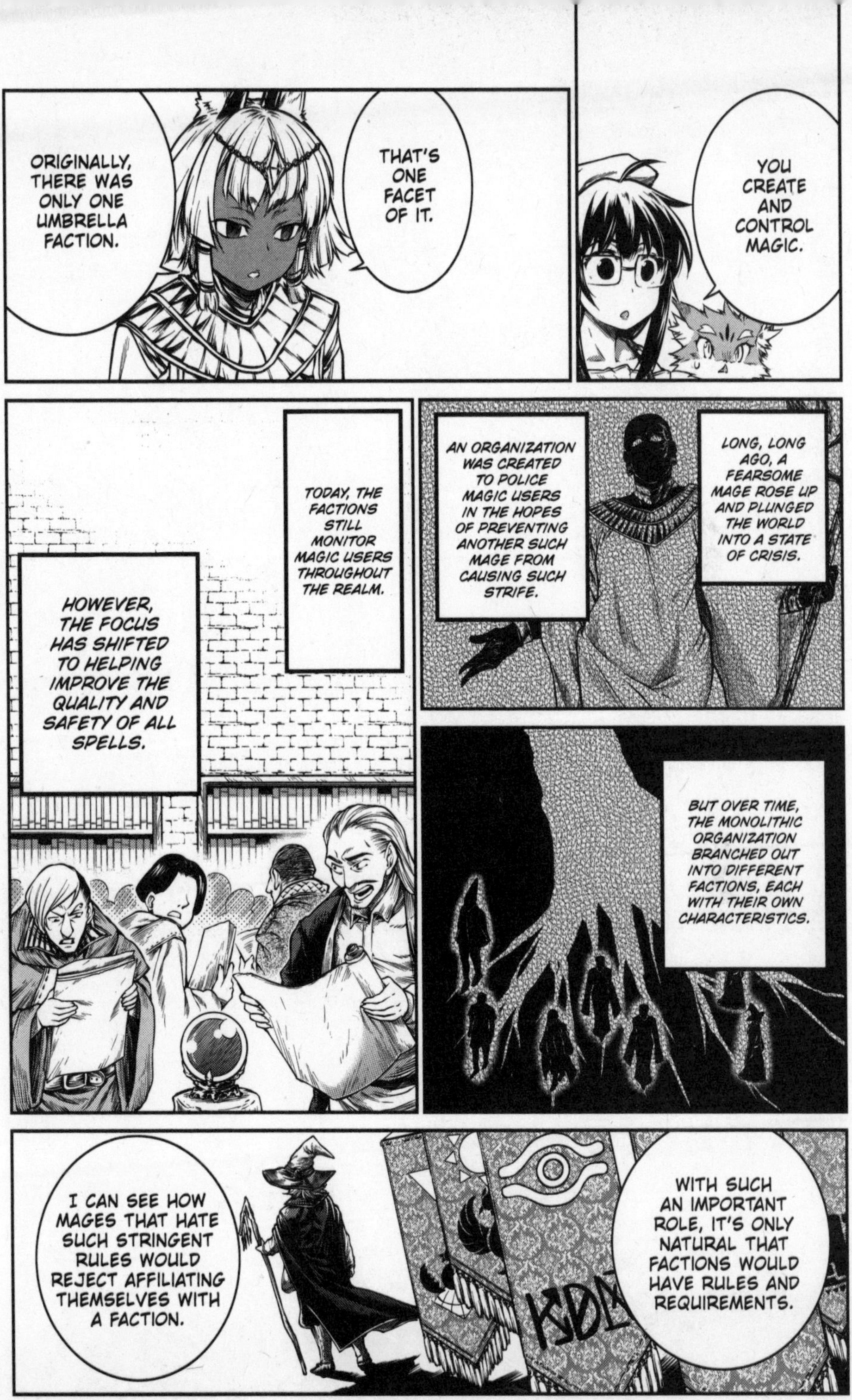

YOU CREATE AND CONTROL MAGIC.
THAT'S ONE FACET OF IT.
ORIGINALLY, THERE WAS ONLY ONE UMBRELLA FACTION.
LONG, LONG AGO, A FEARSOME MAGE ROSE UP AND PLUNGED THE WORLD INTO A STATE OF CRISIS.
AN ORGANIZATION WAS CREATED TO POLICE MAGIC USERS IN THE HOPES OF PREVENTING ANOTHER SUCH MAGE FROM CAUSING SUCH STRIFE.
BUT OVER TIME, THE MONOLITHIC ORGANIZATION BRANCHED OUT INTO DIFFERENT FACTIONS, EACH WITH THEIR OWN CHARACTERISTICS.
TODAY, THE FACTIONS STILL MONITOR MAGIC USERS THROUGHOUT THE REALM.
HOWEVER, THE FOCUS HAS SHIFTED TO HELPING IMPROVE THE QUALITY AND SAFETY OF ALL SPELLS.
WITH SUCH AN IMPORTANT ROLE, IT'S ONLY NATURAL THAT FACTIONS WOULD HAVE RULES AND REQUIREMENTS.
I CAN SEE HOW MAGES THAT HATE SUCH STRINGENT RULES WOULD REJECT AFFILIATING THEMSELVES WITH A FACTION.

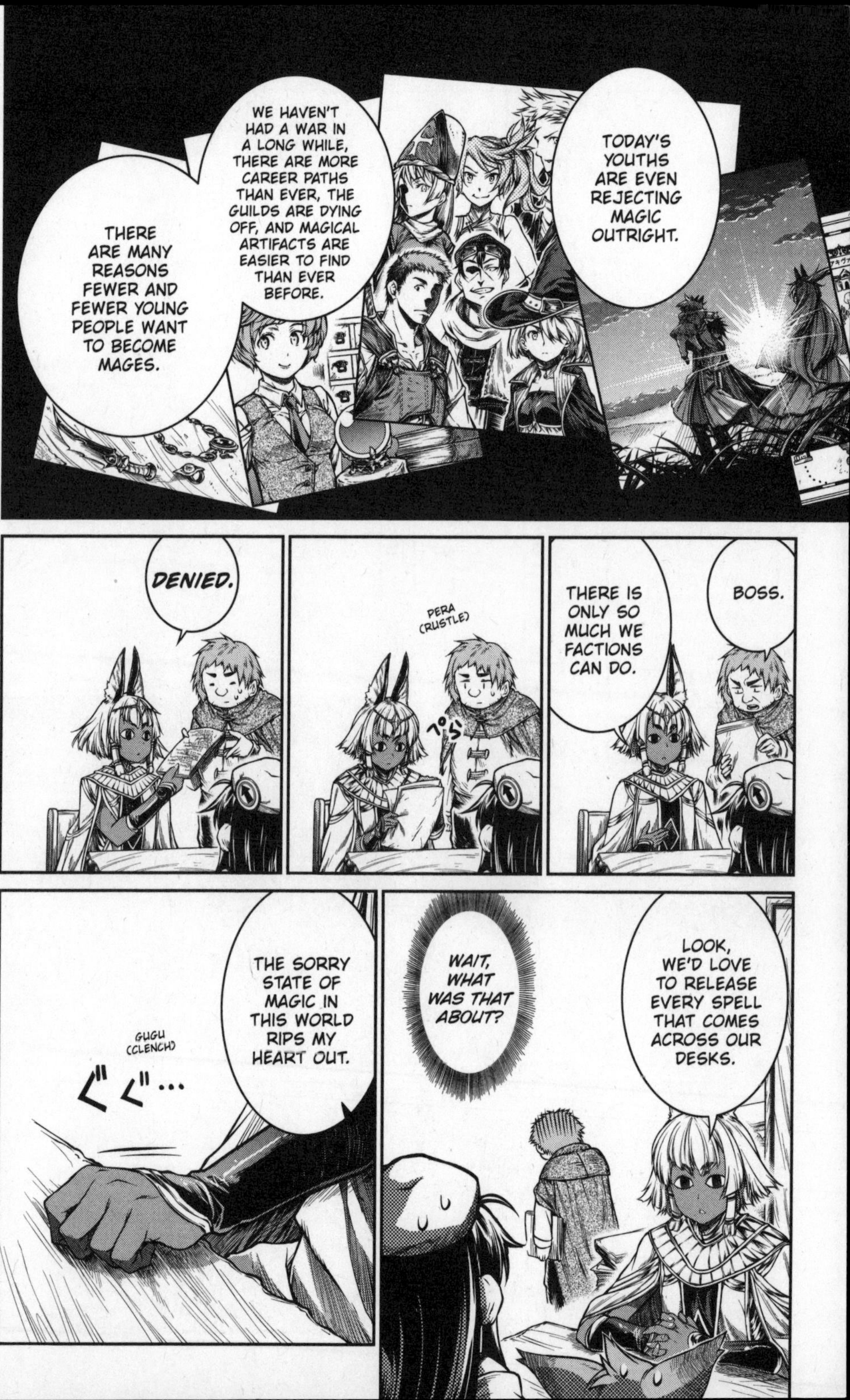
TODAY'S YOUTHS ARE EVEN REJECTING MAGIC OUTRIGHT.
WE HAVEN'T HAD A WAR IN A LONG WHILE, THERE ARE MORE CAREER PATHS THAN EVER, THE GUILDS ARE DYING OFF, AND MAGICAL ARTIFACTS ARE EASIER TO FIND THAN EVER BEFORE.
THERE ARE MANY REASONS FEWER AND FEWER YOUNG PEOPLE WANT TO BECOME MAGES.
BOSS.
THERE IS ONLY SO MUCH WE FACTIONS CAN DO.
PERA (RUSTLE)
ぺら
DENIED.
LOOK, WE'D LOVE TO RELEASE EVERY SPELL THAT COMES ACROSS OUR DESKS.
WAIT, WHAT WAS THAT ABOUT?
THE SORRY STATE OF MAGIC IN THIS WORLD RIPS MY HEART OUT.
GUGU (CLENCH)
ぐぐ…

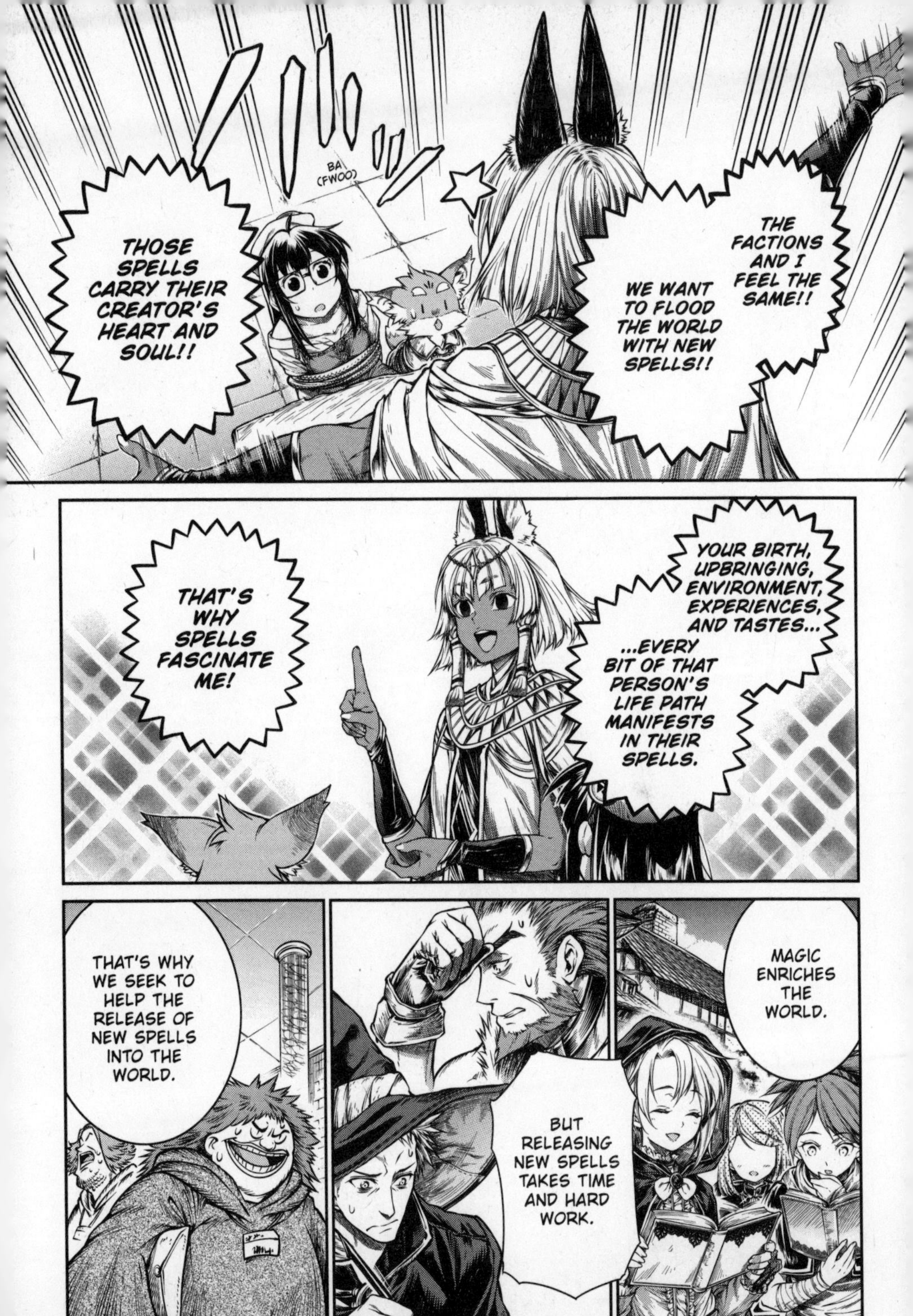
THE FACTIONS AND I FEEL THE SAME!!
WE WANT TO FLOOD THE WORLD WITH NEW SPELLS!!
BA (FWOO)
THOSE SPELLS CARRY THEIR CREATOR'S HEART AND SOUL!!
YOUR BIRTH, UPBRINGING, ENVIRONMENT, EXPERIENCES, AND TASTES...
...EVERY BIT OF THAT PERSON'S LIFE PATH MANIFESTS IN THEIR SPELLS.
THAT'S WHY SPELLS FASCINATE ME!
MAGIC ENRICHES THE WORLD.
BUT RELEASING NEW SPELLS TAKES TIME AND HARD WORK.
THAT'S WHY WE SEEK TO HELP THE RELEASE OF NEW SPELLS INTO THE WORLD.

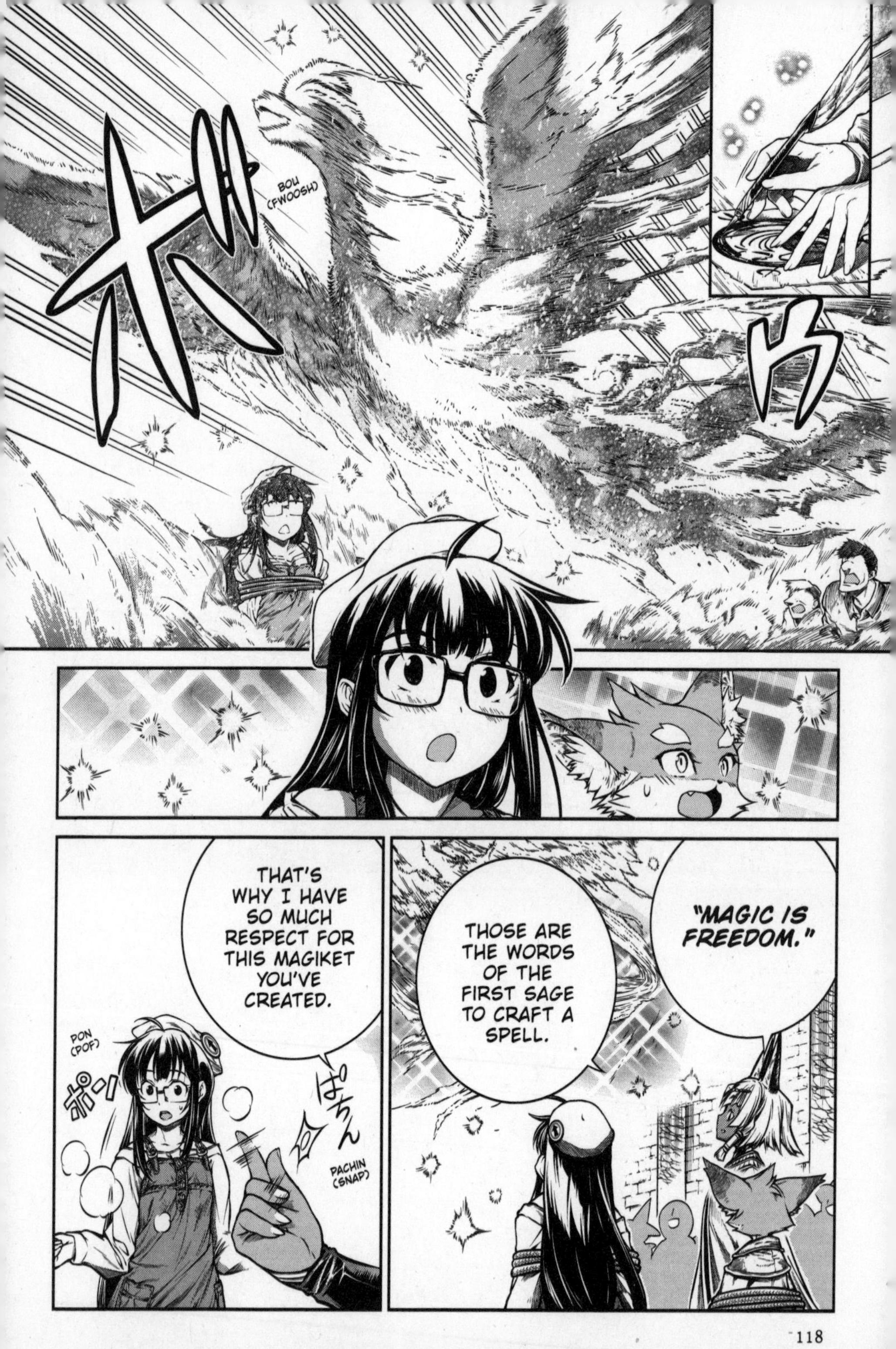
BOU
(FWOOSH)
"MAGIC IS FREEDOM."
THOSE ARE THE WORDS OF THE FIRST SAGE TO CRAFT A SPELL.
THAT'S WHY I HAVE SO MUCH RESPECT FOR THIS MAGIKET YOU'VE CREATED.
PON
(POF)
ぱちん
PACHIN
(SNAP)

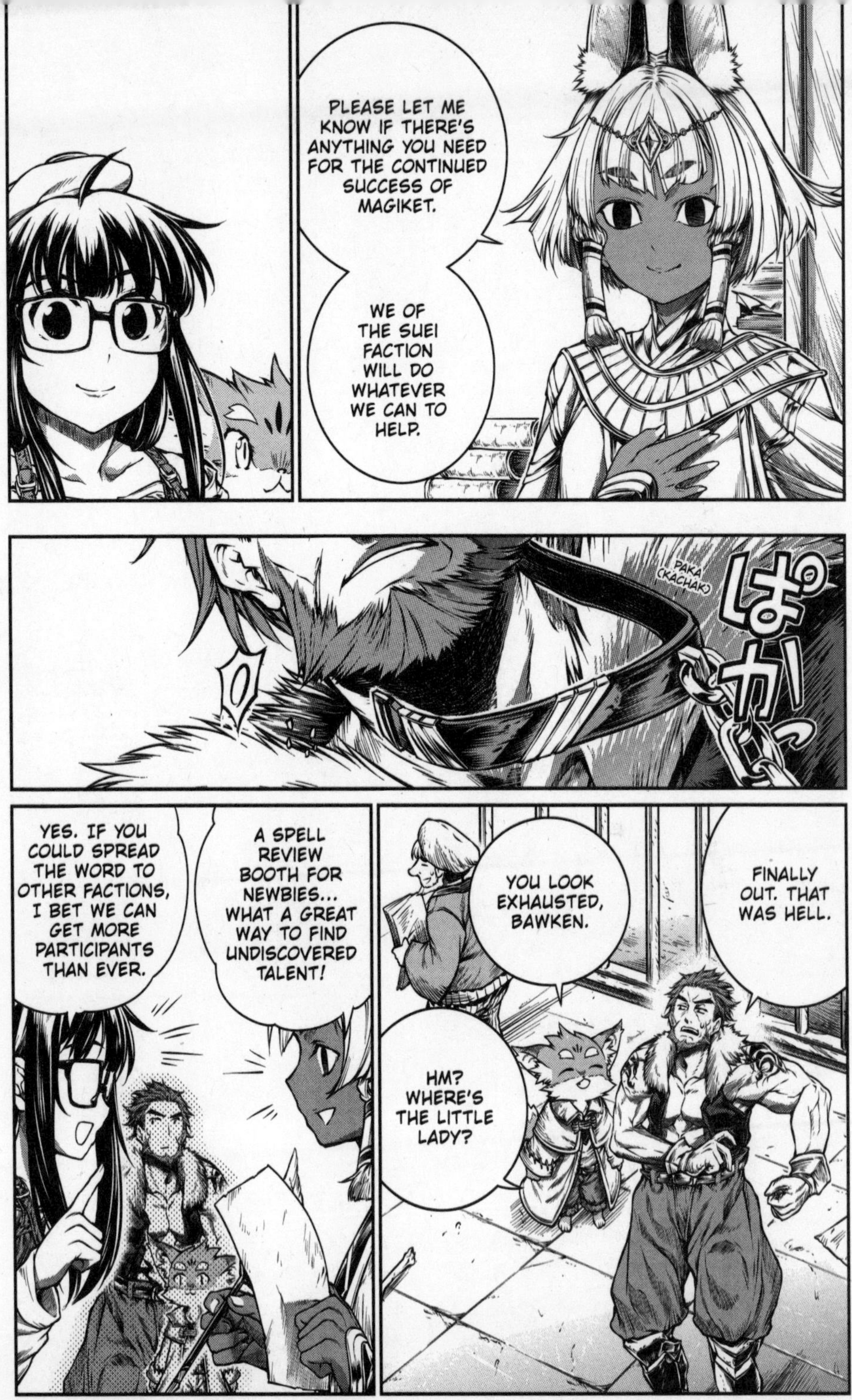
PLEASE LET ME KNOW IF THERE'S ANYTHING YOU NEED FOR THE CONTINUED SUCCESS OF MAGIKET.
WE OF THE SUEI FACTION WILL DO WHATEVER WE CAN TO HELP.
PAKA (KACHAK)
ぱかっ
FINALLY OUT. THAT WAS HELL.
YOU LOOK EXHAUSTED, BAWKEN.
HM? WHERE'S THE LITTLE LADY?
A SPELL REVIEW BOOTH FOR NEWBIES... WHAT A GREAT WAY TO FIND UNDISCOVERED TALENT!
YES. IF YOU COULD SPREAD THE WORD TO OTHER FACTIONS, I BET WE CAN GET MORE PARTICIPANTS THAN EVER.

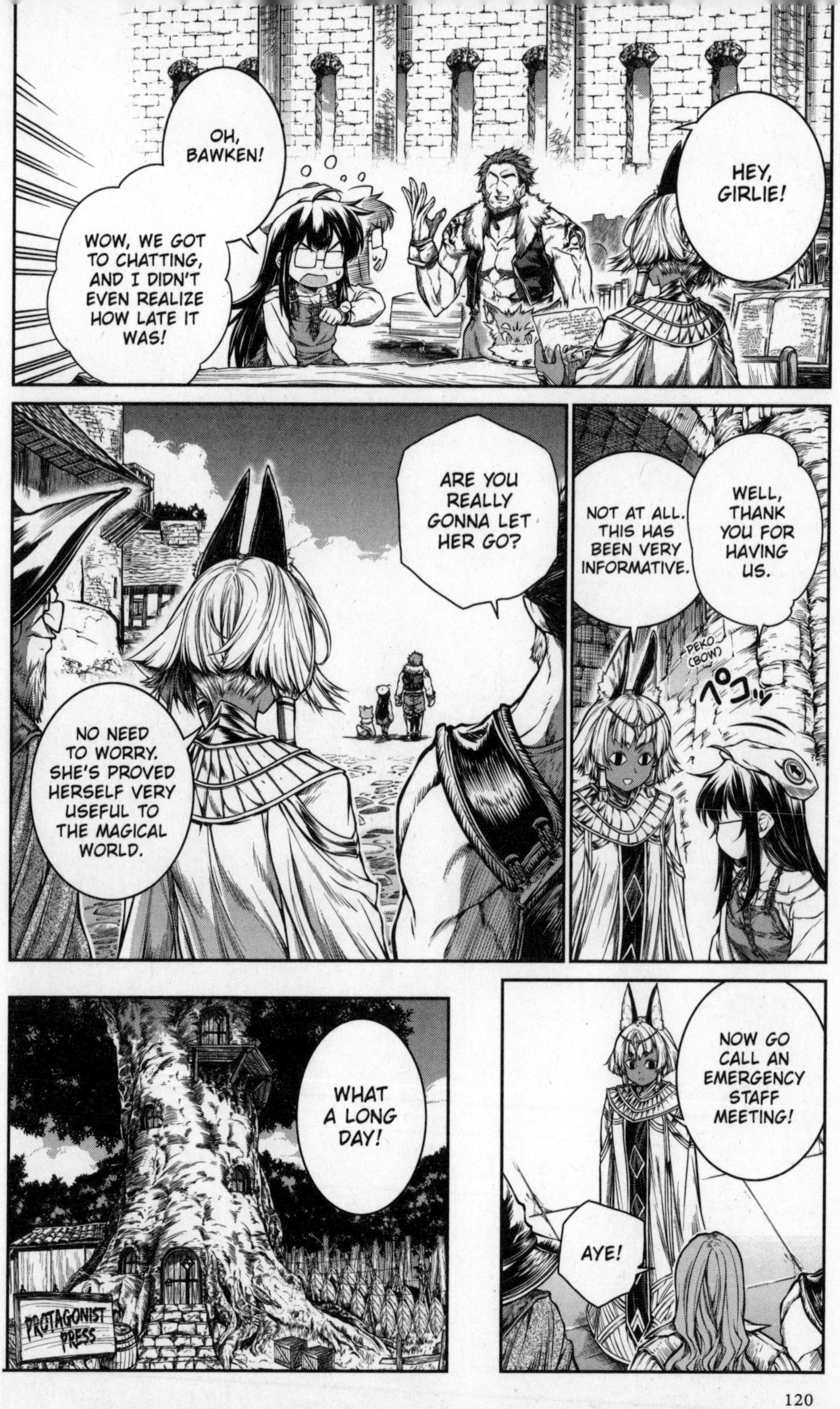
HEY, GIRLIE!
OH, BAWKEN!
WOW, WE GOT TO CHATTING, AND I DIDN'T EVEN REALIZE HOW LATE IT WAS!
WELL, THANK YOU FOR HAVING US.
NOT AT ALL. THIS HAS BEEN VERY INFORMATIVE.
PEKO (BOW)
ペコッ
ARE YOU REALLY GONNA LET HER GO?
NO NEED TO WORRY. SHE'S PROVED HERSELF VERY USEFUL TO THE MAGICAL WORLD.
NOW GO CALL AN EMERGENCY STAFF MEETING!
AYE!
WHAT A LONG DAY!
PROTAGONIST PRESS

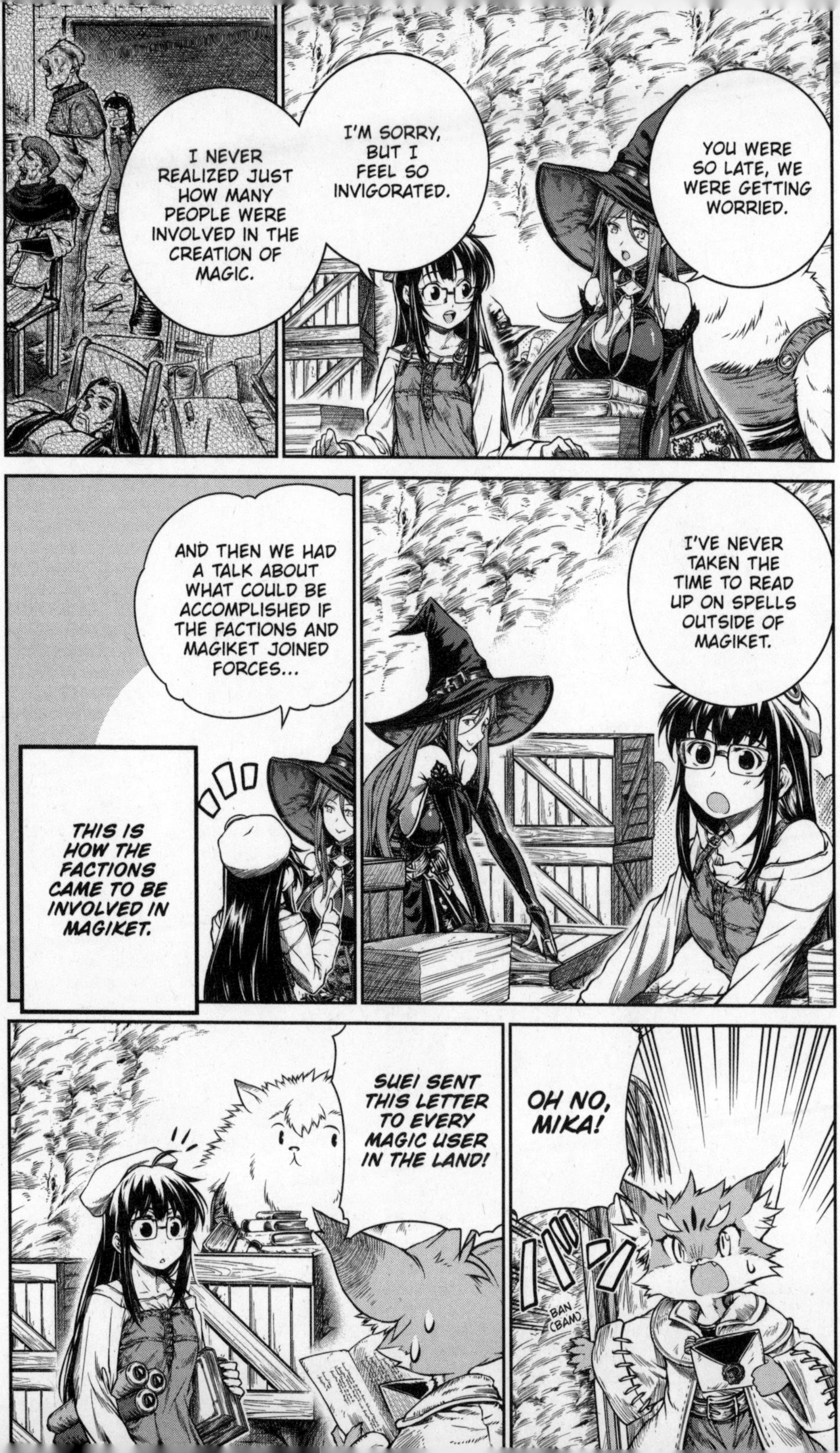

YOU WERE SO LATE, WE WERE GETTING WORRIED.
I'M SORRY, BUT I FEEL SO INVIGORATED.
I NEVER REALIZED JUST HOW MANY PEOPLE WERE INVOLVED IN THE CREATION OF MAGIC.
I'VE NEVER TAKEN THE TIME TO READ UP ON SPELLS OUTSIDE OF MAGIKET.
AND THEN WE HAD A TALK ABOUT WHAT COULD BE ACCOMPLISHED IF THE FACTIONS AND MAGIKET JOINED FORCES...
THIS IS HOW THE FACTIONS CAME TO BE INVOLVED IN MAGIKET.
OH NO, MIKA!
BAN (BAM)
SUEI SENT THIS LETTER TO EVERY MAGIC USER IN THE LAND!

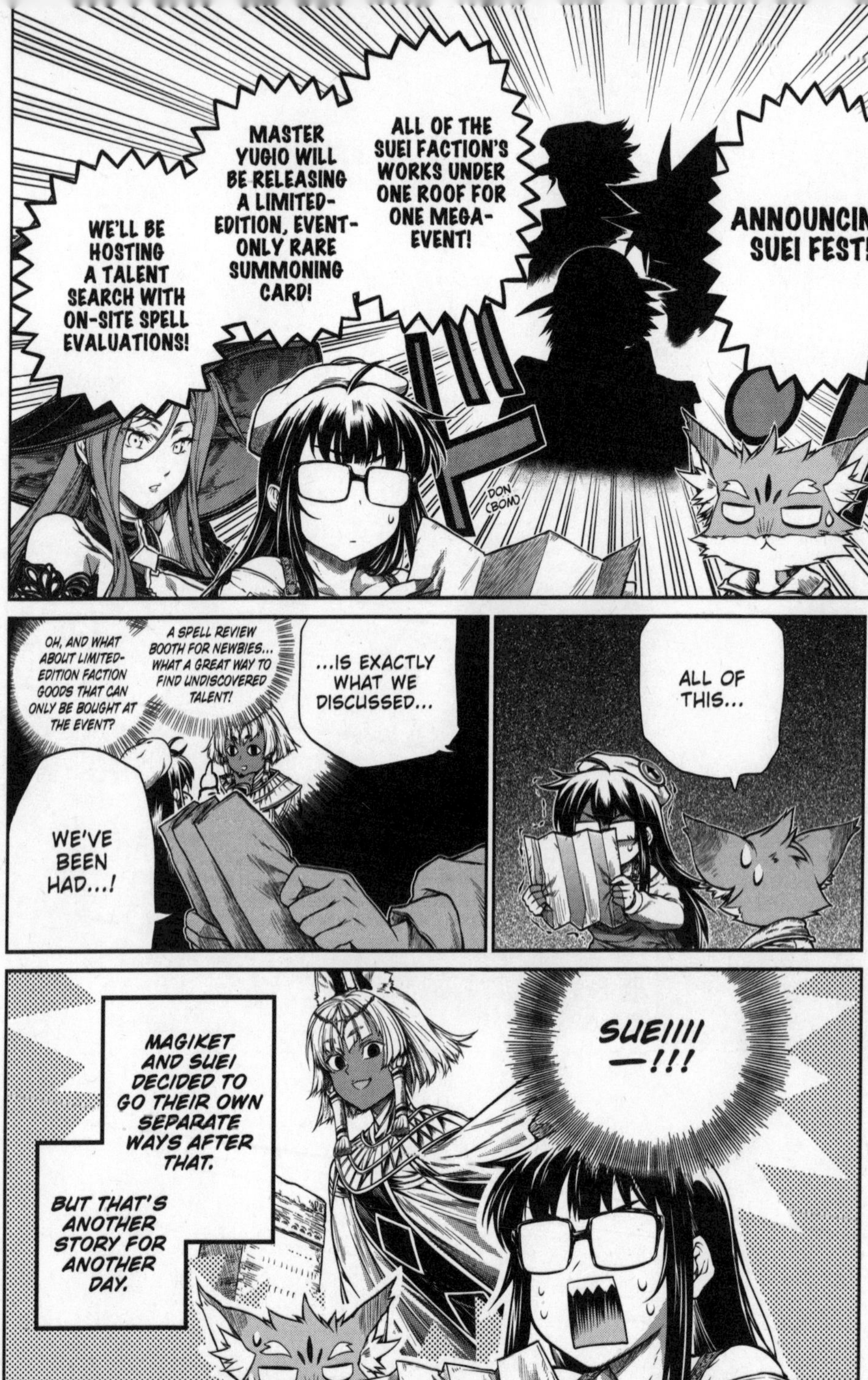
ANNOUNCING SUEI FEST!
ALL OF THE SUEI FACTION'S WORKS UNDER ONE ROOF FOR ONE MEGA-EVENT!
MASTER YUGIO WILL BE RELEASING A LIMITED-EDITION, EVENT-ONLY RARE SUMMONING CARD!
WE'LL BE HOSTING A TALENT SEARCH WITH ON-SITE SPELL EVALUATIONS!
DON (BOM)
ALL OF THIS...
...IS EXACTLY WHAT WE DISCUSSED...
A SPELL REVIEW BOOTH FOR NEWBIES... WHAT A GREAT WAY TO FIND UNDISCOVERED TALENT!
OH, AND WHAT ABOUT LIMITED-EDITION FACTION GOODS THAT CAN ONLY BE BOUGHT AT THE EVENT?
WE'VE BEEN HAD...!
SUEI!!!! —!!!
MAGIKET AND SUEI DECIDED TO GO THEIR OWN SEPARATE WAYS AFTER THAT.
BUT THAT'S ANOTHER STORY FOR ANOTHER DAY.

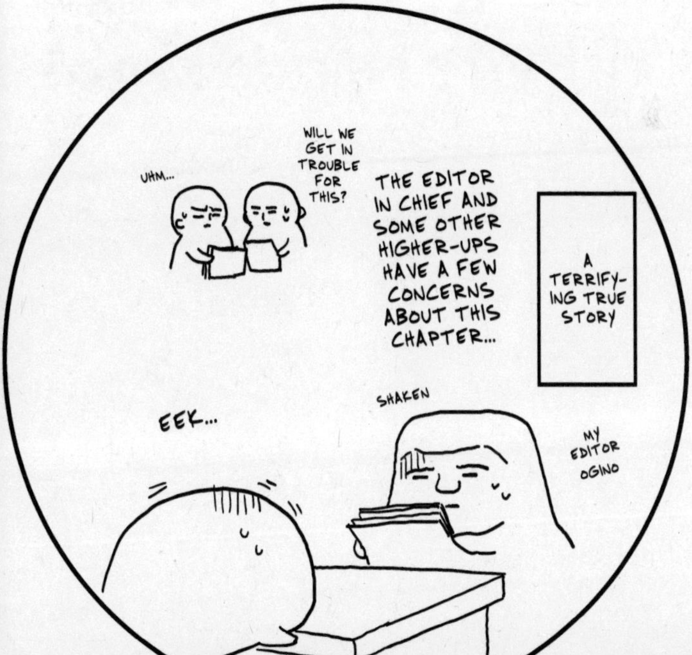
A TERRIFYING TRUE STORY
THE EDITOR IN CHIEF AND SOME OTHER HIGHER-UPS HAVE A FEW CONCERNS ABOUT THIS CHAPTER...
WILL WE GET IN TROUBLE FOR THIS?
UHM...
MY EDITOR OGINO
SHAKEN
EEK...

A WITCH'S
PRINTING OFFICE

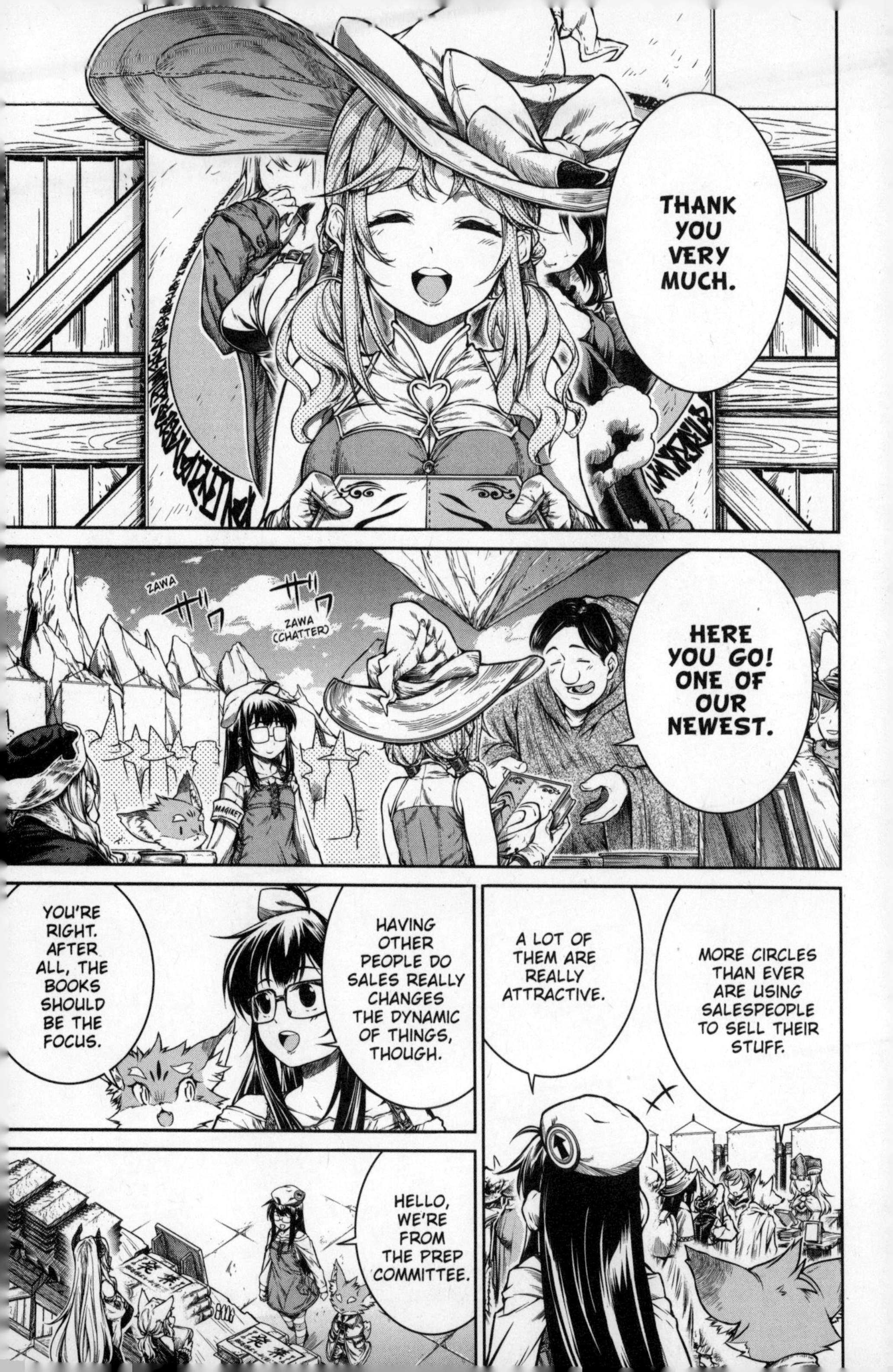
THANK YOU VERY MUCH.
HERE YOU GO! ONE OF OUR NEWEST.
ZAWA (CHATTER)
ZAWA
MAGIKET
MORE CIRCLES THAN EVER ARE USING SALESPEOPLE TO SELL THEIR STUFF.
A LOT OF THEM ARE REALLY ATTRACTIVE.
HAVING OTHER PEOPLE DO SALES REALLY CHANGES THE DYNAMIC OF THINGS, THOUGH.
YOU'RE RIGHT. AFTER ALL, THE BOOKS SHOULD BE THE FOCUS.
HELLO, WE'RE FROM THE PREP COMMITTEE.

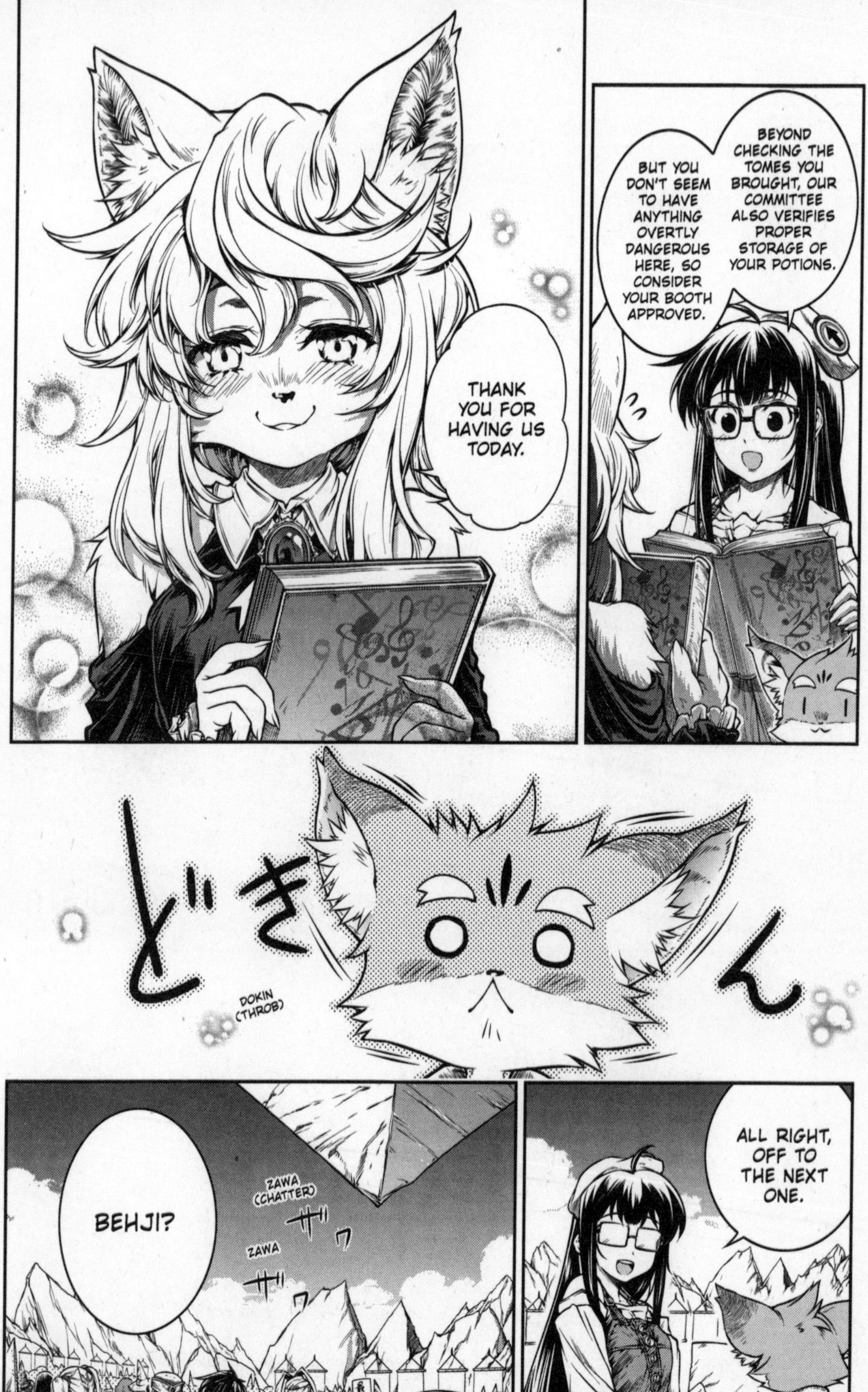
BEYOND CHECKING THE TOMES YOU BROUGHT, OUR COMMITTEE ALSO VERIFIES PROPER STORAGE OF YOUR POTIONS.
BUT YOU DON'T SEEM TO HAVE ANYTHING OVERTLY DANGEROUS HERE, SO CONSIDER YOUR BOOTH APPROVED.
THANK YOU FOR HAVING US TODAY.
どきん
DOKIN (THROB)
ALL RIGHT, OFF TO THE NEXT ONE.
ZAWA (CHATTER)
ザワ
ZAWA
ザワ
BEHJI?

Chapter 18

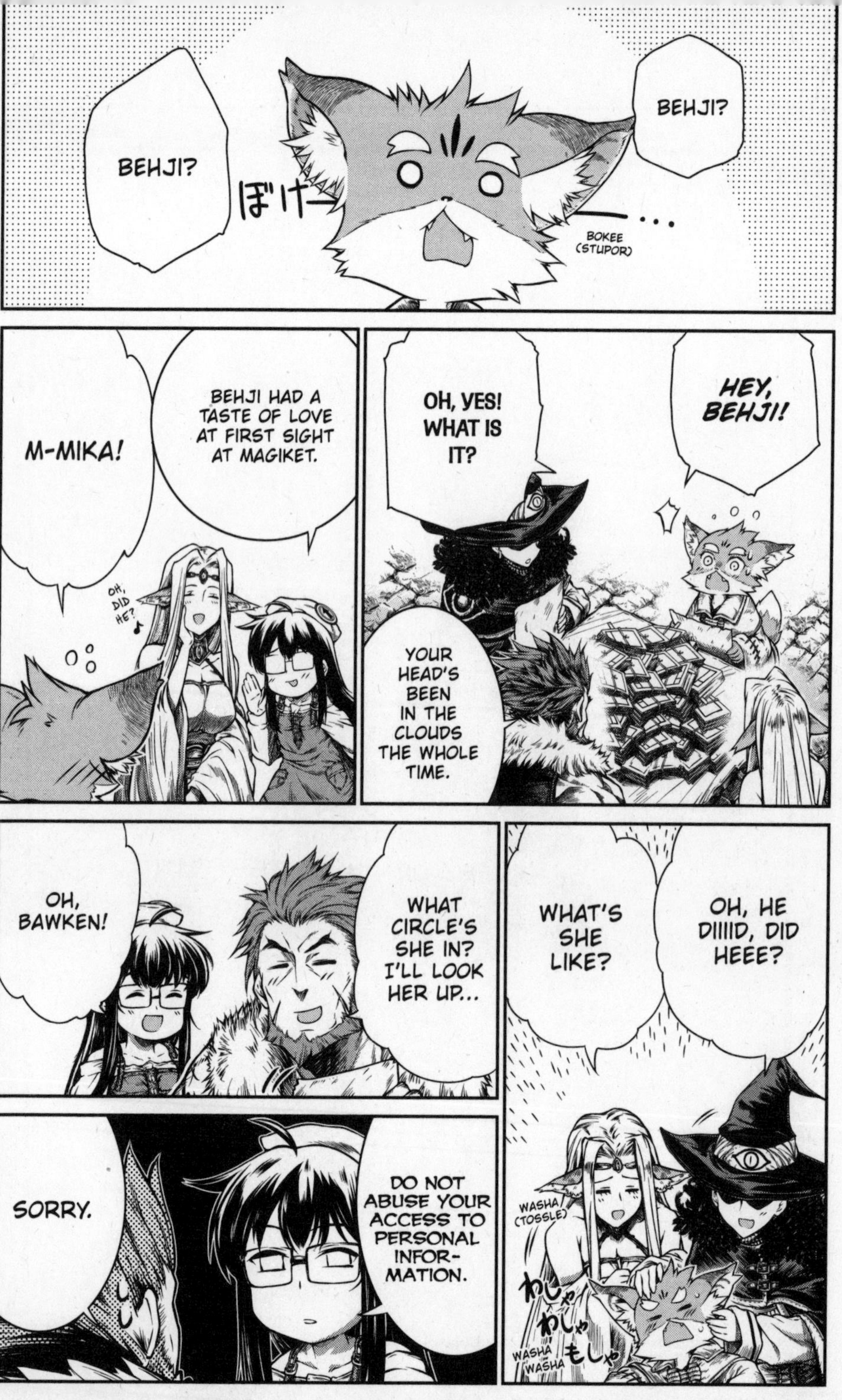
BEHJI?
BEHJI?
ぼけー
—...
BOKEE (STUPOR)
HEY, BEHJI!
OH, YES! WHAT IS IT?
YOUR HEAD'S BEEN IN THE CLOUDS THE WHOLE TIME.
BEHJI HAD A TASTE OF LOVE AT FIRST SIGHT AT MAGIKET.
M-MIKA!
OH, DID HE? ♪
OH, HE DIIIID, DID HEEE?
WHAT'S SHE LIKE?
WASHA (TOSSLE)
わしゃわしゃ もしゃ
WASHA WASHA
WHAT CIRCLE'S SHE IN? I'LL LOOK HER UP...
OH, BAWKEN!
DO NOT ABUSE YOUR ACCESS TO PERSONAL INFORMATION.
SORRY.

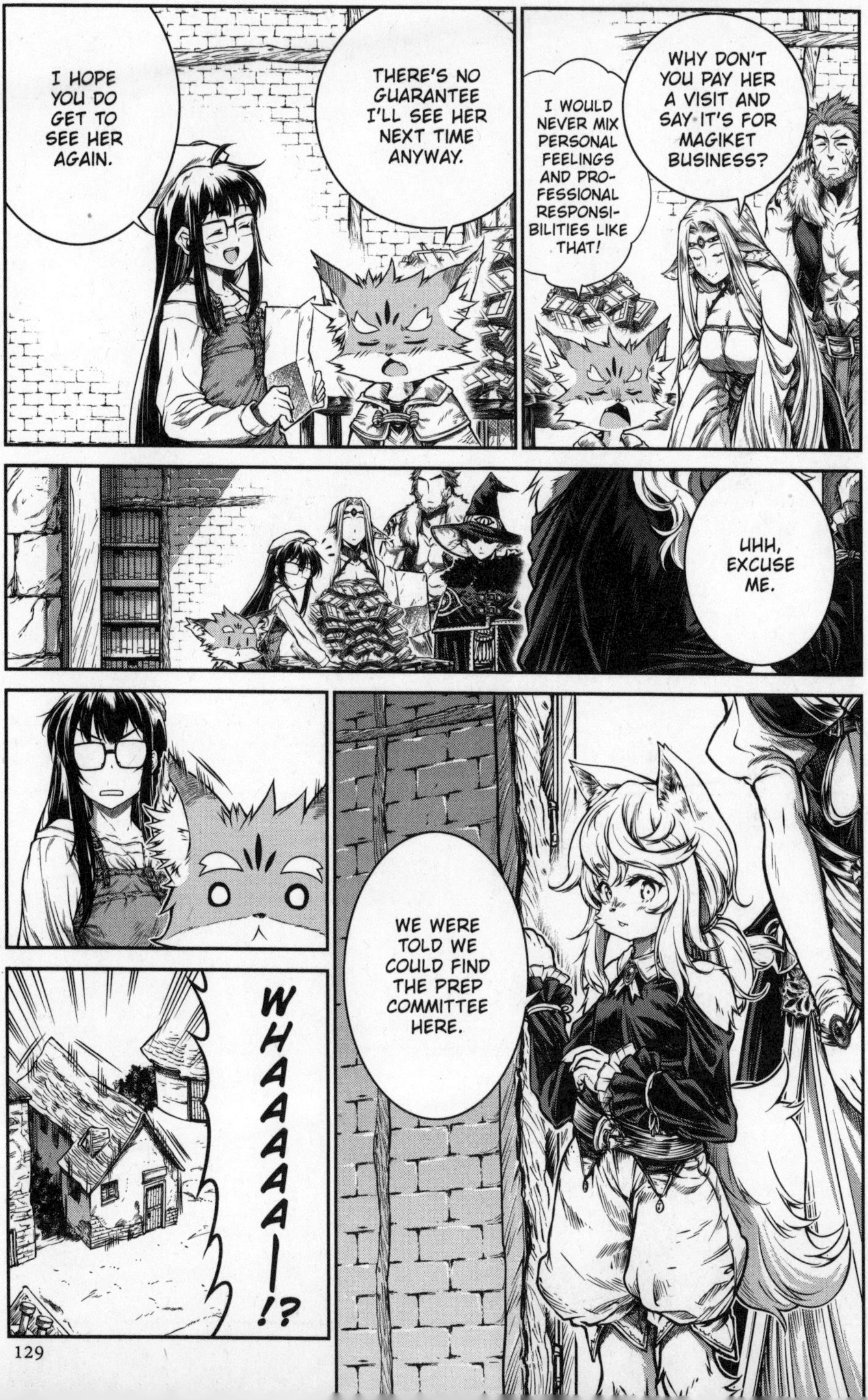

WHY DON'T YOU PAY HER A VISIT AND SAY IT'S FOR MAGIKET BUSINESS?
I WOULD NEVER MIX PERSONAL FEELINGS AND PRO-FESSIONAL RESPONSI-BILITIES LIKE THAT!
THERE'S NO GUARANTEE I'LL SEE HER NEXT TIME ANYWAY.
I HOPE YOU DO GET TO SEE HER AGAIN.
UHH, EXCUSE ME.
WE WERE TOLD WE COULD FIND THE PREP COMMITTEE HERE.
WHAAAAAA!?

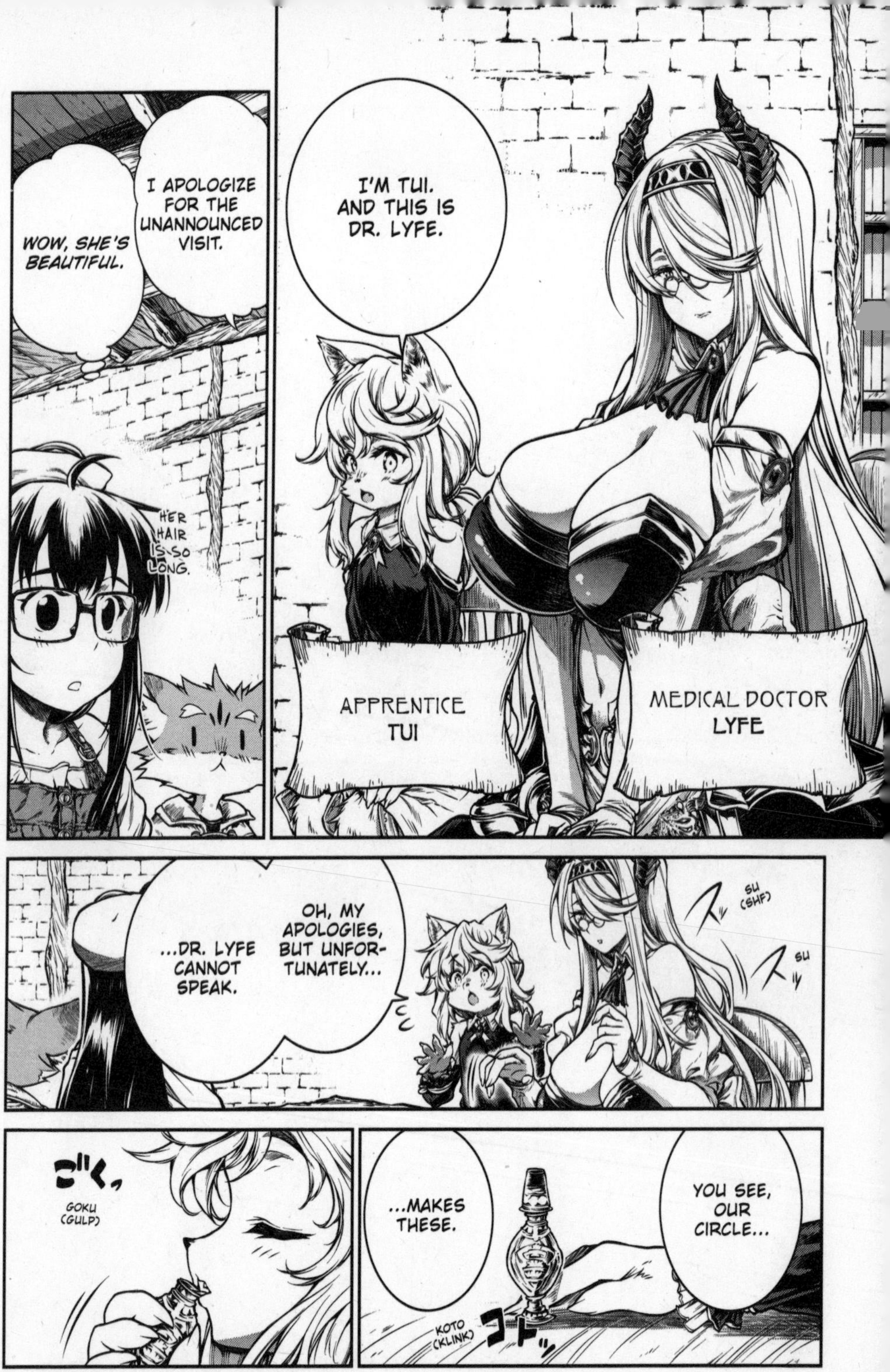
I'M TUI. AND THIS IS DR. LYFE.
MEDICAL DOCTOR LYFE
APPRENTICE TUI
I APOLOGIZE FOR THE UNANNOUNCED VISIT.
WOW, SHE'S BEAUTIFUL.
HER HAIR IS SO LONG.
SU (SHF)
SU
OH, MY APOLOGIES, BUT UNFORTUNATELY...
...DR. LYFE CANNOT SPEAK.
YOU SEE, OUR CIRCLE...
...MAKES THESE.
KOTO (KLINK)
GOKU (GULP)

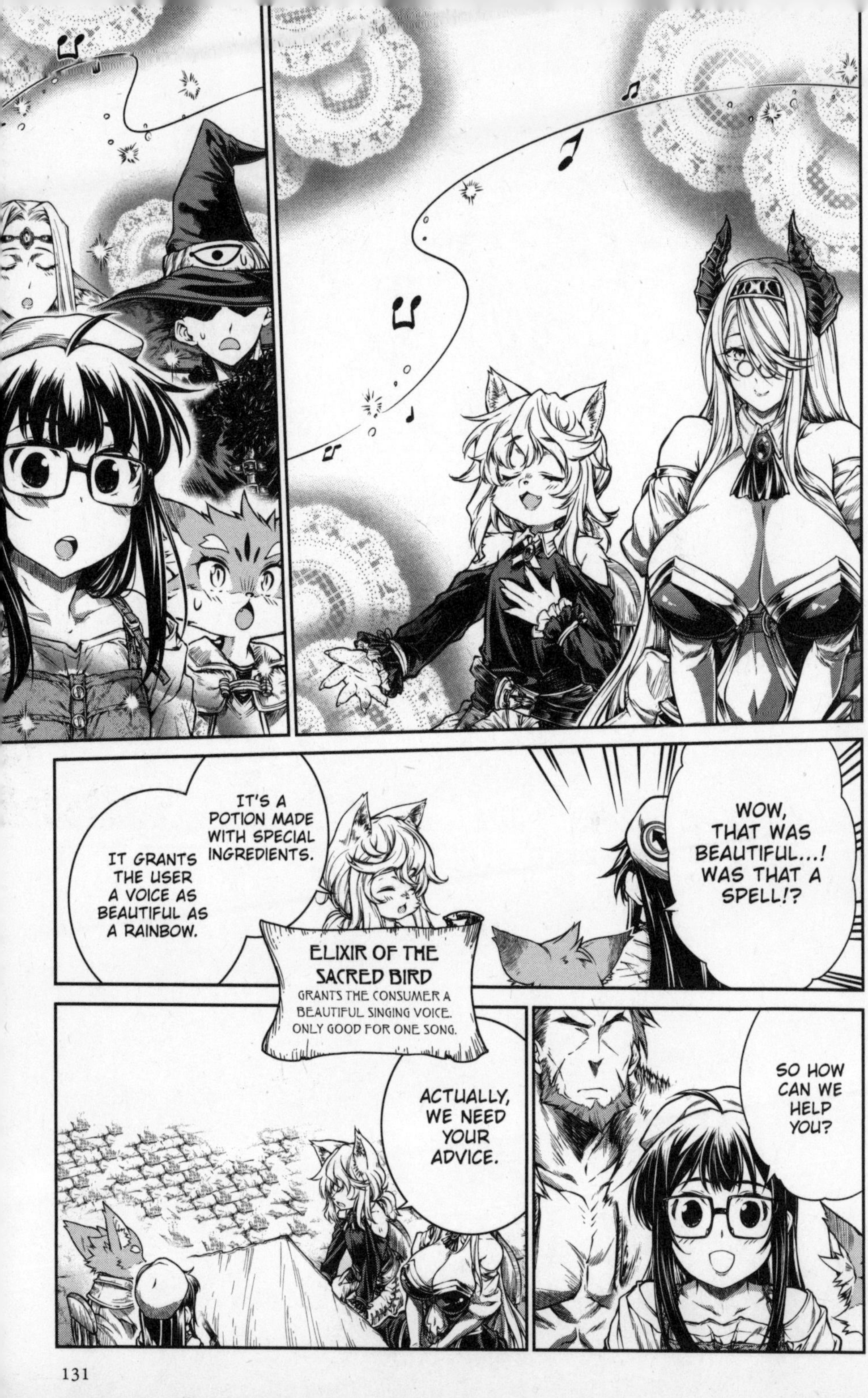
WOW, THAT WAS BEAUTIFUL...! WAS THAT A SPELL!?
IT'S A POTION MADE WITH SPECIAL INGREDIENTS.
IT GRANTS THE USER A VOICE AS BEAUTIFUL AS A RAINBOW.
ELIXIR OF THE SACRED BIRD
GRANTS THE CONSUMER A BEAUTIFUL SINGING VOICE. ONLY GOOD FOR ONE SONG.
SO HOW CAN WE HELP YOU?
ACTUALLY, WE NEED YOUR ADVICE.

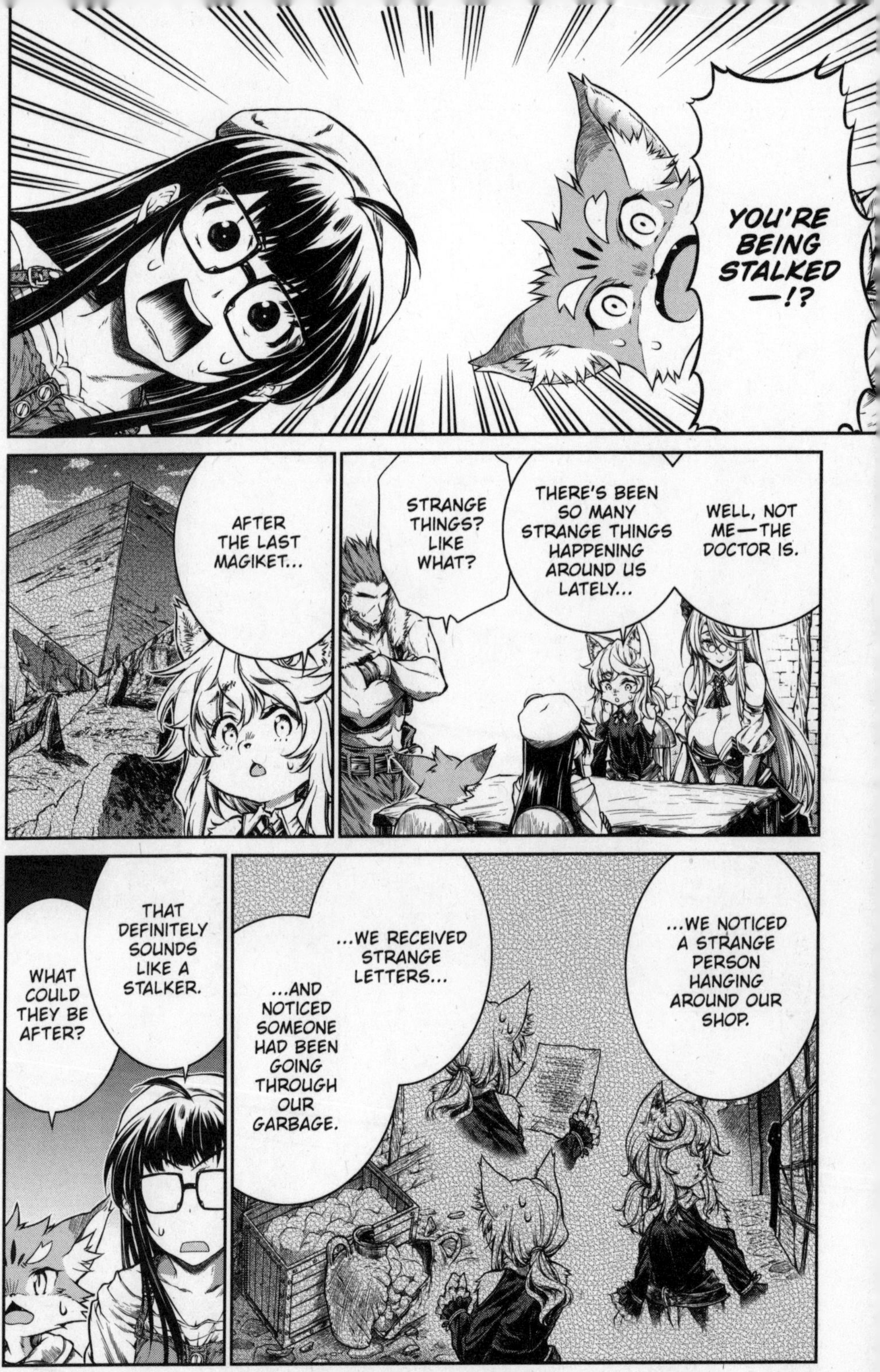
YOU'RE BEING STALKED—!?
WELL, NOT ME—THE DOCTOR IS.
THERE'S BEEN SO MANY STRANGE THINGS HAPPENING AROUND US LATELY...
STRANGE THINGS? LIKE WHAT?
AFTER THE LAST MAGIKET...
...WE NOTICED A STRANGE PERSON HANGING AROUND OUR SHOP.
...WE RECEIVED STRANGE LETTERS...
...AND NOTICED SOMEONE HAD BEEN GOING THROUGH OUR GARBAGE.
THAT DEFINITELY SOUNDS LIKE A STALKER.
WHAT COULD THEY BE AFTER?

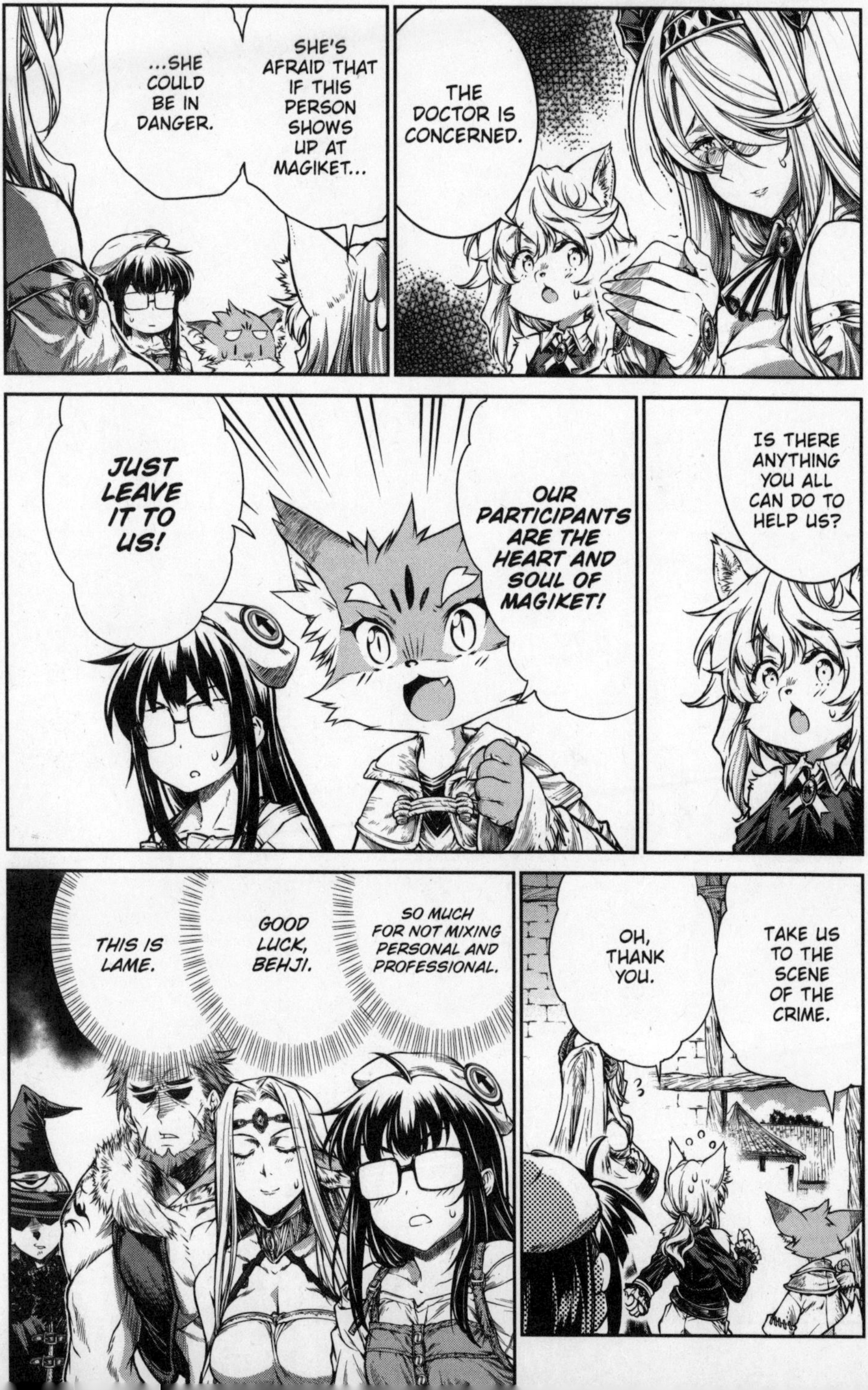
THE DOCTOR IS CONCERNED.
SHE'S AFRAID THAT IF THIS PERSON SHOWS UP AT MAGIKET...
...SHE COULD BE IN DANGER.
IS THERE ANYTHING YOU ALL CAN DO TO HELP US?
OUR PARTICIPANTS ARE THE HEART AND SOUL OF MAGIKET!
JUST LEAVE IT TO US!
TAKE US TO THE SCENE OF THE CRIME.
OH, THANK YOU.
SO MUCH FOR NOT MIXING PERSONAL AND PROFESSIONAL.
GOOD LUCK, BEHJI.
THIS IS LAME.

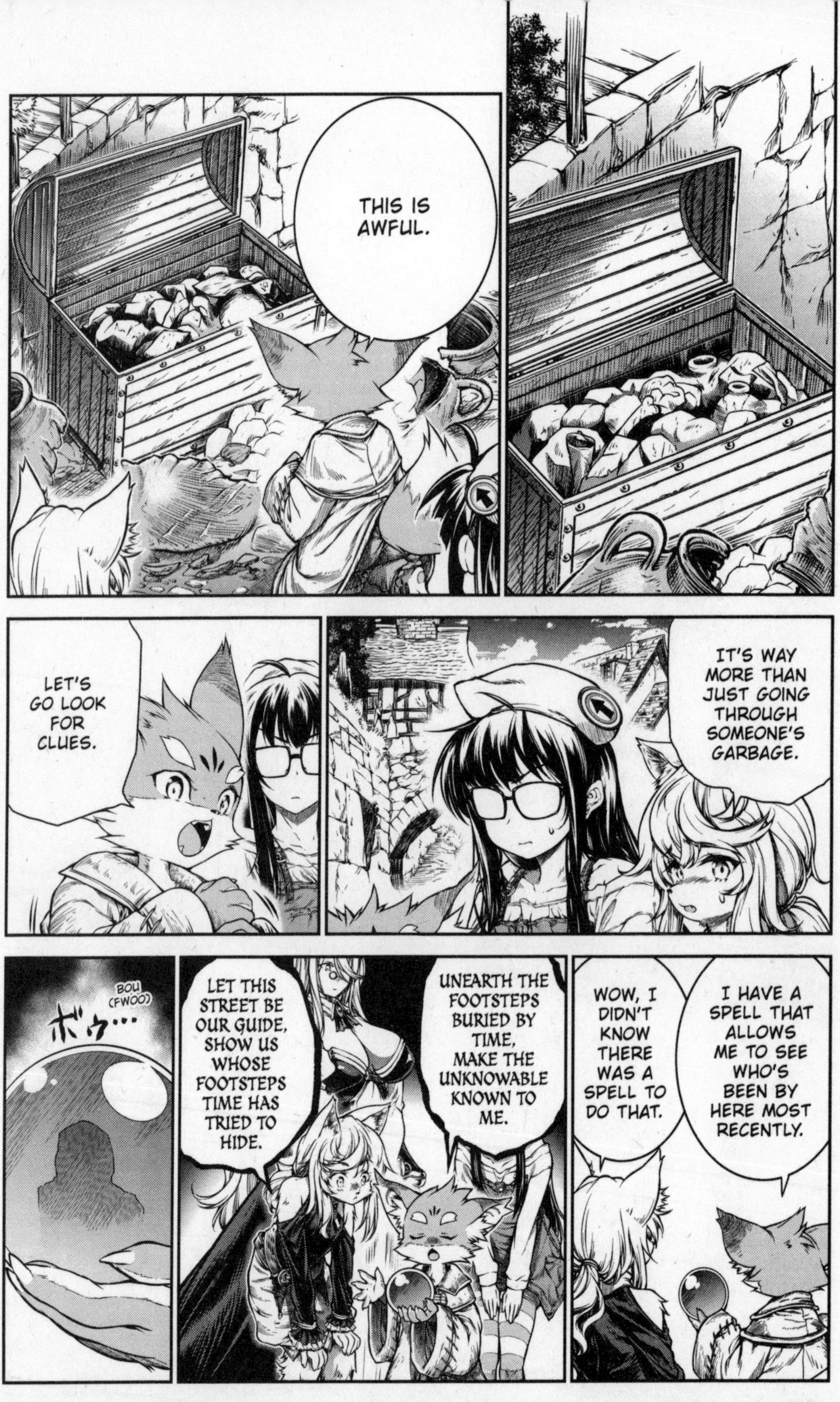
THIS IS AWFUL.
IT'S WAY MORE THAN JUST GOING THROUGH SOMEONE'S GARBAGE.
LET'S GO LOOK FOR CLUES.
I HAVE A SPELL THAT ALLOWS ME TO SEE WHO'S BEEN BY HERE MOST RECENTLY.
WOW, I DIDN'T KNOW THERE WAS A SPELL TO DO THAT.
UNEARTH THE FOOTSTEPS BURIED BY TIME, MAKE THE UNKNOWABLE KNOWN TO ME.
LET THIS STREET BE OUR GUIDE, SHOW US WHOSE FOOTSTEPS TIME HAS TRIED TO HIDE.
ボウ…
BOU (FWOO)

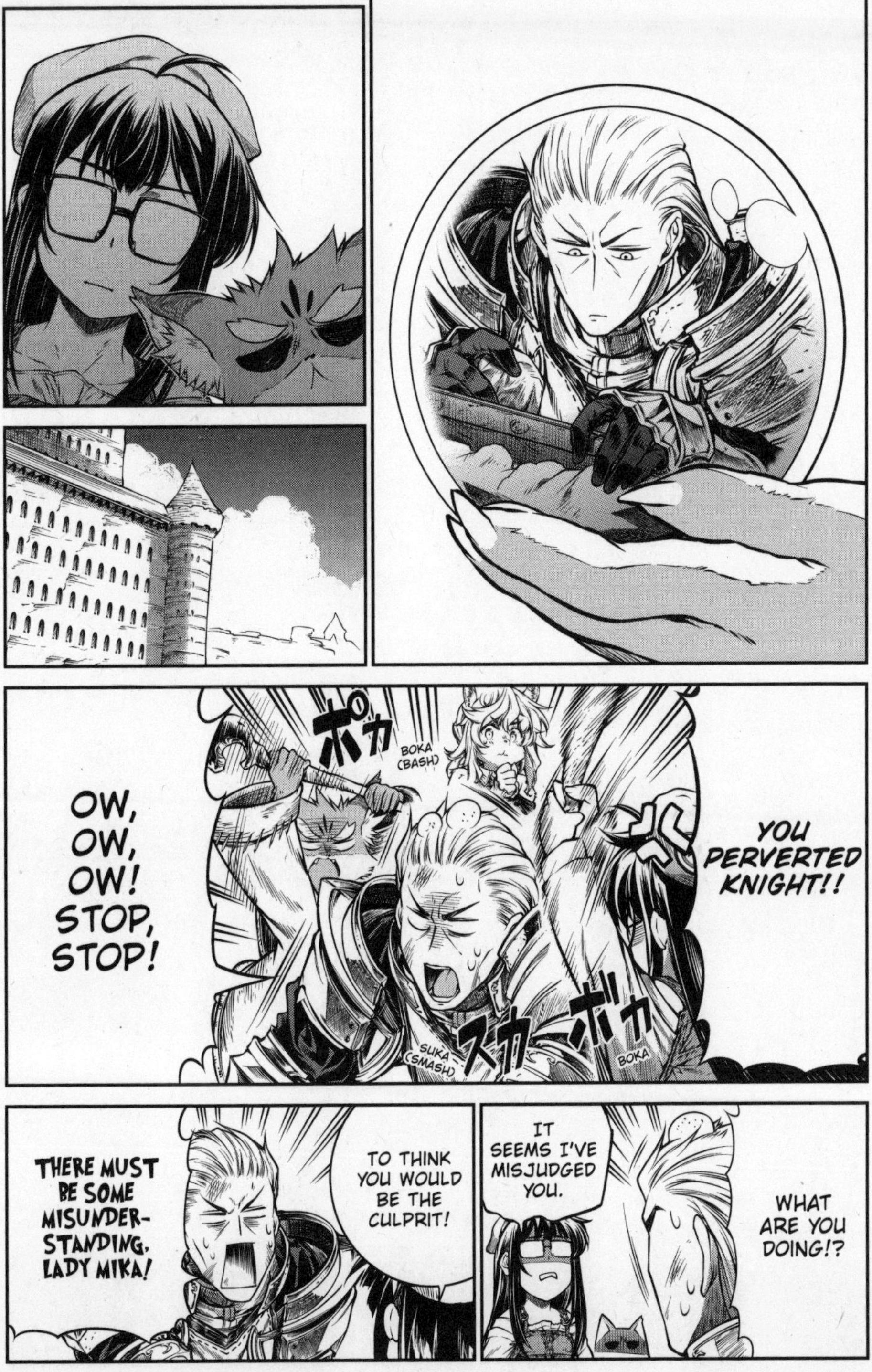

YOU PERVERTED KNIGHT!!
ポカ
BOKA (BASH)
OW, OW, OW! STOP, STOP!
ボカ
BOKA
スカ
SUKA (SMASH)
WHAT ARE YOU DOING!?
IT SEEMS I'VE MISJUDGED YOU.
TO THINK YOU WOULD BE THE CULPRIT!
THERE MUST BE SOME MISUNDER-STANDING, LADY MIKA!

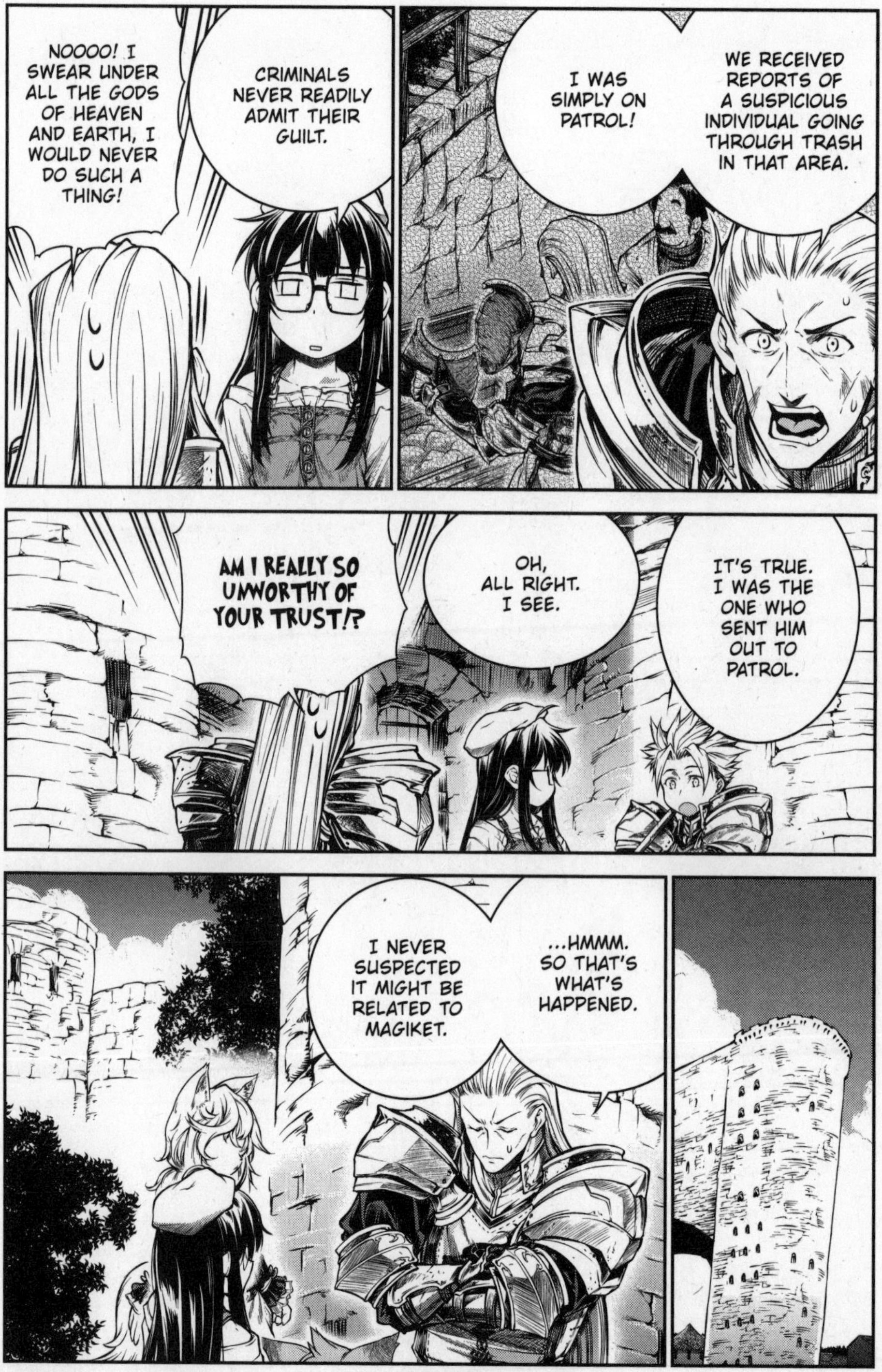
WE RECEIVED REPORTS OF A SUSPICIOUS INDIVIDUAL GOING THROUGH TRASH IN THAT AREA.
I WAS SIMPLY ON PATROL!
CRIMINALS NEVER READILY ADMIT THEIR GUILT.
NOOOO! I SWEAR UNDER ALL THE GODS OF HEAVEN AND EARTH, I WOULD NEVER DO SUCH A THING!
IT'S TRUE. I WAS THE ONE WHO SENT HIM OUT TO PATROL.
OH, ALL RIGHT. I SEE.
AM I REALLY SO UNWORTHY OF YOUR TRUST!?
...HMMM. SO THAT'S WHAT'S HAPPENED.
I NEVER SUSPECTED IT MIGHT BE RELATED TO MAGIKET.

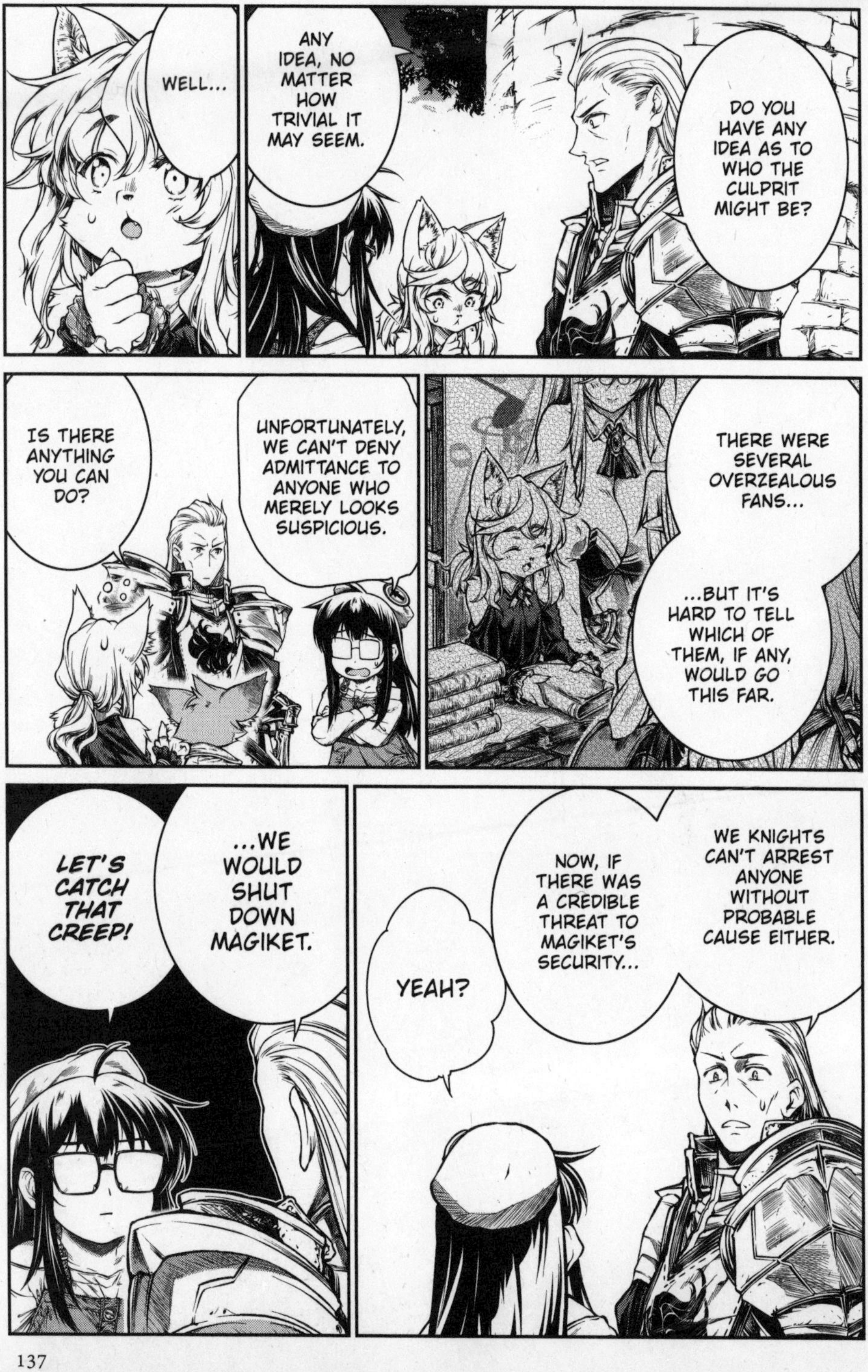
DO YOU HAVE ANY IDEA AS TO WHO THE CULPRIT MIGHT BE?
ANY IDEA, NO MATTER HOW TRIVIAL IT MAY SEEM.
WELL...
THERE WERE SEVERAL OVERZEALOUS FANS...
...BUT IT'S HARD TO TELL WHICH OF THEM, IF ANY, WOULD GO THIS FAR.
UNFORTUNATELY, WE CAN'T DENY ADMITTANCE TO ANYONE WHO MERELY LOOKS SUSPICIOUS.
IS THERE ANYTHING YOU CAN DO?
WE KNIGHTS CAN'T ARREST ANYONE WITHOUT PROBABLE CAUSE EITHER.
NOW, IF THERE WAS A CREDIBLE THREAT TO MAGIKET'S SECURITY...
YEAH?
...WE WOULD SHUT DOWN MAGIKET.
LET'S CATCH THAT CREEP!

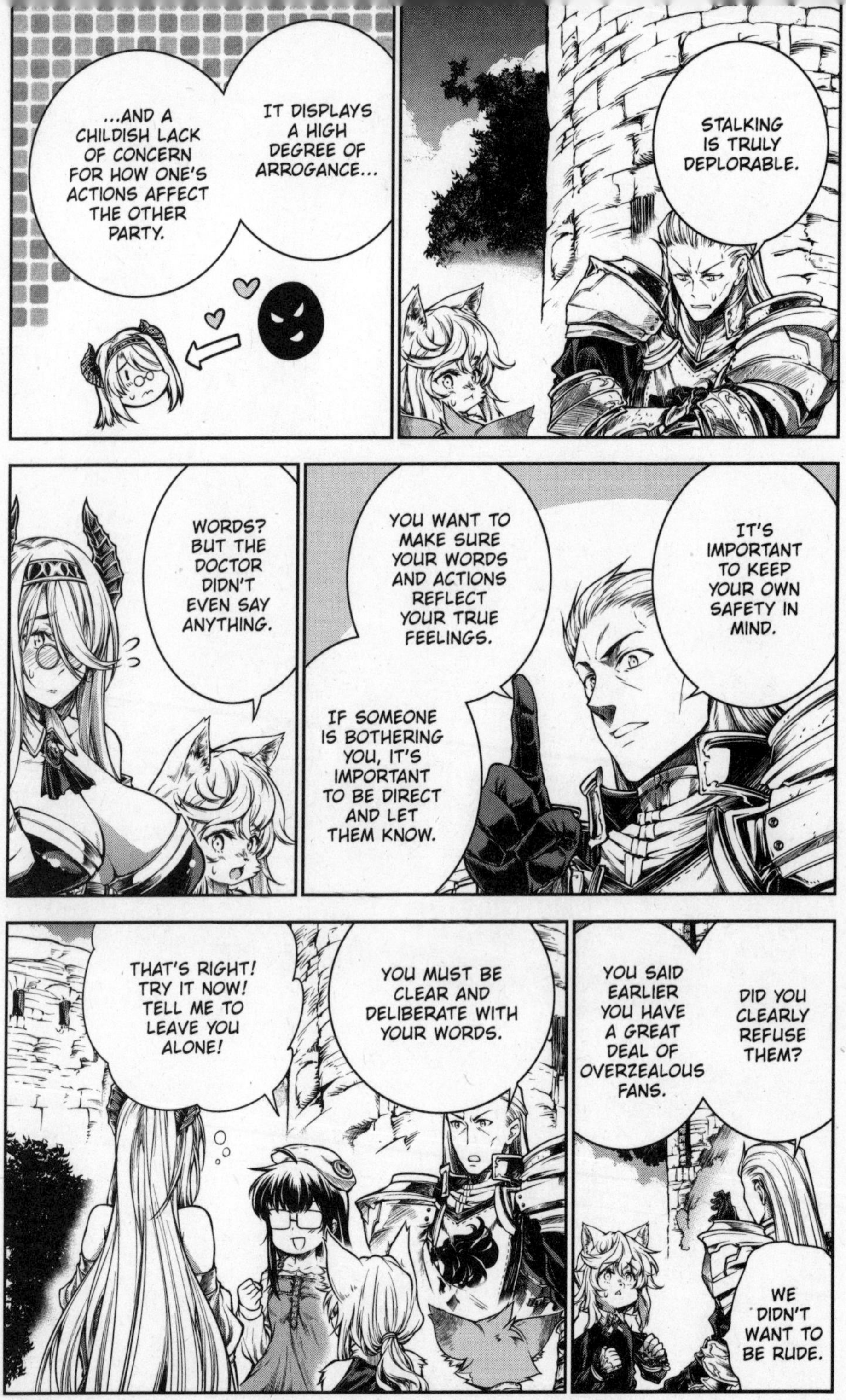
STALKING IS TRULY DEPLORABLE.
IT DISPLAYS A HIGH DEGREE OF ARROGANCE...
...AND A CHILDISH LACK OF CONCERN FOR HOW ONE'S ACTIONS AFFECT THE OTHER PARTY.
IT'S IMPORTANT TO KEEP YOUR OWN SAFETY IN MIND.
YOU WANT TO MAKE SURE YOUR WORDS AND ACTIONS REFLECT YOUR TRUE FEELINGS.
IF SOMEONE IS BOTHERING YOU, IT'S IMPORTANT TO BE DIRECT AND LET THEM KNOW.
WORDS? BUT THE DOCTOR DIDN'T EVEN SAY ANYTHING.
DID YOU CLEARLY REFUSE THEM?
YOU SAID EARLIER YOU HAVE A GREAT DEAL OF OVERZEALOUS FANS.
WE DIDN'T WANT TO BE RUDE.
YOU MUST BE CLEAR AND DELIBERATE WITH YOUR WORDS.
THAT'S RIGHT! TRY IT NOW! TELL ME TO LEAVE YOU ALONE!

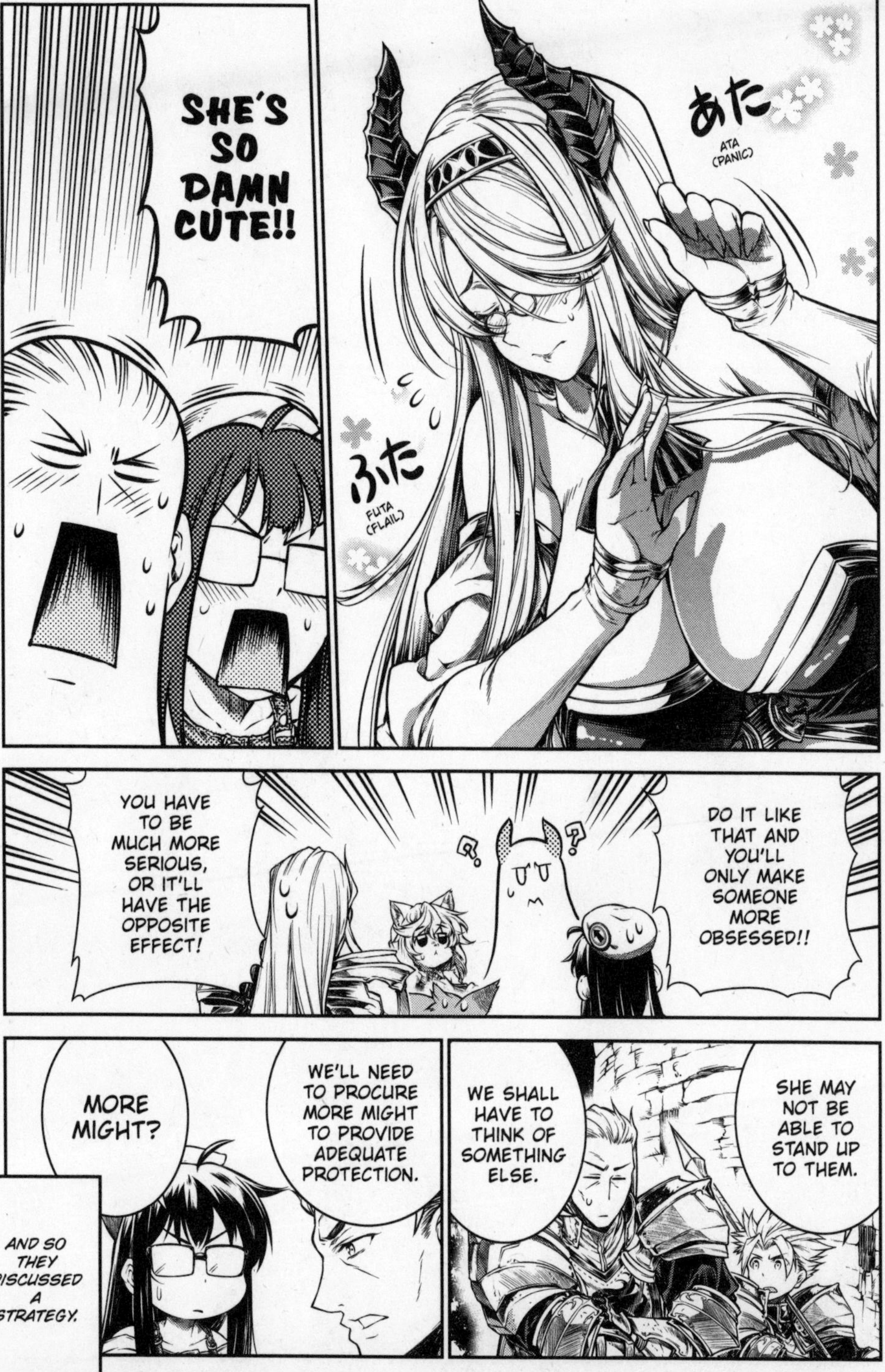
あた
ATA (PANIC)
ふた
FUTA (FLAIL)
SHE'S SO DAMN CUTE!!
DO IT LIKE THAT AND YOU'LL ONLY MAKE SOMEONE MORE OBSESSED!!
YOU HAVE TO BE MUCH MORE SERIOUS, OR IT'LL HAVE THE OPPOSITE EFFECT!
SHE MAY NOT BE ABLE TO STAND UP TO THEM.
WE SHALL HAVE TO THINK OF SOMETHING ELSE.
WE'LL NEED TO PROCURE MORE MIGHT TO PROVIDE ADEQUATE PROTECTION.
MORE MIGHT?
AND SO THEY DISCUSSED A STRATEGY.

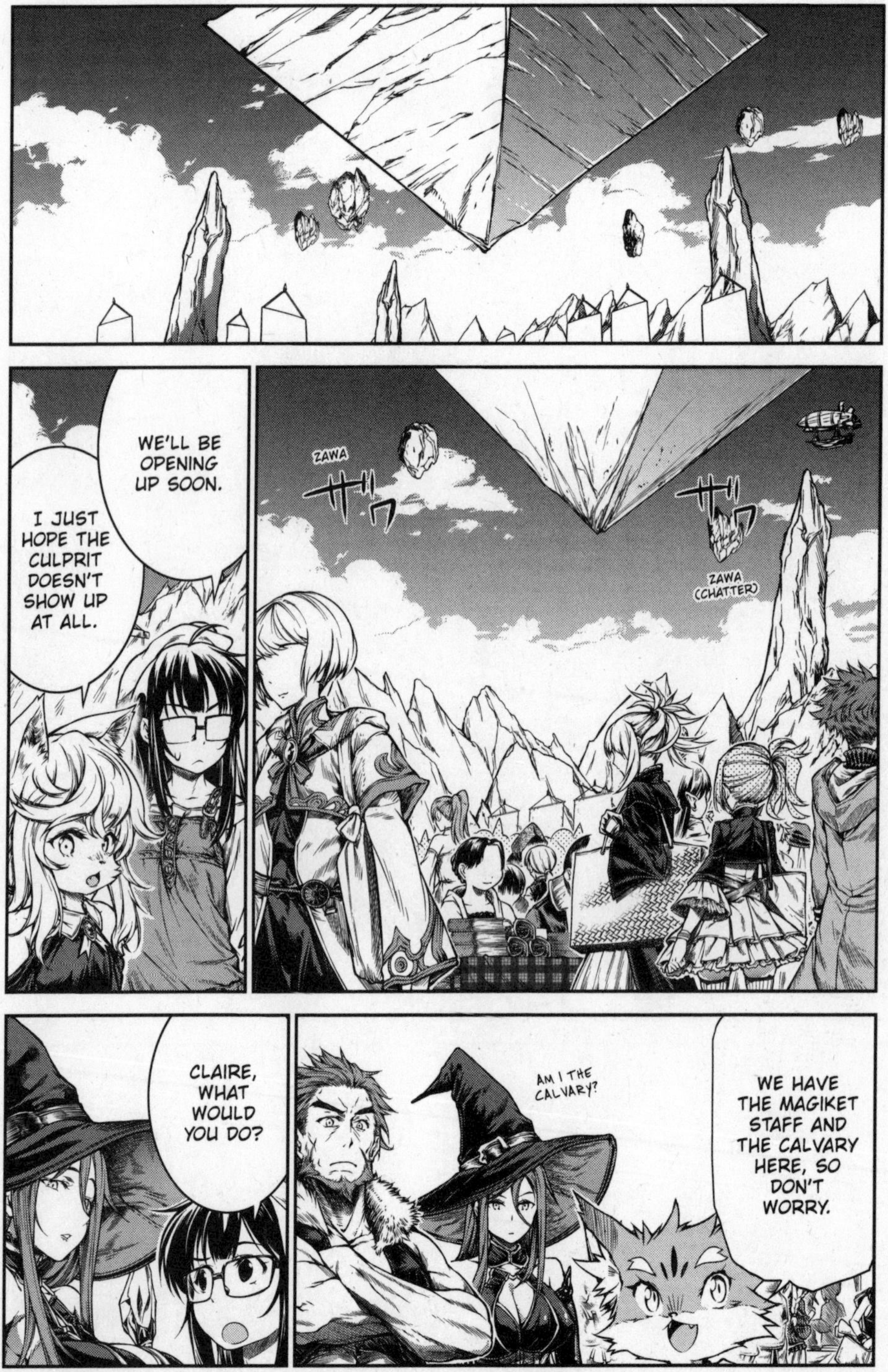
ZAWA
ZAWA (CHATTER)
WE'LL BE OPENING UP SOON.
I JUST HOPE THE CULPRIT DOESN'T SHOW UP AT ALL.
WE HAVE THE MAGIKET STAFF AND THE CALVARY HERE, SO DON'T WORRY.
AM I THE CALVARY?
CLAIRE, WHAT WOULD YOU DO?

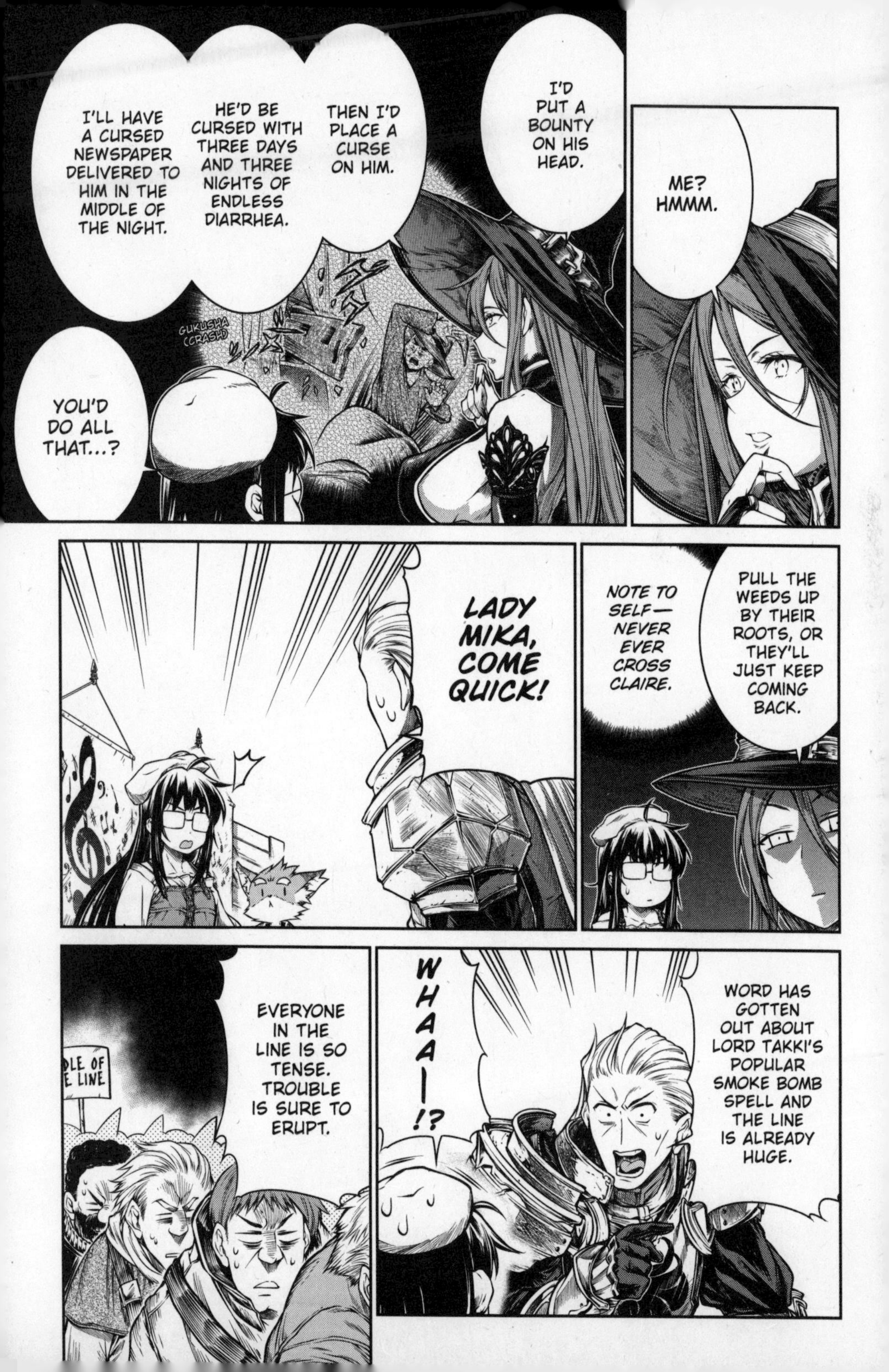
ME? HMMM.
I'D PUT A BOUNTY ON HIS HEAD.
THEN I'D PLACE A CURSE ON HIM.
HE'D BE CURSED WITH THREE DAYS AND THREE NIGHTS OF ENDLESS DIARRHEA.
I'LL HAVE A CURSED NEWSPAPER DELIVERED TO HIM IN THE MIDDLE OF THE NIGHT.
GUKUSHA (CRASH)
YOU'D DO ALL THAT...?
PULL THE WEEDS UP BY THEIR ROOTS, OR THEY'LL JUST KEEP COMING BACK.
NOTE TO SELF— NEVER EVER CROSS CLAIRE.
LADY MIKA, COME QUICK!
WORD HAS GOTTEN OUT ABOUT LORD TAKKI'S POPULAR SMOKE BOMB SPELL AND THE LINE IS ALREADY HUGE.
WHAAA—!?
EVERYONE IN THE LINE IS SO TENSE. TROUBLE IS SURE TO ERUPT.

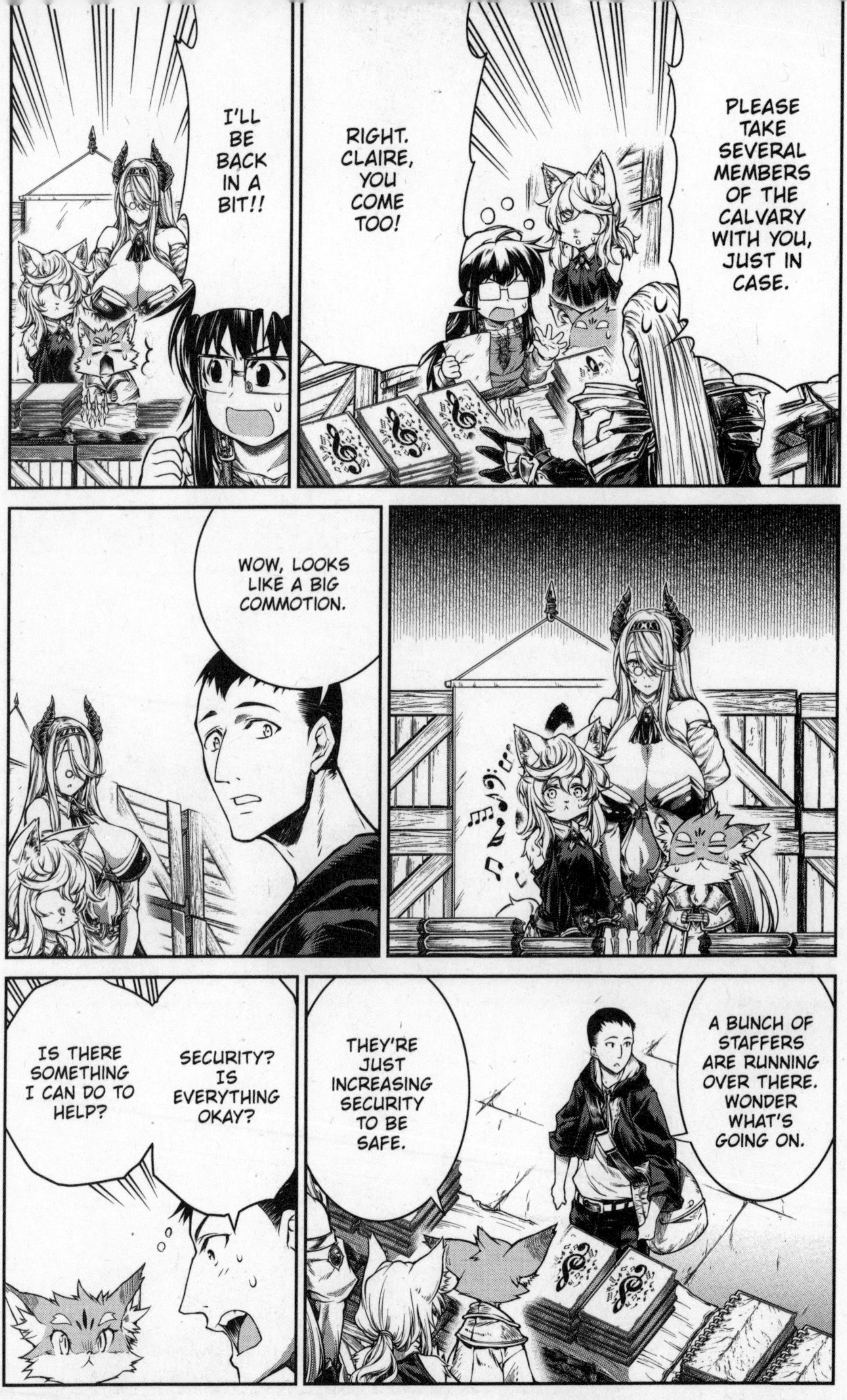
PLEASE TAKE SEVERAL MEMBERS OF THE CALVARY WITH YOU, JUST IN CASE.
RIGHT. CLAIRE, YOU COME TOO!
I'LL BE BACK IN A BIT!!
WOW, LOOKS LIKE A BIG COMMOTION.
A BUNCH OF STAFFERS ARE RUNNING OVER THERE. WONDER WHAT'S GOING ON.
THEY'RE JUST INCREASING SECURITY TO BE SAFE.
SECURITY? IS EVERYTHING OKAY?
IS THERE SOMETHING I CAN DO TO HELP?

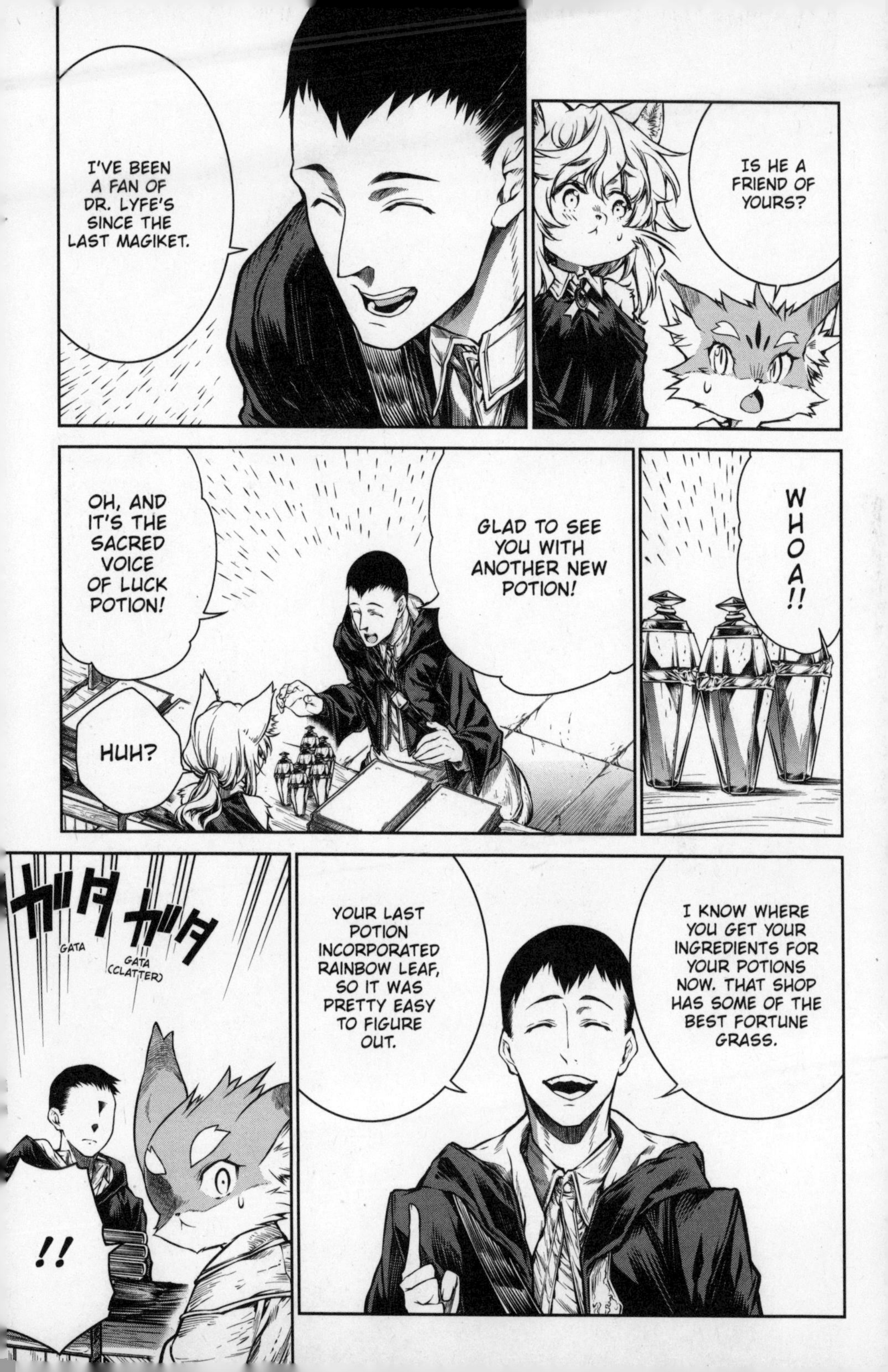
IS HE A FRIEND OF YOURS?
I'VE BEEN A FAN OF DR. LYFE'S SINCE THE LAST MAGIKET.
WHOA!!
GLAD TO SEE YOU WITH ANOTHER NEW POTION!
OH, AND IT'S THE SACRED VOICE OF LUCK POTION!
HUH?
I KNOW WHERE YOU GET YOUR INGREDIENTS FOR YOUR POTIONS NOW. THAT SHOP HAS SOME OF THE BEST FORTUNE GRASS.
YOUR LAST POTION INCORPORATED RAINBOW LEAF, SO IT WAS PRETTY EASY TO FIGURE OUT.
ガタ
GATA
ガタ
GATA (CLATTER)
!!

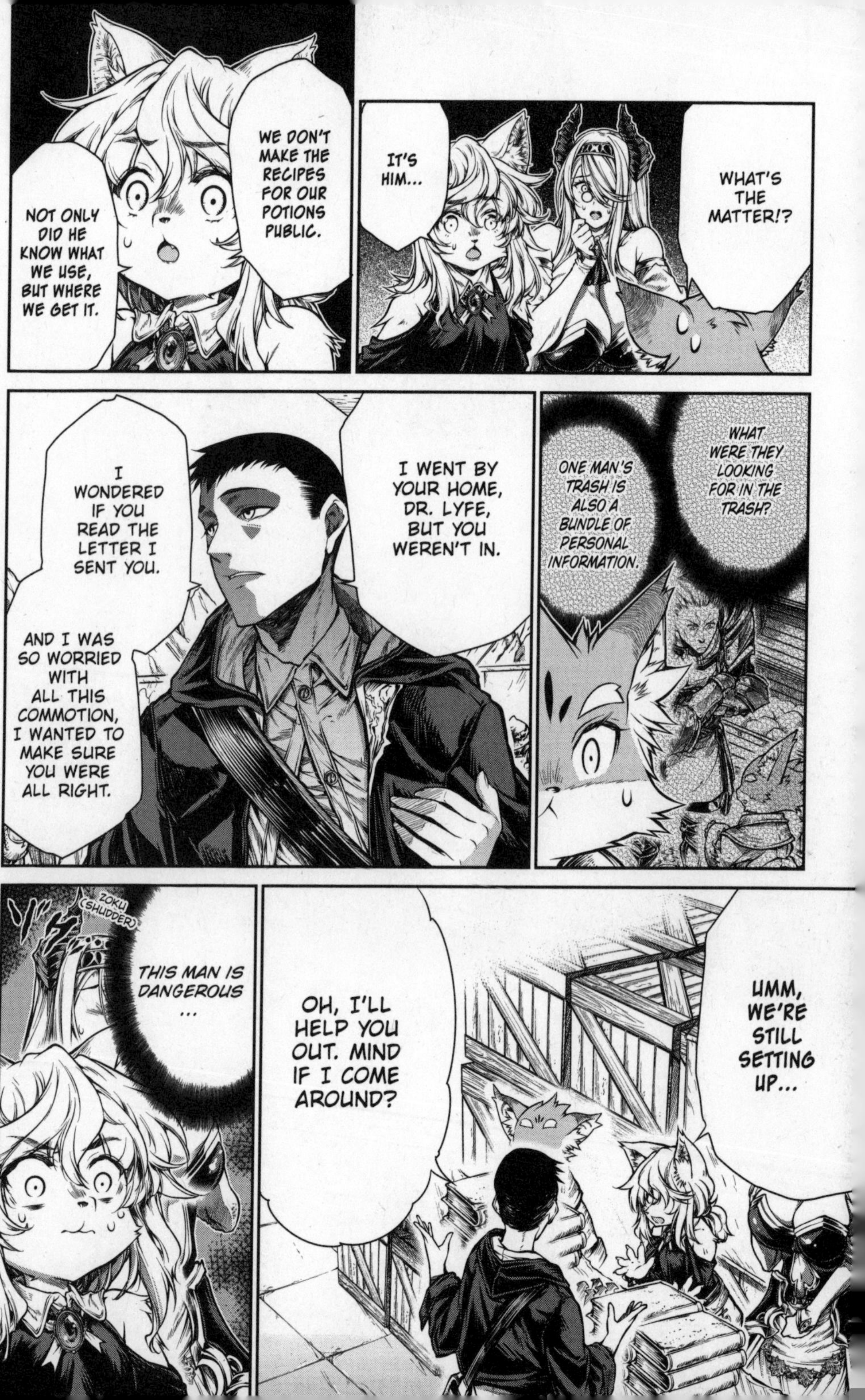
WHAT'S THE MATTER!?
IT'S HIM...
WE DON'T MAKE THE RECIPES FOR OUR POTIONS PUBLIC.
NOT ONLY DID HE KNOW WHAT WE USE, BUT WHERE WE GET IT.
WHAT WERE THEY LOOKING FOR IN THE TRASH?
ONE MAN'S TRASH IS ALSO A BUNDLE OF PERSONAL INFORMATION.
I WENT BY YOUR HOME, DR. LYFE, BUT YOU WEREN'T IN.
I WONDERED IF YOU READ THE LETTER I SENT YOU.
AND I WAS SO WORRIED WITH ALL THIS COMMOTION, I WANTED TO MAKE SURE YOU WERE ALL RIGHT.
UMM, WE'RE STILL SETTING UP...
OH, I'LL HELP YOU OUT. MIND IF I COME AROUND?
ZOKU (SHUDDER)
THIS MAN IS DANGEROUS ...

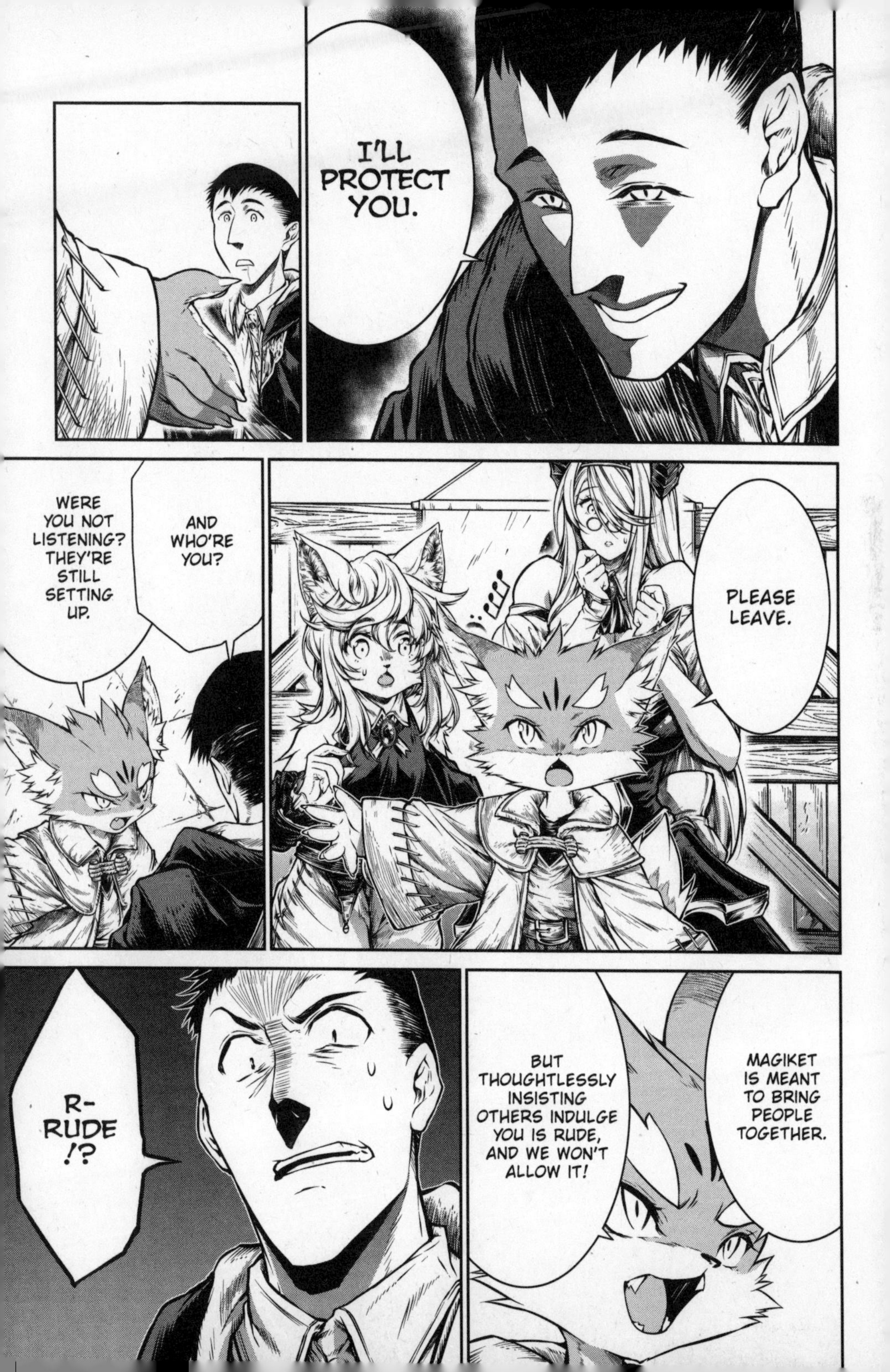
I'LL PROTECT YOU.
PLEASE LEAVE.
AND WHO'RE YOU?
WERE YOU NOT LISTENING? THEY'RE STILL SETTING UP.
MAGIKET IS MEANT TO BRING PEOPLE TOGETHER.
BUT THOUGHTLESSLY INSISTING OTHERS INDULGE YOU IS RUDE, AND WE WON'T ALLOW IT!
R-RUDE!?

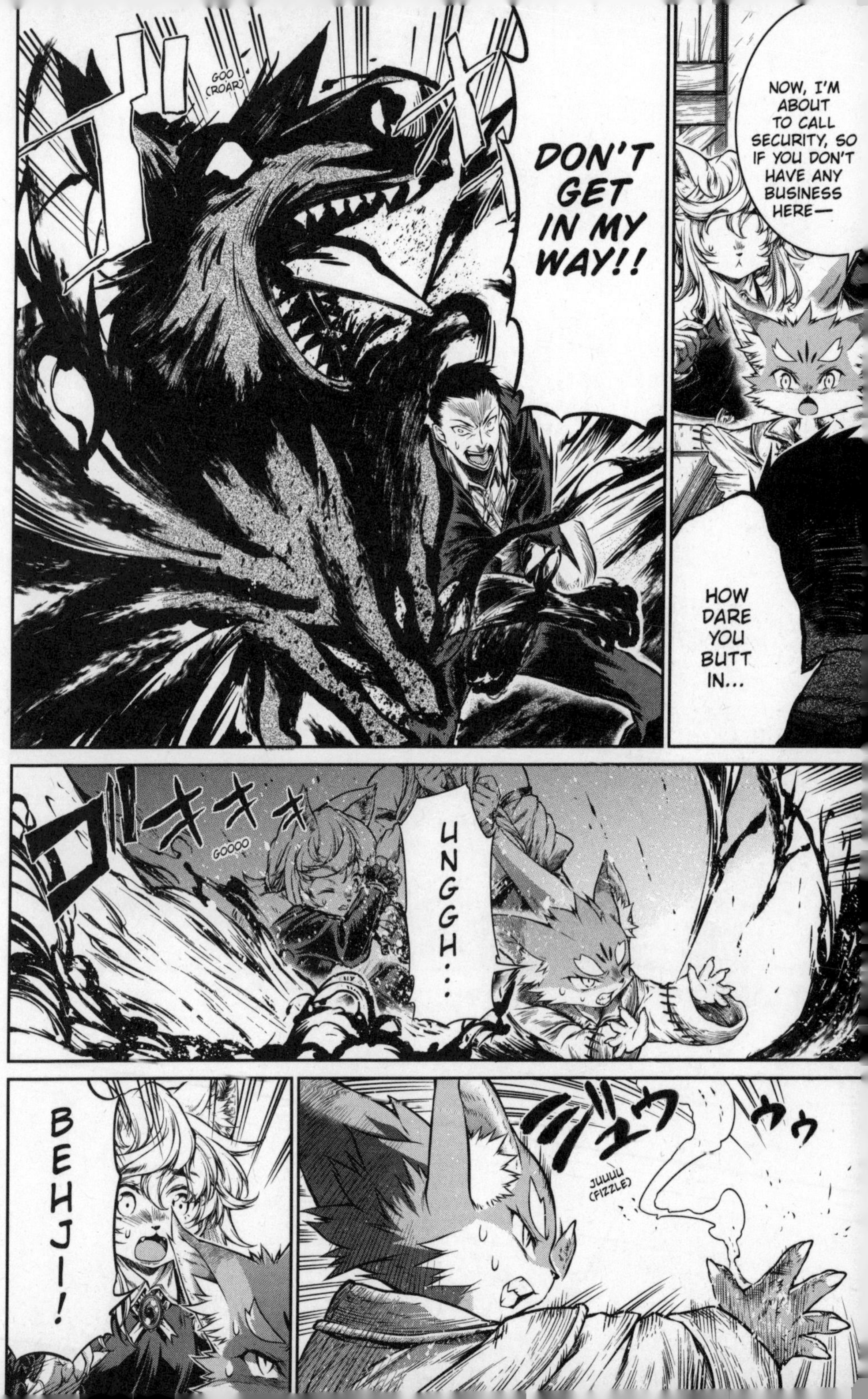
NOW, I'M ABOUT TO CALL SECURITY, SO IF YOU DON'T HAVE ANY BUSINESS HERE—
HOW DARE YOU BUTT IN...
GOO (ROAR)
DON'T GET IN MY WAY!!
UNGGH...
GOOOO
JUUUU (FIZZLE)
BEHJI!

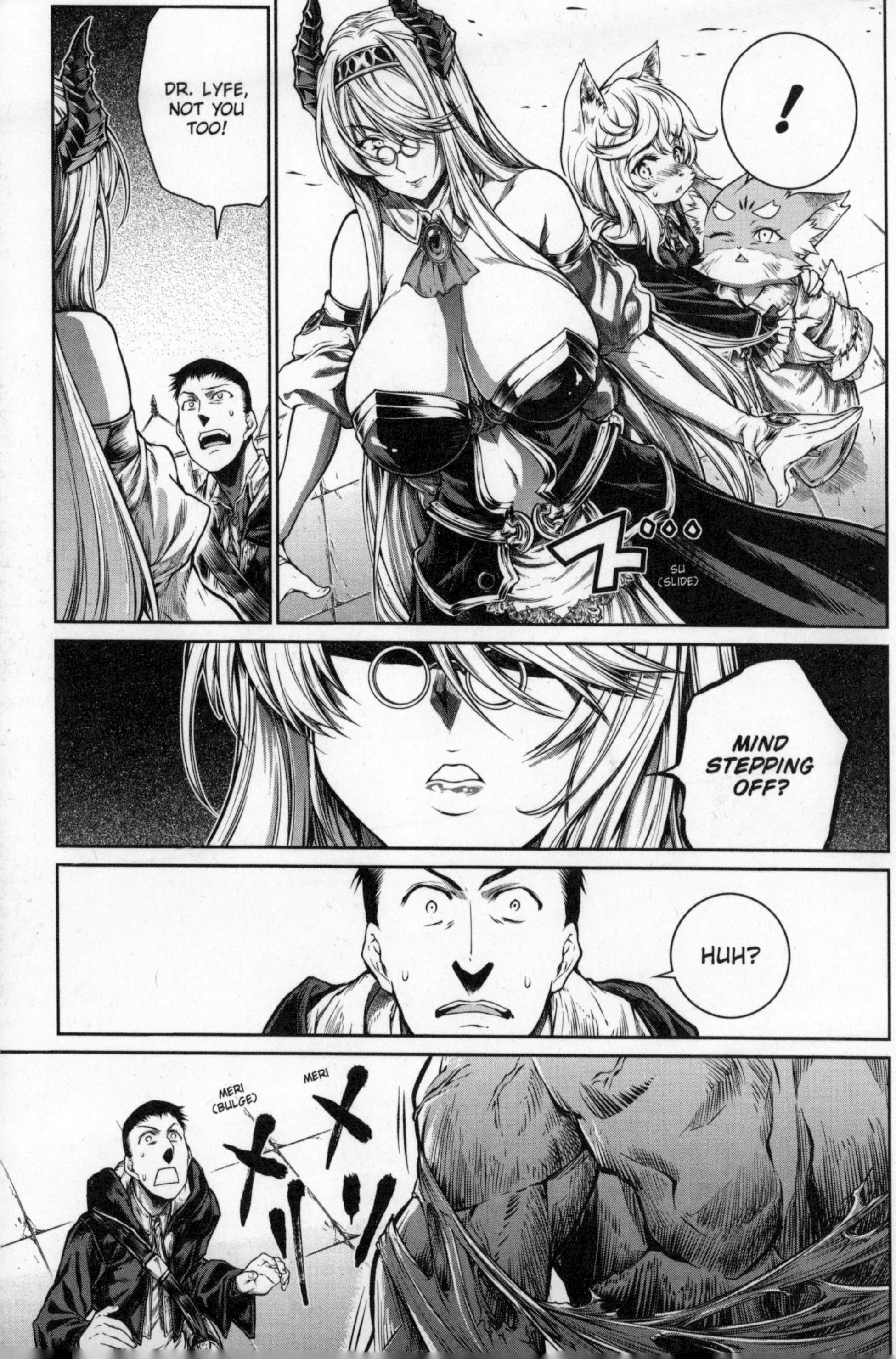
!
SU (SLIDE)
DR. LYFE, NOT YOU TOO!
MIND STEPPING OFF?
HUH?
MERI
MERI (BULGE)

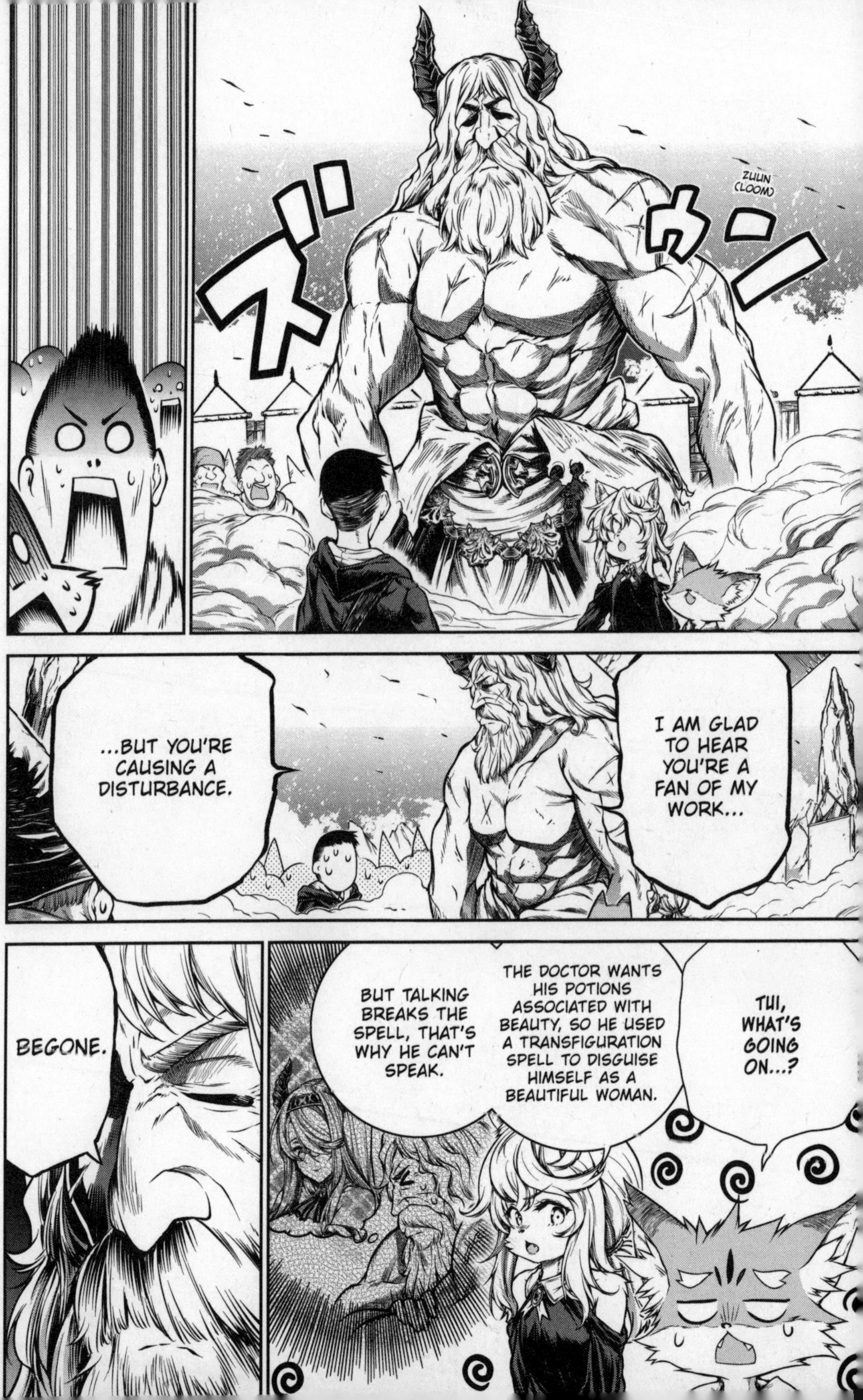
ズゥーン
ZUUN (LOOM)
I AM GLAD TO HEAR YOU'RE A FAN OF MY WORK...
...BUT YOU'RE CAUSING A DISTURBANCE.
TUI, WHAT'S GOING ON...?
THE DOCTOR WANTS HIS POTIONS ASSOCIATED WITH BEAUTY, SO HE USED A TRANSFIGURATION SPELL TO DISGUISE HIMSELF AS A BEAUTIFUL WOMAN.
BUT TALKING BREAKS THE SPELL, THAT'S WHY HE CAN'T SPEAK.
BEGONE.

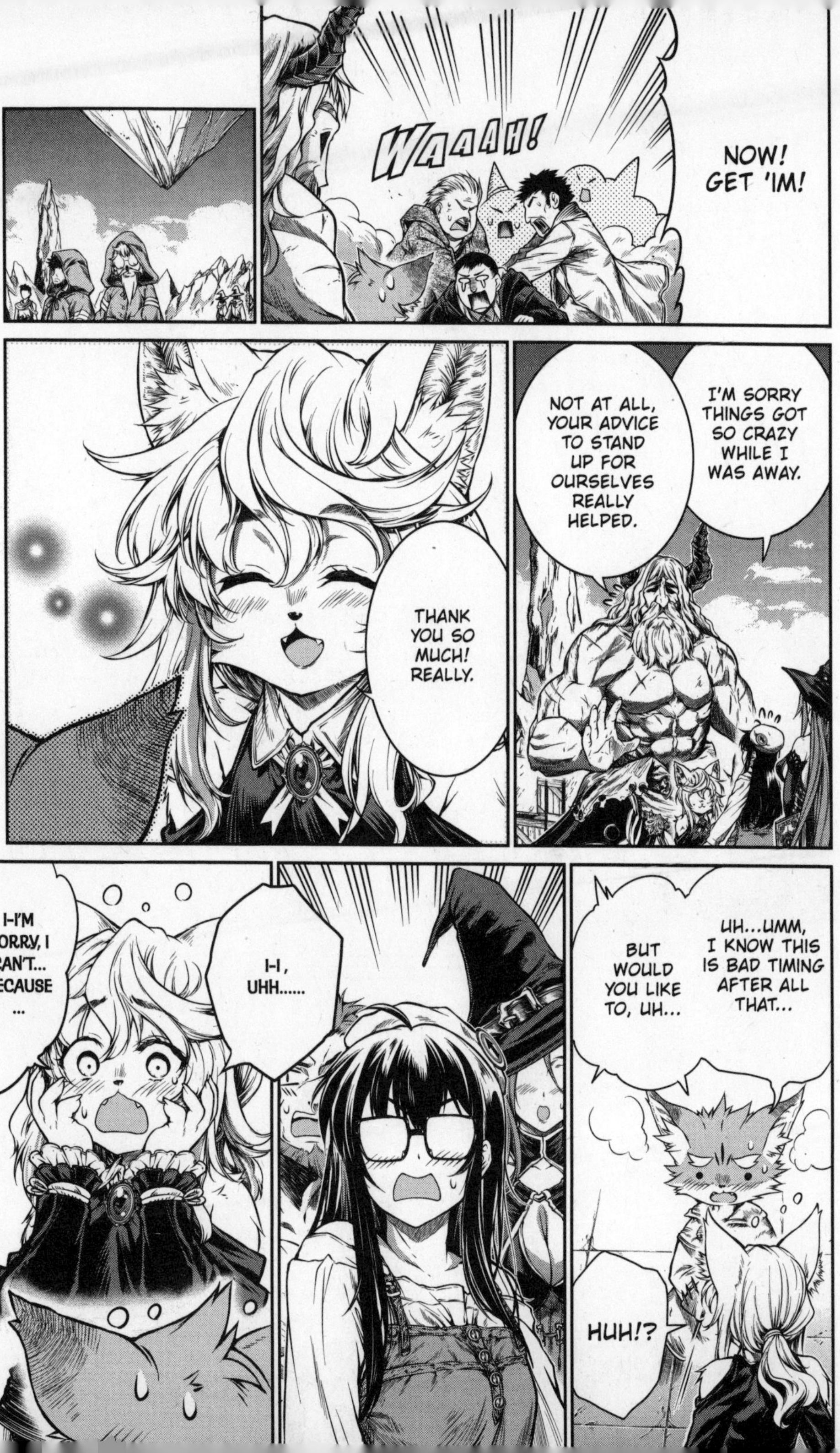
NOW! GET 'IM!
WAAAH!
I'M SORRY THINGS GOT SO CRAZY WHILE I WAS AWAY.
NOT AT ALL, YOUR ADVICE TO STAND UP FOR OURSELVES REALLY HELPED.
THANK YOU SO MUCH! REALLY.
UH...UMM, I KNOW THIS IS BAD TIMING AFTER ALL THAT...
BUT WOULD YOU LIKE TO, UH...
HUH!?
I-I, UHH......
I-I'M SORRY, I CAN'T... BECAUSE ...

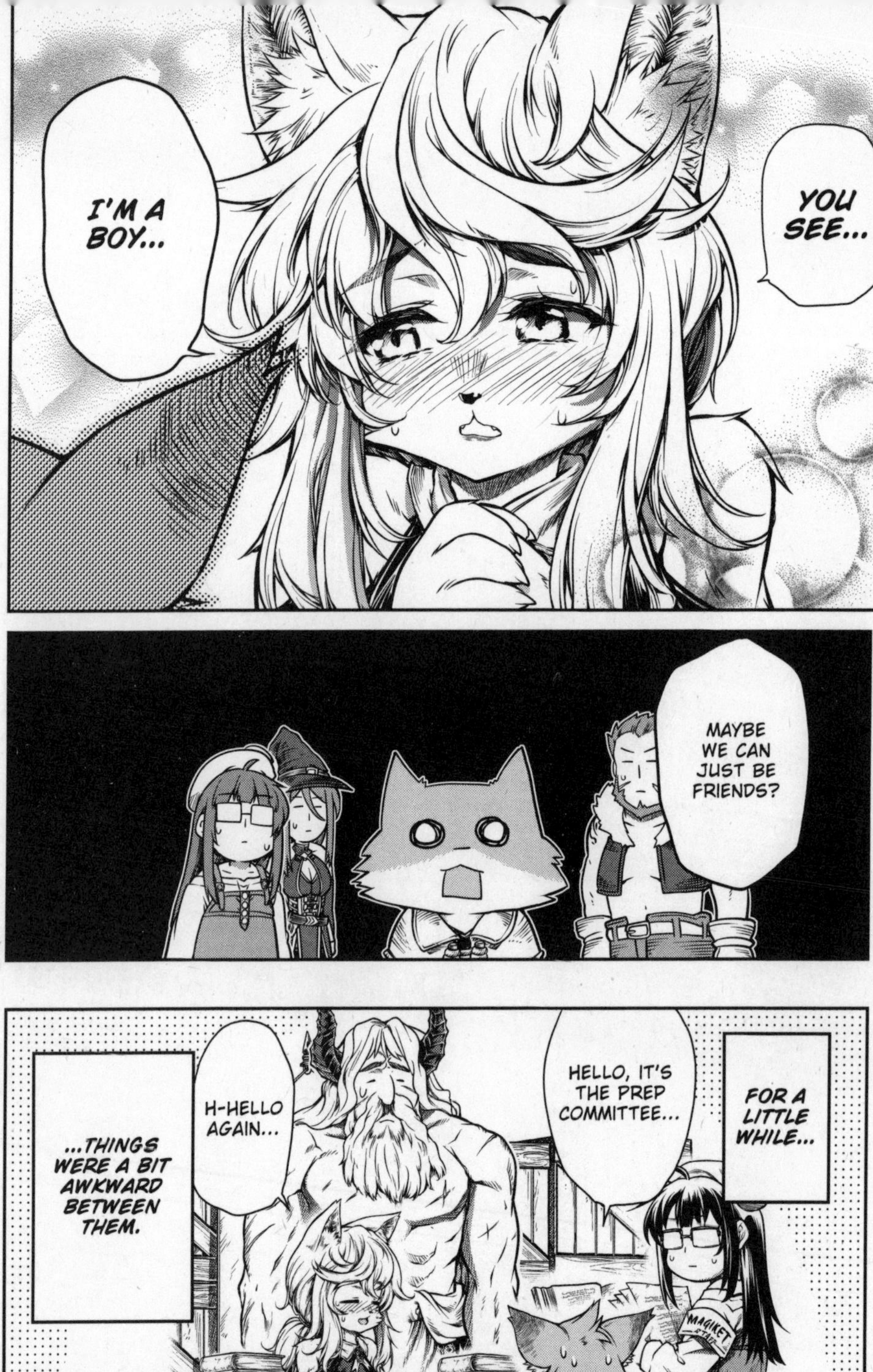
YOU SEE...
I'M A BOY...
MAYBE WE CAN JUST BE FRIENDS?
FOR A LITTLE WHILE...
HELLO, IT'S THE PREP COMMITTEE...
H-HELLO AGAIN...
...THINGS WERE A BIT AWKWARD BETWEEN THEM.
MAGIKET
TO BE CONTINUED IN VOLUME 4...

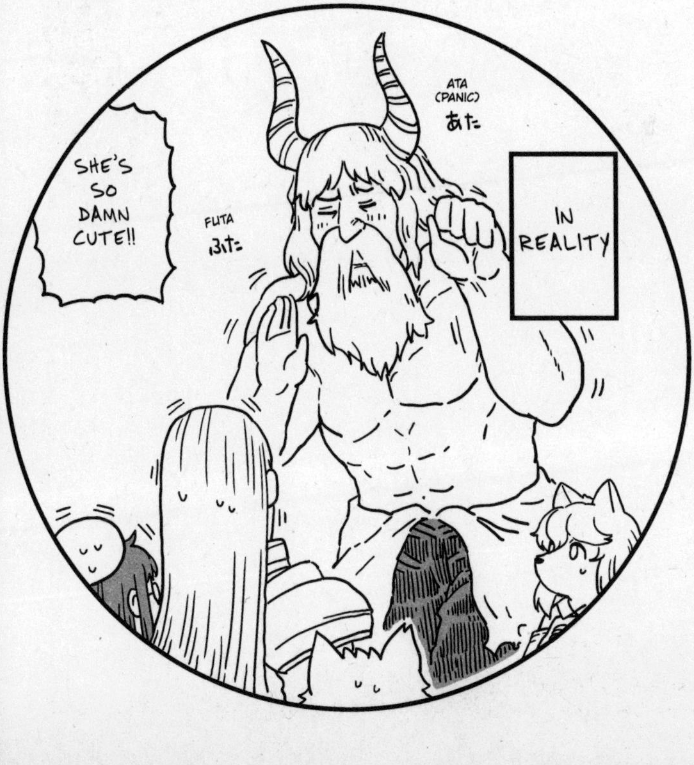

IN REALITY
ATA (PANIC) あた
FUTA ふた
SHE'S SO DAMN CUTE!!

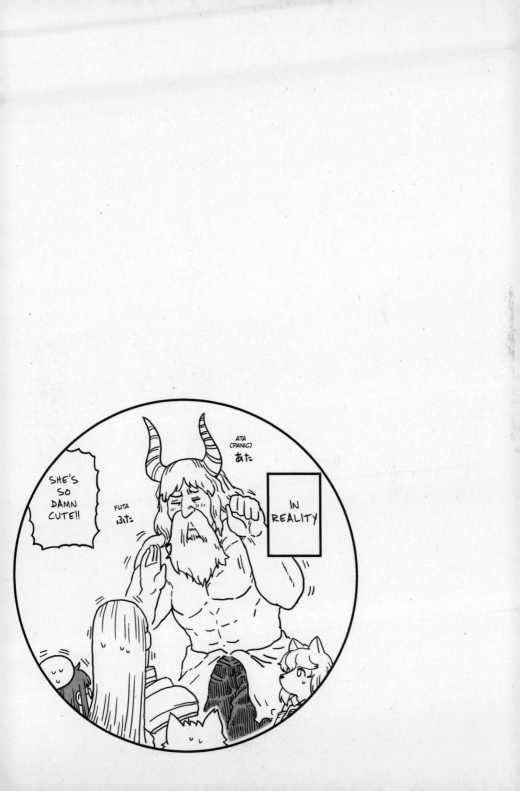

A WITCH'S PRINTING OFFICE

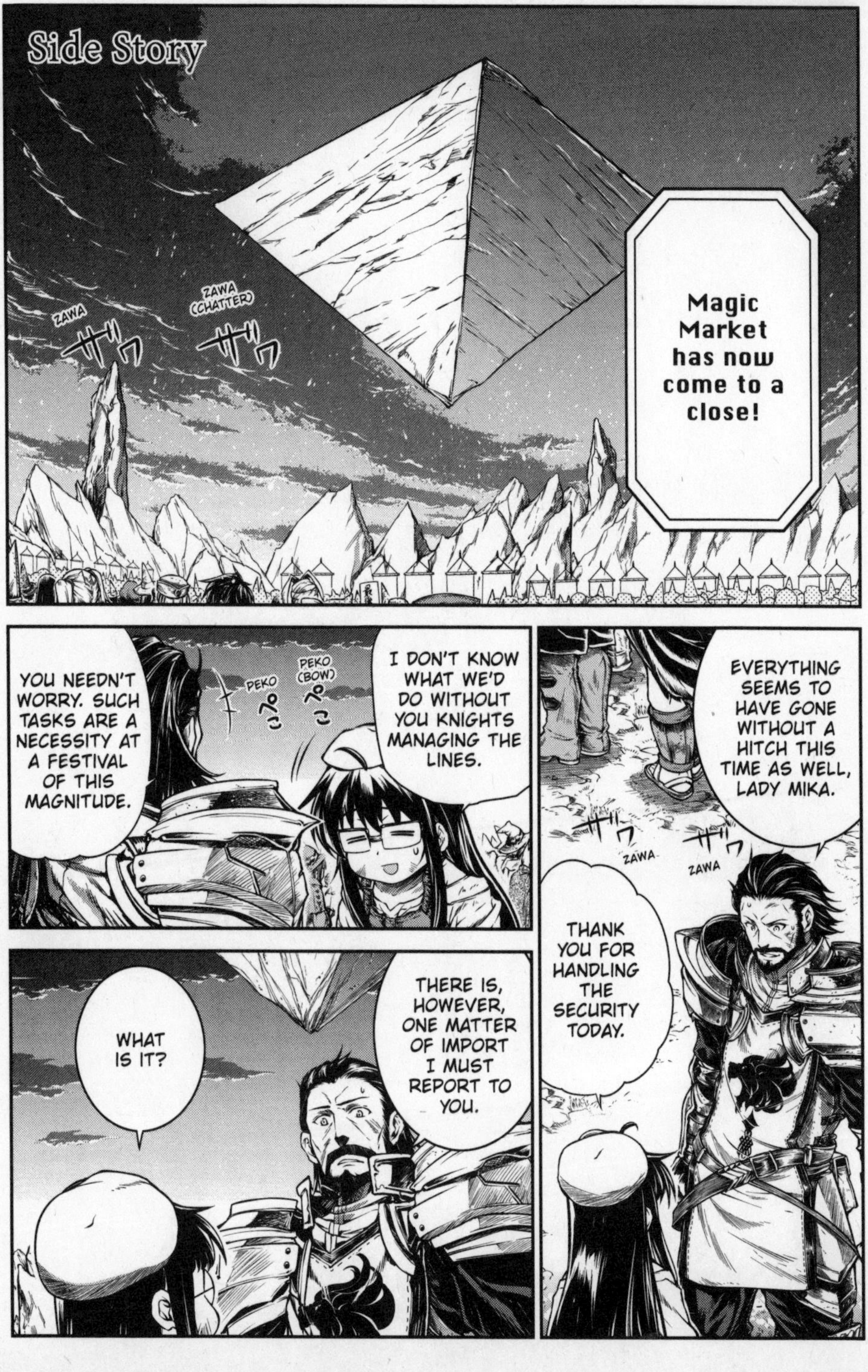

Side Story
Magic Market has now come to a close!
ZAWA (CHATTER)
ZAWA
EVERYTHING SEEMS TO HAVE GONE WITHOUT A HITCH THIS TIME AS WELL, LADY MIKA.
ZAWA
ZAWA
THANK YOU FOR HANDLING THE SECURITY TODAY.
I DON'T KNOW WHAT WE'D DO WITHOUT YOU KNIGHTS MANAGING THE LINES.
PEKO (BOW)
PEKO
YOU NEEDN'T WORRY. SUCH TASKS ARE A NECESSITY AT A FESTIVAL OF THIS MAGNITUDE.
THERE IS, HOWEVER, ONE MATTER OF IMPORT I MUST REPORT TO YOU.
WHAT IS IT?

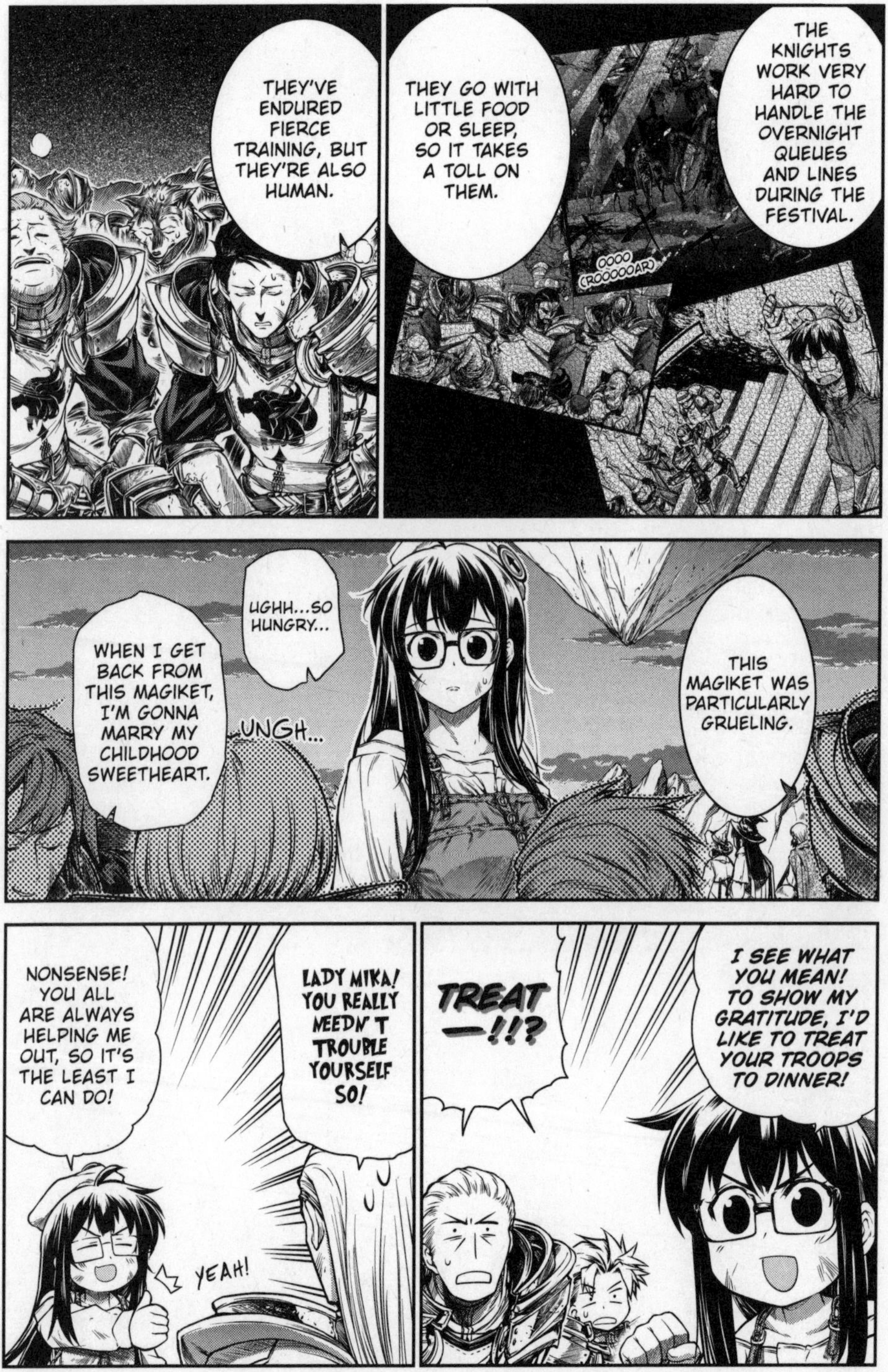
THE KNIGHTS WORK VERY HARD TO HANDLE THE OVERNIGHT QUEUES AND LINES DURING THE FESTIVAL.
THEY GO WITH LITTLE FOOD OR SLEEP, SO IT TAKES A TOLL ON THEM.
OOOO (ROOOOOAR)
THEY'VE ENDURED FIERCE TRAINING, BUT THEY'RE ALSO HUMAN.
THIS MAGIKET WAS PARTICULARLY GRUELING.
UGHH...SO HUNGRY...
UNGH...
WHEN I GET BACK FROM THIS MAGIKET, I'M GONNA MARRY MY CHILDHOOD SWEETHEART.
I SEE WHAT YOU MEAN! TO SHOW MY GRATITUDE, I'D LIKE TO TREAT YOUR TROOPS TO DINNER!
TREAT—!!?
LADY MIKA! YOU REALLY NEEDN'T TROUBLE YOURSELF SO!
NONSENSE! YOU ALL ARE ALWAYS HELPING ME OUT, SO IT'S THE LEAST I CAN DO!
YEAH!

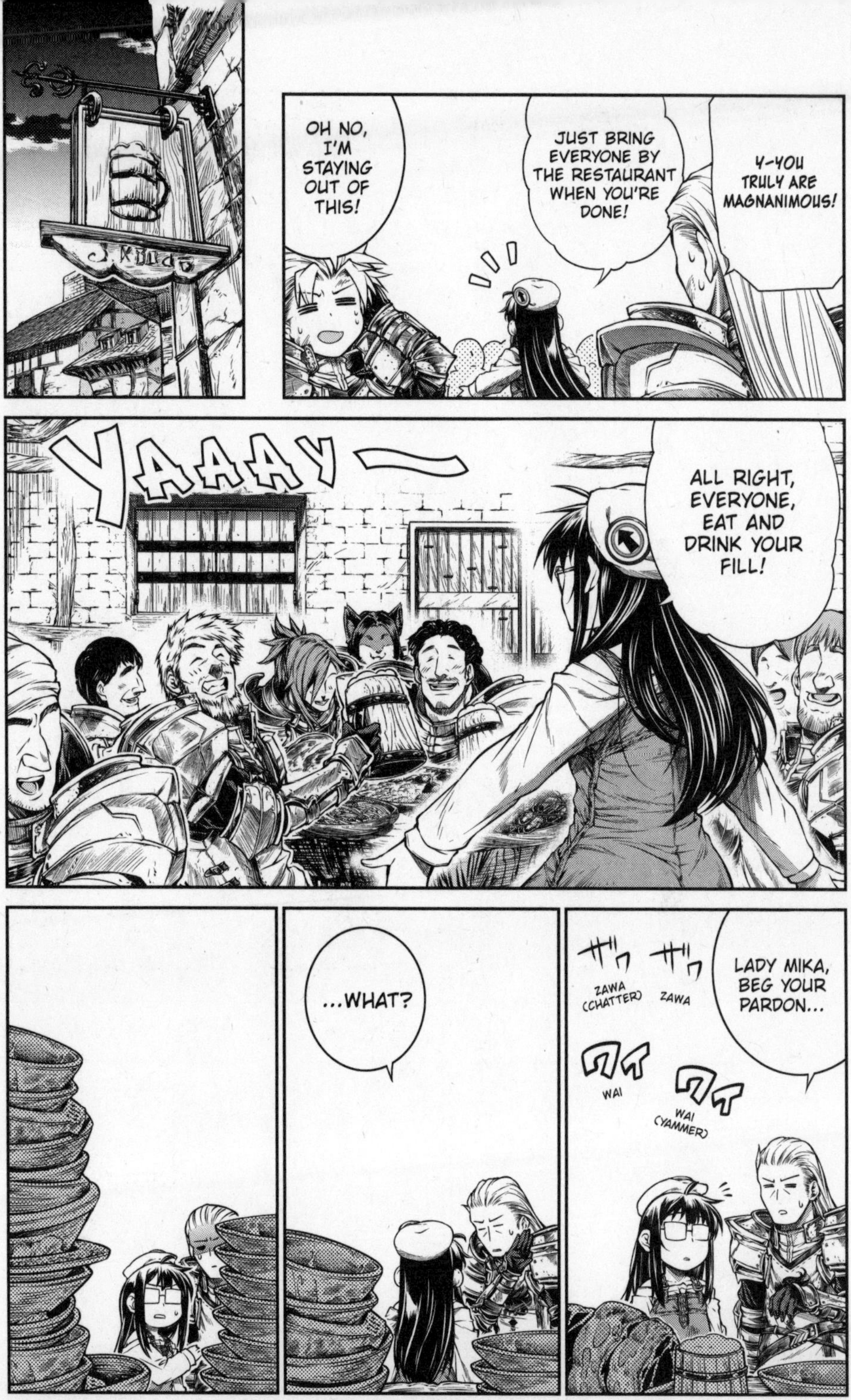
Y-YOU TRULY ARE MAGNANIMOUS!
JUST BRING EVERYONE BY THE RESTAURANT WHEN YOU'RE DONE!
OH NO, I'M STAYING OUT OF THIS!
ALL RIGHT, EVERYONE, EAT AND DRINK YOUR FILL!
YAAAY—
LADY MIKA, BEG YOUR PARDON...
ザワ ザワ
ZAWA (CHATTER) ZAWA
ワイ ワイ
WAI WAI (YAMMER)
...WHAT?

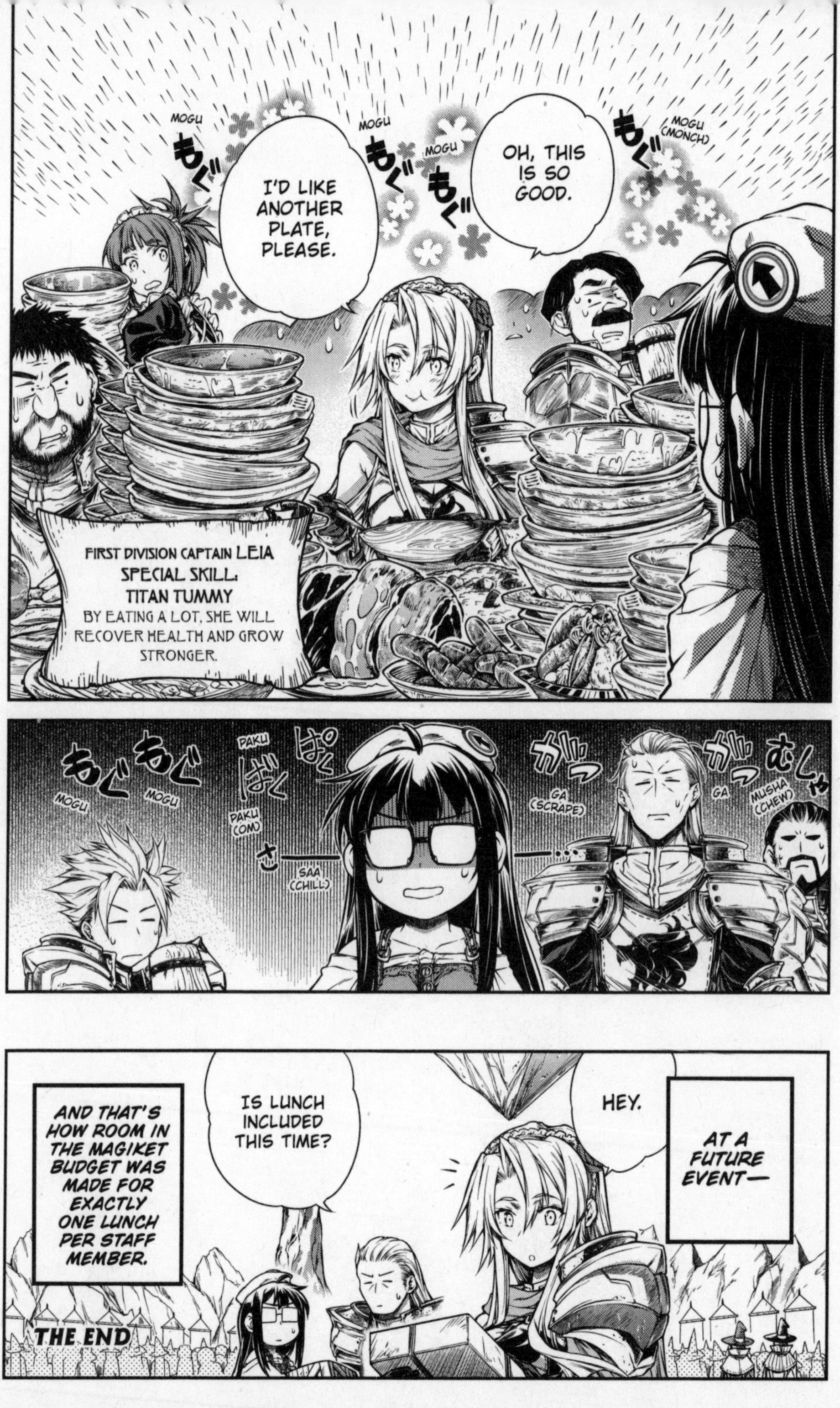
もぐ
MOGU (MONCH)
OH, THIS IS SO GOOD.
もぐ
MOGU
もぐ
MOGU
I'D LIKE ANOTHER PLATE, PLEASE.
もぐ
MOGU
FIRST DIVISION CAPTAIN LEIA
SPECIAL SKILL:
TITAN TUMMY
BY EATING A LOT, SHE WILL RECOVER HEALTH AND GROW STRONGER.
むしゃ
MUSHA (CHEW)
かっ
GA
かっ
GA (SCRAPE)
さー
SAA (CHILL)
ぱく
PAKU
ぱく
PAKU (OM)
もぐ
MOGU
もぐ
MOGU
AT A FUTURE EVENT—
HEY.
IS LUNCH INCLUDED THIS TIME?
AND THAT'S HOW ROOM IN THE MAGIKET BUDGET WAS MADE FOR EXACTLY ONE LUNCH PER STAFF MEMBER.
THE END

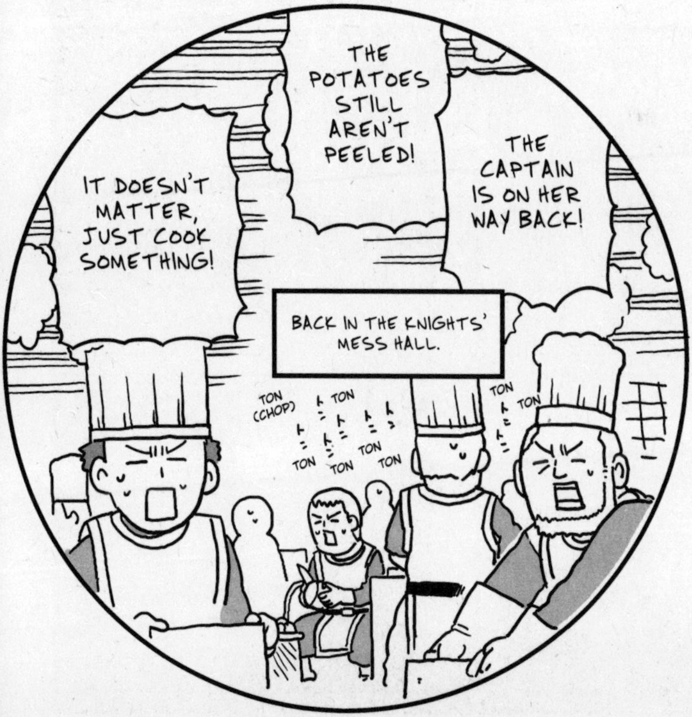
THE CAPTAIN IS ON HER WAY BACK!
THE POTATOES STILL AREN'T PEELED!
IT DOESN'T MATTER, JUST COOK SOMETHING!
BACK IN THE KNIGHTS' MESS HALL.
TON TON
TON (CHOP) TON TON TON TON TON

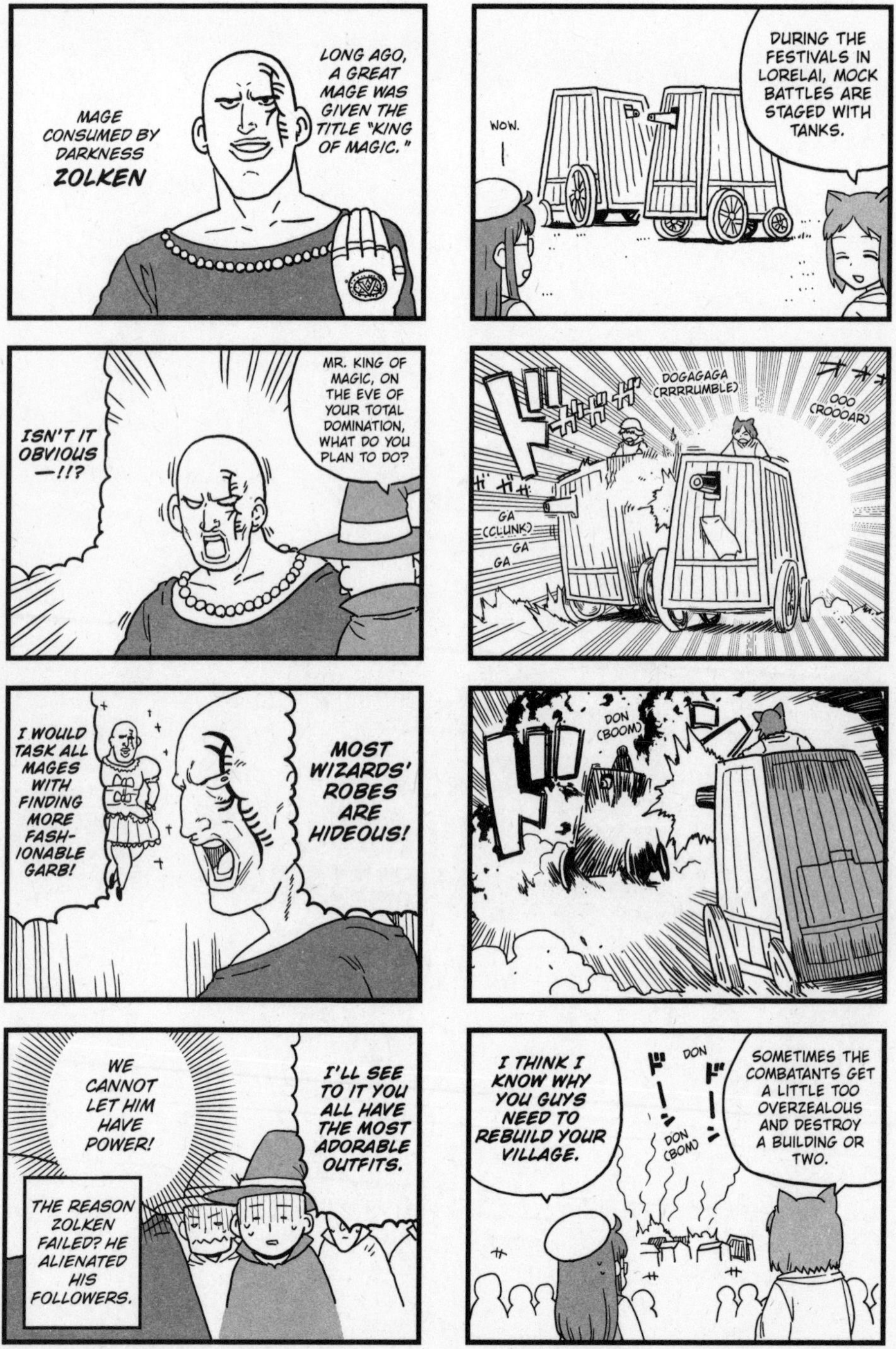
DURING THE FESTIVALS IN LORELAI, MOCK BATTLES ARE STAGED WITH TANKS.
WOW.
OOO (ROOOAR)
DOGAGAGA (RRRRUMBLE)
GA (CLUNK) GA GA
DON (BOOM)
SOMETIMES THE COMBATANTS GET A LITTLE TOO OVERZEALOUS AND DESTROY A BUILDING OR TWO.
DON
DON (BOM)
I THINK I KNOW WHY YOU GUYS NEED TO REBUILD YOUR VILLAGE.
LONG AGO, A GREAT MAGE WAS GIVEN THE TITLE "KING OF MAGIC."
MAGE CONSUMED BY DARKNESS
ZOLKEN
MR. KING OF MAGIC, ON THE EVE OF YOUR TOTAL DOMINATION, WHAT DO YOU PLAN TO DO?
ISN'T IT OBVIOUS—!!?
MOST WIZARDS' ROBES ARE HIDEOUS!
I WOULD TASK ALL MAGES WITH FINDING MORE FASH-IONABLE GARB!
I'LL SEE TO IT YOU ALL HAVE THE MOST ADORABLE OUTFITS.
WE CANNOT LET HIM HAVE POWER!
THE REASON ZOLKEN FAILED? HE ALIENATED HIS FOLLOWERS.

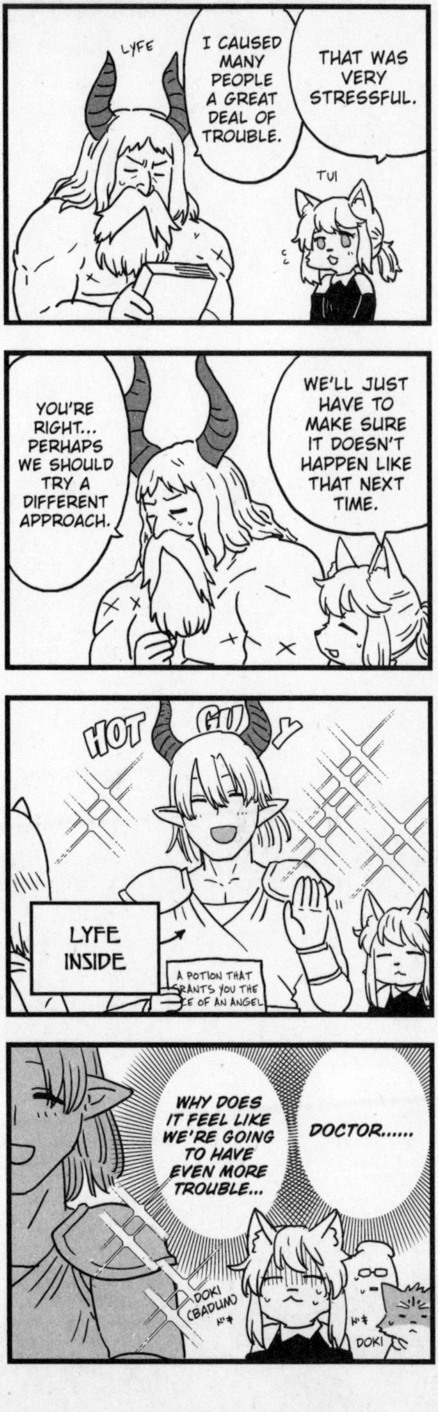
THAT WAS VERY STRESSFUL.
I CAUSED MANY PEOPLE A GREAT DEAL OF TROUBLE.
LYFE
TUI
WE'LL JUST HAVE TO MAKE SURE IT DOESN'T HAPPEN LIKE THAT NEXT TIME.
YOU'RE RIGHT... PERHAPS WE SHOULD TRY A DIFFERENT APPROACH.
HOT GUY
LYFE INSIDE
A POTION THAT GRANTS YOU THE FACE OF AN ANGEL
DOCTOR......
WHY DOES IT FEEL LIKE WE'RE GOING TO HAVE EVEN MORE TROUBLE...
DOKI (BADUM)
DOKI

GREETINGS

THANK YOU FOR PICKING UP A COPY OF VOLUME 3 OF A WITCH'S PRINTING OFFICE. IT'S BEEN TWO YEARS SINCE THE SERIES STARTED SERIALIZATION.

DURING THAT TIME:
THE ORIGINAL MAGAZINE WE WERE PUBLISHED IN, G'S COMICS, HAS CEASED PUBLICATION.
COMIKET HAS EXPANDED TO FOUR DAYS.
THE OLYMPICS ARE COMING TO JAPAN.
AND REALITY HAS BECOME SO MUCH LIKE FANTASY, IT MAKES MY HEAD SPIN.

WHAT AWAITS MIKA AND HER COMPANIONS NEXT?
I HOPE YOU'LL STAY WITH US AND FIND OUT.
SEE YOU AGAIN IN VOLUME 4!

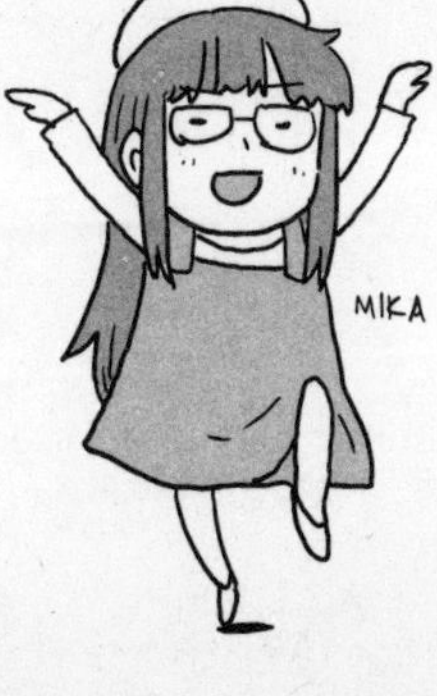
MIKA

ONE DAY IN JULY 2019

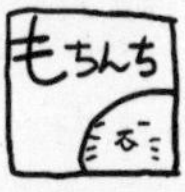
もちんち

MOCHINCHI

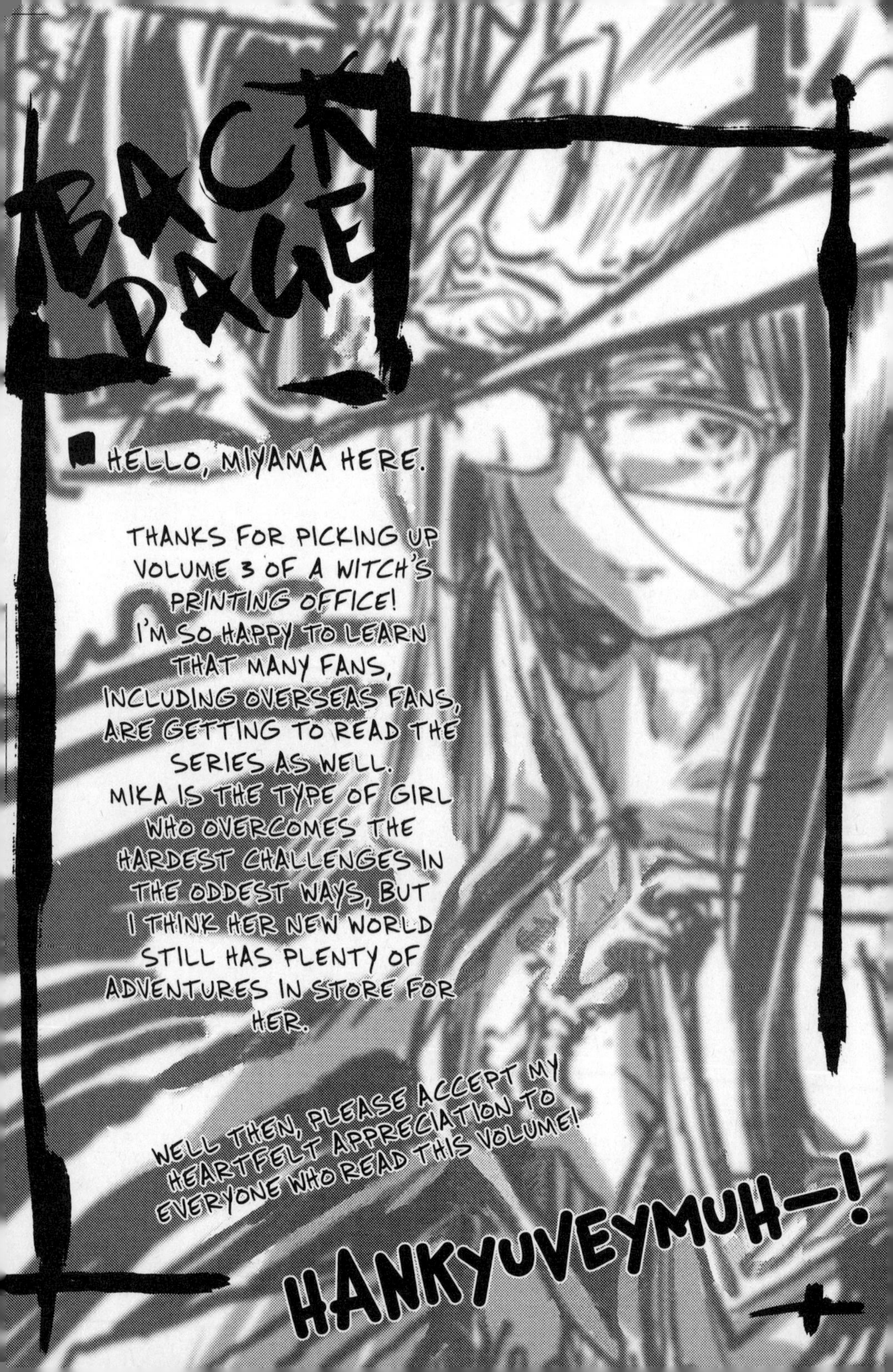

BACK PAGE

■ HELLO, MIYAMA HERE.

THANKS FOR PICKING UP VOLUME 3 OF A WITCH'S PRINTING OFFICE! I'M SO HAPPY TO LEARN THAT MANY FANS, INCLUDING OVERSEAS FANS, ARE GETTING TO READ THE SERIES AS WELL. MIKA IS THE TYPE OF GIRL WHO OVERCOMES THE HARDEST CHALLENGES IN THE ODDEST WAYS, BUT I THINK HER NEW WORLD STILL HAS PLENTY OF ADVENTURES IN STORE FOR HER.

WELL THEN, PLEASE ACCEPT MY HEARTFELT APPRECIATION TO EVERYONE WHO READ THIS VOLUME!

HANKYUVEYMUH—!

A Witch's Printing Office

STORY
MOCHINCHI

ART
YASUHIRO MIYAMA

✦

ORIGINAL COVER DESIGN

SAVA DESIGN

COVER PAINTING
SIOKOJI

COLOR PAGES
KICHIROKU

EDITOR IN CHARGE
KENTARO OGINO

EDITORIAL ASSISTANT
YUSUKE KATO

A WITCH'S PRINTING OFFICE

3

story **Mochinchi** art **Yasuhiro Miyama**

TRANSLATION: AMBER TAMOSAITIS
LETTERING: ERIN HICKMAN

This book is a work of fiction. Names, characters, places, and incidents are the product of the author's imagination or are used fictitiously. Any resemblance to actual events, locales, or persons, living or dead, is coincidental.

MAHOTSUKAI NO INSATSUJO Vol. 3
©Mochinchi 2019
©Yasuhiro Miyama 2019
First published in Japan in 2019 by KADOKAWA CORPORATION, Tokyo.
English translation rights arranged with KADOKAWA CORPORATION, Tokyo
through Tuttle-Mori Agency, Inc., Tokyo.

English translation © 2020 by Yen Press, LLC

The names "Comic Market," "Comiket," and "Comike" are registered trademarks and/or trademarks of Comiket Inc.

Yen Press
150 West 30th Street, 19th Floor
New York, NY 10001

Visit us at yenpress.com
facebook.com/yenpress
twitter.com/yenpress
yenpress.tumblr.com
instagram.com/yenpress

First Yen Press Edition: June 2020

Yen Press is an imprint of Yen Press, LLC.
The Yen Press name and logo are trademarks of Yen Press, LLC.

The publisher is not responsible for websites (or their content) that are not owned by the publisher.

Library of Congress Control Number: 2019947774

ISBNs: 978-1-9753-0993-0 (paperback)
978-1-9753-0994-7 (ebook)

10 9 8 7 6 5 4 3 2 1

WOR

Printed in the United States of America